NOTORIOUSLY NAKED FLAMES

By

Mike Steeden

Published by GBS Publishing, Dover, Kent, United Kingdom

Also by Mike Steeden:

Gentlemen Prefer a Pulse – Poetry with a Hint of Lunacy
The Shop That Sells Kisses – Poetry with a Hint of Magic

NOTORIOUSLY NAKED FLAMES

This book is dedicated to
Rainy Days, Coffee, and Love Letters

"The mind I love must have wild places, a tangled orchard where dark damsons drop in the heavy grass, an overgrown little wood, the chance of a snake or two, a pool that nobody's fathomed the depth of, and paths threaded with flowers planted by the mind."

--Katherine Mansfield

"It is impossible to imagine a more complete fusion with nature than that of the Gypsy."

--Franz Liszt

"I took some pictures of the place [Hitler's residence] and I also got a good night's sleep in Hitler's bed. I even washed off the dirt of Dachau in his tub."

--Lee Miller

PRELUDE

Sometimes, just sometimes, the intoxicated Time devil, drunk on his own success, slumps into a benighted stupor and time itself is fleetingly fractured. It is upon the occasion of such seismic cracks a tsunami of memories comes to flush out what has passed; a double-take much better than before.

By plea of frozen tears, the mind's eye gallery opens its cryptic doors and as mayflies to an ominous dusk, excited habitués race here, there, everywhere to assimilate that which has long since been archived, now dusted off; displayed.

A rendezvous perhaps? Two soon to be lovers, a chance encounter born of fate oblivious as yet of the unsullied bond twixt vivacious flesh and abiding soul, no care in the world over anything or everything, unaware of walking canes and deathbed musings that one-day will unmask a fault in fortune's haughty wheel affording them a brief escape when Time takes of its wasted rest.

Twixt thus far stainless sheets those green lovers and the one circumstance had invited in; the one they had come to love, scramble to discover and invent, knowing then, forgetting now, that sometimes, just sometimes, nothing is impossible.

Notoriously Naked Flames

1.

LATE AUGUST 1938 – PAS-DE-CALAIS, NORTHERN FRANCE

Dog days of summer, gothic spires and cobblestones, a frantic accordion. The plum coloured stains upon simple white tablecloths, spilled house red for the main part. Cigarette butts and chitter chatter, a café full. The clamour of the greedy, the mirth of friends and lovers. A promenade of Mademoiselles, not a table to be had. Inside or out.

They walk on by, hand in hand. She and he sharing the silence of seasoned lovers amidst the affable hiss of the old town.

'I wasn't that hungry anyway'

'Nor me'

A bargain basement auberge. Fan light left open. A little previous the moth mistakes an early evening lit candle for the moon. Clean sheets and privacy.

They live a little in the twilight, live some more after sunset. Divine the transparency of radiant enduring cravings.

2.

8th MAY 1945, PARIS

A standstill, crystal clear night under the amorous impressionism of a chaperon moon's intimate ogling, the lioness and the lamb renew an affair. Cemented almost as one upon Pont de l'Archevêché sharing the last of the Gauloises, looking down and out at the magic of perception over nature that is the alchemy of the Seine, they wish they could turn back time and make different those far apart lost years. Instead, they decide that a discreet left bank boutique hotel too good a thing to neglect now that the white dove has come home, the hawks of war flown away, bloodshed done with.

3.

EARLY SUMMER 1952 – SUSSEX, ENGLAND

Her: She examines her defenceless giant searchingly as he bathes. He, the one who is a portrayal of rare full-fledged innocence, and wonders if the macrocosm inside his head replicates the one outside of hers. She hopes against hope that locked within exists a rainbow's multi-coloured arc, or is all this lost upon the extraordinary self, empty of speech, hearing and sight, unaware that gesture is the only language he bestows. Touch and smell his native inside-out lone connection.

She communicates as best she can. Upon his awakening, she is always there. Her 'hello of sorts' a lover's tangled tongue kiss. No passion though, they are no longer the passing lovers they once were. More that the sharing of her unique taste serves to let him perceive her, recognize her. Always has him gift a beaming smile just for her. She wears the self-same perfume each new day also, it helps him identify her proximity.

With no great difficulty she aids him out of the bath, warm towels, warm heart care. Time for drying and dressing, though the palaver of dressing irks him, induces a frown. Regardless he is immune to nakedness within his ambushed consciousness, his curious dominion. Not for him the embarrassment of the earthly collective.

The sun shone the day before. Albeit keeping a caring eye open, she chose to let him wander the lawn, uncovered. From nowhere a summer storm brewed, small hailstones. She watched as he held out his palms, threw his head back, greeted the spheres of water ice, an air of amazement, no suffering.

The eternal 'what next' frustrates her day; muddles her mood. She undresses, calculates he may have no recollection that human beings come in two packages. Her hands upon his chest, fingers spread wide, sensation of touch inviting. Invitation accepted, he mirrors her actions, stroke for stroke, his look curious, questioning, captivated. No folly in innocent exploration.

A telephone outside of his realm rings. Might be important, she pulls away. Notices he sheds a single loaded tear, from which continent of emotion it heralds, likely she will never unearth.

He has been this way ever since she rescued him.

Him: The zest of a lemon, a sugar-coated wafer, foul odour, euphoric aroma and the emptiness of the barren void. Unstimulating insignificance, turmoil, sudden cramps, heartache for reasons unknown and pulsating vital organs. Rough textures from smooth; smooth from rough, the pleasure that gravity affords. Heedless of the nature of sex and sexuality. Two directional manipulation by way of touch. The perception of longitudinal and transverse waves communicating as best they can. These, and these alone, were all I believed I ever knew. These were the pittance, delusions had endowed. Yet all this was when I was God, God of all I could evaluate, sat august on my throne and out of reach. That was when I was the entire universe. That was when elation was, what fatalistic happenstance brought forth.

Perhaps I exaggerate a little. A new-found enthusiasm does that. It would be an idiocy to say I was not alive to the existence of anything else. Breathing phenomenon's whose presence outside of me would add to my alien self. For instance, they applied heavy wrappings that warmed me when cold, flimsy ones that cooled me when too hot. As to exactly what living things they might be, I had not the vaguest concept save that they might have been the viable flotsam and jetsam serving my continuum. Whatever, those who breathed delivered sustenance and cleanliness.

Whether she found me, or had been gifted me I have yet to determine. All I know is that prior to the event I was that macrocosm, just a solitary star in a curved and bent blackened retreat. Cold hearted instinct had declared I was a pulsating, living thing seemingly born into a realm of muddled isolation. Of that I was chaotically aware. That aside, an eternal abyss of my own making was my possessor and only possession. That, I believe, is the way of God wherever one might find Him.

Come her perfume, all would change. She has shown me that within her realm of balance I cannot speak, nor hear, nor see whereas, in her equivalent, such senses are taken for granted. Now I am savvy to the simple verifiable truth that I am no God. That I would find the legendary unicorn alive and well, an easier thing than unravelling the puzzle of impossible omnipotence.

Through touch and tongue she has transposed images in my mind of her past and current, her hopes and dreams as clearly as if I had eyes that see. I do not think she is aware she has this capacity within her. Her words of knowledge sit inside the library she has contrived inside my head. Were I not mute I would tell her of her energy. I perceive visions of her life through hopeless eyes. I hear her speak on stage in a theatre named Cerebrum. Could I conjure spoken words and viable replies I would debate with her. No longer am I deserted, left to fend alone in an enclave of instability, unaware of predators and poisonous plants.

If I could live out the simplicity of my flawless dream then I would climb the highest mountain, cast my net and harvest a sky full of storm clouds, hide them away and gift her, her very own wild blue yonder.

Her: 'How does one balance the subjectivity of ethics, of incorruptibility, against the primeval, innate response to the simplicity of human touch now that he understands desire? Now that he has an appetite for more of the same?' Simple enough questions to answer were she an adept physiologist. Regrettably, she is not. One thing is for certain, for beyond doubt she knows that when death's door finally invites, he must journey beside her. He would never survive abandoned.

Damage done? A fallible catastrophe? A naiveté abused? A grownup innocence corrupted? Or, rather a goodness courtesy of love's own curious offerings? She decides that, against all odds, in spite of all the unanswerable questions, she has discovered in her damaged 'lost but now found again' lover, an inexperienced, gentle giant, a perhaps calculable yet nevertheless inexplicable rekindled love. The kiss they shared on Pont de l'Archevêché, Paris the night the war ended comes fervently to mind. That kiss had sparked a spree of indulgence like no other before or since. But that was a time before he was broken. She pulls herself together, determines her duty henceforth is simply to ensure he is kept out of harm's way.

What had begun as inquisitive compulsion, an honest enough nocturnal unmasking had spawned her quandary, as was obvious in hindsight. That it had led to exploration of shared hearts, minds and inevitably unbaked sex, a predictable thing? A vital element in his progression or her self-indulgent manipulation toward an immodest end? In part, she sees herself as she-devil, the perpetrator of an intimacy akin to incest. In part, an angel of mercy fulfilling the cause of sexual virtue. Surely only believers would feel such guilt? She holds no beliefs. Why then does guilt overwhelm her? So many questions, none that she can answer.

While he still sleeps she carefully climbs across his bare torso, mindful not to disturb. A difficult task performed upon a single bed. Before bathing she telephones through an order for a king-sized bed from the department store in town. The antique gruff proprietor, in a typical huff, suggests she visits and chooses one to her exact liking. She tells him who she is and that his most expensive bed will suffice. Her mind and future made up. Nothing further to discuss save that he should put it on her account. He huffs no more and agrees delivery for the next-day.

Enlightened instinct marks that this new day, her now deaf, mute and blind giants grasp on all things, not just the carnal, will be by far and away greater than yesterday's.

Outside it is warm and getting warmer. Her privacy is assured. Little point in getting dressed. She keeps a vigilant ear out for when he stirs. French toast and a cup of black tea outside on the patio. A quizzical recollection from late into last night, 'It is as if the tip of his tongue upon my belly is trying to spell out words, as much as anything else'. The intuition born of being female argues that a rare magic is afoot.

Cambridge had taught her the reflective ways of philosophy; likewise, covert operations had taught her to think on the hoof. It is thus that contradicting her previous well thought through 'theory of his full-time protection' she concludes she needs a space within in which to think. Hence a little later, mid-mornings prospect of strong coffee only just on the horizon, her gentle giant still fast asleep, she sneaks out for a jaunt around the rambling pathways within the deciduous laden grounds. An old Dutch roadster bicycle that must once have belonged to whomsoever, her preference over Shanks's pony. She notes that the swallows have returned from the tropics and are now nesting in the eaves. Of absolute necessity she dons a wide-brimmed floral print sunhat, ever irked that for it to remain about her person an ungainly chinstrap is required. Is sure not to forget matching sunglasses also. For sake of common-sense comfort rests a small feather stuffed cushion, held in place with a multitude of new-fangled elasticated hairbands, upon an unyielding saddle, and is off.   Her secret emancipated female allows senses to take leave of absence. Sound reasoning belongs to sunshine days like these.

At the lake the cygnets are fast becoming swans, the ducklings almost ducks. The cycle at rest against a weeping willow she first dips her toes in the water, then paddles, speculates that in lands where barter holds sway over hard currency then life in such a place must be cheap. Unable to support such premise with fact learnt, or personal experience, it is dismissed tout de suite. Thoughts stray, 'Have I found perfect in imperfection'. The thought lingers, refuses the offer of safe passage to sempiternity. Guilt tugs at heartstrings. She must return before he rouses.

A dog days' wasp, posturing as if it were an enraged fading 'fallen apples drunkard' stings her butt as she attempts to settle upon her crudely adapted saddle. It hurts like hell. Perhaps French knickers would have been a prudent accompaniment for the sunhat, her immediate thought. She sees the funny side, laughs and heads back to the house. Besides, with her condition too many rays can spell trouble. The sting lingers on.

4.

BERLIN 1936 – MUSINGS OF A FORMER LOVER

How very young she was. A crime, almost. Yet come the days of retribution, the days when the remnants of shameless evil would be tracked down, hopefully eradicated, Argentina she thought might become her home from home. That was then. As of now, the unbearable midsummer dusty dry heat, a thing the medics had long since insisted that, with her specific condition, she should avoid, plus the foulest stench of fermenting acre upon acre upon acre of cattle dung meant she simply had to get away.

Her initial intention was to wish upon a star. In the event, she was spoilt for choice and decided to run with gut instinct and return to the tantalising decadence of Berlin. However, with the dawning of her 'when it suits' fatherlands National Socialism epoch where blond locks and blue eyes were the safest bet, being unusual, an albino reliant upon a smokescreen mousey brown wig, darkest sunglasses and heavy make-up during daylight hours posed certain potential pitfalls of which she was aware, yet cared not.

I am blind now. My own condition has worsened, reached its finality. All I can see these days are memories long since deposited within. Some fade a little, others get embellished, yet one, just the one never changes. That night when I first laid my then functioning eyes upon her. The night she both wept and danced unmasked to the plainsong of a clumsy fiddle in a blue, blue fog loaded freaks paradise beneath Kurfürstendamm. She would later tell me her tears were nothing more than her disappointment that the only food left over for dancers was salted cashew nuts. She was allergic to those and had gone starving rotten hungry.

Inevitably, being of insanely enticing skin and bone, stark snow-white all-over, amid the throng of the grotesque powdered and rouged she was to become the very symbol of the unashamed immodesty that was the Kabarett, the talk of the waning 'Golden Age of Weimar'. Was it the fusion of the saucy cat calls of the well-fed faces coupled with her own devilment that ensured she became notorious for dancing naked on stage? Likely it was. Also, she led an excessive style of life back then dominated by schnapps, opium and her bisexuality. How was I to know that one day soon she had it in her to become an accomplished and later, much fabled assassin within espionage echelons? Upon reflection, we must have made an absurd pairing. Me, the stereotypical reticent old school Englishman, she the wildest, whitest creature, game for anything and everything.

Oh dear, my jocular nurse now tells me, blood pressure non-existent, brain function just adequate. A regular pulse would be a plus. Pulses should be bonded as brother and sister, yet mine are so far apart they are akin to warring siblings. What use my sanity in a sealed envelope?

Where was I? I do tend to ramble with the passage of time. Whatever, I left her behind the day I climbed Everest. Her new preference, rich tea biscuits and Darjeeling plus, inevitably, the pretty little hotel waitress she was keen on bedding in my absence. Sadly, in her enthusiasm she had not realized that the gal was not of that particular persuasion.

Back in the day she once told me that she hated sharing a decent bottle of Chablis with anyone. How she stayed so slight is quite beyond me. Funny, the odd things one keeps in the locker. Regardless, it was while I was trudging up to base camp, she sought the solace, then allegedly the casting couch (perhaps vice-versa, one could never tell with her) of the sauntering American we had spotted in the bar the night previous. US Secret Service chappie on a Nepalese jaunt with buddies by all accounts. He must have seen in her the potential for the clandestine. The rest, for me at least, is sad history. I never saw or even spoke on the wire with her again. I will say this of her though, she was kind to the luckless, an oppressor of the wicked. I think of her often.

5.

EARLY SUMMER 1952 – SUSSEX, ENGLAND

Him: Can I hear as she does? Not now, likely not ever, conceptually though, the ability to absorb sound as something more feasible than the ripple of waves was a foreign notion until this moment. Somehow, I imbibe both her almost every feeling, illustration and speculation. It is thus, I could not but help to perceive her envisage, 'He sleeps the sleep of the dead' before she left for wherever it was she went. I worried not, save for her safety, as I by some means knew she would return sooner rather than later. The one-way telepathy she possesses, if that is what it is, feeds such instinct. No matter, she had left me the lucid glory of a dream in her wake. If only she knew the pace at which the stimulant, ethereal legacies afford me, left behind as keepsakes. If only. My mind races. Am I collecting the whole of her knowledge and dissecting her language at a swift pace? 'He's a quick learner in more ways than one', her bedtime whimsy now embedded in my head. Likely, most probably certainly, I grasp too much at one sitting for my own good.

More sixth sense than hunch, a rare thing for one like me, blessed with just smell and touch. I feel my dream was no illusion. Something intangible speaks, while something tangible paints a picture of a version of me before I came to be damaged so. Is that it? Yes, something from before nags, something from before she rescued me. Rescued? I need to fathom how to confirm, or otherwise that I am on the right track. Did she really 'rescue me'? Was I once as unambiguous as she? For the moment, though, I must recount my dream, for dreams most often fly away to God knows where.

"There is a magnetic corner of the globe, somewhere south of here and north of there, that is visible only from within. There are those who are unconsciously attracted to this land, others may guilelessly chance upon it. Some however, are abductees from abroad held captive as mere chattels, skivvy's and such like, marooned in the service of the better off citizens. It is thus that any and all would do well to take heed of my warning that in this place not everything is as it first seems. There is no movable feast in an unvarnished Hell cleverly disguised as vestal dreamland.

To the inept eye all is possible in this impossible corner boasting, as it does, a society built on unlikely 'either/or' bedfellow foundations born of frailty and virtue, namely, malice and benevolence. As to which of those twins holds sway at any given time is dependent upon the capricious pendulum of fate. Once when eavesdropping, I heard tell that after 'The Book of Impossible Things' – a tome all citizens once held dear – was unwittingly 'misplaced' nothing was ever the same. Needless to say, 'malice' reigns supreme pro-tem.

During my ill-fated stay here I have concluded any native tongue is understood by one and all in their own mother language and vice versa. Those peopling this most cosmopolitan of places are much varied. Black, white and a painter's pallet mix of pigmentations in between, effectively chronicling the all sorts assortment that is mankind.

Being of tropical clime, the season never changes. An unremitting summer persists, trapped as she is under the prevailing rainforest canopy. Additionally, daytime is forever overbearingly hot and sticky, humid, intolerable, yet beyond the witching hour the swelter remains much the same only scarcely less so.

I was delivered up by unenviable circumstance and am now a much-altered version of my former self. The revenant me longs to be homeward bound, to the place from whence I began. However, since the one whose name I am not privy to robbed me of my station in time and claimed me as her glorified bondservant I have been lost to the virtuous world.

I am now known by just a number, 107345. That is all there is, 'que sera, sera' as the fatalist might say."

There was, nay is, a surreal reality within the threads collected of slumber that signifies much more remains unsaid, is still to unfold. I sense her return. She will bestow further secrets of past, present and self. Already I grasp that she is petite, of purest white skin and locks, whereas I tower over her. When joined as one, it is as if restoration from before lingers on via her Morse code tongue. A journey revisited? The question nags at me.

Her: Hang his regular bath for a change. What use a new-fangled pristine double shower all the way from America not shared? She washes for two, careful not to get soap in vacant eyes that may not see, yet may well still smart. The concept of leaning forward to apply shampoo to cleanse his mass of curls seems beyond him. Understandable. The soapy task falls to her. She struggles, he senses her difficulty, lifts her up as if she weighed thin air. From lofty heights, she succeeds, makes sure all is rinsed away. He softly places her back upon the wet tiles. The lifting of her is a surprising new addition to his ever-growing list of realised talents. She contemplates the rapture of breakneck union, yet becomes lost in deepest thought, him now perched upon an old wooden bathroom stool, while shaving her much cherished strapping colossus's morning-shadow chin. She so wants to let her mind slip back in time. Back to where their story began, yet a gut-wrenching trauma of harsh memories bookends such train of thought.

Afternoon now, a scorcher. Outside not an option for one with lack of skin pigmentation. A shame. Regardless, she, a neo-Nightingale of sorts, has not bothered to dress either herself nor him. Little point in the circumstances. Besides, there is a certain virtue when she plays palpable Eve, and he the unwitting Adam, notwithstanding the absence of the silly fig leaf.

Supine upon the settee, eyes shut tight she rests, Beethoven's beast, Symphony No. 9, his final piece of excellence, the one composed when a complete deafness had finally taken Ludwig into a new domain. She holds on tight for the arrival of the final movement and its vocal soloists and chorus. The grandfather clock ticks too loudly when all is still, yet this day the volume just, only just, drowns the antique. For his part he sits cross-legged in front of the gramophone the palms of each hand glued to butterscotch plastic mesh speaker soaking up amplified vibrations, the slight muffling of sound this causes, a thing she could not but forgive.

Eyes open, she turns her head a little, looks over and at him, double takes and thinks, 'Shit, you've been through so much, my beautiful creature'. His capacity for perception amazes yet again. Plainly he knows she is gawping. How so? Plainly, he knows exactly where she rests, for as if loyal canine, he crawls on hands and knees toward her, kneels at her side. It is as if he is examining her with eyes not blind. Intently she watches as his left hand locates her bare belly. Then, using the tip of forefinger as marker she feels him trace the letters making up the short invisible sentence all lovers take for granted, 'I Love You'. That such words were written upside down, as if he expected her to read them as print, a surprise. A combination of amazement tinged with an abstract panic overwhelms. 'How the fuck did you do that?' No answer expected, none given. In the mini crisis of the moment she sheds uncontrollable tears of elation. A breakthrough. A credible impromptu connection beyond just the pleasures of the flesh has been accomplished. She had quite forgotten he was left handed.

Beethoven be damned, she takes the deepest breath, slips off the settee, rests a pliable him upon his back atop the supple woven rug specially imported from China. Mimicking his own about-face action, she scribes, 'I Love You Too' across his muscled stomach. In return, he bestows an unmistakeable expression full of tenderness and a knowing, repetitive nod of acceptance. Something understood. She thanks the Lord they chose not to put on clothing this day. Needs a handkerchief to wipe away more teardrops. The back of her hand must suffice. The possibilities and the enormity of rapport via finger-coded alphabet too much to ingest in an instant.

Him: A barrier was broken today. I am beginning to remember things, most often vaguest things, of a shared past, and now shared presence. The end of a something, the starting point for something else. Inexact history blended with flawed recollection. A fog persists, smothering my consciousness. Then a wide-awake precise past representation as if of these times. Me, she and Paris at war's end. Crystal clear. Then I am denied, for the memory takes shelter in the shadows almost as quickly as it showed up, is replaced with the overwhelming tiredness, a tiredness that takes no prisoners, offers up what is likely deceitful retrospection. I need to fathom a method of discerning facts from the stagnant pond of fiction that are nothing more than bogus memoir;

Nimble invasion then timeless occupation. To the bloated victorious the spoils of war. Bars of gold, works of art, champagne and any fine lady, more of the same, more of the same, then some more. It irked her that, surprisingly, his wallet was empty. Yet by way of fortunate recompense, the street wise working girl had had the foresight to steal the cavalry jackboots from the fetid feet of the soft bellied general lying there in a schnapps induced drunken stupor, snoring away like the fat pig he was.

She had heard tell that southeast of The Alps and faraway there was a place prone to the occasional earthquake, where the locals ate seafood, made their own fresh spaghetti, drunk white wines aplenty and paddled in the warm enclosed ocean as and when the fancy took. Also, she understood that the sun always shone there. Certainly, the Quartier Pigalle did not feel like home presently, and when word got out regarding her theft there would be hell to pay if she stayed put. It was clear she should leave the city without delay.

She determined that such a land as she had learned of would make for a perfect getaway save for the fact that she had not the official papers granting her leave of travel, and regardless she had not sufficient money for the train fare. Still, upon reflection and notwithstanding the potential for blizzards at high altitudes she could travel by foot. After all, the stolen cavalry jackboots looked to be expensive and as good as new and would serve her well on her long and, as an alpinist devotee had once made mention of, potentially treacherous journey. Moreover, it was somewhat fortuitous and perhaps a good omen that she shared the same shoe size as the previous incumbent of the boots. Indeed, having given them a trial she had concluded that they rather suited her, especially so when undressed for work. Additionally, in terms of marketing her exclusive services to all of mankind her new best 'up to the thigh' footwear would, she had little doubt, tickle the fetish fantasy of many a red-blooded businessman or give a delightful twist on comfort's take for any lonely soldier boy.

From the evidence of his wallet, it was a given that the slumbering, lumbering general plainly had no intent in paying her for both time and body. So, for good measure she stole his pistol also, then tied his feet together in case he awoke in order that she could safely make good her exit. It was thus that she followed in Hannibal's footsteps across the mountain range only pausing to pick edelweiss and nibble upon rye-breads and strange looking cheese with holes in it gifted to her by grateful goat herders and yodellers in traditional garb she had fallen across along the way. She had a tendency in that regard.

However, as is inevitably the case when the rabid untamed beasts of war are on the rampage and home-grown heroes still wear short trousers, when she reached rainbows end all she found was another city of the vanquished. A place where there was little need for the all-conquering to transact with the oft times timid, sometimes impulsive, now neutered populous. Yet by way of trading subjugation and subordination for blindfolds and sweet promises she found she made an income better than most others. Her thieved cavalry jackboots and her realization of wild fetishes served her well...and, at least the sun shone all the time.

Come evening, after a meal, we take fresh air, sit under a slouching yet commensurate heat. By way of touch, I note she is lightly clad. I am as was. For now no more finger language or the perplexing telepathy of her kiss. Matters not, we hold hands from our respective positions. She to my left. Every so often she raises a glass to my lips. Unique oaked flavours tell me this must be Rioja Alta. How so? I have no idea, yet memories of fine wine almost triggered. Rioja Alta always my preference back when. When? My head whispers Spain, my heart beats fast. For an instant I prepare to die a cryptic death. Then all is calm once more.

She must have noticed, she squeezes tight. Her tenacious tiny hand a fine match for my cold fear trembling one. Nothing comforts more than the one who loves. We remain thus until the heat abates and I chill a little.

We have a new bed it seems. A big one. Springy mattress. No coded finger messages required, our place of slumber duly christened. Energy spent, fast asleep, her body is appetizingly limp. For me, constant pillar to post reflections of Spain provoke a more than just a restless sleep. Spain of old is trying to speak with me, of that I feel certain. I beg of dreams that they tell me no more lies. They deny me even that small favour, only within these lies I have been granted the faculties I am now denied;

Here I have no tag of stereotype, here I am unique, here I am locked-in, here, within the lemon sandstone walls of a timeworn, breathless Moorish fortification I live a little, dream a lot, suffer, eat, wash and shit.

I am looking out through a barred window, elbows upon sill, crossed fingers supporting my chin, my back to her. Heard her footsteps as she approached. Noted she was alone for once. Out of choice I did not turn about face, did not acknowledge her presence.

For her part, she observed I had lost a little weight. Even from behind protruding ribs told their own story. The unsuspecting often took my blasé indifference toward all and sundry as a sign of resignation, maybe outright defeat, or perhaps just that my fabled genius had finally played out. How little they knew, for such apathy was merely a façade. A fact she was well aware of.

"Here, I have clothing for you...just an old gandoora...it'll have to do. I couldn't find any sandals. The thing is we can't have you...well...not like this...not today"

In the blue times twixt constant contemplation vis-a-vis my passion for lost causes, and the equally irksome conspiracy of idiots focused on inflammatory design, I, the prisoner here, would lay down and wait in anticipation of a Popular Front parade.

"I'll leave the gandoora folded on your bed. What are you so engrossed thinking about?"

Still I did not turn around. "For no good reason, other than perhaps the subliminal, I resolved that I would see if I could count up to one billion in whispers and wondered just how long such a challenge would take. Too long I reckon. You see, having determined that there are 86,400 seconds in a day it would take more or less 11,574 days, which works out at nearly 32 years to achieve such a quest, and that is assuming I take no sleep for the duration and only allowing one second to speak each number. Plainly I would need the occasional rest and further, as the numbers got bigger they would take more than one second to say. Given that I would likely pop my clogs, or be disposed of prior to completion I am thinking it for the best to abort the mission at this embryonic stage...by the way, why favour me with clothing after all this time? Since when has compassion been within your gift? And what's so bloody important about today?"

At home, she would watch, sometimes even play with the antennae of bristling ants that owned her garden. Yet in this place, she reigned supreme, played no silly games.

"Look at me, face me." Be that an order or request I cared not, studiously I ignored her. "Have it your way then," an out of character statement by any standard, the iron rod her usual preference, "You are free to leave...obviously, you can't leave as you are." She found herself wishing for storm clouds to match her imperfect mood.

At last I relented, changed position, looked her in the eye, "How so?"

She knew well that her cigarettes would kill before they cured, a presumption of her own private subjugation. Looking at me stood there stark naked I could virtually read her mind as the thought struck, and was then spelt out in words, that, 'spellbound are the idealists, the others are in their graves'. She announces she might write that down a little later. She made audible note that she could see my bruising was fading, though the scars were eternal, ensuring memory of her would live on in my worst nightmares. Then, "In Burgos, just yesterday, Franco was publicly proclaimed as Generalísimo of the National army and Jefe del Estado, Head of State. The civil war as good as over. For reasons I am not privy to, you are to be released forthwith. As to whether you'll ever be 'free in spirit', I doubt." I sensed that the words 'free in spirit' she spat out had left a bitter taste.

"So, all Godfearing fascists, so very fond of The White Terror can now sit back and count their pesetas, and one day claim they knew nothing about anything?"

She wore a phony smile, "You should know my preference would have been to have your head on a platter...excuse the metaphor...we never did break you; dehumanise you, you 'the one who got away'...still, I feel sure we'll meet again one day. Come, make haste, you will be escorted all the way to the French border."

Was this 'she' the one who brutally fashioned me thus? Weary in body, clouded clarity of thought defies evaluation when fact lays claim to be fiction's sibling.

6.

AMSTERDAM 1942 – A LIASON WITH A RESISTANCE FIGHTER

Her: The uninvited weasel occupying appropriated lodgings had had better days. Certainly, none worse. So much for the mouth-watering anticipation of red light potential and the sheer delight snapshots of 'spring again' tulips would bring to loved ones back home.

Deathly quiet within four walls, yet in the street below the sissing of cyclists, the chitter-chatter of panicking stale bread hunters was broken only by the blunt decrees of the hard-nosed uniformed playmaker directing gun totting subordinates toward likely attics and basements where the fearful hid or were hidden, the clatter of jackboots upon cobblestone and the odd terrorized scream of female distress. 1942 in Amsterdam a place where those not quislings were either taken on a free train ride, left weeping or resisting the best they knew how.

She could not help but to absorb the grandeur of his purloined surroundings. Albeit that he was a high-ranking officer he was, in the global plan of things, of arguable consequence, he had certainly done alright for himself. Highest ceilings flaunting crystal chandeliers she would, in different circumstances, readily swing from. Delicious sweeping views of the city from the balcony, a Dutch Master or two adorning aesthetically pleasing walls.

Ever the compassionate assassin, that he was on his knees, hands tied fast behind his back, feet tethered similar, her revolver as good as glued to his temple, she had afforded him the decency of retaining his socks. That that small modesty made him look ridiculous pleased her. Apt revenge for the evil he had orchestrated? She believed that to be the case, besides if God was reticent in coming out to play, then she would play God.

A little earlier, more out of boredom than anything else, she had, with painstaking care, removed from the bridge of his debatable Aryan nose his wire framed spectacles, placed them upon the sumptuous carpet, then, with the heel of his own forsaken boot, smashed them to smithereens before his screwed-up, searching eyes.

She already had all his secrets, and some more. The chapter was near complete. Tilting her head mockingly, her giveaway violet eyes drawn to his near unsighted equivalents, "You really are not as I imagined. All sinewy, half blind, a skinny little fully paid-up member of the self-proclaimed master race."

Now looking sheepishly at the floor, he mumbled as would a small child caught scrumping apples, "They'll catch you and kill you...you know that?"

"Maybe, maybe not."

Without the benefit of lenses, his now reluctant eyes struggled to interpret exactly what she was up to as she slipped on a rubberised glove, upon the palm of which she placed a thin-walled glass oval capsule, the size of a pea. "Stick out your tongue like a good soldier if you wouldn't mind." Although now aware of what was coming, his overwhelming desire to cling to dear life just a little longer ensured he almost voluntarily complied. With theatrical aplomb, her rubber protected thumb crushed the cyanide pill against his tongue. Insofar as she allowed, he squirmed a moment as she slammed shut his mouth, holding on tight, locking his jaw. Within just minutes' consciousness had taken its leave for someplace else. Shortly thereafter the heartbeat followed on behind.

Bagging up his clothing she paused to take a last look at her dead adversary. The thought struck that for his gestapo uniform to be complete, to be authentic, she needed the socks. A pity really, her artistry spoiled. Needs must when the devil drives, the socks she had to have.

It was evening when she returned to the scabby garret they shared on the other side of town.

"Success?" he asked.

"Of course, here, a genuine gestapo officers uniform, boots and all, for your chums in the Resistance for covert activities."

"Did you get it out of him as to just how much he knows of our whereabouts and operational plans?"

"You wish to debrief me so soon?"

"What do you think?"

A long and not unpleasant post-witching hour sharing both privileged information and each other came to pass. In times of war, he found, as did she, one takes what one can get double-quick.

7.

MIDSUMMER 1952 – SUSSEX, ENGLAND

Her: 'Red sky at morning, sailors take warning'. Tuesday has become Wednesday; the weather has turned. A promise of clouds and the odd shower of rain that suits those of sensitive skin. She brushes her hair before cheval glass mirror. Contemplates snow-white pig tails. Thinks of times before he enrolled in her list of lovers. Of the time before he entered her life;

'Cairo smelt of sweet dates, sweat, camels dung, hashish and tangible fear. White noise barter and banter in the bazaars irked her more than a little. Also, she noticed that the wily toffs, those gaudy suited moneyed ones donned the reddest fezzes, wore 'hammer and sickle' fashioned cufflinks. Bewildered she took the last ocean liner out of Alexandria, across The Med, home to timeworn England's pastures green. Within her productive invention she saw towering evergreens mask a nest of ferns disguising an undergrowth of helpless pinecones marooned within a permanent eventide that would never betray a murder, self-destruction or a clandestine union of thickest skinned untamed carefree true lovers.

Now safe and sound, the bespectacled librarian lookalike read Shakespeare and counted pennies. She loathed bigots, arranged marriages and Chaucer and, although her mousey disposition indicated otherwise, virginity was an irrelevant thing she could not claim as her own, less spoken of, timid virtue. On those days when not shuffling dust ridden books she played the banjo, badly initially, not so later. Craved the safe-haven of wonderful, wonderful Copenhagen before a beefy John Bull came chasing. Were he not a self-absorbed egotist insofar as the world at large was concerned he could have had her knickers off in a flash. Perhaps that was why she adored him from afar?

The year the angry mob sang the monsters praises in the graveyard, where the good and the great rested, stirrings from high above had the deceased turning in their graves wondering just how such an event could have happened. It was a long since lost to time Wednesday in late autumn when she concluded here, there and everywhere there would be a price to pay for this. Come the spilt blood of Western Europe's repetitive revolution, willing martyrs, since time began, live that dream. Self-same Wednesday, a cloudless night of moonbeams and salty spray, she waltzed with an imaginary lover at the end of the outcast pier to the heart-stopping gnarly waves inherited orchestration and the 'stay up late' choir of libertine gull's own savvy chorus. Wondered if a foetus knew of fear and laughed in its face? She was pregnant, of course. By whom? That was the question. Nothing came of the child. A miscarriage long forgotten, occasionally remembered.'

Perhaps in a while we shall take a drive out somewhere more interesting than somewhere just 'nice'. Perhaps not. The potential for distress in his hour of partial recovery sways her decision. She decides to walk with him to the lake. He would like that she supposes. Recalls he once swam The English Channel. Maybe they could take a dip. Let not the chill of cold waters interrupt, let them inspire.

In his brand-new pastel blue gandoora and Roman sandals he has the look of a flawed Messiah about him. Summons to mind the day, not that long ago, she had retrieved him. All he wore, all he possessed even, was just a blood, sweat and excrement stained, once white gandoora, an item now washed, ironed and stored away in the hidden box of memories. For her part the wide-brimmed floral print sunhat suffices, the golden orb no threat to her wellbeing this day.

The seclusion of the estate, save for the days when the groundsman and his squad are at work, affords a life more Bohemian than in current vogue. They hold hands, share a kiss here, a kiss there as she guides him across a vast lawn down to lakeside. Once there she feeds him by hand wild cherries and Scottish raspberries from a small wicker hamper she had had the foresight to carry with her. Ever the territorial bird a cock robin makes his presence known.

He drops to his knees pats terra-firma seeking softest grass. She keeps a weather-eye as he slips out of his single item, lies face down on the turf and executes a hundred press-ups or more. Impressive, inspiring. A certain brazenness almost overwhelms as she wishes to lie twixt he and grassland beneath; that she be exertion's amorous foil. Laughs at the very thought of it. Perspiration's very own beads dripping from his brow to hers would make her urge. Bad idea, though one worth the thought.

Later, swimming, she stays scrupulously at his side. The water is pretty deep in places, she must take great care all remains well in his world. No need for concern, he still swims like a fish. Foolishly, she has forgotten to bring towels. She ought to be angry with herself, yet cares not a jot. Upon exiting the lake, much shivering and chattering teeth. Nought an inseparable, enduring embrace cannot cure.

On their backs, side by side, she shifts her body a quadrant, supports her raised head in open palm. Almost 'Thinker' pose, she reaches over, rigid digit at the ready, pens a question upon his abdomen, 'ARE YOU REMEMBERING THINGS?' She notes the etching of the 'question mark' clearly tickles. He sits up, seeks out her forehead, prints, 'YES. MANY THINGS'. Eagerly, she responds, 'BEST WE GO BACK AND SPEAK SOME MORE'.

Some days seem never to end. This is not such a day. Time is adamant that it will not stand still. Through unique calligraphy the pair exchange questions and answers, answers and more questions, giving scope for momentum in his cerebral restoration. Instinct advises she should not rush. Small steps are best when handling the wounded, more so as she suspects recollection of one specific memory will be so horrible that if and when it is recovered it may destroy him for eternity. Besides, the day is waning. She changes tack. Playtime allowed, school is out for break time.

Twilight is now keen to birth darkness gifting small glimmer to soft-hued quarters a bleary-eyed sun has kissed goodnight. A time when reckless silhouettes oust unnerved shadows and horizons are lost to goodbye's opaque puzzle. Extravagant moths, wily bats and stay out late swifts come to play, kindling ponderous fresh lover's fragile fancy, so sweet l'heure bleue of crepuscular invention. In such surroundings their world belongs to a soothing moon, sometimes daring, sometimes sheepish, now and then shining, other times blue. Captivating twilight, you are sovereign. As it should be in times such as this, the sympathetic

Chinese carpet once more plays host to the cavort of the infatuated. The ticking of the grandfather clock, the gullible metronome.

Afterwards, she spoons feeds him French onion soup and rustic bread. Albeit engrossed in the task, and gratified he is woofing it down with relish, an idea. Childs play in its simplicity, yet likely adrenalizing for the one, who until now had been stuck within his own lost world. They take to the new bed where, until a tiredness overwhelms, they scribe noughts and crosses upon each other's bare flesh. Given her gift of sight trumps his of blindness, she even lets him win a game or two. Smiles from both, much laughter from one. His best day so far? Likely that is so. Before sleep takes hold, her finger asks of his chest if he had any recollection of the occasion they met for the very first time. 'I DO' his hasty response.

The longest day arrives, the day a stand up straight and tall sun cloaks itself in grey cloud as to deliberately disappoint. Matters not, she has a great scheme afoot.

Ever that loyal canine, he lets her lead him to the bedroom. Once settled comfortably on his back upon the eiderdown she pulls up an occasional chair, sits to his right, and thus is comfortable inscribing invisible words upon his torso, starting from pelvis then up toward scapula, so as his dead eyes might read as a book if afforded a magic spark.

Ever so slowly, with gentle precision, 'NOW IS THE TIME FOR YOU TO TELL ME OUR STORY. THE FIRST TIME WE MET. DO YOU FEEL ABLE TO DO THIS?' A nod of concurrence. She continues, 'TAKE AS LONG AS YOU NEED. I SHALL PLAY BLACKBOARD TO YOUR CHALK'.

Him: As she asked for an answer to her question the whispering voice inside my head spoke up, reminding me in concrete detail that, yes, I well-remembered the first time I cast my eyes upon my free spirited, blanched angel. A cardinal lust at first sight, a sweltering love followed on not far behind. Against all odds given my experience thus far my memories are this time, unpolluted. As the bankers might say in terms of a blue-chip potential client, 'undoubted'.

However, the modus of communication twixt her and I surely will render a full transmission a hopeless task.

Notwithstanding the matinee hosting the dramatics from the reels of a motion picture playing inside of my Theatre Skull I resolve to provide, best I can, just salient points and landmark still frames, via capital letters traced upon her bare belly. So long as I establish, to her satisfaction, that I am closer now to becoming who I once was, her heart will rest easy. Who would have thought that, what on the face of it looks to be nothing other than silly erotic playfulness, is my means of contacting the outside world? A small virtue of naked connection. Even from my locked-in perspective, this whole exercise is both bizarre and not without a beautiful symmetry. It is said, 'where there is a will there's a way' and she and I have proven such throwaway line as accurate through our own exclusive mode of exchanging information. Every so often, I detect my finger has slipped into the tiny crater that is her belly-button. It is then she wiggles, probably giggles, and I must start again from the top, but not before acquainting her with the fact that exercise might take all day and well into the night. 'NOT AN ISSUE TO WORRY YOURSELF ABOUT' her gently engraved riposte.

Several times I try, several times I fail. My forefinger is willing, the complexities of long-winded storytelling say 'no'. The more I think, the longer and more exclusive what was meant to be anecdote becomes. A dictionary worthy of The Oxford tag fills a brain that until now has been in rediscovery mode. Despite best endeavours, the task is beyond me. As any experienced agent knows, when a plan is falling apart, then the plan must be aborted. Yet, as any experienced agent also knows, without a contingency strategy he is dead in the water.

I sense her concern that my words are not flowing. My finger pens the unseen yet understood words, 'THIS IS TOO MUCH FOR ME,' then adding, 'MY TALE IS COLOSSAL. I REMEMBER EVERYTHING EXCEPT HOW I CAME TO BE HERE.' I detect that she sits up, then stands wobbling precariously upon a playful mattress. Instinctively I also stand, locate her naked hips and hold her steady. The face with eyes that see all, now faces my darkness beholden equivalents. Resting her petite hands upon my shoulders, she draws me forward just a little. Then an everlasting kiss, taking care not to entwine our tongues to the extent that disentanglement becomes insurmountable. When raw passion dedicates itself to pure love's cause, a crescendo like no other follows in its wake. Such hasty lovemaking makes for a sticky iridescence. We shower, a routine best shared. She pens the promise, 'LEAVE IT TO ME. MAYBE, I CANNOT BE EASEL TO YOUR CHALK. BUT A BLACKBOARD AND CHALK I CAN BUY FOR YOU. ARE YOU ABLE TO WRITE DOWN OUR STORY? I CAN GUIDE YOU IF THE WORDS CROSS EACH OTHER.' I answer a simple, 'YES'. 'THEN I WILL GO INTO TOWN AND BUY ALL YOU NEED'. She leads me back to bed wanting me to rest there until her safe return, kisses me once more. I can feel the smooth material of her the clothing she must have just put on.

Her: Albeit loathing being at the wheel, a thing she has always found tedious, she keeps an old Jaguar Mark IV as a ridiculously excessive run-around. Now late afternoon and day long cautious shadows are beginning to stretch their limbs, this is not an early closing Wednesday so the hardware store is still open for business. It is at that store she parks up and makes her purchases of both slate and the, to her at least ever since childhood, mystical rock formed from sediment, fashioned into chalk sticks.

Understandably keen to return home as soon as possible she is irked to find that upon attempting to start her vehicle the engine merely grunts and futz. Hopeless rain clouds replace the threatening grey clouds that had lingered all day. A summer storm brews. She has no umbrella nor suitable coat with her for when the clouds finally burst. Despite the prospect of the days third metaphorical shower, she has little choice but to take the walk to the local garage on the edge of town to seek assistance. She estimates it is a half a mile walk. It is along the way, via the High Street, then taking the shortcut through St Mary's Church graveyard her very own 'in the beginning' Bohemian flashback arrives to say an almost, but not quite welcome, 'hello' even though her faulty engine should be her thinking priority;

'Before the delivery of abstraction and castles in the air, when untamed filaments deemed nakedness as an impossible perception there was a conscious void, where eat, sleep and breed was all. Come metamorphosis, come the arrival of flesh unadorned, then come the nativity of an alive and kicking thing, later to be known as 'art'.

In her malleable days of fresh courage, her wild secret never shared, she had declared herself a living art form. As such she determined she would live life accordingly, blind to ominous power shifts threatening the hitherto established, convivial order of all things. Such changes would find chaos reigning supreme, for humankind now came to see only the dancer, not her dance, caring not that such creativity as would satisfy the senses was about to become nought but art's rotting corpse; a mere metaphor for the ways of war.

On sunny days, in the privacy of a stone walled garden, upon the greenest buttercup and daisy lawn, surrounded by extrinsic Romanesque mirrors she prepared herself in mind and body. In a flight of fancy, unravelled her interpretations of what she would become when outside of reflexive self. She found the answer in completeness.

Blanched whiter than snowfall, mouth wateringly clad in just the unwieldy papier-mâché fashioned wings of a mute swan she danced a lonely ballet, while in the shadows a timeworn virtuoso caressed a disinfected violin before a spellbound congregation of neo aggressors. For their sins, the soulless gathered together within the smouldering theatre of life, had eyes only for a perceived naked tart, not the sublime artist at play.

Before such cruellest intrusion, the self-same venue was an avant-garde meeting parlour, where wasted artists chose to pickle their livers, speak of rhymes and reasons, sometimes to tussle each other for the limp hand or unmentionables of the one who might become muse, lover or last port in a storm. Within the audience, a medallion laden Field Marshall, a clichéd monocle sporting conqueror to boot, in the company of subordinate stooges, a man renowned for taking what he pleased for pleasure or for profit.

"Who is this albino freak? She is stunning beyond belief. I must have her."

With palm covering tell-tale mouth, thwarting any prying lipreaders, his second in command advises, "I understand the girl caused quite a storm in the months before we arrived. She is held in high regard in artistic circles."

"Is she really...have her arrested for public nudity the moment her performance ends."

"Is such a thing against the law in these parts, Sir?"

"I neither know nor care."

Each holding an arm in crushing vice like grip, a brace of lackeys frogmarch the live art form from floodlit stage to the dimness of a Field Marshall's table. Laid bare before him, she protests that with wings intact she cannot be considered naked and has thus not broken any laws. Upon a nod and the click of his fingers, she is no longer a swan. *"There then...wings clipped...you are now outside of the law...I'd be obliged if you fellows would take her to my vehicle. Keep guard of her...no funny business. I'll join you shortly."* She requests that she collects threads of modesty from her dressing room. Such request falls upon deaf ears, then they bustle her away, she spitting profanities to the backdrop of stamping jackboots and cries of 'encore'.

3AM in what would be a paradise mansion were it not for its gross incumbent, her restless sleep is broken. She finds herself queerly unrestrained, sharing the bed of one who had both taken her to this place and later 'taken her' there. A paradox not lost. A careless Field Marshall now sleeps the sleep of the dead, immune to his frailty. In the drawer of a bedside cabinet she discovers just a revolver and a uniform regalia dagger. Her choice the latter. No time wasted in his transformation from man to starfish, his limbs now rigidly secured to points of the compass bedposts, mouth stuffed with smelly socks and dress tie gagged.

She pinches his nostrils together, causing his startled return to stark reality. The dagger begins its journey of quest at his jugular, pauses a while for melodramatic effect, then its razor tip scores his frozen torso from chest bone down to sex. His castration her culinary masterpiece. She leaves her tormentor, still squirming, fighting a losing fight with the ties that bind, to bleed an unhurried, tortuous death. Due punishment for heinous crime enacted. From the bedroom veranda, his testes are thrown away. 'Carrion for the magpies' she thinks, she smiles.

From that night and forever, she ceases to be an art form and becomes a fledged assassin whose name would one day come to be spoken in whispered esteem throughout intelligence circles across the globe. Moreover, as to exactly how a naked girl carrying a Field

Marshall's private briefcase full of secrets, that she would later sell to the highest bidder, made her escape she never did tell. Yet escape unscathed she did.'

Was that memory her future career defining moment? Likely it was.

The man at the garage was known to her. A friendly enough middle-aged bearded, chubby chap, who could most probably do with a few lessons when it came to personal hygiene, enthusiastic about matters mechanical and ever willing to retain the goodwill of his customers. Only recently he had serviced the Jag. To have it breakdown not that long after such servicing was unacceptable. That he could only apologize and agree to have her car towed back to the garage for an overnight repair plainly embarrassed him. Noting her displeasure at the prospect of making her own way home and then having to go back into town the next day to collect her car, the 'man at the garage' was quick to offer the loan of his own vehicle overnight. He points out that the loan car is parked just 200 yards up the street from the garage. Bidding him goodbye she commences the short stroll toward a rather uninteresting Ford Prefect. It would have to do.

The English weather can be as unkind as it is unpredictable. No sooner has she started walking, the heavens open and spontaneously soak her to the skin. That she wears only a cream lace long sleeved button down the front dress that becomes instantly see-through at least brings forth a controlling smile. Not such a smile from the local vicar, somewhat taken aback when making due mental note that if 'see-through' was bad enough, the stark truth that she wore nothing underneath was even worse. Tutting to himself he walks on by. Regardless, she collects the little Ford and returns to the hardware store where she had had the foresight to leave the blackboard and chalks in the care of the manager and out of inclement weather's way. It tickles her sense of humour that said manager, unlike the shocked vicar, could not but help feast his eyes upon the as good as naked apparition stood before him in the now totally translucent dress. Fortunately, to a nonconformist girl who had both done and seen all that the human body in art and reality can display, puerile modesty is, always was, a largely immaterial thing. Even so, given the practical and climatic difficulties of the afternoon adventure she is surprised her mood remains good. 'It must be because my giant is well again in his head. He is functioning again' her fleeting verdict as to her upbeat disposition.

The drive homeward, through the ever-worsening storm provoking flash floods and mayhem a tricky business in a tricky to drive arguable rust bucket fails to nag at her demeanour. She makes a point to park as close to the door as is possible, thus ensuring rainwater has a minimal effect on the blackboard and relatively vast quantity of chalk sticks. The cacophony of nature's chosen storm muffles all other sound as she struggles with purchases carried in one hand, a front door key in the other. Once safely ensconced in the hallway she rests the gift that will make for better communication aside the telephone table.   Now behind closed doors the impossible thought that she hears music dismissed as daft. Her priority is to check on her giant of crippled senses.

To her astonishment, she finds him in the drawing room, sat unveiled at her Steinway grand piano playing Beethoven's Moonlight Sonata, a rendition defining perfectness. In awe of, and conscious that he neither can see nor hear, she sheds intoxicated tears of wonderment. How so? Back in the days of intrigue he was all thumbs, could not play but a single note.

He stops playing immediately, no doubt feeling the draft as she opened the door making him aware of her return. Sullen, with the look of guilt about him he sits head bowed upon the piano stool. Rejoicing still in what she just heard, what she just saw with her own eyes, she rushes over to where her giant sits, planting a thousand kisses upon his face and head, crying out an ecstatic 'bravo' only she could perceive. Inevitably, beyond her wild enthusiasm, the quizzical perspective within demands she know more.

Remaining seated, he reaches out for her. She sees that he is unsurprisingly startled to discover she is drenched wet through and more than a little covered in chilly goose bumps. Gently, and with the self-same purity applied to the piano's keys he unbuttons the dress that clings, top to bottom, finally slipping it slowly off her shoulders, tugging it a little down over her arms, lastly allowing it to drop crumpled and dripping to the floor. Enveloping his arms around her, holding her as close as is possible, he transmits his body heat, hugs her back warm once more. Then they are as one. That a little later her fourth and his third 'shower' of the day would be a necessity, a worthy price to pay, whatever the answers to questions still to be sought. For now, Beethoven can be put on ice.

The giant's propensity to grasp the methodology of the translation into chalked words on slate of his initial memories, beyond all expectation. Plainly, his soul had not been as permanently damaged as his sensory faculties.   With a modicum of bleeding-heart guidance at the outset, he was now able to make known to her a memory of events far more detailed than even those she had recollection of. That such communication was one-way traffic, an inconvenient irritation. For her part, her only way to convey information or raise questions remained tactile finger spelling upon on bare belly.

First thing, each day, every day was to get him to cast words, words that she would transcribe in a journal kept exclusive. As the blackboard filled, studiously she would wipe away the evidence, have him pen the next piece. His memory as to where he had left off, of where he had to carry forward from was both immense and impressive. Afternoons were kept free. Mostly they were spent together outside of the house, as weather allowed. The project of putting memory into words was all-consuming. She had decided it for the best that they stayed naked. It had become a wide-eyed habit born of part desire and part the need to exchange small talk using their own invention, namely the rub of fingertip upon sensitive skin, the latter being unworkable clothed. Often, she wished he could see her as she saw him, yet from the content of his written account she found it to her liking that somewhere in a gallery inside his head held still frames of her every which way. Often, she mulled over which 'she' he thought of when they made love.

It had taken the best part of what was left of June, into a balmy July before his story of the circumstances of their first meeting was fully told. He had, to her mind, not missed a single thing. Purposely, waking up in the early hours the morning after its completion to read it in its whole, uninterrupted, chalk dust free entirely, was a day she had looked forward to seemingly for an eternity.

Him: My mind is, I find, sharper than ever before. I was no slouch but the writing down of our story has been a therapy like no other. Maybe, this is my very being compensating for the loss of sight, hearing and voice? Maybe. I am still at odds with the universe when it comes to discovering what happened to me, that memory if it still exists within will need to be hunted down. If lost entirely my greatest fear is that there might be too much for her to impart by way of fingertip. I'll not rest easy until I am abreast of what happened, of how I became the freak I often, despite her love and compassion, feel. Whatever it was, I am blessed she found me. For now though, the only story I can tell is of the day I met her.

December 1937 – His reflections of events in Surrey, England

It was nearing Christmas, I recall. An exiled Romanov, a Grand Duke of ill repute, although with inconsonant, strong links with The Fuhrer by all accounts and a subject the Department had long since been interested in, indeed, had tracked far and wide, who had organized this 'no names, no pack drill' illicit event. Given the nature of the gathering, I conclude that the local constabulary must have been offered a considerable donation funding this year's policeman's ball and, more importantly, to turn a blind eye. Whatever, this is for all intents and purposes an evening of fisticuffs and fanny in the company of empirical suits. A fine way to celebrate the season of goodwill in a wretched, soulless waning epoch tainted with the stench of brewing war across Europe, maybe beyond. By hand delivered 'private invitation only', the arrogant well-heeled elite, defining old money values, and the morals of good for nothing scoundrels gathered together. That the Grand Duke had included me on his guest list, an unexpected thing yet too good an opportunity to turn down. He surely must have known full well who I was; what I did to earn an honest crust. Sometimes, those who aspire toward newfound greatness, or retrieval of greatness lost in a tidal wave of self-possession, believe they are sacrosanct and lose life's plot. Such, I suspected was the case with our blue-blooded, filthy rich host with a finger in every forbidden pie. That he kept a high public profile and had yet to be assassinated by the Soviets let alone any other interested parties remained an unanswerable question.

Regardless, I accepted his offer of an 'Evening of Gentlemen's Entertainment' at a place somewhere in the bowels of garish Surrey in an instant. As to which one of us would be predator and which one prey I was yet to ascertain, although my hunch was that I might be the latter. It mattered not, such dilemmas are par for the course in the game that is espionage;

Spotlights illuminate a ring without ropes. Beyond its invisible boundaries, save for the soft glowing crimson halos of the glowing crimson cigar tips and the occasional tepid mayfly flames of obligatory cigarette lighters, the recently fashioned in haste auditorium is in darkness. On top of the prodigious raised circular platform, for it certainly is no boxing ring, no ropes, no neutral corners, under a fog of tar and nicotine particles trapped by the glare of the overhead lights a young man is taking a beating. Pandemonium infests a baying throng. The bare-knuckle fight lasts only a single minute. The pretentious toff audience, now an angry mob, want more blood, more gore.   The fight a mismatch. An incidental referee surprisingly intervenes to save the boy taking unnecessary extra punishment. Presumably, he takes the view that the Grand Duke would not take kindly to having dispose of a corpse of irrelevant consequence.

The victor, clearly familiar with the rules laid down by the Marquis of Queensberry, seeks a neutrality of sorts, a rostrum's edge, until the referee beckons him to centre of what is truly a ring more suited, perhaps, to the wrestling fraternity. A hand painted with the sticky claret of the loser's blood is raised aloft confirming triumph. The winner has not broken sweat.   There is a ripple of applause acknowledging the victorious one that is barely a white noise, hardly discernible against a wall of heckling and catcalls. Cyclops and Elephant Man, both in boiler suit overalls assist the bewildered also-ran off stage. From the vanquished blood flows bountiful, his face a swollen ruin.   Illumination is restored. The plush punters quieten down. Only the rumble of a thousand conversations randomly pollutes the salacious guffawing of the demonstrative.   Scantily clad waitresses bring out more champagne. One screams aloud as a drunken slug pinches her curvesome bottom. She drops her tin bar tray. It clatters as it hits the stone floor. Glass shatters all about. She makes out to slap the slug's face yet thinks twice. Thinks better of the idea. The slug stuffs a fistful a "five jacks" down the girl's cleavage.   A score is amicably settled. A semblance of order is restored amongst a sea of testosterone charged masculinity sat, a dozen to each round table, all in best bib and tucker. Bow ties abound. No gallantry here.

The night is drawing to its inevitable close. Only the one act left before curtain fall. A lewd comedian, better suited to Chiswick Empire variety theatre for the common man, his Italian lookalike suit shimmering silver over a purple waistcoat, microphone in hand, returns. After tripping on its lead and almost falling flat on his back he combines all that is erudite and smutty as he unleashes a tirade of wisecracks. The comedian has, at every opportunity, been spouting off thus all evening. He is our Master of Ceremonies. I find his bawdy tales all but amusing. He announces that a brace of strippers, the pair who had provided virtuoso performances earlier, and whose cascading tresses, swollen knockers and curvaceous chassis' we had feasted upon then will now mingle with the audience. That they mingle unclothed, selling raffle tickets for some charity or another, a predictable thing. By the same token, that they are also the 'prize' will readily ensure ticket sales beat usual expectations.

The finale, the crowning glory. Our less than illustrious compere promises something most 'special'. He grins the worldly grin of the consummate bore. The drift of his words not lost on this audience. He exits to small hand-clapping. Once more, the lights extinguished, only the stage remains in a foggy glow. All is still as the gathered company waits in quiet anticipation. One could hear the drop of a pin. The wait seems to last forever. Suddenly, there is fine music, not emanating from the gallery as previous. Not the big band imitators who played with pomposity for the previous strippers. Just the elegance of an aging pianist sat at his piano, edge of stage, waiting his moment. His presence there as if by magic.

A single, blessed shaft of frigid light plays tricks with eyes wide-opened, pans, then descends first upon the far reaches where the pianist remains, then swiftly transfers centre-stage exposing just you, you as otherworldly ballerina, stood as statue on tippy toes, plainly awaiting your moment of glory. Collective heavy breathing, for you wear not a thing in the interest of modesty. Indeed, I am quick to note you chose not to favour body hair. There is no soft bell-shaped romantic tutu for thee my love, for you are clad in nought but simple pink ballet slippers, a tempting single garter belt and a pancake tutu affording a scandalous view, your snow-white hair in a loose bun, pantalettes an option abandoned.   That you are quite the most superlative female specimen I have laid my eyes on leaves me stupefied. I am unconditionally engrossed. What is more, your perfectly formed configuration, of small stature, tempting albino skin so remarkably, yet so agreeably ghostly pale, and even from where I sit, your engaging violet eyes bewitch, though you, the angel who had chosen to take the fall, notice me not.

So preoccupied with you am I that the split second the pianist commences his performance I am taken aback. He plays the smoothest piano arrangement of Tchaikovsky's, the Nutcracker pas de deux, the "Dance of the Sugar Plum Fairy". A solo dance for a ballerina, and dance you do, though not before loosening your ridiculous, grotesque even, tutu, allowing it the slip to the floor, stepping out of and over the tragic thing thus ensuring what might have been putrid pornography becomes accomplished tactile art, the retention of that garter belt perhaps the licentious key to such art. The music almost lingual you dance both shamelessly and sensually ensuring an achievement that is faultless, contradictory and filled with a scorched purity, the like of which previously unknown to this seasoned observer of the fairer sex. There is no sadness, no desperation in what you do. Remarkable, furthermore that you are, traced throughout by a roving beam of light, the icing on the cake. I am witnessing way beyond the subjective, the exploration of the possible, the exquisite capabilities of the female frame in dance. I wonder if any of the others here see art beyond the person dancing as I do? Unlikely, all things considered. Philistine's them all.

As your own take upon the depiction of classic ballet ends the cry goes out for more, more, more. Those roars of approval abound about the place; so loud I think that they might bring down the roof.

Outside, deep midwinter's after-dark freeze, inside a more than comfortable virility enhanced fever.

As you allow your erotic novelty to fade into a legitimate bareness the crowd comes to life, roars its inebriated approval. No longer do they lurk in the shadows of barbarous hush.

The prance now done with you, the albino girl and her pianist hold hands, bow to your audience to further cries of 'encore, bravo, encore'. The pianist whisper indiscernible words in your ear, takes of his lonely leave. Now you stand proud, stand alone, seemingly captivated by the roars of undoubted approval. It is as if the naked you is absorbing the very life energy of your drooling patrons, feasting upon your own omnipotence, enjoying yourself beyond measure. You, as invincible predator have them begging to be your exclusive prey. Eventually, as I suppose you must, you turn to exit. I detect a certain reluctance on your part. You have the look of a girl who has revelled in herself beyond measure. It is then, seemingly unannounced, the Grand Duke himself makes an appearance. A fine bouquet of white tea roses in hand. Without hesitation, you, back on firm ground, accept his worthy gift, even peck your benefactor upon his bristly cheek, taking the delicate flowers to the place edge of stage where rests your discarded tutu. With greatest care, you go down on one respectful knee, lay the bouquet upon the floor. Then, in a flash, drawn from the rim of your pancake fashioned garment lying there, what I immediately presume to be a circus throwing knife. You make direct eye contact for an instant with the Grand Duke before propelling the knife in his proximate direction. He collapses in a heap on stage. So impressively skilled are you in the art, for your accuracy and the sheer power of impact delivered leads me to conclude our host would have died in what my American chums would name 'a New York minute', the offending blade cemented into his now cold heart. As assassinations go, a blueblood taken out by a naked albino before a riotous audience takes some beating. A melodramatic moment of the first order has just been unveiled by one unveiled. I find myself wondering just, 'who the fuck is this girl?' and determine that I must find out.

Little time to think on as anarchy and commotion prevails. Without delay full illumination of the venue is restored. Enormous bodyguards, brutes and accessories surround pocket-sized you. Still, you stand your ground, head tilted as one in quizzical thought, the look on your face one of insane curiosity. Then, as abrupt as an antelope being run down by a pack of wolves, a most wily you races away through the surrounding circle of muscular would be captors, through the panic stricken gathered throng, and are off and out, pushing aside all that stand in your way, off into the freezing cold of night. Surely, tenacity must be your middle name?

For a moment or two I remain calmly seated enjoying the mayhem, just sipping on my glass of Bolly, reflecting upon the astounding event that had just unfolded before my very eyes. That your slaying of the Grand Duke, for most certainly he was a dead as the proverbial Dodo, was as clearly planned and premeditated as it was sensationally brazenly breath-taking in its execution notwithstanding the outwardly foolish absence of a blueprint for a safe escape. The idea strikes me that surely you must be in the employ of The Soviets, yet panache and Soviets are rare bedfellows. Impromptu, I resolve to recover you before the predatory henchman of the deceased intercept and bring you to ground. For reasons bordering on abject lunacy and odds ostensibly stacked against a successful outcome does not deter me from being the chivalrous knight questing to save the life of a damsel in distress.

That the herd now also stampede toward the main exit, a given. My own preference is a fire exit come side door leading to the copse within the grounds, spotted upon arrival here. I have long since discovered that in my line of business one does not last long without making note of artful ways out of any building, and if I'm not mistaken your obvious guile would take you out of this place and make for those small woodlands aside the mansion. That is, in similar circumstance what I would do. Both my choice and guess are sound for outside, away from the brouhaha, where tarmac gives way to pine trees, under moonlight, I find you, my beautiful bare-skinned ballerina held fast by a brute while his accomplice, his face in yours, plainly reads you the riot act. I take the view that they are awaiting the arrival of someone more senior prior to taking further action. I check the lie of the land for any stray onlookers and noting that fortunately there are none, I clinically disable the pair of them pronto, leaving them out cold on a prickly bed of pine needles. Aghast, your frowning eyes and crinkled thinking brow dart first at the bodies lying prone, then directly at me. You are not too sure if I am friend or foe. It seems you choose the latter, as you start to make a run for it.

I pride myself on nothing if not my fitness. After all, I can run the 100-yard dash in just a little over 10 seconds and have swum The English Channel on two previous occasions. In short, I am much too fast for you, and even though you do not presently see me as that rescuing Arthurian knight in white armour I am quick to grab a flyweight you, throwing you over my shoulder head first, though 'without so much as a by your leave' you act most unlike any rescued damsel in distress in all of history. I feel your tiny yet most effective fists pummelling my back. By way of physical riposte I slap your delicious bare arse' and announce that, "I am on your side" and that for your well-being you would be well advised to, "shut up, and play dead", if you wish to get out of this situation in one piece.

I apologise for what you no doubt see as my lack of chivalry in throwing you over my shoulder like a market traders sack of spuds, adding, "Young lady, you are plainly in a bit of a pickle, I am merely trying to rescue you. I am versed in these matters. You are in safe hands now. I will carry you as we make our way to the front of the building and through the inevitable panicking throng to where my driver and vehicle awaits. I shall simply make it known to one and all that I am on official business and have you under arrest."

"Are you Special Branch? I take it you are? Well, Mr Plod, you can put me down, I had the whole matter under control until you arrived." I choose to deny you that request pointing out, "It certainly didn't look like it was 'under control' with you at the mercy of those two thugs? And no I'm not Special Branch, although to an extent you are on the right track."

"Look there's no time to lose. Just let me go. I'll explain all another time, say The American Bar at the Savoy Hotel, 5PM tomorrow for cocktails, you can pay. And by the way should you ever slap my backside again I'll fucking kill you."

"Gosh, you really are a spirited little thing. Least you forget I've already incapacitated those gorillas who had you in their grasp..."

You interrupt. "Those two 'gorillas' as you call them are my minders, playacting as assailants, leaving others to presume I have been apprehended, thus assisting me in my escape...a complicated tale, yet true. I don't know you from Adam, Sir. Now put me down. I am quite capable of looking after myself."

I accede to your stern request and carefully place you upon freezing dry land. Without the hint of delay, and as a freshly ringed bird returned to freedom, you head for the trees at pace, only taking time to turn about for an instant to remind me, "The Savoy, 5PM tomorrow."

I casually stroll back into the building via the fire exit and take of my leave by the main door. Outside, beyond the masses, my driver has the engine running, thankfully the heater on high. "Bit of trouble at the do, Sir?". "You could say that, not sure what it was all about if the truth be told." We depart. It is only then, sat lounging upon the back seat enjoying a cigarette, I recall my much-cherished herringbone overcoat had, by necessity, been left behind in the cloakroom as I gave chase. The word 'bollocks' springs to mind. Deciding to return to collect it would be pointless and sure there was nothing of great importance within its pockets I see no reason to bother my driver to return to recover it.

All the way back to Belgravia all I can think of is you, the pretty little thing with the will to kill, yet, on the face of it, so perversely innocent on the eye. Off you scamper into a wooded darkness outrageously clad in just ballet shoes, the self-fashioned Naked Nymph of the Pine Forest of the Night. I am perplexed as to just how you will make good that escape in such circumstances. One thing for certain though, and that is that without fail I shall attend The Savoy tomorrow at the agreed time. Certainly, the image of that edible, petite bare-bottom of yours as you fled, I knew would linger on. Delightful. If flesh alone could leave one besotted then you are the living proof of such a thing.

I am keen to continue the passing on of our story. She says a firm 'No'. Kisses my forehead, says we both need a break for food and drink. Asks if I could tell the next part of the tale as a traditional story, akin to a novel, not as a mission debrief in the first person, as she finds it a little irksome. She adds that she is impressed beyond measure. Also, if I have a complete recollection as to all that 'happened next' then she will cry tears of joy knowing that once more we truly belong to each other in not just body, yet mind and soul. That she will find a way to magic a full life for me out of just my sense of smell and touch. She is testing my abilities I think. Before I resume, she pens, almost clawing my torso with her fingernails in enthusiasm, that she has 'that' garter belt still;

The American Bar within D'Oyly Carte's glazed brickwork creation that is The Savoy Hotel, bounded by Art Deco's own butterscotch ivory's uniform variations and favoured by the likes of Bogart, Marlene, de Gaulle and Winnie himself, a glamorous venue. Certainly, one suited to those of magnetic charisma over the grouchy academics engrossed in testing their expertise against a slumberous Times Crossword Puzzle in an exclusive Gentlemen's Club. In a corner, seated under portraits of old stars and new starlets, sits a tall, handsome man of athletic build, dressed in Saville Row's finest, sipping a Daiquiri and outshining the immaculate tie-and-jacketed waiters, so well versed in the care of their wellborn clientele. It is 5.07PM. Thrice he has impatiently looked at his Rolex. She set the time for their meet at 5.00PM. She is late; he is a stickler for time. Lighting up yet another Dunhill he decides to give her just ten more minutes. If she has not turned up by then he will be off.

Outside, in The Strand, in a frozen to the core London Town, reliant upon overhead Christmas sparkling lights, neon shop frontages and fluorescent street lamps pollution for illumination, a diminutive girl outwardly contrived of snow crystals hurries toward The Savoy well aware that she is not on time for her appointment. That she is caught in a crush of bowler hats heading homeward bound from daytime duties in The City, all rushing in the direction of Charing Cross Station, a vexing thing.

"It's 5.15! You're late young lady?" Not that he is much older than she. She cares not a jot, merely affords him an unconcerned shrug and a frown from a forehead almost masked under the mesh veil of her black fascinator. If looks could kill then such hallmarks belong to her. Remaining stood resolutely still, in anticipation of good manners, she is disinclined to offer a reason for her tardiness. Suddenly, aware his usual politeness has deserted him, he stands erect and offers her the seat opposite his. A waiter spontaneously materializes prompting him to ask of her, "What would you care to drink?" She addresses only the waiter, not he who posed the question, "I'll take my usual 'White Lady', Marcel."

"Of course, your wish is my command, Mademoiselle Éloise."

From this brief interplay twixt girl and garcon feeds her self-styled chaperon with specific personal information, namely that she is unmarried; is a regular client of The American Bar and that her name is Éloise. Calming a little, and gladdened beyond sensible measure, he asks, "I take it you're a regular here? May I call you Éloise? My name is..." She stops him in his track, hastily interrupts, "Wrong on both counts. And, no you may not call me, Éloise for that is not my name. Additionally, it may be for the best in the circumstances that we do not share names. I should stay with 'young lady' if I were you."

Plainly put in his place the couple sit in stony formal silence, her eyes darting this way and that as if on the lookout for brigands. For his part, and typical of the male species, he cannot help himself but feast his eyes upon due south of the veil. She wears a vanilla coloured Pinctada oyster pearl necklace complimenting her blanched complexion, and certainly fills with an aphrodisiacal completeness the low cut black velvet dress, one fashioned in the burlesque style. Curiosity leaves him to wonder if the black seamless nylons he observed as she arrived are embellished with last evenings garter. He hopes that that is so. That one so slight wears pitch-dark flat shoes with a diamante buckle surprises a little. A statement of belief in oneself perhaps? Nevertheless, come the arrival of her appropriately named 'White Lady' cocktail a silence is broken.

"Your eyes linger too long, Sir."

"I meant no offence. My humble apologies...young lady"

"Worry not, it happens all the time, for a number of reasons, one such reason obvious, others plain irritating. You like what you see?"

"At the risk of sounding a tad untoward, I like both what I see before me now, and the, how shall I put it? Perhaps best said, 'the animate apparition wearing just a smile' that was you last evening. By the way, I see you bite your fingernails!" From beneath her veil he detects the hint of a satisfied smirk. Disregarding that small giveaway as to her charmed disposition, she pointedly ignores his last remark, as he ignored her override viz a viz exchanging first names.

"Don't laugh, and bear in mind it was my late mother's ridiculous choice, yet I go by the name Titan, by the way. It is fortuitous I stand six feet, seven inches...I can sense that you will still not impart your own name. Matters not." She fails to respond in either words or body language, allowing another pregnant pause. Eventually, she pipes up, "You very nearly got me killed yesterday. You realize that if the Grand Duke's men had caught up with me I would have been done for."

"I understand that now, of course I do. However, put yourself in my position. I had only minutes previous to confront your perceived plight and react to what was unfolding before my eyes. My intention was to quiz you later as to what provoked the deed and exactly why."

"Do you not 'think' things through before you act?"

"As I've just explained, I did think. You must see that. Besides, you called this meeting; you suggested both time and place. What pray do you have to say?"

"True enough. I feel I need to know why, exactly why you tried to intervene on my behalf last night. I am aware you must be an MI5 man. However, you cannot have been that well informed from up above, otherwise you would have left me well alone."

"You've guessed correctly, there is little point in keeping that a secret at this juncture, I am MI5. Moving on though, I take it that clearly your knife wielding exploits causing the Grand Duke to shed his mortal coil was more assassination than plain murder?"

"Any fool could have worked that out."

"Who exactly are you working for then?"

"Ask your bosses."

Gobsmacked, he responds, "There was certainly no mention of you being on our payroll made at the debriefing this morning."

"Good. In truth I am not exactly on MI5's payroll. I will share with you what should be plain as the nose on your face, namely the fact that I am a freelancer. You will be aware there are a few of us out there willing to support a worthy cause when the price is right. Your seniors came to me with an offer I could hardly refuse."

"Why you?"

"Put simply, they had sound reasons for wanting the Grand Duke liquidated in public view. I have a certain reputation in that regard. The Director General specifically requested I make my mission a 'piece of outrageous theatre'. I think you'll agree that I accomplished that with a certain élan."

"I must admit I am rather miffed to have been kept in the dark, but yes you certainly fulfilled the terms of your brief. Tell me though, how on God's earth did you come up with a plan such as you implemented. I mean to say, dancing naked as ballerina to the music of The Sugar Plum Fairy of all things before a mob of virile, well-oiled gents; taking the old blueblood Russian fellow out with a circus knife...one hell of an impressive throw of the knife I might add...then making an escape off out into a frozen night in the buff with every chance of being captured?"

"Success would only be a certainty if my target had no idea whatsoever what was coming to him. As a naked dancer, he would see with his own eyes I carried no weapon, that I was merely a 'weak and feeble' woman and was thus no threat to him. In his eyes all he would have seen was a better than average striptease artist; in his mind he'd be hoping that I might well be his upmarket prostitute for later on. You men are all the same...easy to manipulate. Also, I should add that the only danger I was in was when you intervened. As I said earlier, you nearly got me killed."

"Leaving that impasse aside, how did you affect your escape? I'm curious."

"Well, after your botched efforts I had to think on the hoot. I had no time to extract the torch from one of my pole-axed minders pockets because of you. So, I hotfooted it through the woods guessing that sooner or later I'd reach the private road that runs through the venues estate, where I'd find my driver, a vehicle and a thick fur coat awaiting me."

"Your pianist was, I take it, your getaway driver?"

"He is much, much more to me than just a driver, yet my lips are sealed. I'll have to leave you guessing on that one, although admittedly it is a clever observation on your part."

"I'm not as stupid as I look! Tell me another thing if you would. This is just my idle inquisitiveness. Did you take pleasure in dancing naked? You certainly looked as though you did. Were you not just the tiniest bit embarrassed?"

"I enjoyed every last minute of it. I am well aware, and not blowing my own trumpet, when I say that I am a most capable and creative erotic performance artist when the fancy takes."

"I am tempted to ask you how you can have 'enjoyed every last minute', yet will shelve that thought for now, however, I am still wondering why the boys upstairs wanted such an execution in front of the gathered high and mighty. I'd been on the Grand Dukes case for months trying to unravel his connections. I was getting so close."

"They wanted to separate the wheat from the chaff. You will know yourself that within the devotees in attendance were many of his partners in both crime and espionage. Since I dealt with their main man, I think you'll find even as we enjoy our cocktails, all over London arrests are being made and even as far away as Paris and Berlin associates of the late Grand Duke are being bumped off or interrogated."

"So, you succeeded where I failed?"

"I succeeded, yes. Whether or not you failed I cannot say. I only met you last night in the most unusual of circumstances...what's wrong? You are looking overly thoughtful."

"I'm just pondering the point that my lot must think me a failure, in which case there's every chance my card is marked and I'm on the way out. Given that I know where all the bodies are buried, 'out' might mean a little more than, 'you're dismissed', if you understand what I mean?"

Understanding exactly the point and predicament she thinks it well to leave alone the subject and not to answer his question. As conversation twixt 'young lady' and 'under threat of unemployment' (or worse) MI5 operative takes a breather, an insightful waiter asks if more of the same cocktails are required. A nod confirms that they are. Moreover, a little later a further repeat order for more of the same was forthcoming. Being increasingly under the abstract influence of alcohol makes, she found, for a more pliable relationship as cold light of day inhibitions are cast aside.   Such was the case when she purposely posed a question of her own, one conveying an unambiguous palpable and pressing yearning. She chose her words as carefully as intoxicant would permit a bitch on heat, yet attempting not to be seen as pleading her case, "Earlier you implied that last evening, 'you liked what you saw'. How does a repeat performance, a one to one reprise with extra special benefits sound to you?"

Her appealing appeal falls not on deafest ears. A tawdry pessimism evaporates, his mood changes for the much better. "Young lady, you certainly are not backward in coming forward."

At last she lifts her veil, overtly fluttering her eye lids Bettie Boop style in time with her now fast pulsating heartbeat, responds fittingly as only a torchbearer female seeking surrender's own carnal abandonment can, "I love it when you call me, 'young lady'. Come on, it will have to be your place rather than mine for reasons I shan't bore you with presently. Does that sound good? Will that cheer you up a little?"

Her signal without metaphors prompts a hasty, perhaps too hasty response, "Why not, 'young lady', why the hell not. I'll have them call us a cab." A victory fed and shared surpasses the banality of the starving vanquished. As he would soon to discover, and as ever, she got her own way, "Do remember, I will have to kill you If you slap my bare bum again...then again, who knows, maybe I won't!"

The next day is Christmas Eve. To the ever so thirsty, giddy participants of a new-born tryst the choice of rendezvous is, for the main part, inconsequential. Be the venue a calculated extravagant nest of reddest roses, black satin and champagne on ice or a spontaneous daredevil assignation in a passageway off lover's lane, both can serve the same ends. The methodology of wedding burning need with triumphant gratification can either spark the quest for more of the same, or may herald an apathy that rarely bothers a wave goodbye.

It was within the confines of the black cab, Belgravia bound, that the white waif had made clear her contradiction. Namely, that whereas the rigours of day to day life of a practised assassin necessitate that she must be in total control always, the vagaries of the love making antithesis was a space in which she much preferred to be acquiescent and, however he wished to interpret it, 'restrained'.

"Then that, if I understand you correctly young lady is most fortuitous. My personal taste in matters of intimacy certainly fit your brief."

"I had a hunch that that would be the case. With that in mind, Sir you will understand that until time is called I shall be your very own harem slave to do with as you wish. No formalities expected, no quarter given."

He cottons on to her little game with the due promptness, a manic expectancy worthy of a seasoned rake, sternly cautioning her, "Then you must defer the calling of 'time' to me, me alone and further I detect a contradiction upon a contradiction, young lady. For by naming me 'Sir' in such bashful manner you have gifted me the subservience that I should demand of you. You are plainly seeking to retain an element of strategic control." She laughs as he laughs and pauses for further thought, while she sits silent with legs crossed starring aimlessly into the spasmodic flashes of London's plane trees and neon lights along the roadside drive by night. "In the light of your misdemeanour I do believe you deserve due punishment, young lady." He leans across, whispers in her ear the words, "For your violation of the rules I command of you to remove immediately and thereafter hand me all that touches your bare skin, including your precious pearl necklace."

Without misgivings, she purges herself of all underclothing, albeit within the confines of a cab, an uneasy task to administer with any seductive grace. Undeterred, and paying no attention to the prospect of the driver noticing their shenanigans, having obediently obeyed his initial request she folds neatly the removed items, then hands over the entirety of her underclothing, plus fascinator, veil, pearls and ever so chic shoes. He was gratified to note that within the assortment there lies the prophesized garter belt.

She finds herself bewildered as he shakes his head, proffering the stern words, "I asked of you to remove all that touches your bare skin."

Still confused, for she had already done as he asked, she turns her face toward his, believing her compliance an obvious thing. After all he had firm evidence upon his swollen lap. Clarity is soon forthcoming, "Did I not make myself clear? Your dress, young lady, your dress...it touches your bare skin now."

She takes a little breathing space, perhaps contemplating for a moment if she still wants to play this game, then decides she most definitely does. In the twinkling of an eye, the black velvet dress is in his clutch, and she now entirely naked, legs no longer crossed. Aware of their antics, an angry, offended cabbie pulls over and parks up aside the curb announcing that he will not tolerate such behaviour in his vehicle. Having already anticipated such an event, the one who is now 'master' hands over two crisp £5 notes and advises the cabbie to keep his mouth shut and his peepers to himself. The driver readily accepts the bargain afforded him and stays schtum; continuing onward and upward to Belgravia, ignoring the very presence of his ribald passengers.

With the need to whisper expunged she responds without protest to his next directive that she should swivel about face and offer up her hands behind her bare back. With her own stockings, he ties those hands tight together whereupon small pain causes her to recoil just a little, then with her own garter belt she is blindfolded. That she offers no resistance, a delight. Upon arriving at their destination he leaves (save for her handbag containing likely important personal possessions along with the necklace neither of which are part of the game) her clothing in the cab to be returned later. "Keep this stuff safe old chap and deliver it back here some time tomorrow. PM would be good. She'll not need any of it until then. I'm the top flat, you'll be well compensated I assure you."

"You don't want to trade places, Sir?"

"Not on your life, matey."

Upon alighting the vehicle he makes sure to check that there are no preying eyes then gathers up his, as of now, authentic slave from the backseat and swiftly throws her over his muscular shoulder in the knowledge that with hands tied any resistance on her part would be scrumptiously futile. As before, only this time out of devilment, he slaps her bare backside with undue zeal. She squeals vociferously growling, "Oh, yes," time and again.

Out of the elevator and back home in his flat, with a long night's unadulterated lust feast ahead of them, sleep is put on hold until dawn decides to interrupt. Come such daylight, before sharing his bed for its primary purpose, his young bondwoman asserts, "You had yourself an early Christmas present."

"And, young lady, likely the best gift I've ever had, or will ever have. Did I fulfil your specific requirements to your satisfaction?"

"What do you think? Would I still be here had you not?"

"You realize I am under your spell?"

"Likewise."

"Maybe I'll phone the cab rank, get a message to the cabbie, ask him to come back another day?"

"Don't you dare. I'm off to Berlin the day after Boxing day."

"Dressed or undressed?"

"Dressed this time, unless events demand otherwise."

Later, now bestowed the gift of winters dubious natural early light, over a breakfast of just strawberry jam on toasted sliced baguette washed down with copious cups of fresh ground coffee, she is compelled to ask how it is he gets to wear a dressing gown, she not a stitch.

"Forgive my ignorance. As I've said before, I am nothing if not a gentleman, were you not of such slight build I would, of course I would, offer you my own gown, yet I stand six feet seven, you barely five feet. I tend to think you'd trip over the hem of the gown and land flat on your face if you wore it. Besides, I am enjoying the view...there are bath towels you can cover yourself up with. Shall I fetch you one?"

"It matters not. Thankfully, it's warm here in your flat so I'm not at all cold. Although with our game done and dusted for the time-being, and as the gentleman you claim to be I expect you to remove your dressing gown and thus ensure we are equals and I also have a view to 'enjoy'.   He duly acquiesces to her perfectly reasonable demand of him.

"Even with the lived-out fantasy consigned to the vat of treasured memories to feast upon later, would it be pushing my luck too far if I asked if I have permission to plant a lover's kiss on your lips?"

"You may, forever and a day, should that be your wish. And rest easy, I won't allow 'the others' to do you any harm."

"I think you'll find I am more than capable of looking after myself."

"I promise I can look after you better than you can yourself. I hope above all hope I'll never have to prove the truth in what I say, yet truth it is."

"Is this a good time to ask of you your name?"

"You may, if you wish call me...Eliza...yes, I like that name. I shall be your Eliza. As to you, I already know your name, yet as of the experiences of last night, I will always think of, and call you, 'My Giant'. Shall we have that kiss at last, Titan, My Giant?"

It was thus upon a Christmas Eve devoid of a Silent Night, the day after her cloak and dagger bent for exotic surrender begat pure romance, a common ground was discovered. An out of the ordinary pairing became lovers. By Christmas Day, the chemistry was such that they were very much in love.'

Back in the 'now', the tale told, I awake to the dripping of salty tears upon my face as she smoothers me in brand-new kisses. I take it that she had set the alarm clock I cannot hear and read without pause or interruption the page upon page of notes she had made from my chalking. She lets me know that she is impressed beyond measure. Adding that, if I have a complete recollection as to all that 'happened in hell' then she will cry tears of joy for a whole day, and that she will find a way to magic a full life for me out of just my two remaining senses. She is testing my abilities I think. Before we venture toward breakfast she adds, excitedly clawing at my very being in uncondensed enthusiasm, reminding me once again that she has 'that' precious garter belt still. I roll her over and pen upon her bare bottom that next time we make love she should wear it upon her eyes and join me in the land of blindness.

She never objects when I choose to be lost in thought. She understands it is a way for me to recover as much of what I have lost as is possible. In many ways that feeling I have had all along, that feeling that she owns a telepathy of sorts persists. The word I tag her with, 'otherworldly' seems even more appropriate now. Thinking time for me, we have agreed, is free time for her. Lately, by keeping furnishings and such like in self-same positions I can guide myself around the house, although the grounds still pose me some difficulties I need to overcome. Sometimes when thinking, I embellish an event. That way it is as if I am at a cinema or am in the good company of a storyteller. I never overlook that what I am perceiving, or telling myself is fact, never fiction, despite the fact I embroider it a little. I am compelled to keep memories as real as possible, as with my cerebral play on an event that, even with the lapse of time reminds me of assassination and Gitanes, for all its misty contradictions. I have no doubt she will remember this escapade. Soon I must have her write it down for posterity;

'No other capital city in the world can do grey quite like London,' her passing thought. A thought dismissed almost as soon as it arrived. For as of now there was the little matter of the naked Ambassador lying as prone as prone could be upon his back atop a plainly hideously expensive Afghan rug to attend to. Clearly, her stiletto heel dug into his pudgy chest bone was causing the gratifying discomfort intended. Moreover, that he knew exactly what was coming

next. Not that he needed a clue, the silencer affixed to her pistol and aimed at his forehead was, regardless, the giveaway. Was that a tear in his eye? Mattered not. She wondered how he might beg for mercy had it been the case that he had not been adeptly gagged. How so naked? Her trademark of course, her panache, her cultivated style.

"Gosh it's so very bitter outside. I truly thought I'd die of cold walking The Embankment on my way here. Still, your office is so lovely and warm." Her English was perfect. She paused, took a good look at him one last time, "Heart or head...decisions, decisions?" A dull thud, a trickle of blood, a ruined carpet, job done.

Cool as a cucumber she took the grand old Victorian lift, an original by the look of it, down to the lobby of the embassy, gave the Cheshire cat grinning boy behind the desk her sexiest smile, checked her reflection in the reinforced glass of the elegant doorway and was gone.

By nightfall, she found herself in a bath of bubbles in a swanky hotel in Deauville, occupied France. It was with an element of regret that she had had to ditch the bleached blond wig of human hair in a City of London cast iron litter bin. Albeit tarty, she had grown fond of the covert article of disguise, was rather smitten with it. Whatever, now ensconced in Women in Love, Lawrence's masterpiece, a bottle of bubbly at her side, a small fortune in Nazi gold confirmed transferred to her Swiss bank account, all was well in her world. The prospect of the casino downstairs had some appeal for later.

One could only hazard a guess as to whether it was the grandest come-hither canyon of her cleavage or the ridiculous measure of her winnings that had the croupier in such a ruffled state. Likely both. In any event I had guessed correctly that I would find her here, she the undeniable dazzling, sultry unfolding legend no matter what side of the warring nations one was positioned. The Abwehr every so often claimed her as one of their own, the pride of the German intelligence agency, yet this gal, albeit much fabled, was in truth a freelance operator.

To a backdrop of a La Môme Piaf cabaret sound-alike singing 'Mon coeur est au coin d'une rue' we shared fine cognac and smoked unfiltered Gitanes in the Art Deco signature bar. She reminded me that 'gitanes' English translation was 'gypsy women'.

I suggested, given that by then we had become rather close allies in more way than one, that she may think it pertinent to keep us posted as to her missions, especially so on my own home territory.

"What's in it for me?" A fair enough question.

"Well, you get to live a whole lot longer and have carte blanche to work for whomsoever you wish...my lot will leave you well and truly alone...until the next time, of course!"

There was that familiar look of doubt I knew so well on her face, "No fee?"

"Afraid not this time, you've been pushing your luck recently as the London Evening Standard has already confirmed...an Ambassador of all people! Really, what were you thinking of? Still, if it helps seal the deal, your welcome the return of this wig. You looked ever so reluctant to part with it in the City this morning." As they say in the East End, the return of the wig was 'the clincher'.

"You followed me?"

"All the way."

"What a loveable bastard you are. Anyway, it's off to Coyoacán, Mexico for me on a freebie then? Why on earth do you Brits want rid of this Leon chap? What interest do you have in him?"

"I don't recall saying this job was one of MI5's, dearest Éloise, or whatever your real name is. Take it as read that we do have an interest in the matter...hence this little chap. I can say no more on the subject though."

Although very much in the throes of a 'new love found' back then, we were professional to both letter and French Letter.

8.

LATER, SAME SUMMER 1952 – SUSSEX, 1952

Her: Three long weeks gone since she chanced upon the him playing spellbinding piano virtuoso. Although very much on hold, the question, 'how so?' endures. He has not been near the thing since that day. Now that her giant has made titanic strides perhaps today would be a good time to quiz him on the subject. To have cornered him back then might have slowed the rate of retrospection. A clattering letter box diverts her attention momentarily taking her away to see just what the postman has delivered. Sure enough, a customary letter. The post mark is stamped 'Paris'. Nothing excites like Paris, or anything deriving from it. The letter she just knows will be from her dear friend, once named Catalina, now by necessity, called Zada. Pro tempore she sets it aside, choosing to savour its content later. First things first.

Commonplace these days, she finds that, as is his current want, that he has made his own safe passage to the small study she granted him when writing the biography of their first untamed encounter. It seems his new-found talents have no end. Upon the blackboard he has chalked an impression of her nude, save for her ballet shoes. That it is certainly, 'a scene from the Grand Duke's soiree' drawn so skilfully reveals a sublime aptitude on the artists part. Its beauty leaves her as speechless as the artist himself.

As ever, an opening of a door confirms her presence in the room. Instinctively he turns toward her, a proud smile of satisfaction on his face. As naked as her ballerina self in the drawing he writes upon her the words, 'DO YOU LIKE?'. Her response plainly in the positive. She reflects that she really must get him used to wearing clothes again soon. Winter is not that far away, plus he is perhaps ready now for a few outings. The bouquet, the feel even, of new places may aid and hurry his recovery. It was only because her early foiled attempts to dress an 'always protesting at the prospect of getting dressed' him when first taking charge of his care had caused her to leave this most mundane things on the backburner. After all, they rarely had visitors to offend save for the occasional visit from the local doctor checking his progress. Indeed, it was that doctor who had agreed with her to let him be for the present in terms of the socially acceptable merits of dressing. Maybe they might have a day out in London soon. She will buy him a brand-new set of clothes. He certainly needed something new, an old gandoora, a pair of sandals and one or two items bought in a rush hardly constitutes a wardrobe.

From his bearing, it becomes clear that he is franticly anxious to impart further information. Assisting in that regard, still she stays dead still. She fathoms that he himself has no idea where these gifts of music and art emanate from and that he is reluctant to wipe away her chalked depiction. A second blackboard is required it seems as he wants to keep the artwork he will never see. Further he would surely like brushes, different coloured oil paints, a canvass and whatever else she thinks he might need. Those items she advises she will acquire for him later in the day. As she pauses, wanting to ask more of him, before leaving him for the shops, he chalks best he can on the wall, 'I THINK THE SENSES I AM LEFT WITH ARE COMPENSATING FOR THOSE I HAVE LOST. EITHER THAT, OR I HAVE A GIFT FROM A GOD I DO NOT BELIEVE IN'. The former point made, a strong possibility, the latter not so in her mind, at least.

Heeding those words of material request and affording them the priority they deserve, she responds upon his breastplate this time, 'I WILL FETCH ALL YOU NEED RIGHT NOW, THAT WAY WE CAN TALK MORE AND YOUR DRAWINGS CAN BE KEPT SAFE AND TREASURED'. The prospect of what prize they might deliver up demands of her that she must not interfere. Answers in respect of the nagging question, once more on hold.

As ever, true to her word and with a now fully functioning vehicle she, having remembered to get dressed à la mode per her usual choice of a chic that is only just the cusp of prosaic decency, then checking for unlikely rainclouds interrupting weather set fair, she heads for town. It is with conspicuous ease she obtains all that she wants from the unlikely stationers aside the local museum of all things banal. She very nearly forgets a palette, an easel he already has. In a clothing shop a little further down the High Street she has the foresight to acquire suitable aprons and from the hardware store equally suitable products to clean both brushes and himself. She laughs out loud at the thought of an otherwise naked, deaf, dumb and blind artist clad in just an apron. "What a photograph that would make," she mumbles to herself. That those out walking the street who might overhear and would assume her quite mad matters to her not a jot. However, there is still one important thing to do before returning home. Within her handbag rests the letter postmarked 'Paris'.

In a full bloom scented flower garden at the rear of a tweedy old lady's Dickensian themed tea shop, a place so traditional that the very concept of expresso has yet to be been explored, she sits and drinks Earl Grey, smoking a much-needed cigarette, envelope at the ready.

The letter is assuredly from Zada who she still occasionally thinks of as Catalina. Its content is brief and to the point. That it is written in passable French something of a surprise for when Zada had left for France just 8 weeks previous she barely had a glimmer of that language to her name. Impressive.

Dear Eliza,

I hope you still answer to that name? One can never tell with you and your secrets of necessity.

Paris is all that you said it would be. I have found an employment of sorts modelling for an artist, although not one you recommended. The letters of introduction you gave me have certainly served me well though. My artist was a friend, of a friend, of a friend of one who knows you well. I think it fair to say I am in demand! Also, I have found suitable accommodation in the very place you said I would, Montparnasse. How it is I have got to live there is a little complicated. I love it and will tell you more when I see you.

The thing is I think of you and your giant all the time, wondering how you both are getting along.

I have a ten-day break in my working schedule coming up as all the artists, well pretty much all Parisians, as you will know, take flight from Paris during the month of August. Put simply, with both time and need on my side, I feel the impulse to visit you both and help out in any way I can.

I still owe you for all the help and assistance you gave me in those dark days, so please say 'yes' and confirm I can come to stay.

In case you are thinking me the fastest ever learner of a foreign language I must admit that a girlfriend, French obviously, has helped me out writing this letter. So, if you are thinking 'impressive' you are on the wrong track.

I miss you both desperately.

Your true friend for eternity,

Zada

Not that she minded, but time had dragged a little of late, the burden of requirement caring for her giant, albeit it the most laudable loving pursuit of her life, could sometimes be mentally draining hence a new face about the place had great appeal. Certainly, she could come stay for as long as she wished. The prospect positively thrilled.

He was evidently elated with his gifts, requesting that she lay out upon the 'soon to be covered with a protective sheet of whatever she thought might do' desk top, in strict order from left to right, first the oils of the colours of a primary rainbow, then list for him by usual messaging procedure her chosen order for the rest of the tubes. If possible that they should be placed in such an order that the first letters of such colours spelt a word he could memorize. Once that was ready and done that he would take great care of them and would be at pains to keep them that way.

Initially confused, her trying out of the new pure white apron, one that barely reached his knees, upon him brought forth similar laughter to that which she had shared with passing strangers in the High Street earlier. Looking at him covered thus she thought him rather sexy and, in their own silent speak, she told him so. Bewildered that she was still fully clothed, her bare belly off limits, he could only but reach out to locate and grab hold of her hand impressing upon the palm the cheeky letters, 'I S-H-A-L-L F-E-A-S-T O-N Y-O-U L-A-T-E-R' atop each other, prompting a nonplus blush that he would never be aware of. It mattered not for she already had in mind the will to be feasted upon later.

Come evening the pair dine on dripping red blood rarest steak and a simple seasonal leaf salad, washed down with a classy Château Margaux, the apron apparently still a must for him, nought at all her own choice.   The tactile approach of fingertip to palm he had seemingly invented earlier that day in the study was one she adopted over the dinner table. A first ever simple mode of connection enabling them to chat while enjoying a meal together. It is on his palm that she explains that shortly they would have a guest staying with them for a few days, a guest he may recall from the days when he had first arrived at this place. Moreover, that this young lady, like him, had been damaged by the same evil sorceress who had near ruined him. The young lady, she continued, was named Catalina yet is now known as Zada. Unlike her giant Zada's senses remained intact. The damage she suffered was of a cruel sexual nature, although as of now she seems to have made a full recovery.

In reply, he pointedly 'remarks' that he still had no recollection of not just how the 'damage' was inflicted or even where such events took place, and that until some of his key memories have chosen to return he has not the faintest idea as to how he found himself here. Commenting on 'the sorceress' he could but only shape a question mark upon her palm.

In order to make what was of necessity long-winded conversation easier the couple adjourn to the study. He with chalk and board at the ready, she has helped him out of his much-treasured apron ensuring her conversational task was a little easier.

The key point she endeavours to get across is that Zada's account of her predicament might just bring about his final important memory recovery, namely that of his obvious torture and subsequent rescue. That Zada had accompanied them here and subsequently helped with his nursing, if she were to impart her own story, then that might just be the trigger. In short, she wants to know if he feels both ready and up to meeting Zada; that she wants to confirm if the time is right to delve deep into the dark recesses of his mind. He confirms that he shares her wish.

More wine, more chit chat. In his own unique way he supposes that with a new lady in the house it might be best if he was suitably attired. Whilst taking his point she is compelled to let slip that pretty much all the time Zada had helped nurse him he had been as naked as a new born, so there was no worry on that front. He need not feel embarrassed in her company. However, she agreed some proper clothing would, for a galaxy of reasons, soon be a necessity. So, the next fine day they would go into London and she would choose for him the best that money could buy, maybe even take lunch at The Savoy, a place that meant of lot to the both of them; a place that he remembered in finite detail. To the next point he made, that being to the effect of, "What the fuck will I wear travelling to and in London itself?" has the pair falling apart, she howling with laughter, him mouthing a dumb equivalent. Certainly, neither the apron nor the gandoora would do. Still mirth ridden, two lovers make for the bedroom with a raw carnal feast in mind.

She wishes she had realized the fast pace of his mental recovery sooner for had she acted upon a thought that had nagged at her for weeks it may have become a reality much sooner. Originally, following his rescue it was generally thought that so scarred was his brain function that any form of communication would be impossible. Yet of now, using just fingertips and his new found chalking words on slate skills had made for a satisfactory element of connection viable. However, their ability to commune with each other was out of kilter. He would write whole chapters on the blackboard, yet she could only contact him and impart whatever she felt was required using the fingertip method. That he had once owned a full set of faculties and thus knew of the regular reality outside of his head meant that he had every prospect of adapting to the special device she had had the foresight to order.

On the day the recently invented Perkins Brailler arrived all the way from Massachusetts, USA, a whole new world arrived with it. In essence, the Perkins Brailler was a glorified typewriter. Each key of its keyboard corresponded to each of the six dots of the braille code, a space key, a backspace key, and a line space key. Like a manual typewriter it has two side knobs to advance paper through the machine and a carriage return lever above the keys. Additionally, only she would have to learn the braille code and become familiar with decoding documents written in braille into the regular form of English she could read easily. For his part her giant had, he assured her, been something of a braille expert during WW2 when on covert night-time missions behind enemy lines it served many an agent well as a means to communicate silently in situations denied a light source. As with his new-found musical and artistic skills, lately he never ceased to amaze. That it took him merely a few hours to master the six keys when typing came as no surprise. Although it took until just prior to Zada's anticipated arrival to familiarize herself with both the language of braille and the functioning of the Perkins Brailler, her determination to learn and discover ceaseless. Her goal achieved to an acceptable level, all she needed now was her friend from Paris in order that together they could compare notes whereupon she would be able to document all they knew of his plight and subsequent rescue.

As to the trip to London, and for days after suggesting it, despite confirming it a fine idea he was on constant edge. The proposed outing would not come to fruition. Too many good memories he did not want tarnished, his tearful reasoning. For the time being his desire was to stay put with her at home, although stressing she should take any and all the time outside of the property she either wanted or needed as he well understood the pressure she must be under caring for him. As far as she was concerned, yes there was pressure yet nothing she could not deal with, and besides their ceaseless lovemaking made up for whatever shortcomings life had thrust their way. That their respective sex drives were perfectly matched represented a top prize many couples would never win. As to new clothes and shoes it was nothing a little off-the-peg shopping locally could not remedy. Not ideal, little panache in such stores, yet fit for purpose nevertheless. At one stage during that shopping trip she found she had nearly opted to buy him pyjamas, then thought better of the idea.

By habitual mode she asks, "Now that you have the Brailler are you going to write your autobiography one day?"

Him: Within my locked-in domain surprise is a thing I have had to adapt to. Everything is a surprise, even those things I expect to happen sometimes feel like a bombshell. Timing is the key. For all my new-found memories I have no knowledge or recollection of this Romanian girl now known by the name of Zada.

At the very heart of the matter deep down inside I perceive a certain Godly 'trinity in unity' apropos the desecration of my senses. An injustice that can never be remedied, a sacrifice reluctantly accepted. Yet, as of now and through my lover's love I can at least communicate with her fully. She has purchased her own Perkins Brailler, studied and learned the language of the blind to a passable level. She says her machine is exactly as the one I use. Conversation in depth via raised dots on a page and fingertips; idle chat, instant thoughts and messages through bare belly's fingertip scribing's. How could I ever have known that the humble fingertip would open the door to a world I once took for granted. When I read her words, in a surreal way I hear her words, for her voice is forever with me. Short of taking my life my dementor whomsoever that was failed to expunge the sound of her voice when severing my ties with the outside world. I see that my one small victory.

Once, years ago when my faculties were in union, and more than a little drunk in some salubrious bar in Soho discussing this and that with colleagues the question, seemingly a silly 'what if?' question was posed of me. Namely, if I had to choose on pain of death what to give up, be it my eyes, ears or tongue what would be my choice. At the time, I opted for eyes, figuring that if I could still both hear and speak I would manage to somehow get by. Yet since losing all three capabilities armed with a very real perspective it is clear to me that presently my choice should have been the ability to see. Both speech and sound are bonuses, sight the most valuable of all. I know in my mind however quickly or slowly she may age she will always be as she was the very first time I saw her, my naked, beautiful, brave angel with the will to inflict harsh justice to those deserving of due punishment. My plaintive cry would be, always will be, to see her as she is today, tomorrow, next year, the year after. Knowing I never will often births a despondency I will never concede to have inherited. Nevertheless, it persists; is now part of me.

Her first effort with the Brailler was to write me a short poem. I still do not entirely understand exactly what it is about, what any hidden meanings within may be, save to say I wept tears of joy upon finishing her tale, likely because the shirt she handed me was she advised 'Breton'.

THE MAN IN THE BRETON SHIRT

All her life she had wanted legs
Proper legs with feet, ankles, calves, knees and thighs
Yet circumstance had afforded her nought but wheels
Small wheels at that
Little wrought iron ones
Wheels that required constant care, oiling and such like

Notwithstanding her shortcomings
She got out and about best she could
That is, until the day the local town hall people had something of a retro brainwave
They cobblestoned the market square
She lived in a house on market square
So now she prayed for tarmac
As well as feet, ankles, calves, knees and thighs

Then one day quite out of the blue
The sailor arrived in town
Breton shirt, beer belly
He drank vast quantities of rum
Farted constantly
Belched with pride, gusto even

They met in a smoke laden bar
She in a wheelchair (her wizened auntie had taken her out for some fresh air. Why she chose to go to a bar no one ever knew)

The sailor was singing a ribald sea shanty at the time
To the accompaniment of an accordion
He amused her; she caught his eye
The accordionist noticed too
A deafening silence ensued
A galaxy of drunkards turned about face
Embarrassing her more than a little

A harlot, hanging on to the sailor's arm for dear life
Flinched at his rancid breath, yet still held fast
Such is the fate of a girl short of gilders (perversely, she cast a jealous
eye at the girl)
Regardless his 'Popeye on spinach' forearm
Thrashed the harlot to Kingdom come

In an instant, the sailor sobered up
Whereas he should have stumbled, he straightened himself
Walked over to the girl and planted
The mother of all kisses upon her virgin lips
Clicked his fingers
Bellowed skyward at the heavens
And miraculously the girl had legs, with feet, ankles, calves, knees and
thighs

With great care, and eyes shut tight
The girl ran her hands over her new limbs
They felt ever so fine
When she opened them again
She found herself on a yacht
On the wide-open sea
In the company of a handsome young man in a Breton shirt
From his place at the helm
He winked and blew her a kiss
All was well in her world

A metaphor in reverse? Oh, that that thought be one proven an actuality.

Another fine late summer's day. Warm enough for us to take once more to the lake. She had marked my stomach with the words,

'SKINNY DIPPY?". Plainly I replied upon her palm, 'YES PLEASE!!!'. Swimming has done wonders for my physical health. She keeps an eye on me, saying there are hidden dangers I should be aware of, overlooking that for me hidden dangers lie everywhere. That she is so protective reassures.

Her: Unattainable to habitually pigeonholed mortals yet living the unconventional, archetypical Bohemian life was never an act of fabricated exhibitionism on her part. It was simply a facet of her psyche. The way she happened to live, rather than had chosen to live. That to the outside world the contrary view likely applied she had never given such a thing a second thought. Save for Monday mornings when the gardeners came to do whatever gardeners do, for the grounds were extensive and in constant need of 'this and that' thus keeping them pristine. On such Mondays, the day that for inexplicable yet bordering on romantic reasons, 'belonged to the moon' she would be sure to remember to cover-up and do 'demure' the best she could; ensure her giant was obscured, safe indoors; keep herself to herself until the lawns and flowerbeds had been rejuvenated and natures leavings tidied up, liquidated or composted. Thankfully, the Friday afternoon grocery delivery was made by one of kindred spirit. A hardy, timeless soul of artistic bent, never one for chitchat, simply funding his passion for his craft delivering customers' orders far and wide about the county. Those times aside, and subject to the vagaries of the English climate, the house and grounds were their exclusive discreet playground.

This day was a Tuesday, and a fine one at that. No longer could she dance to please the one of penned in awareness, instead she now danced with him. A little way back from her treasured lake upon an oversized rug of hardy grass lived a granite stone picnic table. It was upon that table she had set an ancient portable gramophone. Undeterred that her partner in dance was without hearing, sightless and had terminally lost his tongue she and he, as vulnerable as the day they arrived in the world of the conscious, whirled to a loud, crackly Waltz of the Flowers, carefree in every which way.

Before, when he was still inwardly whole, they had waltzed from dusk to dawn on the floodlit deck of a Danube pleasure cruiser, oblivious to the prying eyes of night owls and troubadours under

Vienna's starriest sky. For this reprise, it would be under a Mad Dogs and Englishmen brightest star scorcher. It mattered not.

Initially she had been concerned, insofar as she ever became concerned over trifling matters, that given the giants hellish suffering she may have to lead the dance. Not so, even lost within himself he had not lost his flexibility, his coordination nor appetite for the transparent eroticism of the dance. Ever the master in every which way. She simply shut her eyes tight, let him be her champion, his mind's eye governing her every step in a space so ample that it intuitively felt both safe and in reach of infinity.

The dance done with, ever conscious of the effect of sun rays upon those like her with an absence of pigment in the skin, she prudently donned a simple white cotton smock and the inevitable wide-brimmed straw hat. Not so her man. He chose to lay flat on his back looking skyward as if sun gazing, eyes wide open in the face of an orb ablaze; one that he perceived could no longer do him harm. Notwithstanding, she slaps him about the wrists, as mother to disobedient child, by way of a scolding reminding him that the medics, although asserting that the blindness was an eternal thing, had never been able to diagnose exactly why he could not see.

For her part, she finds herself debating with thin air as to whether China tea scored over Indian varieties. Coming to no satisfactory conclusion she opts for champagne. In truth champagne had always been first choice. Also, before tripping the light fantastic she had had the foresight to leave a magnum chilling in an ice bucket in the shade of the weeping willow, lakeside. In order that he knew of her intent she writes in letters per usual upon his stomach detailing where she is off to and what for. His smile in return confirms her message has been received and understood.

It is just as she is making for the bubbly, a crunching noise from the direction of the long driveway catches her attention. Turning about face she notes a 'dragged through a hedge backwards' looking Zada struggling with a sizeable suitcase, its wheels not best pleased to be lugged ever onward along an unforgiving drive. Zada has arrived a day earlier than anticipated! Excited, she runs over to her completely overlooking that fact that bare feet and white limestone gravel could never be bosom buddies.

"Jesus, that hurt."

In broken French, "You're glad to see me then? Can we speak in Romanian, it seems like an age since I spoke in my mother tongue?"

"Of course we can." They share the hugs and kisses of dearest confidants, then, "Sorry, so sorry Zada. I think I've drawn a little blood on the soles of my feet. Anyway, you're a day early, we were expecting you tomorrow. How are you dear girl? You look a little worse for wear."

Now, both sat cross-legged upon the lawn aside the driveway she scrutinises her tootsies for offending items, Zada helping out, picking little pieces of sharp stone that are reluctant to abandon ship. A thought strikes home, "How on earth did you get through the gates? I always keep them locked."

"I climbed over. I decided to surprise you both."

"Climbed over? You are as mad as ever Zada. How did you manage to do that? I mean, your case must weigh a ton. You could have seriously injured yourself climbing up, plus the spikes at the top. They're really deadly."

Zada proudly explains in finite detail her Herculean assault upon the wrought iron adversary. First, she had had to mount the gates all the time battling with her suitcase. Upon reaching the summit she managed to lob it overboard then made her own descent, ever conscious that spikes were likely candidates threatening her mortality. In any event, the undertaking had been a success. Mission accomplished.

"I could use a shower though, I'm all sweaty and sticky after that."

"Of course, Zada. Why not bathe in the lake? You know the water is clear and it's not that cold today. By the time you've had a swim and dried off, there will be a glass of champagne waiting for you. I just need to pop back to the house and get another glass."

"That sounds perfect, although I've not packed a swimming costume though."

"Do you need one?"

"I guess not. Can I leave my case here on the edge of the drive for the moment? I'll collect it later."

"Of course you can, I'll help. We can manage it together. Love your outfit by the way. Stand up and give me a twirl."

Zada is all too willing to twirl yet not before explaining both she and it were a tad dishevelled presently. Her dress, a simple charcoal grey and gunmetal sack dress certainly no Dior yet no doubt had cost a small fortune in a Parisian boutique however, as she stood upright all thoughts of a twirl were lost when her gaze suddenly caught the image of the naked giant spread out as if modelling for some sort of surreal crucifixion sunning himself over yonder. Apprehensively to begin with, then with kittenish enthusiasm, "That's him, he's outside with you, I see him over there," all the time, jumping up and down, clapping her hands together as would a child opening a present on Christmas morn, "Tell me how he is, have there been any signs of improvement since I've been gone?"

The quest for the extra champagne flute aborted as the pair make their way toward the giant's resting place, "I'll let you see for yourself, Zada. Many things have changed since you left. The possibility of him remaining in what seemed likely to be a permanent vegetative state is no more. I'll explain more later, yet he and we have, through both chance and later design various means of connecting with one another. Sadly, such connection will be denied you as your language is Romanian and he won't understand you as I do. He remembers more and more each day, yet not his time in Kharkov nor indeed you."

As the pair approach a little closer and not that he has detected their presence, Zada finds herself placing an unnecessary palm across her mouth, all the time trying to supress a giggle seeking freedom, "I see he's pleased to see me! Is this commonplace these days?"

"Thankfully, yes. Whatever she took from him she didn't manage to demean his manliness."

"So, your nights are full of romance then?"

"Most mornings and afternoons also. Not that I'm complaining. Sex is the very spice of life. Give the thing a flick of the finger if it bothers you, he'll get the message sure enough."

"It's probably best if I leave that task to you, I think."

While Zada watches on, carefully, (and not carry out the previously proposed 'flick') so as to not make him jump out of his skin she makes him aware their guest has arrived a day early and is at her side right now. Instantly, he covers his genitalia best as he can with his hands. She explains once again that Zada had nursed him, had seen him naked, even washed him many a time so he should have no qualms about being bare now. At this, he calms, gets to his feet and awaits formal introduction to the one he had forgotten existed.

"Should I cuddle and kiss him? Will that count as a 'hello' in his world?"

"I think he'd like that."

"I was going to undress for the swim. I may as well undress here and now so as he and I shall embrace as equals." With that, Zada hoists her dress over her head and kicks off her shoes.

"No white bits I note, and you've not got the taste for underwear back I see? You look even more gorgeous than ever, by the way. Your skin is as if Aztec Gold. Your hair now as blackest chocolate. You look so lovely I could eat you."

"Thank you and you are correct. I find that artists are not keen on models with unnecessary variations in skin shades, and that gypsy look I have seems to tantalize. I'll tell you more about that later, I've lots of news. Anyway, now for that cuddle"

At that, the giant is treated to his cuddle and a kiss upon his lips greeting. As Zada finally draws away he gently grabs hold of her shoulders keeping her still then sniffs as would a terrier dog picking up on a scent. The girls can almost hear the cogs inside his head ticking over, his facial expression a questioning one. Still holding Zada in place he turns his head toward his lover instinct telling him exactly where she stands watching. With much deliberation he mouths the words, "I REMEMBER HER NOW. SHE WAS HERE IN THIS PLACE WITH YOU. HER COLOGNE, I RECOGNIZE HER COLOGNE."

Afterward, when Zada's swim was done with and the champagne duly polished off the trio share smoke salmon and leavened bread with a simple leaf salad laid out on the dining table. Keeping the Bohemian theme intact a balmy, humid evening, clothing a thing none have opted for. Zada is amazed that he handles a knife and fork as if he had eyes that see, that he knows exactly where his plate sits, even the position of the salad bowl on the table top.

"That's nothing Zada. You'd be surprised at the things he can now accomplish. The strangest thing though is that I found him playing piano to perfection one afternoon not so long ago, yet before all this that would have been way beyond him. I doubt he could play a single note. Add to that he has become an artist. His paintings are remarkable. Painting with oils at that! Instinct seems to tell him what to do and how to do it. His nudes of me born of his memories are phenomenal. I would bet with you that he'd fathom a way of painting you if I asked him and I believe he'd give any Parisian artist a run for their money."

"I think I'd like that."

"I'll ask him shall I?"

"Why not."

Zada watches on fascinated at the fingertip to palm conversation that ensues.

"He has agreed to paint you, it's given him a new project and has made him most happy. He just needs, and he stresses such need is of innocent intent, to run his hands over your body. With you, like me being much shorter than he is, he needs you to stand upon a chair. He will commit to memory the contours of your figure."

"Well, not that he knows it yet, it's fortunate I didn't dress for dinner. Having said that it is getting a little chilly even here indoors."

Once upon a chair he gently runs his hands over her entirety as if to capture only her aura. First her face, then the torso and all the way down to her toes.

"I think he wants you to hold your arms out straight, Zada."

Zada duly obliges, although not without snorting a little as he feels about her armpits. Once done and dusted and clearly in deepest thought he takes of his leave out of the dining room to that small space that is now his studio.

"So, he makes his own way around the house now? That's remarkable. I can barely believe what I'm seeing."

"He can make his way around with ease so long as I make sure to keep everything in the same place. I think the real him, the one from before, is alive and well save for the absence of any memory of the abuse that brought about his impairment. And that Zada is something I need to talk to you about. While you're here with us I'd like to pick your brains. Between us I wish to document his and your plight at the hands of that evil woman and gift it to him as a story. I am hoping that such a thing will serve as the last piece of the jigsaw, will make him as whole as he can ever be."

"Of course, I'd only be too pleased to help. It might do me some good as well. Maybe in doing so the last of my own demons might fade away. You make me wonder though, how will he read such a tale?"

"So sorry, I forgot to explain that bit. Are you familiar with a thing called braille? You are? Good. You see he already reads and I have taught myself the language of braille. We both use a braille typewriter. As we put together the story, I'll type it. When it's finished he'll read it. I think I need to be with him as he reads though just to be one safe side in case memories do come flooding back and he falls apart."

"Just say when you wish to start. I'm ready when you are."

"Tomorrow perhaps. I suspect he'll be busy painting for the next few days, so asap would be good. Now, tell me of your new life in Paris. Tell me how it's all working out."

Before continuing the conversation Zada decides the evening drop in temperature now demands she finds her dressing gown. It is only then that both girls in unison remember that her suitcase is out by the drive. Together they take a walk under the new born stars, holding hands and marvelling at the glimpse of a barn owl out hunting, a bat out eating the small insects that did not have to foresight to make for home as the sun went down. Soon, all is well. The suitcase retrieved, the dressing gown now warming Zada, her hostess still content as was.

Together they snuggle up on the lounge settee as Zada tells all. She has a lover, a young artist of rich parentage. That he shares with her the monthly endowment his father gifts him in return that she be his exclusive muse, a Godsend, plus she lives with him in his garret overlooking Luxembourg Gardens saving her from any rental costs she would incur living elsewhere, "I should have added that bit when I wrote you the letter saying I was coming to visit, but I wanted to keep it a surprise. Anyway as an artist he is yet to hit the pinnacles of success yet critics speak well of him. That is the reason I am able to get away for a while, in order that he can prepare for his exhibition at a desirable venue on The Left Bank," adding that most of the paintings going on show are of her, a thing she is proud of.

"All nudes?"

"Mostly, yet not universally, I'm wearing a hat in one!" a cheeky riposte.

"So, you are happy and in love?"

"Happy? Yes, I am. In love? Possibly, he is kind, good-looking, talented...all those things...yet, I worry that when he gets tired of me he'll be off searching for a new muse. He says that that will never happen, that he is besotted with me, but...well, you never know."

"In life, Zada, I find you must take things day by day. Just enjoy yourself. Make the most of everything. There are no rules as far as I am concerned...well, you know that of me already. By the way, did you ever pursue that belly dancing idea?"

"Not yet. I haven't needed to, although I've practised and practised."

"You didn't mention your artist's name."

"Jacques, Jacques Carbonneau. His father is..."

"Of Élysée Palace Council of Ministers fame. Antoine, the Minister of the Interior."

"You know him?"

"It would not be fair on you for me to answer that question although so as to stop you worrying over my motives in saying what I've just said, you can rest assured I never had any liaison with him, or, I have to add, his son, your lover."

Over what turns out to be the entirety of Zada's stay, talking of and about the unhappy events affecting so severely, yet in different ways, both Zada and the one robbed of senses, as they recall them, and at the same time collating their respective recollections, using just mere pen and ink upon paper, the girls work in chorus, each in turn imparting their in many ways speculative take on the happenings from his imprisonment, and latterly his rescue. Additionally, as something of an offshoot, yet still relevant to the whole event, Zada reiterates the story of her own harrowing abuse at the same hands as the one who had stolen the giant's formative senses. She and Zada agree with her decision to assemble such a tome, for a tome it would become and convert it to a set of braille documentation following Zada's departure. She finds herself living in hope that they may gather a sufficient chronology and factual account of those awful times that might just trigger a comprehensive restoration of his memories and thus make him whole again although, that meant as whole as he ever could be.

The pair work hours on end, sustenance sometimes forgotten not so the thought provoking red wine, often through the fading of natural light and late into the dark of night. The giant so heavily engrossed in his paintings he seems not to care a jot about any additional isolation. By now he regards such a state of being as his reality. In short, he has learned to come to terms with what others would regard as segregation; yet he is, had never been in hindsight, like those others. More so than ever before living only inside his head is now an acceptable, almost preferred way of life.

Twixt the two girls, their timing, an unplanned perfection. The tale is completed just the evening prior to Zada's return to Paris and her artist lover whose company she seems not to miss unduly. Indeed, it was his planned exhibition of paintings themed on her nakedness that entices her return to France the most.

It is on that last evening, both girls dressed to the nines, although not so the artist giant who with as much flurry and flair as he can muster presents to his lover his large canvas depicting a scene of an Istanbul slave auction from back in the day. Both lover and Zada giggle with guilty, lascivious delight when noting the raunchy nature of the work laid before them. There, centre stage is his whiter than white skinned beautifully proportioned girl stripped down for meticulous inspection of a host of eager potential purchasers. Then close by a shamed Zada, also bereft of clothing perched provocatively at the side of the giant himself, he in the guise of the suave Arabian sheik 'highest bidder'. Through tried and tested technique he announces that the painting has been fashioned in the style of The Orientalists. A smirking Zada suggests to her friend it is more likely fashioned in the style of a hedonist with an obscene imagination and making known that categorically the quality and skill of the blind giant's work to be the match of any sighted artist she had met thus far in Paris. Both girls marvel at not just the detail of the scene exposed before them, but also wondering just how a man in his condition could construct such an implausible masterpiece of an oil painting. Additionally, for Zada only, to take home with her, a small painted canvas of her as a traditional reclining nude. Via his lover Zada is advised that the work has been moulded from the image of her stored within his head from the night she had arrived; the night he had been allowed to feel with fingers and palms every inch. She notes and marvels at the exact depiction of her face. To Zada it was almost beyond belief that he had captured her features faultlessly as only an artist with an exacting functioning eye could be expected to do.

The night being still young, the wine still flowing, the threesome take leave of memories and paintings, deciding that a piano solo, with him the only choice as pianist, and they, the generally vociferous girls would stay politely schtum and form his appreciative audience. He is at odds to explain by finger on palm that for the next two hours he would perform all twenty-one of Chopin's Nocturnes. Asked how he knew of such a thing, as well as intending to play the same as soloist, he replies he has no idea whatsoever. Bewildered and bewitched two enthralled girls sit back and soak up the perfection that is his sublime performance. It is well after the witching hour they finally take to their respective bedrooms.

Having made good her farewells, Zada readies herself for her journey home only this time setting aside any thoughts she may have had regarding the climbing of the perimeter gate as she had done upon arrival. Instead, she is driven to the station by her host, the one she still calls Eliza, arriving only moments before her train is due to depart. There is only time for a short chat upon the station platform before boarding.

"Look Eliza, I'm being serious when I say that I can see just how much you and he are in love, yet the toll upon you caring for him night and day must be hard, so should you ever need a break and getaway then rest assured I will willingly sit in for you. I think they call it compassionate leave in military circles, respite care by any other name. All you have to do is ask. I know that in many ways he is self-sufficient, yet left alone, you know better than me, it could all go wrong for him. Think about it."

"You are too kind, Zada, yet on the horizon there is a thing, an important thing I feel compelled to undertake. Your offer of assistance is one I might just take up."

"You're not intending to return to work are you? It is so dangerous what you do. I presumed you'd given all that up?"

"One last job while I'm still relatively young. Not that I am short of money in any way, yet this one last matter I'd like to attend to will pay a significant fee; one that will leave us more than comfortable for the rest of our lives. Presently, I'm just thinking about it, soon they will insist I respond."

"Have you told him?"

"Not yet, I haven't decided if I'm going to accept, although I'm under great pressure to do so."

"I hope you reject the offer, yet as I said, if you need me I'll be there for you at the drop of a hat."

"You have become Zada quite my dearest friend. Thank you again."

With that, and amid the growl and fog of the steam train straining to depart, Zada is away, yet leaning out of the window waving a constant goodbye until finally out of view.

Him: For reasons I'm not sure of I find myself worrying that Zada may be late for her train. I think I shall miss her. Also, that Zada is a name she has taken leaving her birth name Catalina consigned to the past intrigues. My feeling is that having her here has helped. She has plainly given my lover a new lease of life, a much-needed foil to take her mind off me and my inevitable care, a thing that sometimes leaves me guilt ridden. I often think it might have been a better thing to have been born as I am now, a freak of nature. Were that the case I would not know of the alternatives a full deck of capabilities offers. Would not know the pressures my very being places on the one I love.

Were it the case I had been as I am since birth, for example, my tendency toward nakedness would be even more meaningless to me than it is now. In days gone by there would have been no circumstances, save perhaps when in the company of lovers old and new, where I would have chosen to tarry unclothed. Now? I care not a jot. As the chill of the evening descends, or when early morning's bite of cold comes to visit she makes sure to cover me in one thing or another. Mainly warm blankets, sometimes she slips just that Breton shirt over me saying I look 'sweet' dressed that way. It makes her happy and that is all that concerns me. I must be hard work, yet rarely is it that she gets exasperated. She understands that I try my level best and, with her guidance and loyalty, I have come on leaps and bounds. Perhaps I whinge too much for still I have my shining memories of her frozen in time; the rhythm of her spoken words in an accent impossible to pin down to the neck of any wood; my touch upon her petit, perfect body; the risqué simplicity of adventures we shared. I simply want to see her as she is now. In my heart and head I know she remains the most beautiful creature, after all not that much time has elapsed since I last cast my gaze upon her. Am I greedy in wanting more? Some healthy men live life and die a lonely death, having suffered an incompleteness of sensuality. Yes, in some ways I am the luckiest man.

Yesterday, and quite out of the blue, she took the decision with autumn just around the corner I needed more clothing. Suitable clothing reflecting the change of season. Once again I refused the trip to London with both she and Zada. I could not face being a one-man monstrosity in the middle of crowds of commuters and tourists. It matters not, I have my painting to keep me amused, plus the new-found joy of the piano and my surprise as to what piece of music materialises in my lap to play each day. Besides, I know my way around the place now and sustenance was assured when she left me a pint glass of water and a Cornish Pasty on an unbreakable enamel plate for my lunch. The pair took the fast train into Town and were only away a few hours. The time flew.

The odd thing has been, whereas I can paint my lover with consummate ease, Zada has posed certain difficulties. I do have recollection of her but not so distinct that I can see her in my mind. My palms over her body have captured her physical essence, yet not her very being. There is a picture in my head yet it had felt incomplete. Then, when the girls returned from their shopping trip as if by magic everything literally fell into place.

The clothes the pair had chosen for me were, to say the very least, unusual. Plainly, all I could do was imagine what I might look like. Even as I thought up such images I realized how much I miss the explicitness of my reflection in a mirror. It seems on the journey up to London, and taking account of my condition, she determined that my new clothing should enable me to be as independent as possible and that the things I wear should be items that allow me to dress myself with ease. Taking that into account, they went for an Arabian theme of all things. As that point became clear to me I laughed a silent laugh.

In substance, they had for me an assortment of items, although excluding any underwear as she sees no call for it in the here and now. To her you cover yourself up if cold or going out somewhere significant, whereas in the privacy of one's own space why wear anything if one is warm, least of all underwear. Fundamentally, my own space is where I exist anyway. Regardless, my new wardrobe includes a number of thobes, one for each season, these being a garment tailored as a shirt, yet ankle length, loose and most comfortable. As the weather turns for the worse I have also a number of items known as bishts. Again, these are ankle length and worn over a thobe. Beyond that I have socks, sandals, Wellington Boots, slippers even. The piece de resistance being my new winter hat. A skull cap over which the turban Zada has painstakingly made me sits comfortably. Her theory in buying such an outlandish range being that the Arabs have panache and are used to drastic variations in temperature twixt day and night, plus, as I have alluded to already, I will be able to dress myself saving her the job of doing up fly buttons, a thing for all my rediscovered coordination I know I would struggle with. Clever girl.

Regardless, and over more than a little shared wine, they set about dressing me up in this and that as if I were a toy doll, and they excited children. I could sense, yet obviously not hear their screams of delight as they mixed and matched the new items with my existing stock. She let it be known to me that whilst her favourite was me, once more in that Breton shirt, but this time with the addition of just Wellington Boots. However, when they finally had me in the almost full regalia of Turban, white Thobe and sandals she scribed onto my palm that really a man dressed as such a handsome sheik should have a harem of slave girls. That was when the thought struck me of schooldays boyish fantasies. I remembered that back then the closest us lads ever got to a naked girl were from a well-thumbed book in the school library of the work of The Orientalist painters, Gerome in particular. Gerome had painted many a scene of naked white girls up for auction in the Middle Eastern slave markets. In current times, some boffins would say of this accomplished artist that his work verges upon pornography and, of course, pornography was the very thing a bunch of 14-year-old boys dined out on. As I recall, and to be fair on the artist, he claimed it merely erotic. I also recall the huddle of pubescent schoolboys, me included, thumbing through that book while the class weakling was charged with the duty of standing by the door keeping a watchful eye out for prefects or, even worse, a master turning up. Anyway, suddenly I knew exactly how to paint Zada. Indeed, I would include both my lover, Zada and I in my conceptualized erotic scene of a slave market with me the highest bidder. In a hurry, I left them to their wine, making for my studio in order to set about the painting that was now crystal clear, if rather indelicate, in my mind's eye. I felt I was beginning to be my old self once again. A rare feeling indeed. What is more, while I knew not the ways and workings of Zada's carnal apparitions, I certainly was well aware of my lover's regular need to escape from the role of a decision wielding Goddess; that necessary need to do whatever it takes to exact the conclusion her client's brief had demanded, or, in my case, to keep me alive and as well as possible. Her determination in such regard I always found, indeed still find, extraordinary. It is thus sometimes she has to let go of herself, has to be the quarry not the huntress. That she achieves this by way of seeking playtime's luscious sexual humiliation as that, she has told me made for her a place where she felt free of the outside world; free of decision making. Unquestionably, were I to paint my chosen scene to perfection her desires in that regard would come out to play once more, a thought I would like to think might become an actuality, as I too have my own dark places, the polar opposite of hers. That we have opposing needs is most likely the spine of our relationship. Opposites, I have heard tell, frequently attract.

The substantial task before me in manufacturing the painting meant it took days on end of old fashioned graft to achieve. Yet unshackled of convention and unable to take reality for granted I was not ruled by the latent restrictions of the unmistakeable obvious uninspiring multitudes. Perceptions of rationale although without conscious realization that that was so, my imagination took liberties for the sake of my art. My raison d'etre firmly fixed upon mirroring on canvas the visions born of the viscera of my godforsaken mind.

If nothing else, I still had my sense of touch, a sense more viral than before my downfall. Perhaps such a thing was courtesy of the God I do not believe in's pity; His atonement for looking the other way when I needed him most? Come what may, my newfound dexterous gift of ingenuity was one I held precious.

Through the sorcery of touch I sensed within Zada's being a vulnerability. When musing as to how to best present the girl on canvas vulnerability would be my watch word if the final product were to reproduce every inch of her image undamaged.

Layers upon layers of energetic rumination had led me to conclude that naturally, as any vincible creature should be, Zada must be painted nude yet more than that her susceptibility would have added impact were she painted within a mindboggling scenario of menacing pitfall.   That is how I came to decide she would be the bargain had, whereas my strong-willed lover would be the bargain still to be bartered for.

The rule of thumb I had evolved when structuring the painting was cut from the same cloth as Ernest Hemingway's writing equivalent, 'Write drunk, edit sober' although this artists version, were it the case he had a voice would have been, 'Sketch drunk, paint sober'.

Picturing the girls thus would be a representation of nefarious pleasure's flight of fancy, namely that of buying and selling desirable women. A voyeur's delight, erotic in the world of make believe, vile in reality. There were other things I worried about also. I knew my lover would likely be more than pleased with the end result, yet would Zada be offended or thrilled? Then there was the matter of plagiarism. Is such plagiarism of content the stealing the Orientalist's thunder? Not so if done better than the originals.

9.

AUTUMN 1952 – SUSSEX ENGLAND

Her: With Zada long gone, having taken summer with her, it was as if the extensive gardens to the estate had been commandeered by a chilly Poseidon. The delivery man had telephoned the previous evening to advise it unlikely he would be able to discharge his usual duties and deliver provisions the next day as an overnight unseasonal blizzard of some magnitude was anticipated. His estimation was proven accurate, for come daylight the landscape had turned into a sea of crystal white more than matching her own outer layer. Albeit only October, the easterly winds born of Mother Russia had carried an ocean of snow all the way to the southern shires of England.

As might a child, and given that rarely do children feel the cold, his pliable lover adored the still of a snowfall. Adored it especially at that time when an early morning ever so excited sun pops up to spotlight the sheer beauty of Mother Nature's artistic prowess; that time prior to it all turning into a horrid slushy mess. Were it not that she might freeze alive she had often thought that to be naked upon a blanket of snow would be her perfect camouflage. An all-white personage upon an all-white landscape. Maybe her violet eyes would be her giveaway? Maybe not. Nonetheless, she took the view it was there to be enjoyed. As such, she dressed her man in his thickest thobe and bhist, his turban along with an ex-military trench coat so ugly it was beautiful she had come across at the church jumble sale and, of course, his Wellington boots. She thought he looked as exotic as exotic can be. Plainly she had communicated to him the weather conditions and sought his approval as to his venturing outside with her. He seemed keen enough in that regard. She thought him the most handsome fellow.

It was thus, the one who thought she had quit the espionage game by design held hands with her lover, the one who had retired hurt from the self-same game and together they made evidential footprints in the snow. She wondered if the lake had frozen over, certainly in the near distance it was clear that the weeping willow felt irritatingly burdened from the sheer weight of its new cloak of frozen vapour.

The pair had only reached the edge of the snow screened lawn when he sensed that his guide, standing full height at only an inch above five feet, was struggling wading through what felt like a good foot of whiteness to make progress toward the lake she had always favoured when out on a jaunt. In his head the property, both inside and out, was mapped out. He had come to know his way about not just the living quarters but of late the grounds also. Armed with such a ground map stored within he had no hesitation in simply lifting her up and holding her in his arms. That she was clothed for once a shock, although given the weather conditions perhaps such a thing was hardly surprising. Moreover, that she felt as if she were a little cuddly animal was unexpected until he recalled the fur she was encased within was the full length with a hood, hideously expensive white mink coat he had gifted her upon her birthday just a few years previous. His guess that she wore nothing beneath the fur, a given. Long-time past she had once explained her fascination toward her own preference viz a viz carefree nudity was a thing that separated her from the crowd and that she could never fathom why others, the general public, were so protective of or offended by the naked human form. That to her such a thing whatever ones' shape or size was a work of sublime evolutionary art. Even when dancing ballet the night of the assassination of the Grand Duke her nakedness was completely lost to her, her performance was paramount, the only thing she cared about...well that and the feeling of purest power her nudity gave her over the assembled sick salivating male throng.

She felt terrible that when dreaming up his new wardrobe she had entirely overlooked buying him winter gloves especially so as she was warm and snug in her mink fur muffins. The thought struck that if only they could easily communicate with each other whilst out in the snow they could talk of love not just be in love. Additionally, she also wished there was a photographer onsite to arrest their image, together dressed as they were. It would make for the finest picture.

Intuitively, her giant knew just when to put on the brakes as they reached water's edge. He placed her back on pastures white. The lake had not frozen over; ducks, coots and a single black swan were making as merry as possible, while lakeside now domiciled in England, circumspect Canada geese looked on jealously from the shore. Even so, a disappointment in many ways. The thought of walking upon thin ice was a thing she had got used to in her professional life and to make real the metaphor felt strangely enticing. She determined to advise him of that piece of information later, when back in the comfort of indoors, sat in front of a raging log fire.

For what seemed like an age the pair stood huddled and cuddling each other, occasionally sharing a kiss, both with eyes cast upon the lake, hers omnipotent, his impotent. Such inequality mattered not to lovers glued together as if as one.

In the muffled silence unique to a snowy landscape all felt deliciously still, the odd noise here and there of wildlife at play or seeking sustenance was all that she could hear. Out of nowhere she thought of his painting of the slave market, she and Zada, the collateral up for purchase by any of the robed bidders on the lookout for fresh flesh, he the striking ever so debonair sheik, the puritanical man of faith, buyer of both she and Zada, the pair of brazen infidels, unworthy of any respect within his community to do with as he wished. The picture-framer in town had looked more than a little shocked when she had delivered the canvas for framing, yet said nothing, accepted his extortionate upfront fee without a murmur. That astonished, perhaps even appalled face he wore, the face of a tedious worst sort of prudish bore would stay with her forever. At the time, she had had trouble controlling her strong desire to laugh out loud; laugh in his goody-two shoes face. Evidently, he recognized her from the painting, stood upon an auction platform wearing nothing but a leather collar and held fast by a male Bantu eunuch, such was her giant's erotic imaginings in setting the scene. As to Zada, she had already been bartered for and was painted sat, indecently crossed-legged, head bowed at her new master's side. The scene set in an old Istanbul bazaar, a word defined in native tongue as 'women's market', a gem. The hustle and bustle; the throng of would-be slave buyers baying for fresher whitest flesh. Just how a blind man could come up with such a thing, such expertise, a miracle quite beyond her, although his capacity to do so obviously to tickle her fancy no doubt the reasoning behind the picture. At the very thought of this the urge for a little roleplay in front of that log fire later had a tingling in places due south, appeal. In any case, it was about time she gave up control for a while and lost herself in masochistic fantasy, played the pretend dominated fresh virgin. Besides, her man, she knew well, would jump at the opportunity to play such a wild and wonderful game. It would have been his motive from the outset, of that she had no doubt. A simple kiss sealed the deal as if by sixth sense.

As he once more chose to chivalrously carry her away they headed back to the house. Another silent journey, a good time to let her mind wander in the wonderland of fantasy. The thought of being owned, having decisions made for her and spelt out in unequivocal orders; to give the whole of herself over as his slave girl, fulfilling to the letter on pain of death her master's wishes, the pinnacle of playful fatalism - accepting, of course, that such things only worked in the realm of seductive delusion, never in real life. Also, such masochism was one she only favoured in the company of man. When it came to female lovers, and she had had many, mysteriously the reverse was the case, domination, lovingly predatory had always been the order of the day. She had felt that way regarding Zada who sadly, thus far, had spurned all things Sapphic. Nevertheless, the prospect of being her giants slave for the night was a delicious feeling, and in a transparent way, the very best present she could gift him and he her, namely that of living out their collective wildest, outlandish dreams.

As to sex itself, she considered it a matter of fact thing marvelling that so many made an issue of the act of fornication, made-up rules, straight-laced etiquette. To her the orgasm, the finality of the game that is sex was merely, as the French put it 'la petite mort', that brief, heavenly relief in a loss of conscious inhibition likened to the moment of death.

That night, his painting became a place in which they took up residence. She the actress; he the actor. They both favoured the method acting approach; the closest thing to reality known to the theatrical fraternity. That his role play was unseeing and silent, was a nothing, for the scene was set firm in his mind. Orders issued by a click of his fingers, a mandatory knowing nod, then a sharp slap upon her easily detected bare backside if she dared pretend to misunderstand his commands. She pretended not to understand with some regularity. He had, after all, summoned up the scene; the playground they were in; he knew she needed that relief from forever having to be in control of others and events, both now in her personal life looking after his well-being and before, in those times she participated in the tournament that is espionage.

For two of a kind who idolize one another a long night heralded but a token sleep. Ceaseless adventure upon the well-trodden boards within the theatre of raw passion often reveals itself thus, and more often than not as the ever-watchful sun rises come first light it begs an encore.

Later, still bedded yet now sharing mugs of piping hot black tea she finds that perhaps now is time to impart the thing that has been playing on her mind, the thing she had kept on the back-burner perhaps too long. Certainly it felt overdue.

Her composition of his and Zada's wretched tale into the form of a short, hopefully very decipherable, story, much longer than she had originally intended, now accomplished, the time had arrived when it should be left to him to read. She determined to sit with him always during such reading in case, just in case of any negative reactions. With fingers, legs and anything else that could be crossed duly crossed the manuscript was handed over as he was sat comfortably in his studio. He was clearly keen to get started yet before doing so kissed the forehead of the author and mouthed the words, 'Thank you'.

10.

OF KHARKO AND INSTANBUL

Her: Oppressors who find themselves incapable of mastering hypnosis generally further their nefarious ambitions by way of implementing the contrived premise, 'supremacy by way of inflicting terror upon the general populous'. Insofar as the highly-prized prisoner was concerned, he served that purpose well. In essence, he was an example and a warning to one and all. Moreover, Stalin the great falsifier of history had ordered he be broken in body and spirit but kept alive, occasionally given public view as an objective living lesson any outspoken detractors of the regime would be well advised to make due note of.

It was within the humongous fortress prison in Kharkov, Ukraine an incorrectly perceived interloper was dragged bloodied and naked through the cold, stark corridors of the gaol to the rousing marching tune of a penny whistle Red Army orchestra. That for public consumption his crime was deemed a treacherous breach of faith by 'one of their own' had ensured his fate; validated his torture and subsequent demise. That that was a timely lie with a purpose, a given, for 'he' was in truth no more than a Cold War British spy abandoned by his own as collateral damage. Yet, at this juncture the great communist leader required that his true circumstances be kept under wraps. Little point in giving the Brits something to shout from the rooftops about when presently there were bigger fish to fry.

Upon arrival, the prisoner found his cell was of the type named a 'Kishka', arguably the worst of its kind ever contrived. In native tongue 'Kishka' meant 'gut' and like an intestine its dimensions were tall and narrow. From the outside it had the look of a coffin. Forsaken, locked within, he could only stand upright, nought else, no creature comforts. * In such an environment, with barely room to breathe, let alone afford the opulence of a slop bucket, the conditions for the inmate were patently hideous. Worse still, the inventively sadistic bigwig Major a large, markedly plain-featured woman who had the ear of The Man of Steel himself had been charged with the task of tormentor-in-chief. She was most accomplished in that regard. The prisoner, a giant fellow, would be hauled out of the cell each day, hosed down and delivered up for what was named interrogation, yet in truth was skilful mutilation before a salivating audience of novice intimidators. Even in the times after he had been blinded, his vocal chords severed, his ear drums rent asunder, the daily visitations continued unabated.

(* The Long Walk by Sławomir Rawicz 1956)

To a gifted cloak and dagger freelancer sometimes an impossible, outrageous manoeuvre outshined the best thought through one. She had, more often than not, found that an element of surprise contrived in an instant inevitably trumped planned design. However, in this specific instance, when minded to rescue alive the gentle giant she had long since claimed as her one and only true love something more visionary was called for. An 'on the hoof' tactic would, for certain, minimize the chances of a successful outcome.

Upon the rickety balcony of the small hotel room situated in Old Kharkov craning her neck just a little she could catch glimpses of the Drobitskiy Yar Botanical Gardens. It was spring, the sun-chasing morning blossom awe-inspiring. However, needs must when the Devil drives and her imagination was running rampant. Having arrived at this glorified boarding-house armed with a key facet of intelligence sourced on a 'no names, no pack drill' basis from a malleable CIA agent licensed to dabble in Soviet affairs, a material scheme was developing agreeably.

A little later over a breakfast of nicotine, strong black coffee, and the debatable local delicacy of mashed potato pancakes at an adequate, yet not sparkling, street café just up from her hotel she considered in some depth the sequence of events required to achieve her aim. When the pair had teamed up in Leningrad a few weeks previous Uncle Sam's under-cover man abroad had intimated by way of discreet chitter-chatter that the sadistic Major had an exclusive appetite for only those of her own sex, indeed had a lover installed in her flat in the opulent – insofar as Kharkov did opulence - part of the city and not just that for he had also provided both the address of the 'couple' and a print of a photograph of the pair in, how did he put it? "Something way beyond just intimate embrace". Better still, in said pornographic snap the camera had fortuitously captured in startling focus not just their lustful antics but also their startled faces. Recognition of either would be unproblematic. Her eyes lingered longer than anticipated upon, not the disagreeable to the eye ample Major, but her admittedly alluring lover. She had that certain something about her. Perhaps a different time, a different place she might have been smitten with her for a day or two? A thought shelved almost as quickly as it arrived for she was nothing if not professional.

Where the less creative would perhaps consider good old-fashioned blackmail the route to take toward their desired end she had something far more extravagant on her mind. She would kidnap the lover, a pretty little coffee complexion creature with a mass of jet black hair, difficult to put an age on, likely in her late teens or early twenties, certainly far younger than the burly Major, hold her hostage, trade her in exchange for her busted giant.

Late that same morning back in her hotel room the time had arrived to disguise her natural aura of unconditional whiteness from any prying eyes and ready herself for the task at hand. A blend-in, rather than stand out camouflage was deemed appropriate. Having applied a dark-hued make-up befitting of the geography of the event to unfold she took great care in separating and pinning her snow-white hair tight to her skull as a pre-requisite to fitting her tame dull brown wig of human hair. Her violet eyes, eyes that marked her as albino, as ever, posed a problem. Her preferred fashionable sunglasses seemed inappropriate. Fortunately, she had had the foresight to carry with her a pair of uninspiring clear lens spectacles, beseeming the drabbest librarian. The heavy black frames would mask and take the focus away from her tell-tale iris's. Once in character she checked herself out in the timeworn bathroom mirror in dire need of re-silvering. Satisfied with what she saw in her reflection she slipped into a non-event assortment of stereotypical dull togs that would blend in with the surrounding dullness of the city and its ever-weary occupants. The phrase 'brown and blue will never do' came to mind. For a girl so impassioned by style, the complete lack of that certain élan ensured her banal outfit was perfection itself; would proclaim to all that she was merely part of the humdrum native flock.

It was via the self-same blossom bejewelled botanical gardens she had made note of earlier in the day, she would saunter to the depot and take a tram ride cross-city to be delivered up in close proximity to the block of flats where the Major's presumably lesbian lover would be in-situ. Covert surveillance plus a little tactful probing of locals over several days had satisfied her that her target never left the building; was always behind closed doors.

Before finally departing the hotel she took a reflective backward glance in the mirror, saw a version of self that might well have been kindred to that of her incarcerated lover. In that moment, she perceived herself as him, fumbling and defenceless, only pride intact, knowing full well that when caged one must abandon all insecurities and memories of both tainted and pure love affairs. It was the way of things when survival was the quest.

Istanbul, the place where Byzantine and Ottoman architecture hold infatuated hands, still managed to cling on to its cosmopolitan impression despite the establishment of the Turkish Republic some 30 years past. It was upon the warmest moonlit evening under oblivious stars, sat at a table set outside of a culinary shrine in the form of a much exalted sea food restaurant in the Kumkapı district of the city, overlooking the Sea of Marmara that two, by the look of them carefree, pretty young ladies took particular delight in stuffing stuffed calamari as well finding amusement in the animated, vociferous, overburdened waiters, itinerant vagabonds and the skilled, yet wildly surreal one-legged musician playing his accordion and occasionally giving them 'the eye'.

The girls made the oddest couple, one a snow-white slender kidnapper, the other her plausible, yet only days before actual hostage, a sultry, tawny fully ripened Romanian named Catalina. To passers-by and for all intents and purposes the pair were best of good buddies. Indeed, that is what they had almost become over the previous four days of arduous travel together from Kharkov, across the Ukraine into Crimea, through the effectively closed city, and home of the Soviet naval fleet, of Sebastopol, then across The Black Sea courtesy of a tame fisherman, en-route to Istanbul. Reflecting upon the events of those previous 96 hours the kidnapper, sipping upon illicit yet widely available Chardonnay, had found it an amazing, although not entirely unexpected, thing how audacious bribery of railway and border officials had allowed to convert what would otherwise have been a much more onerous journey into one of relatively easy passage.

Having perhaps taken one too many glasses of wine, and in retrospect, a willingly shanghaied Catalina was clearly keen to fill in the blanks insofar as her personal history was concerned. She had alluded to her tale when travelling yet now with the bravado born of alcohol had the courage to put flesh on the bone. Nevertheless, her abductor was not herself so tipsy as to realize that were it not for both the wording of the ransom note and explicit photograph left behind at the flat in Kharkov for the not so good 'Miss' Major to discover when returning home from her prison duties, the escape to Istanbul would have been significantly more dangerous than it had been. In the event that the stipulations of that note and the assured blind fear reaction of the Major should her Sapphic predilection be published far and wide meant that the journey had been free of any police or military giving chase. The old boot had kept schtum. In short, the matter of barter, the exchange of the broken giant she loved for the return of Catalina had become a very private matter twixt kidnapper and Major.

Fortunately for the kidnapper she was fluent in the Romance language that is Romanian. Catalina, her husky voice a delight to the ear, explained she was an indigenous Hutsul and that until two years gone she had resided with her loving family in an impoverished village placed indelicately upon native foothills, namely those of The Eastern Carpathians. One unusually humid new seasons day, having spent the whole morning gathering wild mushrooms, she was walking the well-used tarmacked track, homeward bound when, quite out of the blue an automobile pulled up aside her. The aged driver, a man in military uniform afforded her a strained sneer come smirk. On the rear seat within, the one she would so soon know only as 'The Major'. Taken aback, for they did not see many cars let alone pristine black limousines where she lived, she was somewhat overwhelmed. The driver had exited the la-di-da vehicle and walked over ostensibly to ask directions to a place Catalina had never heard of anyway. When she had advised that she could not assist it became clear that his posing a question of her was nothing less than a ruse to get up 'nice and close'.

"That is when all of a sudden he grabbed hold of my arm and frog-marched me to the car. He shoved me onto the back seat alongside who I was soon to discover was the Major and told me that if I knew what was best for me I'd sit still 'like a good girl' and not say a word. I was shaking and petrified so did what I was told. We travelled in silence for what seemed and probably was hours. The Major studiously ignored my presence the whole way. She had slept much of the time during the journey. She snored like a pig. By night-time, probably well after midnight I guess, we had ended up on the outskirts of Kharkov, a place I'd never been to before. In fact, I'd never been to any big city previously apart from Istanbul with you today...I've loved every minute of it by the way. Eventually we reached what I now know was the prison complex. The Major let the driver go off home and had the guard at the entrance handcuff my hands behind my back. That really scared me and I still had no idea of what was going on; of what they wanted of me. It was then she led me all the way up to what she said was her office and in no uncertain terms advised that I was to be her new 'plaything' and that should I object she would have me locked in a cell to rot forevermore. I didn't understand what she meant by 'plaything' yet was afraid to ask. At the time all I could think of was my parents who had no idea what had happened to me or where in the world I was, or even if I was alive. They still don't know."

"Did you object? Oh, pardon me, bad manners Catalina, shall I have the waiter to top up your glass?"

"Yes, to both. Thank you. What's your name, by the way? It feels ungracious of me not to call you by your name."

"You may call me Eliza, Catalina."

"Anyway, Eliza, in a panic I pleaded with her to set me free telling her I'd go down on my knees and beg if she wished. I just wanted to go back home. She showed not the slightest compassion and was having none of my, what she called, 'whining'. At this point she told me that a couple of days in a cell might make me more 'responsive'. Again, I appealed for my freedom through a waterfall of tears. I just wanted to go home. It was then that she ordered me to undress. Without thinking, and as a Godfearing modest girl, I instantaneously refused, revolted at the thought of taking my clothes off for, and in front of, her or anybody else. And even if I had agreed I wouldn't have been able to with my arms still cuffed behind me. She must have known that. She did know that, for next she smiled, chuckled to herself, got up from her desk chair, casually walked over to the door and called for guards. Two guards arrived in no time. They were both male. It was explained to the pair that I was a whore and a common thief proving to be a noncompliant 'customer'. Simply by clicking her fingers then pointing at me, and waving a forefinger up and down she had the guards tear off every stitch of clothing I wore. My dress, everything was torn to shreds and scattered over the floor before my eyes. I couldn't even try to cover myself up with my hands fixed as they were. I was so scared and ashamed."

"Then?"

"Then, having been told in the plainest terms not to even think about raping me the guards escorted me down staircase after staircase, along corridors and passageways, finally throwing me in a cell without any windows or any lighting. Before locking the door, and in the dimness of the corridors illumination, my handcuffs were removed. I was given just a blanket and a glass of water. I fumbled with both as I was shaking all-over, spilling a little of what I was soon to discover was water more precious than I'd ever thought water could be. They just left me there to stew for what I guess must have been a couple of days; I'm not sure how long really, certainly a long time. I know I was so weak, thirsty and hungry when she finally came for me. When she opened the cell door she shone a torch in my face. It blinded me for a moment as I had been confined in the pitch black for so long. She grabbed my wrist, told me I stank and then pulled me by my hair into the empty, freezing cold corridor and back up to her office where there was an open wooden coffin. The whole event unfolding was beyond bizarre. Just the very sight of that coffin made me scream, made me cry my eyes out, for I thought she was about to kill me. She stood there just watching me immobilized with the dread of everything going on. I became hysterical. I could tell she was enjoying my humiliation. She had got a riding crop out from somewhere and when I tried to cover myself with my hands she lashed my backside, insisting I put my arms out straight. I couldn't stop crying, my arms were aching from being outstretched. After that she slapped my face as hard as she could and, as she put it, brought me 'to my senses'. It worked to an extent. Eventually the tears ran dry. As I calmed a little she ordered me to climb into the coffin and lie down. I did what I was told and climbed in, but not before she had gagged me. Prior to closing the lid on me she told me not to worry as she had no plans to kill me just yet, adding that if I knew what was good for me I should lie still and play dead. The very last thing I remember was the thump of the coffin lid being shut. Well that and hearing her talking to at least two, maybe three or four others, I don't really know how many, saying that the coffin contained her dear mother, that it had been mistakenly delivered to her office by some stupid undertakers when she was out performing other duties and that it was to be delivered forthwith to her flat and that she would meet them there to let them in."

"So basically she bundled you into the coffin and that was that? Clearly, she was keeping you a secret from the Party, her bosses and co-workers as well as the world at large. Hang on though, I find it hard to believe no one noticed a naked you being escorted along those various corridors and up flights of stairs on your way to her office."

"Truly, there were no others anywhere that I saw. The place seemed totally empty."

Self-styled Eliza thought this a good time to settle the restaurant account and head back with Catalina to their twin bedroom in the exclusive hotel she had booked where the pair had dropped off their belongings earlier in the day. That the driver of the cab they hailed, donning a fez, chain smoking a brand of cigarette that gave off a thick aroma of chocolate vanilla had charged massively over the odds did not go unnoticed although she decided it was not worth arguing over at this time. Their chosen room afforded well-deserved sumptuous twin beds, both of the wrought iron framed canopy type. Purposefully, in that whilst she had built up a level of trust with Catalina it could not be overlooked that the girl was integral to the return of her lover. Separate bedrooms would have given Catalina the realizable ability to make good an escape in the unlikely event she was prepared to take that route, without papers, passport or currency let alone any worthwhile knowledge of exactly where she was or where she might go.

The bellhop had already delivered the requested nightcap of crème liqueurs and departed when, noticing Catalina looked exhausted, Eliza suggested that they talk some more in the morning when they would be refreshed after a decent night's sleep, pointing out that while they did get some modicum of rest on the train journey they had had little since. With that the pair finished their respective drinks and got ready for bed. Curiously perhaps, 'Eliza' made due note of the fact that Catalina without a nightdress displayed no reticence at all over the fact that she had no choice but to sleep in the raw.

"I'm ever so sorry Catalina, and although I trust you, you are my key ingredient in this exchange and I can't take any chances. Originally, I had assumed you would be problematic. Those who are kidnapped understandably often are somewhat peeved to say the very least. It is an unusual thing for the victim of a kidnap to be pleased to be captured in my experience. I truly thought I'd have to keep you sedated, bound and sealed uptight in a cellar or such like. Although I have with me all the apparatus and, of course, Chloroform to cover any situation, and seeing as we get along so well we'll just settle for the leather collar and slim chain restraint. And, just in case you think me weird these items are not connected with any strange fetishes! They will, however, help me relax knowing you're not going to be able to make a run for it. I'll padlock the chain, it's quite long, to the bedpost. It shouldn't cause you any discomfort, stress, or impede any nocturnal mattress wanderings while you sleep."

With that Catalina acceded to the request with surprising, yet due erotic humility, even kneeling upon the bedroom carpet bowing her head and then offering up her neck in submission to make the task of fitting the collar a breeze, adding with a girly satirical giggle, "This is like being at home with the Major."

Studying Catalina lying delectably vulnerable upon a wafer-thin eiderdown waiting to be covered up and tucked in for the night her kidnapper could not help but cheekily observe, "You look so gorgeous by the way. The collar suits. The fact that the chain is fastened to the rails of the bed head I also find very, how shall I put it? Sensual, yes sensual. You really are very beautiful. Perhaps, maybe?"

"You might not believe me, and I'll tell you more tomorrow, but seriously I am not what you think I am. Not at all."

"Oh well, my loss. Sleep well, Catalina."

With only the soft light of a hesitant gibbous moon sneaking in through the open window, before she dropped off, Catalina uttered the imploring words, "You're not going to give me back to the Major, are you? Please don't do that." Her kidnapper refrained from replying, yet her mind buzzed well into the early hours searching for a potential Plan B that might afford Catalina some assurance in that regard. Before she could decide exactly what she should do to possibly help her quarry would be dependent upon hearing the rest of her tale come the new day.

Tomorrow had arrived with a flourish, an eager sun shone as proudly as only an arrogant golden orb is capable of. Catalina's transfer of tangible guardianship back to the Major was just three more days away. Her abductor concluded a little culture would provide light relief and was much in order. She suspected her hostage had never seen beauty fashioned by man akin to that which Sultan Selim III had designed for his dear mother. It was thus both girls took to Yildiz Park in the Beşiktaş district of the city, with its two beautiful old pavilions, the view of the Bosporus, waterfalls and ponds as well the stunning gardens and mass of established trees, all guardians of history's unfinished secrets. Out of choice, both wearing respectful headscarves, they strolled aimlessly, favouring chance over design.

"Eliza, this place is so beautiful, I've never seen anywhere like it in my life."

"It is lovely, I agree wholeheartedly."

"Have you been here before?"

"Yes, just the once with my lover; my lover, the one that despicable Major of yours has, I understand, all but destroyed."

"Oh, I thought from what you said to me at bedtime last night you preferred the fairer sex. Did I get it all wrong then?"

"Not really, let's just say my personal preferences are not confined only to the males of your species."

"Your species?"

"Slip of the tongue, nothing more."

"You said, 'that Major of yours'. Truly, the Major isn't mine. I admit that I am hers but not out of free-will as I have explained to you."

"Try explaining some more. The tale of your maltreatment is like no other I've ever heard."

The heat was soaring as midday approached so the girls took to sitting in the shade of a lonely Japanese cherry tree surrounded by absurdly green lawns. Prior to explaining 'some more' a worried, or perhaps just quizzical, Catalina expressed her concern that wherever they went people were staring at her companion. Notwithstanding the answer being plainly obvious, 'Eliza' replied saying that she was used to random stares; that it was the way of things for albino's; that that was why she generally took to wearing both a sunhat and sunglasses, notwithstanding substituting the scarf for the sunhat as of now, her bleached complexion was a giveaway, hence still they gawp.

"Anyway, before I answer your question about the Major, first you tell me how you broke into the flat. I've been trying to work it out but can't. I'd been locked in day after day for the two years she'd held me captive there, and tried to open the door a million times just to see if I could, yet you just waltzed in like you owned the place. You did the same with my wardrobe door, for that was always locked to me also."

"Tricks of the trade. Let's just say I have a certain way with locks. Besides, when I arrived you didn't have a stitch on. I could hardly snatch you stark naked. Opening the wardrobe so you could get dressed was something of a priority don't you think? I don't believe that even the biggest of bribes would have got us first-class seats on the train with you stark naked! Anyway, carry on with your story, I'd love to get chapter and verse from you."

"Where shall I start?"

"Why not where you left off last night. If I remember you'd been dispatched to the Major's flat, without a stitch on and stuck inside a coffin. What happened next?"

"Well, I'll come to why I was naked later but as far as me ending up in her flat, I'll explain that first. To put it simply, she opened the coffin lid and said, 'get up'. I could sense her scrutinizing my body as I clambered out. Then, much like she did at the prison, she yanked me by my hair and dragged me off to her bathroom, ordering me to take a thing called a shower as I 'stunk to high heaven' to the extent she wanted to vomit. My problem was that I didn't know what a shower was. Truly. Up until that point I'd never seen or heard of such a thing. We didn't have such things in rural Romania and I had no idea how to turn it on or what to do or even what it was actually for. It just felt like a weird glass box and me an exhibit like a zoo animal. Anyway, that's when she just gave a shake of her head, got undressed, and joined me in the shower. I still remember how blubbery her ugly belly was. Then she washed me all over, and I mean 'all over' then, well then, I'd rather not talk about it."

"I understand. From what you said you are not homoerotic. Sorry I got that all wrong last night. How on earth did you cope being her, being her what? Lover? Mistress? What?"

"Wife. Believe it or not, she eventually made me her wife, although there was no actual wedding or anything like that. She professed undying love for me. Said I was everything to her. She even gave me a wedding ring. I have the ring in the suitcase you made me pack before we left the flat. I was so scared when you showed me the pistol in your hand, saying that if I made one false move 'now or ever' you'd kill me. I thought you really were going to kill me at the time. I just thought, 'oh no, not again, please God not again'. A satirical smile, adding, "I'm glad you didn't shoot me," then continuing, "Going back to the Major, I had little choice but to do whatever she wanted of me. I had been warned that if I refused even her smallest request or instruction she would have my family back in Romania tortured and murdered."

"Bitch."

"Yes, a bitch with an inexhaustible, disgusting sexual appetite. She once, early on in our 'relationship', pointed out that I could if I so wished play-up and be sent back to the prison where she would use my body for experimental new methods of torture, or I could stay in the flat with her and accept daily humiliation as a way of life. I agreed to be good and stay with her. It was the only logical choice. As to knowing how to humiliate me she was a maestro."

"How so?"

"I don't want to go into the precise specifics, I really don't, although you may have noticed when I packed my suitcase that I didn't pack any under garments. Remember, when I stepped out of that coffin I had nothing in the world, no clothes, no nothing. Well that's how I stayed for the first few days of being with her. She'd go off to work and leave me naked, expecting me to be her slave...you know, cooking for her, keeping the place spotless and always reminding me without fail that my life and the lives of my family depended upon me fulfilling any and every command she issued. So, I remained the good little girl and did everything asked of me without complaint. She'd come back home, then it was constant sex, deviant sex I might add, me forced to do unspeakable things I'll never tell anyone except my Maker one day in the hope He makes her burn in Hell. Then the day came when she returned home with bags of beautiful expensive low-cut dresses, high heeled shoes, stockings and suspender belts for me. How she had acquired such expensive things in a place like the Ukraine I have no idea. Whatever, she had me try them all on in front of her as she sat by the fire sipping whisky, nodding in approval. She called it her 'fashion parade'. I asked if there was any underwear to which she simply replied, 'what do you think?'. I took that as a 'no'. Because of her I haven't got underwear on today as you will probably have guessed."

"Sorry to interrupt but I had noticed. I was just being polite not mentioning it. Carry on please."

"Well that's about it, my story is told. Sex, sex, sex, slavery and more sex. I couldn't do anything other than play along with her. She scared the living daylights out of me. At last, on this day, this gorgeous day, and yes, I know it may only be for a short time, yet I suddenly feel free again. I don't want to lose that feeling, please find a way, please."

"I will try my best to think of something. You must understand though that my lover is my priority, but I'll do my best for you, Catalina. I think you know that?"

"Thank you. Oh, for the sake of explaining the relationship as it evolved I should add that the Major and I shared the same bed, shared kisses, sometimes she'd be tender, mostly not, but I know for certain she was besotted with me. She even got down on one knee when she put the wedding ring on my finger and pronounced me her darling wife who she would cherish and be loyal to until the end of time. That night she concocted a particularly all-night long horrid way of consummating what she had called 'our marriage'. Even so, every single day she went into work, or on the times she was out of the city for days on end, doing whatever she did out of the city my new clothes were locked away in the wardrobe leaving me naked for the whole time. She told me that the thought of me left at home with nothing on awaiting her return when she was away excited her beyond measure. I think by that she meant...well, I'll let you guess that! I suppose I was lucky she kept the flat so warm as winter can be especially cold in Kharkov."

"You really have been though a nightmare Catalina. Your script reads like a Grimm's fairy tale only worse. Pray tell me my lovely, already you have heard me talk of the, at best, indecent photograph of you both. Someone must have taken that picture. Did you never have guests at the flat? My own covert investigations reveal that others in the tower block and nearby understood just the two of you lived in that flat."

"Oh yes, we'd both sometimes sit outside on the balcony on summer evenings sharing vodka and caviar. Generally, well always, she kept the door to the balcony locked-up tight save for those 'special treat' times. We were not directly overlooked and it didn't ever seem to worry her to have me sit with her, although she insisted we always kept a good distance apart so as any prying eyes wouldn't put two and two together. For that reason, I was always as fully dressed as she allowed me my clothes for those occasions, naturally. I quite liked...maybe 'liked' isn't the right word, but you know what I mean...those times, they were the closest to a kind of normality I ever had with her. There was never a threat of violence or disgusting sex. And, although not that often, we did have house guests. As you will have seen the flat is enormous and very grand, certainly grander than anything I could have imagined from my former life. Sometimes people, important people would come over for dinner parties. At those times she had me dress up prim and proper as a waitress, although still without underwear under an authentic uniform and I was always introduced as her 'live-in' housekeeper, come cook, come waitress. I was not allowed to speak to the guests unless spoken to, and even then, I should keep my eyes firmly fixed to the floor, head bowed and keep any reply short, polite and use just plain words. She often got very drunk at those parties. I hated it when the guests had left, especially the night she thought I'd overstepped the mark when asking some politician who seemed very important and who clearly liked his drink, if I should top up his glass. That was the night when she threw me face down on the bed and whipped my backside with her dreaded riding crop. Every time she whipped me I screamed like a banshee in pain but she said if I carried on like that the neighbours would hear and she'd have to be done with me. Then she changed her mind and said she'd carry on beating me until I stopped screaming. Somehow, I'll never know how, I stopped my racket and I just laid there sobbing until she was finished. She always seemed to get a thrill when I cried. By the way, I still have the scars on my butt from that night and am surprised you didn't notice them when you kidnapped me? Anyway, she was very contrite and even apologized the next day. I think she'd been crying herself, her eyes were red. That was the one and only time she ever showed weakness or said sorry for what she had done to me. She is an evil woman and I hate her so much."

"That's awful, and no I didn't notice your scars. That's unlike me, yet I was rather busy catching my prey, namely you. Anyway, you can always show me later. The truth is you were nothing but a sex slave to her. I am amazed, honestly I am, that she didn't break you. Most would have cracked; gone insane."

"I just want to live to see my family once more, that's all I wanted then, that's all I want now. She made sure by constantly humiliating me that I was prepared to do anything, anything at all, however vile, in the hope that one day my dream would come true. From then on I made double sure I did whatever she wanted of me. Not long after she declared herself 'husband' to my 'wife' she complained I never had an orgasm when with her, so I learned to fake them. Once she complained that I never told her I loved her, so I told her I loved her with all my heart. When she wondered why I never instigated love-making I even started encouraging her to pleasure me."

"Wow, oh wow. That is so bad. Look, seriously and sorry to sound so indifferent, but going back to the photograph, what is the story behind that picture? It could be important as to how your future pans out."

"The Frenchman."

"Pardon?"

"She called him just that, the Frenchman. I never knew his real name yet it was he who took the photographs. There were many more than just the one photo you talk about, yet apart from that risqué 'one' of the two of us, all the rest were just of sweet little me. You see, following our 'marriage' I was told a professional photographer was to visit, his purpose to create a portfolio of 'artistic' images of me so that my beautiful body would be frozen in time and become her priceless forever keepsake."

"That's when The Frenchman came in then? He was the photographer?"

"Yes, she said he was a Communist who had defected to the Soviets and who worked, well I think that's what she said, for the State newspaper and sometimes at the prison, although what he photographed at the prison I have no idea."

"I do, but we'll leave it at that. Carry on please."

"Apart from what I think was his murder, there's not a lot to it really. He turned up with her one night a few days after she'd mentioned she wanted the 'portfolio' of me, with a leather bag full of what I was soon to find out was his camera, lenses and other various pieces of equipment. I didn't realize straight away it was him. I just remember hearing her arrive with a male guest. So, I played by the rules and stayed out of the way in the bedroom until summoned. You must remember that until she got home and unlocked the wardrobe for me I was, as ever, comically and entirely naked. I can't even say I was dressed in just a wedding ring, even that was taken from me each day and placed on the wardrobe shelf locked away with my clothes until she came back home as she preferred me to be completely undressed. I eavesdropped and they, that is she and the 'him', were deep in conversation regarding where to set up his camera and I then fathomed that the he must be the photographer. They had decided, from what I overheard, to have me pose in the lounge upon the beautiful red velvet chaise longue I'd never been allowed to touch, or even dust, let alone sit on before."

"Yes, I noticed the chaise longue when snatching you. It is clearly an antique, a very expensive one at that. A murder you say. Tell me more, I like a good murder story."

"I'll get to that in a moment, I promise. Right, where was I? Oh yes, next she called out for me. Having nothing on, and she obviously knew that, she shouted at the top of her voice, 'COME HERE RIGHT NOW, DO YOU HEAR ME, RIGHT NOW IF YOU KNOW WHAT'S GOOD FOR YOU'. I didn't fully know what was going on and whether she wanted me dressed before meeting the photographer, but was afraid to ask for fear of upsetting her, so I just made an entrance as was. I didn't even dare try to protect what was left of my modesty...well insofar as well-placed hands can protect modesty... in case she had one of her bouts of wickedness. And that, in the buff, was how pathetic subservient me made my entrance and was inevitably photographed. On a chaise lounge spread this way and that per his and her sick demands.   The shame of it all. Everything that happened, that has happened, all of it, will haunt me forever. I just have to put on a brave face and pray that everything changes."

"That must have been so distressing for you? I don't want to diminish In any way that part of your story, yet can't wait for the murder, you're keeping me in suspense too long."

"OK, OK I'm getting there. You know, once it would have been distressing, embarrassing even, but by then I'd given up caring. After the photographs were taken, we all sat around the dining room table, me still bare, drinking champagne until we were totally inebriated. The Frenchman was falling over drunk. The Major said he could stay the night in the spare bedroom. After that we all went to bed. As I had guessed earlier the Major would be keen on sex with the lights on as always before sleep. It was during that sex that The Frenchman, totally unannounced and still very drunk, entered the bedroom, said 'Smile please' and I'm guessing that that was when the picture you talk about was taken. I remember the flashlight on his camera made me jump out of my skin. The Major, roly-poly naked herself got into a fit of rage and shoved The Frenchman out of the bedroom, shutting the door behind her leaving me alone. I heard a massive crunch as he fell backwards onto the floor, then a noise like he was suffocating, then just silence. She was a good while, but eventually came back to bed and we fell asleep. I was up before her next day and went to make her usual strong black coffee, yet come that morning there was no trace of The Frenchman to be seen, just his camera and equipment. She never mentioned him again and I didn't feel it was my place to ask about him."

"That's some story. It sounds like she magicked him to heaven or hell. She's obviously cunning as well as evil. I shall have to remain aware of that for later. Anyhow, how did those photo's come into being without The Frenchman. How did the pictures get developed?"

"I have no idea. All I can say is that about a week later she arrived home, insisted I got dressed immediately, then presented me with a leather-bound album of what she referred to as, 'the best and most imaginative shots'. She said she obviously had her own treasured copy of the album that she would always take on her travels to remind her of me and that I could keep this one and that it was a loving gift from her to me. I took one look in the album and died a thousand deaths."

"Did you keep it?"

"I think she would have killed me as well if I'd said no. There were only a dozen or so blown-up photos in the album and it also got locked away on that wardrobe shelf with the wedding ring whenever she wasn't at home. For some strange subliminal reason, I can't explain to you, I put the album in my suitcase also when you came for me. Would you like to see it? I don't mind, really I don't."

"Part of me says 'yes please' the other part says, only if you are sure you want to. Are you sure?"

"I am sure. If anything, it's a blessing I packed them. The album is the only thing, apart from the scars on my bottom, that validates all the things I told you."

"OK then we'll run through the album later. For now it's best we take a break. The heat is becoming intense here. A café and a cold drink is called for I think. We can discuss some more later."

In a silence that sought no translation, two girls walked through and out of the park in the quest to find a café in shade. An essentially, but not quite intimate hush. More, one born of her arguable saviour mulling over the barbaric ordeal of Catalina's misfortune. That Catalina could prove with hard evidence and certainly to her satisfaction that she had been telling the truth changed the rules of the game. That being the case it meant, without any shadow of a doubt, Miss Major would have to suffer for her sins, and at the same time not just her Titan giant, but Catalina also must be 'rescued'. With that decision made a methodology of enactment to be resolved and a shady café happened upon, the girls spent the rest of that day being just girls eventually ending up in the undercover elephantine Grand Bazaar of 60 streets and 5,000 shops. By the end of the day it was an overjoyed Catalina crying tears of both gratitude and pure joy at, to her at any rate, the experience of her lifetime and the gifts she had received. So precious to her, the evil eye amulet to wear in her luscious hair to ward off evil spirits, so much silver jewellery, and even a skimpy belly dance costume just for the sake of harmless fun. Sadly, and not that she said she particularly cared, no suitable undergarments were found.

"Perhaps you'll belly dance for me later, Catalina? You looked deliciously exotic when you tried it on in the shop."

"I don't know how to."

"I'll teach you if you like?"

"I would like. But how will you teach me. You haven't got a costume of your own, have you?"

"Sadly, not one with me in Istanbul, but who said getting appropriately dressed for the occasion was compulsory? Perhaps we can ask that one-legged accordionist we saw at the restaurant to play the music. Not authentic music I know but anything lively and playful with the right rhythm will do. Having said that, perhaps not. Maybe when this 'thing' is all over we can make merry." At that Catalina blushed just a little, nevertheless a bona fide blush.

On the taxi ride back to their hotel a contemplative Catalina could not help but beseech, "You're not sending me back to the bitch, are you? You wouldn't have spent all this money on me if you were. Thank you, a thousand, thousand times, thank you, thank you, thank you. I've never had a day like this in my life." With that she cried some more, especially so when the reply came back, "Not on your life. This all ends the day after tomorrow, you can count on it. Just be aware that you must trust me like you've never trusted any one before. You can do that? Anyway, I shall try not to get you involved in the matter if at all possible."

"Yes. Of course. I'll do whatever you say. I'm used to doing whatever she said so I don't need to practice how to obey instructions."

"Don't be so silly. You know exactly what I mean. Be strong. Stronger than you've ever been before. It may not be easy, but trust me, it will be done. Be braver, be more courageous than you ever dreamed you could be, not just in the now, but forevermore."

The chilling of the evening, although not an especially cold chill, prompted two fed, watered and wasted girls now back in their hotel bedroom earlier than anticipated. Both were so tired. Catalina in particular. Before finally retiring for the night they shared the big bubble bath in the exquisite ceramic tiled interconnected bathroom. Innocent fun, nothing more. Catalina bid the bath water farewell first saying, "That reminds me of sharing a bath with my sisters back home, only this one is ten times the size and much posher" then playfully, yet pointedly, made to thrust a tempting backside in Eliza's face, giggling, "See the scars on my butt. I don't think they'll ever go away."

Catalina's abductress lingered on in the now bubble free bath water deep in thought fine-tuning her scheme for the exchange now that circumstances had changed. Eventually, albeit reluctantly for she could easily have fallen asleep in the tub, she alighted, wrapped herself in a plush cotton pile towel and returned to the shared bedroom only to find Catalina kneeling atop her own bed, naked save for the collar restraint she had clearly fixed upon herself of her own volition.

"No need for the collar tonight Catalina, you have my trust. I know you won't take flight while I sleep."

"I wanted to wear it for you. You have showered me with gifts and given me not just a taste of freedom but a chance of real freedom also. I have nothing to give in return. No money, no nothing except my body, and you did say you liked girls sometimes. I am all yours if you wish."

A stillness that conveyed incredulity, then, "Catalina, just look at you, you are beautiful, you are thoughtful yet you need to be wise. I am many things, yet to date have never abused a trust, never taken such a liberty, never taken advantage of a good soul, such as you. Likewise, no matter how kind your motive may be, you must never prostitute yourself ever again. Your world is changing, that thing called 'choice' once more, belongs to you."

"But this is my choice."

"It's not mine. Not like this, anyway." With that she removed Catalina's collar, kissed her upon the forehead, "Sleep well Catalina. The world will soon be your oyster."

11.

A SPRINGTIME OF CARING 1952 – SUSSEX, ENGLAND

Her: Three weeks gone since deceit wedded transposition. It is now spring, and comfortably domiciled in England's pastures green, two twittering young ladies play futile tennis on a court of crushed shale within the ample exclusive grounds of a Cubist masterpiece of classic French design far, far away from the heart of ordinary urban prudence. In a milk and water bedroom, sleeps seemingly forever, a damaged beyond repair convalescent giant. The optimism of those caring for him, his best medicine. Given his trinity of stolen senses, for his own safety when left unattended the physician has recommended he be sympathetically strapped to his bed thus eliminating the risk of further injury to his person. Whilst not for certain, an incontinence diagnosis was unlikely, yet for the sake of prudence, beneath his bedsheet a rubber equivalent ensuring the mattress is not spoiled in the event of little accidents. Regardless, both girls watch over him. Together keep him clean and cared for. As yet, no one can say if his mind still functions in part or at all. Time, protection and watchful analysis alone would likely determine the answer. To that end, and to send out to him the subconscious message that he really was in safest hands, the pair ensure the given gift of gentleness bestowed upon the female is afforded him always. A kiss upon the brow when tucking him in at night, the reassuring holding of his hands when guiding him to the bathroom, the delicate manner of his routine daily shave, the simplicity of a warming cuddle as and when, serves, hopefully to accustom him to the stark fact that he is out of harm's way, safe once more, that times of habitual torment and confinement are forever over.

It was Catalina who had christened him, 'His Royal Highness' just the other day. Now they both address him thus. It matters not a jot that he cannot hear. They share the night-time ritual, sitting at his bedside, watching, waiting for signs of upsurge in his condition. They find the task of tending to him much easier if he is withheld clothing after all when nursing someone in need compassion triumphs over threadbare modesty.

For the moment though, in the name of light relief, both girls have, at huge expense, donned pumps and Tinling's fashioned waffle-piqued flare tennis dresses, notwithstanding that their respective skills in the sport are anything to write home about. A feral black cat on a solo mission stops by to peek at a wayward tennis ball on walkabout that a stringed racket has inadvertently smashed way out of court. Disenchanted, the feline walks on by his mind on greater, hush-hush, neo philosophical things. The girls decide enough is enough and make for the house when finally, and overwhelmingly bored, that just a lucky return of serve constitutes the only rally they could, twixt the pair, manage.

"Providing you don't think it rude of me to ask, tell me Catalina, how much did that jeweller I recommended you in Hatton Garden pay you for the wedding ring? Yellow diamonds mounted in platinum and yellow gold should, I trust, have been worth a pretty penny."

"Of course, I don't mind you asking. £3,000 was what he paid. Apparently, I'd have got much more if I could have provided provenance."

"I presume the Major stole the ring from the wrecked body of one of her victims at the prison, so no provenance. Still, that's a tidy sum. Have you made your mind up to return home to your family yet? If you have, do be careful to keep low key, thus avoiding risks."

"I have, and I shan't be going back just yet, maybe never. I need to find a way to let them know I'm alive and well without putting them in any jeopardy. You know yourself how difficult things can be behind the Iron Curtain. Australia has a certain appeal to me. I've been thinking about it for days. Australia, I'm told, will take me in and give me citizenship plus it's a country free of tyranny. But for now you and His Royal Highness need me and I owe you so much. I will hold dear a place in my heart for the both of you forever and a day."

"Thank you, but I can manage alone Catalina. You are hardly grown-up and have a life to live. Get out there and make that new start on the other side of the world."

"Maybe. Can I give you some of the money I received for the wedding ring? I still feel guilty taking gifts and shelter from you, yet never giving back in return."

"Without you I may never have got His Royal Highness back. If anything, I owe you. There cannot be a price put on love, and as poorly as he is, and probably always will be, he remains the love of my life and believe me, male or female I've done a lot...the lot. He is yet to be bettered as lover or kindred spirit. He is my project; my passion, but I'll tell you what, you can if you really do want to give me a present, you gift me your photograph album, the special one. I know it embarrasses you; I know it is arguably, well let's be fair, an indecent thing, yet The Frenchman was a bloody good photographer, and you Catalina are a bewitching nude muse, even if he went over the top in terms of taking overly graphic shots. Take away the vile circumstances of the photographs coming into being and what's left is just you, a divine piece of erotic art. After all, photographs such as these, lovers have shared with each other since the camera was invented. There is no shame in nudity."

"If that's how you feel then take it as read, the album is yours."

"You know, when you first showed me the album, that fact that they had forced you, insisted you made constant eye contact with the camera was disturbing for it intrusively exposed the whole of you, body and soul, nothing hidden, the sex slave, you the unwilling one, lost in time, whereas without that eye contact the shots would have been an accomplished artistic take on the faultless female form. Then, the more I thought about it, the fact that I now know you well, that I know the nightmare you went through, that those lifeless, conquered eyes of yours staring out of the picture at me, me alone are pleading for me to save you. And save you I did. Although wanting the album makes me a little ashamed, yet I'd be a liar if I'd didn't say I found them carnal in the ravishing extreme. Maybe, it's the effect those eyes of yours have on me, because of the way I am made? Whatever, and I must add that it's a good thing His Royal Highness is blind in some respects. If he were to catch a glimpse of you au naturel you might turn his head and that wouldn't do at all. I'd lose him!"

"You make me want to cover up, even though I'm dressed. I can understand what you're saying, yet simply wish I didn't, or perhaps better put, couldn't understand your words. Please don't take offence. You know how traumatic the whole experience was. Having said that, and just out of interest, tell me which picture did you like best?"

"I'm embarrassed to say but I think you can guess."

"Oh, that one. I think it gave submissive a whole new meaning did that one! It's funny how I can laugh about it now. Why is that?"

"Freedom, Catalina, the pure relief of gaining your freedom counts for a lot and it's a healthy thing to put the worst happenings behind you and be rid of them forever more. I hope one day His Royal Highness will be able to do the same. You're blushing again, Catalina, I adore you even more when you blush."

"You can look, but as we've agreed, never touch."

"Regrettably, I am aware of that, darling girl."

Come the chilling of an enigmatic evening, bathed and changed out of her tennis garb into something with polka dots, Eliza attends to her lost giant while sweaty Catalina, still in Tingling's finest, takes to the kitchen sink to wash-up dinner plates, knives, forks, saucepans, thinking idle thoughts of pastures new. From the floor above, a shrill snake of sound wiggles its way downstairs almost polluting the geometric forms of Cubist design within, "Catalina, come quick, come now," the urgent request. She leaves idle thoughts behind to simmer, rushes up to the bedroom. Enter a puffed out panicking Catalina, "What is it? Has he hurt himself? Why is he sat on the edge of the bed with his head in his hands? Why does he seem to be crying?"

"No, he is not hurt. I believe he is happy. There is nothing to worry about."

"My God, you scared the living daylights out of me, what happened?"

"It's his mind, his mind is active. There is some hope. You see he had woken up and as ever I presumed that after having slept so long he'd need a wee. As I always do, I held his hand and coaxed him from the bed, prepared to guide him across to the bathroom, whereupon he brushed my hand aside and did it all by himself, really, he did. He walked there without any help, did what he had to do, and walked back to his bed, all unaided."

"So, you mean he memorized what he had to do?"

"Yes, he memorized. This is a major breakthrough. He's not a vegetable. A small piece of him has returned. Maybe this is the start of something bigger. I'm so happy for him, Catalina."

"As am I."

The girls, as if excited schoolgirls, clap their hands together, shed salty tears of jubilation, hug each other tight, jump up and down on the spot in delight. Then, frozen still in time, they watch eyes wide open as an incredulous giant deliberately, and without urgency, leans forward resting his palms upon the floor as if to feel that floor vibrate beneath his feet. He tilts his head to one side quizzically as there is nothing save for flooring to feel. They realize what he is trying to do, so jump up and down again, and with more gusto than before, scrutinizing his every move as he absorbs the floor's vibrations as if they were his first breaths of life. He then looks skyward, eyelids shut tight over dead eyes and smiles the smile of holy revelation. Unable to control themselves instinctively, and in unison, the girls each grab an arm and lead a willing patient down the staircase and into the lounge below, "We must celebrate. He must savour his moment."

"Do you think it's warm enough for him here. Should we have tried to dress him first? Maybe if we dressed him, he would one-day work out how to find his clothing and dress himself."

"First things first, Catalina. One step at a time. He'll be confused enough just by being here. He has smell and touch. I think we should introduce him to the things those two senses can appreciate."

However, as schemers scheme best schemes a disoriented giant, collapses to the floor, banging the back of his skull upon the ever so solid Macassar ebony coffee table on the way down. A call from the black Bakelite telephone to the emergency services brings forth an ambulance and he is stretchered away to the hospital, leaving a silence soaked in culpability in its wake.

Three days on, a stitched, bandaged and as of now concussion free Royal Highness is brought back home accompanied by his less than pleased physician. As would a miffed headmaster he gives the girls, only one of whom understands a word he says, a dressing down, calling them, "Bloody fools" adding that only, "A regime of meticulous routine" would have any chance of a morsel of restoration in his being and wellbeing. Duly reprimanded the pair stood side by side holding schoolgirl hands, bowing their heads in shame and commit to the 'will try harder' proposition asked of them.

Following his return, and over the course of the weekend, times of introspection and order, yet finally a degree of healthy mediocrity returns. The mending giant is in hibernation, the house is spic and span, the albino, under the chosen name of Eliza, and Romanian Catalina sit on the veranda enjoying an afternoon treat of Jin Jun Mei tea all the way from China and smoking Lucky Strike cigarettes all the way from America.

"How exactly did you rescue His Royal Highness? I mean, it's obvious you did rescue us, we wouldn't be here otherwise, but you never did tell me the whole story."

"I've often wondered when you were going to ask that question. It's not that interesting in the global plan of things."

"I'd still like to know."

"OK then, here we go. You recall that when I kidnapped you from the Major's flat in Kharkov, on the reasonable presumption that you were her esteemed lover, I left the seedy photograph of you both in, how shall I put it, 'advanced foreplay' plus, what in colloquial terms is called a ransom note together on the pedestal table in the drawing room. The note gave the explicit instructions as to the hurdles she'd have to jump in order to affect your safe return. Even before your capture I had established to my satisfaction that she would not want a word of your actual, and her potential, demise getting out. Hence the power of the picture. You have to take account that Stalin loathes homosexuality as much as he loathes anything, even comparing it to paedophilia and while lesbianism is not itself outlawed, in law, women are increasingly caught up in the psychiatric system, and women who desire other women are inevitably diagnosed with a form of schizophrenia, the self-same diagnosis the authorities would use for political dissidents."

"You mean, if unequivocal evidence of the Major being lesbian got out they would send her off to a frozen archipelago in Siberia never to be heard of again?"

"In essence, yes. The Soviet regime cannot be doing with openly practicing homosexuals whatever their gender. Males have it far, far worse, yet the Major knew well that the thing she was, was her potential failing."

"I see."

"That meant I had her at my mercy right from the start of the operation. My ransom note was crystal clear, I remember its words almost verbatim. These, more or less, are the words I penned;

'You don't know who I am, yet I have in my possession your lover. You've no doubt realized that she is not at home presently. If you wish to ever see her alive again then you will need to comply with my instructions for her safe return.

Presently, you hold against his will prisoner number 107345. You will trade 107345 in exchange for your lover. No currency need change hands, you will merely hand him over at an appropriate time and place and, in return, you get to have your young lover back in your clutches. A simple transaction.

Accompanying this letter, you will note, there is a print of a photograph that will only see light of day and be published far and wide should you not comply with these instructions. Should you decide otherwise, rest assured your Man of Steel and all his cohorts will be posted copies and additionally your lover will die. I feel sure that the content of this photograph and the certainty that any lack of compliance on your behalf will herald the end of your career, the end of your freedom – unless, of course, you have a taste for Siberian winters and prison cells? My trump card, don't you think?

In ten days' time from now – for the sake of clarity, a week next Wednesday coming - at 3pm precisely, you will deliver up 107345 to the British Consulate in Istanbul. The gentleman who upon the steps of the Consulate in public view, will make himself known to you will accept 107345 on my behalf. He is a discreet man and will keep your little secret safe. In case of any doubt, presently, the gentleman at the Consulate has no idea your lover exists.

Then, two days later – the Friday - at the very same time of 3pm you are invited to retrieve your lover. There is a barber's shop in in the Old City of Istanbul. Come alone. If you did not know already, Zürafa Street is infamous for its brothels. I shall have 'eyes' everywhere. If I detect any other persons accompanying you, or anything suspicious then all bets are off. You will wait outside of the shop for as long as it takes for further instructions. That is all you need to know. Nothing convoluted, I assure you.

Do not consider any tricks. Arrive too early, or too late, then the girl dies. If it has crossed your mind, and I do hope it has not, to make a pre-emptive strike on the assumption that the barbers shop is where she will be domiciled twixt now and the date of the hand-over, be aware that she is tucked safely away elsewhere in a place you would never think of finding her. Also, if you are so foolish as to attempt to appropriate her return in the interim period say, while the girl is being transported to Turkey, be aware that the outcome of your folly will give cause to her instant extermination.

*You may be wondering why we both simply
don't meet up and swap prisoners? In layman's terms
I see no good reason to place any trust in you. Hence,
you have no choice in the process of exchange.
Lastly, I hear you wondering if I will keep my side of
the bargain. You don't. That you must place blind
trust in me is your only option.'*

Catalina pauses, in silence gathers her thoughts. "Say I was troublesome like the average snatched person, frightened, enraged, violent, weeping, screaming oh, I don't know whatever kidnapped people act like, how would you have transported me to Istanbul, if Istanbul was your plan from the start?"

"The same way as you travelled here, by rail and sea the only difference is that you'd have had a discreet pistol in your back the whole way. If you're thinking, 'how could she remain awake the whole time on a journey as long as that?' you would have overlooked the fact that I had an accomplice with me the whole time, watching from close-by. You might remember seeing him on the train? The fat Turk with the black patch on his left eye. His name is Ali. I'd rendezvoused with him in Istanbul on my way out to The Ukraine and he had travelled with me to Kharkov before your capture. He stayed in the shadows but was always covering my back."

"He was with us all the way?"

"Yes, only with you it turned out he was there more as a guard than a threat. He's quite a nice man when you get to know him although he does, I admit, have a dark side I don't altogether approve of."

"I never noticed him. Anyway, once in Istanbul where would you have kept me locked up?"

"Ali owns that barbers shop in the red-light district I mentioned in the ransom note. It's just one of his many business interests. There is a large hidden basement that is as good as soundproofed. Back in the day it was used as a storage area for slaves en-route to the markets of Arabia. Pretty girls fetched a good price."

"So, I would have been kept there all along despite what you said in the ransom note?"

"Yes, you would. The only reason you were not kept there and stayed with me in the hotel was simply because circumstances had changed everything. The moment I realized you were as much a prisoner as my own lover I knew an adjustment to my original plan was called for. That is when I decided the Major must pay the ultimate price for her crimes against those I cared for."

"I saw 107345 tattooed on his wrist. So that was his prison number?"

"Yes."

"Tell me, if I had been just a kidnapped pawn in the game, how would you have treated me. It doesn't matter really but I'd like to know."

"Well, the naked are less likely to try to escape, the tied and bound cannot easily escape, the blindfolded cannot see to escape. Those things. That is how you would have been kept."

"A home from home then! In the end would you have killed me?"

"I don't think so. I may or may not have cheated the Major. It was in my mind once His Royal Highness was confirmed safe with my contact at the British Consulate to simply have you thrown onto the street and be done with you."

"What, with no clothes on?"

"Most likely, although Ali is an astute business man with an eye for a profit and associates all over the globe. There remains, even today, a market for slave girls in the Middle East. Maybe, if he asked me nicely I'd have let him sell you. It would have depended on what type of person you were. If you had proved to be like the Major then you can take it as read the slave markets would have been your destination. Fair punishment I think."

"Let's get this clear in my head. I am assuming you'd heard His Royal Highness was in the safe hands of your man at the British Consulate. Then you wait a couple of days until, the Wednesday I think you said; you leave me back in the hotel while you go out to meet with Ali, then later at 3pm you both meet the Major in the street outside the shop. What happened next. I know she died but I'd like to know how. I think that once I know everything my life will really be up and ready to start all over again."

"It wasn't quite as simple as that. Remember we knew what she looked like. Fat, ageing a little and pale walking the streets of the Old City. It wasn't that difficult for one of Ali's many brothers to spot her well before she arrived at the barber's shop. In the hustle and bustle of the street with a well-placed knife shrewdly up the back of the blouse, and a walk to the barber's shop, then to its basement, where she was expecting to find you. She was easy prey for a professional."

"She died in the basement?"

"Yes. Realistically I needn't have been there. Ali could have looked after the whole affair himself. He was outraged when I told him all about the way she had treated you for the past two years. The thing was I wanted to speak with her before she met her Maker. Whilst trusting Ali, I wanted to see; know for certain she was dead. I felt that that was important both to me and you. The funny thing was, right up until we tied her to the chair she still believed, totally believed she was going to have you back in her custody any minute. For some perverted reason in that flawed brain of hers she really thought you loved her. What a trusting fool she was, you'd think with all her experience she would have harboured some doubts regarding your supposed love of her and my intentions insofar as the 'trade' was concerned. She almost deserved to die for her stupidity alone. Still, they say 'love is blind' and in her case it certainly was."

"What happened next? How did she die?"

"She died quickly."

"Is that all you're saying?"

"OK then. I calmly spoke with her. Listed the crimes she had committed turning my man from fit and healthy to deaf, dumb and blind and how she had been responsible for so many cruel deaths and mutilations over many years, plus the sick pleasure she had derived in repeatedly raping you. Ali was stood behind her, his blade at her throat all the time I spoke, when I gave him the nod, he simply slit her neck from ear to ear. A messy but swift death."

"Her body?"

"Let's just say Ali keeps piranha fish."

"Have you assassinated many people in your line of business?"

"Only those who deserved it. Only those ones. No others."

"It pays well from what I see here?"

"It does, when you are as adept as I am. Always remember I believe in compassion. The innocent need have no fear of me, not now; not ever."

"Thank you. I think we ought to check on our patient now, don't you?"

Having spent what was left of the afternoon and into early evening first cleansing, manipulating the limbs of, then feeding their presently most likely still much confused patient in relative busy silence, Catalina harboured freshest thoughts. For her the time was fast approaching when dreams and aspirations must be fulfilled. She had, almost on the spur of the moment, felt the urge to move on and start anew; to leave the past behind. She worried so how the one who had become all but her mentor, certainly her best ever friend, would take the news of her imminent departure. She need not have.

"I can't say just how happy I am for you, Catalina. Overjoyed in fact. Tell me, is it still in Australia you will make your new life?"

"I've changed my mind, it's simply too far away. Do you remember when you first brought your pair of rescued souls, the 'he' and the 'me', here to your wonderful house. First, we concentrated all our efforts making him as safe and comfortable as possible. In what spare time we had you would tell me stories of all the places you'd been to; all the things you've done. Paris stuck in my mind more than anything else. Thanks to you I've realised a worthwhile sum of money from the sale of my so-called wedding ring. It will pay for my new start in Paris until I can get a proper job. I've never been there but you call it 'The City of Love' and make it sound such a magic place. Do you think I'm wise in choosing Paris? Tell me you do."

"I do. Very much so, I do. You'd be well advised to learn how to speak French post haste though. Parisians especially respect those who bother to learn the language. Anyway, what exactly do you propose to do for 'proper' work there?"

"I don't know. I'll have to see when I get there. I have no special skills, no formal education. Sure, I can read and write yet beyond that...well, I'm just a poor farmer's daughter from a remote village in Romania where I'd be expected to marry young and breed early. Maybe I could work as a waitress in a café."

"You should set your ambitions higher than that, Catalina."

"Well what then?"

"Montmartre."

"What is Montmartre?"

"Don't you remember, Catalina? I spoke of it with you. Montmartre is a large hill in the 18th arrondissement of Paris."

"What of it?"

"It is the place where the artists congregate. A magical, bohemian part of the city. Cafes and culture. Anything goes. It's wonderful, a paradise for not just painters but thinkers, writers, sculptors, musicians, you name it, Montmartre is where you'll find them. Presently I hear that Avant-Garde Art, for all its sins, stills thrives as do those new 'Rebel Painters' fresh from America. So many genres. I adore the place with a passion."

"And what would I do there, besides work in a cafe?"

"Think, Catalina, think. First, with the money you have find a place to live. The rental prices for a garret have risen lately I hear, yet in relative terms you can rent there for next to nothing. Then, if I were in your shoes I'd take up modelling for the artists. I am well connected there and can introduce you by letter to all the right people. The well-established artists; not the stony-broke ones and there are a lot of those, by the way. No, you'll need the ones who would pay good money. If you need to you can always top up your income waitressing in cafes, but don't make that your one and only 'proper' job whatever you do."

"Why would they want to paint me, let alone pay me for the privilege?"

"See yourself in the mirror, Catalina? You are not just beautiful as a person. Surely you must know you have an exquisite body. You are perfectly formed and stunning to look at. Have you not ever noticed the way men gawp at you in awe? True artists, the best ones that is, respect the female form, want to capture it in all its glory on canvas. Enter Catalina from Romania, the prettiest girl in all of Paris, maybe all of France."

"Does it mean getting my clothes off?"

"Sometimes, but not always. It would depend on how any painter wanted to portray you. I can understand that after your experiences with that awful woman you might have some reticence in posing nude, yet, and I think you should be ever so proud of yourself, you've put that trauma behind you...that's a big thing you've managed and remember, what you went through would have broken most people into little pieces, never to be put back together again. You are strong, you did what you had to do to stay alive and succeeded. So, don't be ashamed at the prospect of using your body to make an income, it's not as if it's walking the streets at night under red lights or anything like that."

"Well, I suppose I could try. My parents back home must never know of this...well of any of the things that have happened to me...they are strict Romanian Orthodox churchgoers, as I was until I gave up God when I found the Devil in the form of the Major. I would like one day to be able to let them know I'm safe and well, even to be able to send them some money, yet cannot dare write them a letter, the secret police snoop everywhere and I don't want my parents or relatives compromised in any way. I'm lucky that there are no links to my name and the Major. There would have been hell to pay if there were."

"Given that wretched bitch had the infamous now destroyed photograph in her possession in Istanbul your only potential link to her were the driver who picked you up in the first place and the two guards who threw you into the prison cell. From the description you have given me of both events I cannot see that they would be aware of the fact you ended up confined in her flat. After all, you were delivered to that place concealed within a coffin, if I recall. Even so, I myself have often thought exactly how we might make covert contact with your family but have never come up with a worthwhile plan. You see, if they did hear you were OK, in one understandably excited moment they might just sing of their good news to all and sundry. That plus any money you might have sent...and such a currency transfer would not be an easy thing to organise...might just whet the whistle of those secret police you talk of. Even then the link to the Major would not be that easy to fathom, although under torture who could predict what your parents might be forced to say or sign. The Major is, like you are, a 'missing person'. It's best you both stay that 'missing person' for now, you know that, and sadly will have to live with it. In the future who knows, but in the 'now', leave well alone."

"I agree."

"So, you'll give modelling a try then?"

"Why not. I am imagining myself lying naked on a sofa for hours on end getting paid for it. It certainly sounds better than milking goats in a stable on a winters day in the middle of nowhere, because that's what I would be doing back home."

"One other thing I've just thought of. Dancing. If Paris is made for anything it's made for dancing. When I was just 17 I'd sneak away from...well the 'from' must remain my secret...anyway, I'd sneak away to start with until the day came I chose to disappear completely. I had felt stifled at home and just had to discover and live free in the world. I had been trained as a ballet dancer. I'll say it myself, a good one. I needed to earn a living. As albino, the stereotypical view of most people generally meant my kind were thought of as unusual at best, downright vermin at worst...some would think us witches or unworthy beings and lock us away. But I always knew I was something special...those gawping men I mentioned to you earlier, unlike you, I noticed them salivating over me so I took my gift for ballet dancing to, at first, the seedy clubs of pre-war Berlin, later in Paris's not quite so seedy, more haute bohème venues and danced for my public."

"Why would a trained ballet dancer choose to perform in what you call seedy clubs?"

"Oh, Catalina, you are so naïve. I danced naked, of course I did. To some that might sound a terrible thing to do. Shameful, shaming, a sin even but to me quite the opposite. To me, through my choice to dance I soon discovered it as an empowering, overwhelming...a wonderful thing. I found that I had my audience, mainly men but not exclusively, enthralled and in the palm of my hand. I was, I remain, unique. The stunning albino girl dancing ballet without a stitch on. I was the talk of the city before, that is, I got into the espionage business where I, by dint of need, have had to keep a very low profile."

"If you were such a living legend...obviously, I don't doubt a word you say...yet how is it you now work under-cover and no-one knows what you do for a living. 'Eliza' who dances naked; 'Eliza' the spy. It can't be that difficult for your enemies to track you down?"

"Plainly, looking as I do I have to take great care at all times, just let's say that the version of me who pirouetted undressed didn't go by the name Eliza, nor is the name of the spy, Eliza."

"So that's not the name you were christened with?"

"I cannot say. I'm sure you understand. I'll still answer to 'Eliza' for you though. That aside, when were you thinking of leaving for Paris?"

"That's the problem, I don't know. I have no passport or documents. It is as if I don't exist. I don't even know how you got me into England. Did you cast a magic spell?"

"Good God Catalina a passport is the least of you worries. I've already thought of that for I knew that one day you'd need to get away. Leave it all to me. I'll organise the whole thing. All I need are a couple of passport photos, you can keep your clothes on for those, and abracadabra, done! As you might imagine I have a regular requirement for such snaps. It would be for the best if you choose a new name, although that's up to you?"

"Oh, I hadn't thought of that. Yes, I can see what you mean. What name do you think I should have?"

"I tell you what, as and when HRH is asleep, we can take wine and conjure you a new identity. How exciting."

HRH's workout routine takes an age. His would-be, yet just pretending, registered nurses completely immune to his nakedness. Press-ups, trunk curl's and in place of weights even, in the absence of such things, lifting a willing 'Eliza' horizontal on outstretched arms high above his head, she trustingly resting atop the palms of his hands, up and down time and time again. She makes note that each day he gets stronger, fitter. That he derives tangible pleasure from resurrecting his fit body that perhaps out manoeuvres the pace of progress of his mind, yet affords some advancement in his overall recovery affords both girls some hope for his future well-being. Catalina's 'Eliza' suggests that before she leaves for Paris perhaps they should, together, teach him how to dress himself as plainly they cannot take the easy route, leaving him unclothed forevermore. "Privacy is a temporary thing," she notes. Finally, after a second bath of the day, this one to purge his body of perspiration, they get him into his bed, reluctantly fix his safety restraints, tuck him in as one would a small child. His lover sings for him. An old Romanian lullaby Catalina had taught her, 'Tiny you are when you start your sleep'. It matters not he cannot hear. Both girls kiss their adored patient goodnight.

The room temperature tumbles as night stumbles then falls, chilly Catalina and Eliza curl up close together under cover of a giant blanket entwinned upon the settee in the lounge.

"You'll need to get the taste for French wines when in Paris, Catalina. This one you sip on presently is a plain and simple Bordeaux. The grape is of merlot variety and, if I recall, in Romania you grow a little merlot so it might taste familiar to you?"

"Sadly not. Back home we women barely drink at all. Maybe a taste of something home made on special occasions, that's all. I hadn't drunk any alcohol until the Major came along and she never gave me the names of any drink she served...or should I say, 'I served up for her'. This one tastes nice though. 'Bordeaux, Bordeaux, Bordeaux...see, I've said it three times so its name stays in my memory."

"You cannot go wrong with a Bordeaux, Catalina. Any French gentlemen courting you for the first time won't think you too expensive to run if you go for this style of popular wine. Now then to the matter of your new name. I positively love thinking up new names, although this new name will be yours, so only you alone are allowed to think it up. What shall it be?"

"I can't think of anything."

"Perhaps another drink of...you tell me the name."

"Bordeaux."

"Good, you even sounded a little French just saying it! Reach over would you, you can pour us both another glass."

A bottle of wine shared twixt two excited home birds invariably empties with more haste and less decorum than expected of in a good restaurant. Soon the empty bottle is replaced with a full one as the name game continues.

"I've had a brainwave, Eliza. It must be all the wine! Look, you have white hair, you're white, white all over and you are my lovely, best friend. In Romania 'Albus'...even I know that means 'white' in

English...can be a surname. If I call myself that I'll always remember you."

"Thank you, Catalina. I'm not sure everybody would name me 'lovely' yet I'll grab it with both hands this time. That you thought of me thus makes me feel special. A first name; what about a first name?"

"What about Zada, it means 'lucky', and I think Paris will be lucky for me."

"There, you have your brand-new name. Zada Albus. No more given names? I thought where you come from you often have many middle names?"

"We do, but no more names for me, Zada Albus is just fine."

"We shall touch glasses and toast, 'Zada Albus' soon to be the talk of The City of Love."

Catalina has her first blush in the persona of 'Zada'. 'Eliza' cheekily points this fact out. They both burst out laughing. They drink some more.

"A thought just struck me, Eliza. You said you would give me some letters of introduction to important people in Paris. Will you sign them 'Eliza'?"

"Best you wait and see, clever girl!"

A reflective pause for thought as a tipsy tiredness infects. Moreover, they both know that a responsibility sleeps upstairs. No more Bordeaux agreed upon, although not before Zada making mention of one of the key things that she had considered and had in part prompted her moving on, "It's time you had him to yourself."

"I know," her sane yet partially heavyhearted reply.

Body language speaks for itself, Zada swiftly changes the subject matter, "Will you teach me to belly dance before I leave? You never know, it might come in useful in the cafes of Montmartre."

"Of course I will. Tomorrow evening after dinner; after we have him settled I'll commence your speed course in the art of sexy belly dancing. Be aware though, back in Istanbul when I mentioned I didn't have my costume with me I really should have admitted that I have absolutely no idea where it is. I know you have the one we got in the Grand Bazaar so you'll be fine, but as for me, well, you guess!"

"I've guessed. There really is no controlling you!"

"I'll be a work of art, rest assured."

12.

AUTUMN 1952 – SUSSEX, ENGLAND
The Aftermath

Him: It is strange how docile, how voluntarily defenceless she can be when she chooses while on the other hand, how courageous and domineering she can be when the chips are down. Her day to day life, for the main part as a subjugate female, yet just sometimes sublimated as a second-class citizen, she becomes a sublime contradiction. Last evening certainly was one to remember, cherish even.

Over a belated yet much needed breakfast of a brace of poached eggs upon toast she wipes away a little of the runny yoke from my chin, a substance I still have trouble eating without making a mess. She hands me a braille note. Essentially, it read to the effect that where I am in mind and body as of now is probably as good as I will ever get, my recovery is as complete as is possible. That I have through my paintings and musical accomplishments, plus of course our shared love; a purpose and proven beyond a shadow of a doubt that I am compos mentis and that she is both proud of me for getting to this place; proud of herself for taking me there. She makes the deliberately stark comment 'do not expect to anymore, this is it for the rest of your living days. You must understand that.'

Coincidentally, I had come to the very same conclusion myself yet had not thus far imparted such information to her for fear of putting her under even more pressure. After I had painstaking read her words, I placed my open palm on the table where we sat eating, a long since tried and tested signal to her to offer up her own palm, a thing she readily did. Upon that delicate paw I let my fingertip do the talking. 'I know. I am content. Do not worry. I love you'. Moments later a tangled tongue kiss verified that all was well in her world also.

As to the story she wrote me of my time as a prisoner clearly living in a hellhole under the reign of a malevolent beast I still, even having slept on it, recall not a thing. She had sat with me throughout the process of my reading. On occasion she would stand beside me, anxious for my wellbeing, regularly placing her arm over my shoulder or to pursue a lover's right to ruffle the hair of the loved one. Come the final sentence I hated myself for disappointing her. I know just how much she wanted me to recall the circumstances of my downfall. Yet, twenty-four hours on, still not a glimmer of remembrance.

There is one thing, I think an important thing, that did come to me though. I have yet to tell her the exact nature of what it was. Part of me believes she would see me degenerating toward the state I was in, yet the other part is of the opinion that questions she has about me may just be answered. The practical difficulty and by necessity where the subject matter of a conversation is likely to be long-winded we have both long since come to terms that the enquirer must wait patiently for the respondent to produce a braille account to be read and digested. Sometimes I laugh inside as occasionally our discussions over the most banal things take us days to complete when there are more words called for than those that can, realistically, be penned upon a bare belly, or the palm of a hand could possibly cope with. Although not a laughing matter this is one of those happenings. So as not to keep her completely in the dark I have however, let it be known that the matter at hand is one of those episodes.

Until reading the blow by blow drama that bedevilled both Zada and myself I had paid little heed to the stark fact that not only could I not recall my imprisonment and torture, but also the events leading up to it. Anything and everything had been expunged from my consciousness. The very last thing known to me was that I was playing Peter against Paul in attempting to invoke distrust twixt the East German intelligence and their Russian masters and supposed allies. As to how I came to be in the Ukraine per the narrative, I had not a blind clue. Similarly, I have no idea of how I came to be back here in pastures green. The very last thing that I could accurately put my finger on was of enjoying a Stein of hideously strong wheat beer with my new-found comrades in the Stasi HQ, Berlin. My cover, such that it was, was that I was about to defect to the East, based upon MI5's discovery that I was a double agent. Under that guise I had infiltrated their organisation and had a comprehensive list of spies living within the jurisdiction they controlled that I was prepared to share were they minded to afford me sanctuary. To me at that time things were going to plan. They were expressly fascinated by my claim that to my certain knowledge there were a number of KGB working with them who were feeding intelligence directly to the CIA. That aspect was in point of fact the truth. I had such a list. My tidings would be dynamite and when conveyed would generate a distrust of the Russians beyond measure. My Lords and Masters would be euphoric. It seems to be the case that my so called new comrades tipped off the Russians, and it was they who thought it easier to beat the information out of me rather than allow the East Germans to provide me safe shelter in their drab land. I cannot help but wonder if I buckled and spilled the beans under torture. The fact that I ended up deaf, dumb and blind implies they failed to get the better of me. At least I hope that to be the case. There has, she says – and she is well-placed to know these things - been no contact between MI5 or the CIA since my return to England. Likely they still believe me to be in a vegetative state and not worth giving me the time of day. However, what the story before me has invoked recall of is, if accurate and there is any truth in it, astonishing.

I suppose, for I know not for certain, that the event took place within the boundaries of East Berlin for nothing within my recollection fits the geography as explained in my readings of my plight appertaining to the Ukraine.

I think the time has arrived to prove to her and myself that mentally I have recovered.

Dear Nameless Girl,

You know already that I've have been completely engrossed in your story of my near extinction, my extraneous fall from grace. You were, after all, with me all the way. Your presence about me brought great comfort and had me feeling secure as, when left to my own devices the read would have been the darkest thing to have undertaken, never knowing if and when it all would come flowing back to me in a tidal wave of memories sought, yet in hindsight it is probably best that such recollection now wanders harmlessly in hidden time.

Before I forget (as ever a thing that concerns me...I jest) I would be grateful if you would write to Zada on my behalf. I had no idea the poor girl had been subjected to such wicked mental and physical torture. To come out the other side almost unscathed says much for her strength of character. That she is your loyal friend says much for your own compassion when the chips are down. I suggest you pen her a note saying her own story tugged at my heartstrings and I wish her nothing but happiness hereinafter.

Also, I was amused to read that out of simple logic and practicality you girls when nursing me back here in England had chosen, for the main part at least, to keep me naked as the day I left my mother's womb. I picture the scenes and scenarios in my mind. If you see me with a smile on my face for no good reason then you can rest assured that those times are the likely motivation.

At that time, of course, you will well recall I was nought but an empty shell. Not a single memory. Nothing. That I now partially understand what it must be like to have been born thus a bonus. I like to think that one day in the not too distant future I may serve such souls who entered this world deaf, dumb and blind and have no escape, no flashbacks, no subconsciousness of life as a whole person within the human collective. I lived that relatively short period as they live out their entire lives, immune to social etiquette, locked in a body without practical purpose. Well, some might disagree with my conclusions, yet those 'some' have not been to the places I have been. To be seemingly held forever hostage in an unidentified domain of virgin mind games, where only unanswerable questions are posed in aberrant pulses of a self without a habitual language, a traumatic thing to those who have always been aware, of little meaning to those who know of nothing else. For example, my nakedness at the time my being was somewhere elsewhere, was not a nakedness at all. It was, in short, a nothing for without things to compare it to it was and would never be a nakedness at all. I wish so that I could recall that period when you both cared for me as something exact, something with a chronology rather than just through misty sensitivity. I accept that I never will recall those times when you nurtured my recovery of incidents and illusions. Had you not risked all when offering me yourself in both mind and body I can safely say there would have been no recovery. One should never overlook or underestimate the sheer power of the orgasm as a means to repair as well as to elate. There is one question I wish to have answered if you would? Idle curiosity, and perhaps a quest for a little self-deprecating ribald humour demands that I learn if, in my lost status, the erection was a regular or rare thing? You let me know that Zada was somewhat taken aback to find me stretched out upon the lawn the day she arrived and spotted me sporting an involuntary hard-on. That would imply perhaps such an event was no great issue in the season I was lost and under her care?

Now to the meat of the matter. Berlin or at least the place I presume to be Berlin represents a bookend. The venue where all my old memories grind to a halt, before new memories began here with you following my rescue. Certainly, my times of torture as revealed in your writings in Kharkov is and will always be lost to me. So, what of my very last, my final memory prior to the bookend being set in place. I think you may determine it a most important thing in terms of the evolution of the 'me' you have in your safe hands as of now.

As a preamble to this story, you need to understand I had, immediately prior to being moved on by persons unknown, found myself being beaten black and blue by those who I presumed at the time, still do, to be two-faced Stasi agents commencing the less than onerous task of softening me up prior to any real torture in order to get me to spill the beans, to name names. That they only stopped their assault upon me occurred when presumably, a superior officer arrived, and speaking in German told the others that his instructions were that I receive only internal injuries. I recall he gave them a significant telling off for the punches they had thrown, and the kicking's I had suffered. With the punishment done with I was dragged away and taken by motor car only a short distance to where I believe was likely the Berlin Stasi Prison, a detainment camp named 'Special Camp No. 3' and run, unsurprisingly, by the Soviet Secret Police. Once there, they stole from me all clothing and what little I held in the form of possessions, then literally threw me behind bars. As you can imagine I was in much pain, beaten yet not broken. Within the cell was just a filthy, wafer thin blood and piss stained mattress. I recollect crawling across the floor to rest, insofar as I could rest, upon the wretched thing. Beyond my physical reach, not that I could stand up properly and reach, a small barred window. It was the absence of light through that same window that let me understand it was now dark, night had fallen.

Outside of the cell, was a smart, uniformed female guard sat at her desk and typing by candlelight. Occasionally she would look up, and fix her sneering, repellent gaze upon me, then carry on with her business at hand. Despite the pain, I must have fallen asleep at one point as I heard her call over to me. I raised my head, looked in her direction. She had in her hand a mug, or a vessel of sorts. "Wasser?" she shouted. The prospect of water was inspiring as the innards of my mouth had dried out with congealed blood from the beating. At that time I would have given almost anything for sip of Adam's ale. I dragged myself along at a snail's pace the best I could manage until I reached the point where she was stood the other side of the bars. "Steh auf", her grumpy order. There was little prospect of me being able to stand so I just stretched out my arm the best I could in the direction of the mug she held, at which the bitch simply poured the water all over me. It was ice cold. I crumpled where I lay, both exhausted and beyond a shadow of a doubt, defeated. A little later, for she had waited until my consciousness resurfaced, she curled her lip, looked me over distainfully, blew out her candle and departed leaving me with only the dim light of the moon for illumination.

Drifting in and out of an understandably restless sleep and in what must have been the early hours, my teeth chattering from the cold, the feeling of touch lost to me as my fingers were close to being frostbitten I heard, I swear I heard the divine playing of a piano. The music of angels. Serene and warming...sadly not literally warming. With all the energy I could muster I raised myself, looked around to try and establish where the music was coming from. Although still disorientated from my ordeals I saw through the dim light, that at the back of my cell, under the unreachable window sat an old man at a grand piano. Noticing me he first paused, then gave up playing. Then, turning in my direction he spoke. "There are better ways to die than frozen and humbled on a floor of stone, you know." I could sense from the sound of his voice he was most probably Jewish. Maybe not, but probably. I had not the strength or inclination to respond. I was happy to let him do the talking. He seemed a reasonable chap and unlikely to be one of theirs.

"That cat got your tongue, young man. I understand, I've suffered much worse, believe me...or not, it doesn't matter either way."

I was baffled as to exactly what he was blabbering on about. In my condition at the time anything warranting more than a 'yes' or 'no' served as a riddle. Still, I stayed schtum just waiting for him to speak some more.

"Once I was a painter, I worked in oils you know, the whole world outside of Warsaw would soon know my real name, my titled pedigree. Also, I was the pianist who could bring a smile to the face of the

sourest, browbeaten underdog...you think I'm boasting, of course you do, yet I am not. I'm just stating the facts. The world would be my oyster, then the Nazi's came. You need not be told the rest of my story for you know it already I suspect." I managed a slight dip of my head, sufficient for him to detect I was in agreement.

"I imagine you are wondering what on earth I'm doing here? I certainly would be were it the case the tables were turned...and please don't respond, there is no need to nod again, I know it must be hard for you," he hesitated for a moment before continuing, then, "I've been here, there and everywhere looking up at the heavens waiting my turn to escape this realm. Now that I am aware that come morning I shall be gone, as likely as not never to return, it seems a crying shame to take my arty gifts with me to a place where the only sounds are those of cosmic storms and solar flares. Not that you know it now; not that you'll realize it soon, maybe not ever, yet you are a fortunate young man, for I bestow my gifts to you."

With what little clout I could summon I answered, "Why me?"

"Because you are the only worthy cause here and very soon I'll be gone. I told you, that to take with me those skills that have been granted me would be to insult The Almighty, and He has been insulted sufficiently in recent times. Whether you are a believer or not, you have heard my words."

That is the last thing, the very last thing I remember before all memory disappeared. Perhaps I fell back into deep sleep. Certainly, there were no goodbyes and I cannot recall his departure from the cell. Was I hallucinating? Probably. Yet how so, I can now, even in the state I find myself in, both paint and play piano?

Yours forever,
Titan, your 'Giant'

Her: She reads his letter by immature daylight, curtains pulled wide open in the surreal privacy of the estate, lying next to him in bed. He sleeps deeply; often over-sleeps, a thing neither can adequately give sound reason to. In her mind she composes a reply, although at this stage it remains germinal. She will pen it properly later in the day. Fortunately, although her Perkins has taken a beating lately, it still functions perfectly.

"Blink and you will miss me. Me, your lover. I exist in this moment as do you my Titan giant. Too soon both you and I will be the dust of cosmic storms. Our purpose, whatever it may have been as unsure of itself and as mystical as in the now. Before long we shall say adieu to our memories for memories have no substance. They are not of the carbon matter of all other things; things that are finite, floating in this infinite universe, they are a nothing existing only in our heads and only while we live. In a twinkling of an eye mankind will be gone from this place. Yet while the thinking mind subsists the lessons of history have some meaning. Profound, or seemingly of little significance, all of our recollections have value. Messages from the past once digested play a part in how we serve out the sentence that is our existence. You have lost a segment of your past, a mere nothing in the ecumenical plan of things. That you have seized hold of a vignette from your time in a Berlin prison explaining by way of the magic of esoteric narration that throws light on new found competence and dexterity as unbelievable as it may be to fully understand, a wondrous thing.

You wonder if you were hallucinating as events unfolded? I think not, as magical as it may seem, the evidence is there for me to see and hear even if you, the artist, are deprived of such pleasures. I suspect you would prefer it differently yet I truly believe that within you, you have created a paradise in which to live. It was always out there, you are the one who has found it. You no longer need to chart a course as I do, your new perception has taken you there. Part of me is jealous, believe it or not!"

'There, that or similar, expanded upon perhaps will do. He'll understand all is well, all is good,' her concluding thought. Pleased with herself she lays back down, head resting on pillow staring at the ceiling all the time contemplating the subject of 'memories.' That all memories have minor complications in resurrection of specific detail that can sometimes, but not always, twist the truth as exaggeration or pipe-dream a racing certainty. Even in such circumstances an element of truth's purity shines through generally. Yet to lose such a major facet of personal history, accurate, happy, sad or painful beyond measure entirely is a theft of one's time on Earth, one's time alive. At least she is reconciled to the fact that if her giant was destined to lose in part such a memory it is likely for the best that it be his days of torture and severance of senses. Talking to herself out loud knowing he cannot hear a single word, "If he is content with his lot, then so am I."

Gratified that he came through the account of his torment unscathed, she decides is a good thing. No longer will she dwell on the subject. They have the rest of their Bohemian lives to live together.

However, there is a maturing dark cloud upon the horizon. A thing that she has thus far omitted to discuss with him. The curse of putting something off too long inevitably makes dealing with that 'something' more problematic in mind and deed than it need be. She has one last mission to undertake. An important matter she has yet to tell her lover about. Another case whereby her employers want the target to be taken alive and kicking, much like the matter where similar directives were handed down back in 1944 where she was compelled to leave the target cold stone dead.

Counting the years she has existed, she finds that they number 34. She knows she looks 10 years, if not more, younger. She also knows that it is not for the fee involved, a tidy sum, that made her accept this new mission. Its causation is simply that a justice must be done, due punishment for hideous crimes metered out. Those without clemency or having never owned compassion who then make it their duty to destroy the harmless must be penalized, a thing she learned at a young age. In financial terms she is a wealthy young lady, she knows that good fortune has long since smiled upon her in that regard, yet still the weak must have their metaphorical protectors. She is such a person.

Often, she counts her blessings as was the case when inheriting a vast fortune from her often absent, when he was alive, father. That he was a European monarch and she is his not much talked about love child a twist of fate that worked in her favour, especially so after the deaths of both he, and later his barren queen. In reality, the earnings from her espionage escapades would have been more than sufficient to live on for life even without the addition of an inheritance. She asks of herself, 'Why? Why take on this new assignment?' The answer, as ever, is the same. Dishing out retribution is her eternal compulsion.

Her giant now snores like the proverbial pig. She pauses a moment or two, just looking at him. Her mind meanders eventually gravitating toward the events that materialized in Belgium back in 1944. That her new case had similarities to that of the one in Belgium likely the prompt for such thought.

'In times of war there is no such thing as a fashionable venue. Fortunately, the long years of combat were at last over. Sadly, and of dire necessity in the fall of 1944 during the month-long bombardment in order to gain access to the port facilities at Antwerp, The Allies had, albeit successfully, pounded the living daylights out of Belgium's coastal regions, the net result of which had rather taken the gloss off Léon Stynen's art deco masterpiece, namely the Grand Casino at Knokke Heist. Even so, the municipality of Knokke Heist, stripped almost bare of its original charm at wars end, was once more sneaking back into favour. Some of the cafes had reopened, a few of the fabled sea view apartments with admirable balconies were available to rent again, plus natures survival instinct had guaranteed the silver sand beach was still intact.

At water's edge, as she hoisted up her skirt a little and dipped a most reluctant big toe into the forever ice cold North Sea. The private words, "Brave beyond sensibility," twixt a Canadian couple in bathing costumes, in close proximity allowed her the perverse pleasure of eavesdropping.

"Word has it my dear, that the surrealist master René Magritte himself is to create a giant mural as part of the casino's renovation."

"Oh, that's good, darling. About time too."

As pleasing as that news was, for she had always liked a flutter in a prestigious setting, a distinctly more pressing task occupied her, for she had had the good fortune to have identified her mark, that being the one who had consigned her foetus to a better fate than being alive.

That he was a despicable article, his crimes against humanity repugnant beyond measure ensured her fixed enthusiasm for the task at hand. Moreover, she was well aware of the chink in his armour, namely a fondness for the ladies, the looser the better by all accounts. After all, it was in the sick circumstances of his warped minded creation they had first engaged. She, the abused captive on the occasion of that tortuous adventure.

It was close to midnight in a resurrected piano bar on the sea front she made her presence known. Dressed to the nines, cleavage, black lace, fishnets and heels, in essence the consummate tart, it came as no great shock that making his salivating acquaintance was as easy as pie. Additionally, it helped that he was already in his cups when slipping him the Mickey Finn. She was more than a little vexed that he failed to recognize her from the time she had spent in the death camp, especially given that he had chosen her out of the crowd, claiming ownership of, "This one...I'll take this...the one of rarest worthless pedigree."

Back in his hotel room, immediately prior to his terminal incapacitation, she felt compelled to remind the pig that once she was pregnant. A short-lived thing. Circumstances and mental paralysis of his contrivance saw to that. Whatever, the drug she slipped him in the bar was well chosen. As a pre-requisite to slipping his mortal coil his awareness subsisted, yet his entirety became wholly immobile. As he lay fixed upon the bed he could hear clearly the reading of his ebbing fortune. She found that just sufficient, given that her contented smiling snow-white face was the last thing he would ever see save for the checkmate kiss goodbye she blew.

That her employers had been most specific in wanting him brought in alive in order to stand trial at Nuremberg, a pity. Better for one and all, her summary justice born of personal testimony. Regardless, she had been minded since accepting the mission to sweet talk her way out of any minor complications and blandishment, as was her forte.'

Still her man slept on. The seeming permanency of his hibernation was beginning to vex. Whipping off the sheets, then penning with insistent rigid digit, 'WAKE UP YOU LAZY BASTARD' upon his unadorned belly did the trick. He awoke with a start. Stern faced, he caught hold of her wrist just as she attempted to dismount the bed, pulled her across to his side of the mattress. Putting aside all thoughts of that first cup of rousing coffee she chose the frantic intimacy on glaring offer instead.

Later, while he paints his next impossible pièce de résistance she takes to the grounds her mind set on visiting a corner of her realm where she may fantasize and ponder without interruption. A place her rare visits ensure that it always has the feel of being unspoiled and special. A place where she trades nature's solace for weak knees and second thoughts.

Irresponsibly barefoot and out of immodest election clad only in a flowing black velvet cape insulating her from a tenacious morning chill and its kindred ogling mist she treads carefully. Unshod, one needs to be vigilant as the abscission of the tertiary season commands; that it is not just the time of the fall of the golden leaf for spikes, barbs and thorns tumble also. Cautious yet resolved she tramples onward, her destination, the folly situated deep within a deciduous grove behind the house.

It has been said of follies that they have no purpose other than as an ornament. She had always suspected that hers being of Gothic revival design was perhaps the exception to rule for she found it to be somewhere tailor-made, within which to disentangle and jettison virtuous thoughts then replace them with all manner of intimate seductive imagining's. Always, since her arrival at the estate the year previous she had felt the innards of the folly to be a haunt predisposed to apparitions of illegitimate birthing, death by foul play, private moments twixt clandestine lovers and nightmares realised. With its purposely shrunken walls and monumental, still intact stained-glass windows depicting celestial notions allowing in any and all Divine light the encompassing deciduous woods choose to gift, it was the one whereabouts where when bare-skinned and unarmed she was both aware and bewaring of that fact. A unique feeling of tempting disquiet for one otherwise exempt from the parochial purities of the everyday flock. Besides, and as only Victorian ghostly design bestows, the folly had the feel of Dracula's fangs biting into the unrobed virgin's jugular. In short, a spine-tingling place to spend a little time.

The entrance to the folly was via an arched oak door that had seen better days. It was never kept locked for there was nothing of material value within. Draping her cape purposely on the outside weathered brass door knob and accepting unreservedly that once within the dark, dank folly she, the accidental heiress, would be little more than a vulnerable cluster of goose buds, she set foot in her little house of rarest provocation. She reminded herself that the reason she had chosen this 'eld' nook was in part to think through things important to her everyday life and, importantly, to feel so accessible that she would be reminded of her mortality. In her line of business such a reminder a necessary thing. Added to which she tells herself that the best decisions in life are made when one feels exposed and unable to linger long over this and that. It was for that very reason she came to this ornamental freak of architecture. Often, she had thought about bringing her lover to this unlocked chamber of spider's webs, woodlice, chrysalis and bewildered moths yet thus far reasoned that his very masculine presence would extinguish her very real, and peculiarly desirable, womanish trepidation for ever. Perhaps one day she would change her mind.

With no intent to loiter longer than was necessary, she purposely saunters this way and that, hands behind her back as if an over-confident Princess Regent amid revolutionary subjects, all the time awaiting the executioner in the crowd to step forth and make himself known. Are the ghosts of those evil souls she had destroyed lurking within these walls? Likely not, yet that is how she feels, surrounded by them, every last one of them. Instinctively, she has a rare yearning to cover herself up, a feeling she successfully combats. An unwelcoming coldest stone floor, one not swept clean in decades turn her feet into blocks of ice. That she now shivers so stimulates a flamboyant sexual urge that must be contained prolonging sweet torture. Maybe she will one-day commission a photographer to capture her decadent image within this strange place? Her mind races as to the possibilities. Her body not sure whether she trembles some more because of the acute cold or tingles at the unrealized autoerotic impulse. Likely it is the latter for in this place she is smitten with her own company. Pinching herself, she sets to achieve the very thing she came here for. Perhaps the siren in her will have her own way next time. She pinches herself once more; marshals her thoughts.

The need to advise her giant that she must be away for a few days has to be dealt with sooner rather than later. For certain, given he will know full well that no mission is without risk, he will feel impotent that his condition makes it impossible to afford her any back-up. Additionally, a plan for his care while she is out of the country needs to be fathomed. As to the former of the two issues he will have to take it on the chin. She has already accepted the mission. As to the latter concern, her choices regarding exactly who will care for him, and taken into account his, nay their foibles, are limited to just one option. Within her body politic she has a million acquaintances, a host of former lovers, both male and female, many trusted friends she rarely catches up with these days and no living family she is aware of. Yet there is one person who was apprised of his condition. That person being Zada, uniquely able to take over the tending to him while she is away. 'How atypical that Zada, the one I kidnapped to further my own cause; the one who I nearly sent back into a life of magnified servitude should have become my closet friend and confidante,' a reasoning that mystified as much as it gratified. Zada it would have to be for she alone would be the one who could cope.

"So Zada, you now speak French fluently. I can tell you've worked hard on the language. I'm impressed."

"When in Rome, and all that! I speak the language better than spell it, but I believe I'm getting there."

"You know, I felt so guilty asking you to help out so soon. That you are here out of your own volition eases that guilt more than you know. It will only be for a few days, three at the most as I mentioned in my letter, and while I know you will argue with me, I must insist on paying you. I'll not let you undertake this responsibility any other way."

"I know you well enough than to lock horns with you, and I'll freely admit some extra money would come in useful presently. Don't worry about a thing, he'll be well cared for and I'll wait on him hand and foot."

"I know you will, Zada. He doesn't need that much help these days. So long as the furniture is left where it is he gets around well with no accidents. It's more a cooking, cleaning and keeping an eye on him task. The big plus is that you now have French. Communication with one another will be possible this time. I know the braille method will not be feasible, yet palm, and don't shy away from it, the finger upon belly lettering plus, of course, the blackboard and chalk chats. All those things will keep him close to our reality, and importantly keep his mind stimulated. By the way, I can't let go of your remark that a little extra money would help. Is everything fine? Is Paris letting you down?"

"I don't think Paris could disappoint anyone blessed with heart, soul and passion. It's merely that my lover, the painter with the politician father I told you of last time I was here is now my ex-lover. He is besotted with his newest muse, the daughter of an American entrepreneur. They met at one of his exhibitions. I think presently they are touring the Caribbean. She's rich, blond and beautiful."

"So, he's left you in the lurch. That's heartless men for you, yet they are not all like that. Tell me, where are you living now?"

"In a flat above the Montparnasse café where I now work. After he kicked me out of the place we shared I had little choice in the matter. He did try to pacify me with a couple of paintings that he says will be worth a fortune someday, but 'someday' feels faraway. The modelling work is spasmodic, plus a few of the art circle tell me I'm too skinny for them and won't paint me until I fill out again. I think most are just joking, there's not much in the way of good money for them to earn lately it seems. Anyway, at least I have a roof over my head and that's more than some and I haven't had to take to the streets to stay afloat...not as yet, that is."

"Why on earth didn't you contact me before, Zada. You'll stay here until you've made enough money to choose what you do next rather than 'what you do next' choosing you. You can stay forever if you want, and I'll point out even if it does sound a little cruel, you are as skinny as a rake. That dress hangs on you like a sack."

"You mean that? You mean I can stay awhile? And yes, I am aware I've lost a little weight. Stress and working as a waitress all the hours God made does that to a girl."

"Do I ever not mean what I say? You're staying here, period. I'll have a courier collect all your belongings in Paris and bring them over here."

"Thank you. That's a whole mass of worry off my chest. One other thing. I don't think I've ever seen you keep your clothes on for so long ever. Why so? Change of season?"

"Yes, at this time of the year the drabness of having to keep warm is an inconvenience. This house is so big, although by late afternoon when the fires have been raging all day it does get significantly warmer, then anything goes as the mood takes; the way things should be. Besides, aside from keeping warm there is only one other reason to get dressed, namely to be looked at. In my case to shock others. I've never understood why the human race doesn't see things my way. At least I'm being honest. Still, that's their problem, not mine thankfully. In a nutshell, I like to be a free spirit. Life is easier that way, a little anarchy never hurts."

"Who cleans the ash away under the grates and sets the kindling for a new fire each morning? That's a horrible job, my mother made me do it as a child and I hated the task."

"I do, although I'm thinking of employing a local to come in to do these little annoying tasks for us. It's just a case of finding someone discreet who will put up with our Bohemian lifestyle. Whomsoever I find will have to adapt to us, not us to them."

"Well I can certainly take on the role while you're away and until you find that right person. I'll do the cleaning, washing, cooking even if you want. I'll earn my keep."

"You really are an angel. Thank you, I could use some help with that as well as with him."

"Is he, your lovely giant, suffering from the chill as well?"

"You'll have to wait and see. So far, since the end of summer I've rarely had to assist when he dresses, which frankly isn't that often. He keeps a paraffin heater in the studio when working, and when he is feeling the cold it's usually one of his thobes he goes for. They are easier for him to put on and take off. He put one on back to front the other day and got so angry with himself for making such a silly mistake."

"Will he mind me running my finger over his belly to communicate? He won't think the worse of me, will he? I wouldn't want him thinking I was being overly familiar."

"Zada, he'll positively enjoy it. Someone new to communicate with, and known to him as a pretty girl at that. Do not worry yourself on that front. Besides, you know our chosen lifestyle is flexible in terms of the so-called morals of the boring masses. The main point, and I'll try not to laugh, is will you mind when he needs to reply on your bare belly, or bare anything else?"

"Well it's not as if I've anything he hasn't 'felt' before. I shan't mind. I see my role here is to care for him as well in any which way that helps him; keeps him stimulated. That's perhaps the wrong word but you know what I mean."

"That's all settled them, yet never forget you are also here as a friend, a real friend we both, him (he likes you a lot, he told me so after your last visit) and I care for you more than you perhaps realize. I'll let him know you're here once more and we can chat the best we can over dinner later."

"Does he not know I'm here to look after him then?"

"No. Sadly I took my time thinking through how to approach the subject with him because I know full well he'll be pained that he can't be with me on the mission. He'll worry, I am aware of that."

"Do you think he'll react badly to the news?"

"I think he'll do what he always has done, before the loss of his senses and since. He'll take it on the chin like a man. I suppose it would have been a better thing had I told him earlier, yet what is done is done."

"How is his painting coming along, and his music?"

"Remarkedly well. I'll never understand how he achieves what he does, although after he had read the account you and I put together of his confinement he did tell me the strangest story that perhaps, just perhaps, threw a little light upon his new-found perceptions and abilities. I'll give you chapter and verse on that later on. His physical coordination and mental dexterity when creating art or music is astonishing. His memory as to where his brushes and paints are laid out bewildering. You'll see for yourself. The artwork is all kept safe and sound in the garage. I'll take you over there now if you'd like to see what he's been up to."

"I'd love to. Has he sufficient for an exhibition?"

"Easily enough."

"Perhaps that could be another project for me to help out with. I'd enjoy that, especially if we could find a London gallery to host it. I think Paris has turned me into a city sort of girl."

"I don't see why not, if you don't mind the nude paintings of you in the public eye."

"Not at all, in Paris I've got used to that sort of thing. You should see the two paintings my former lover left me. Positively indecent yet much praised in the art circles."

"Maybe you should put them up for sale in any exhibition also. London buyers pay through the nose, and with you the model being there for all to see in more ways than one...well, who knows how much they'll fetch."

"I think I'd like that. Your giant's nudes of me versus that wretch of a cheat who left me almost high and dry. Oh, importantly, did his memory of those horrific events return after he had read the transcript?"

"No, I don't think they ever will. He is reconciled to that fact, as am I."

"That's a pity, yet even though he can't remember it, at least he now knows all, the best we could explain, even if the account of his days in the prison were based on what the wicked Major boasted about. It must have been she he was referring to, as the injuries she commonly inflicted match his completely. That he now knows what he can't remember must be of some consolation?"

"Believe me, it is. If he'd become distressed I'd know. Presently, he can barely keep his hands off me and that wouldn't be the case if he was feeling down in the dumps. Between you and me we're having a whale of a time together."

"Lucky you."

"Your luck will take a turn for the better, trust me. By the way, did you realize we have conducted this entire conversation in French?"

"Yes. I've barely spoken a word in my mother tongue for months. I wasn't going to learn the language any other way. Plus, it helps me wherever I might one day end up as more people speak French than they do Romanian."

"Shall we head for the garage to see his paintings?"

"Good idea."

Alone, within a congregation of unnerving identical immortals he marvels at a presumed chameleon sky above, ever grateful that when she left him marooned she was at odds to remind him to think well of her.

Those balmy days of sluggish avalanches and an antipathy toward the swarm long gone. They abandoned him the moment she opened her heart and scribed the word, 'Abracadabra'. Already, he misses her honeyed flesh, disrespectful soul and perceptive love making with an abnormal passion.

As of now, every which way horizons frame the roomy prison cell of his person. Tantalising perimeters beyond his ability to touch, let alone see, hear or sing the praises of. A vagrant apiary, walls agonizingly ahead of perception chasing blind eyes. Ties that no longer bind, frigid art forms, unfathomable riddles and a Moorish castle in

Spain. These are the obsessions she takes abroad, fighting the good cause.

He desperately waits for her safe return, yet knows this feeling must never see daylight.

Him: Time procrastinates, reluctant to chart its course toward oblivion when it knows it's got you cornered, when it knows your loved one is faraway. As that concept came to me I had to pinch myself and get real. She has only been gone a single night, and withal I have the new arrival Zada to act as surrogate, insofar as she is able.

I suggested apple crumble. Instead, she made a Romanian apple bread pudding cake. I have to admit it tasted divine. The reason I proposed a cake was born of Zada and I practising the exchange of words written in French upon each other's blank canvas stomachs. I had a distinct recollection that the last occasion I had cause to be in such close proximity to her naked skin was several months previous when, put literally, I was running my hands all over her so as to fix her image in my head prior to painting her. This time around the first thing I perceived was that from the feel of her emaciated rib cage she seemed to have become as skinny as a rake. I had no hesitation in telling her that she needed to fatten up more than a little. That she cooked such a pudding and ate what instinct implies to be a worthwhile chunk told me she had heeded my words. I understand that she has been worn out both mentally and physically in recent times.

I find Zada to be the most agreeable friend. Although I saw no reason why I could not manage a few days alone, it was common-sense that enabled me to agree that the last thing my lover would have wanted would have been to worry about my welfare while on a mission. As with any assignment a clear head is an essential facet in the armoury. To have objected would arguably have left her off guard; placed her in additional danger, a thing I would never do. Having made note of that fact, I am understandably impatient for her safe return.

Zada's spelling in French leaves a lot to be desired, but we get by. As soon as she gains some extra flesh on her bones I think she will feel better. I have made it clear to her that if she wants me to stop insisting that she disrobes each day for me to check her progress in putting on some weight then she must eat, then eat some more. To detect from the rise and fall of her torso she was laughing and then promised to do as I commanded gave me the feeling this deaf, blind, mute had achieved something, notwithstanding her riposte that if we are to continue debating this and that through the means of fingertip upon bare skin than it would be preferable if I could control my haphazard erections. I could only but advise that the penis has a mind of its own and that I have no say in the matter of its status at any given time. From the way she curled into a ball I assume that once more she laughed, for so extreme her spheroid contortions it was as if she were to asphyxiate. Thinking back to the times prior to being as I now am, there would have been no circumstances whereupon I would have been in a situation such as I was with Zada during that tête-à-tête. Some things have plainly improved for the better. Without doubt not giving a damn regarding matters intimate, at any rate things my eyes can never gaze upon represents a new-found openness I treasure. I did conclude by reminding her that she was in safe hands with me, she never need wear a stich if she did not want to as the one thing in life I could never be was an improper voyeur.

Certainly, she works hard. The house has never been as warm as she has ensured it now is. We are only 48 hours into this arrangement yet I am pleased with her and have no problem with her staying on as long as she wishes as has been suggested. Moreover, I must never forget that the poor girl has suffered in many more ways than one. As such we are kindred spirits of sorts.

Right now, as I paint she is outside wrapped up snug and warm, woven basket in hand, beyond the lake to the dank, I presume, shadowy spot near the perimeter walls we walked together earlier when seeking the sheer joy of fresh air. It was there she advised that she had discovered an outcrop of Fairy Ring Champignon ready for the picking. I understand she is to turn them into a Romanian dish, a soup known as Ciorbă de urechiuşe, or wild mushroom sour soup to those like me without a word of her mother tongue. Regrettably I am no longer able to tell one bottle of wine from another, thus I suggested of Zada she go to the wine cellar and be sure to pick out the Chardonnay, a perfect accompaniment to mushrooms. In making that request I had to contact her via the palm of her dainty hand. As to our dinner this evening I have suggested she makes her entrance suitably undressed for the occasion thus being conducive to a form of communication with one another far better than said palm of hand. I feel she saw the funny side of that remark. That naked souls dine together in innocence and without romantic thoughts an unusual thing to say the very least.

In my dreams I am not denied the impediments lost to me in harsh reality. Such dreams are lucid accounts of what might have been. Last night, only a few hours after she had left for Amsterdam and the potential perils her being there might bring, my moonstruck demons portrayed their own masterplan for she and I.

'Come fading glow, vampire bats crisscross a ripe moon, silvered chimney smoke outpaces the silly, chilly moths rushing ever upwards chasing heaven sent white light. A befitting sight worthy of the promise magic bestows upon an otherworldly place few beings know exists. Midsummer day's spawning of the briefest obscurity, so stingy the gratuity of darkness's deepest pockets leaving just wafer-thin messages for the abandoned subdued tidings of those condemned to life in limbo. No time or place for squirreled away final goodbyes solemnized in melancholy words begging guidance. A hint of urgency shrouded back-of cautious tongues, a flock of lost sheep favouring tarmac over lush grass.

Time has no mercy, offers no favours when on the tail of a sleepy sun, hell-bent on tucking itself safe and warm beneath horizons snug blanket of guarded hallucination. A stark moorland tumour, a misshapen granite hideaway. Bad luck, curiosity or wanton kidnap lead to such a place; a last rock of Celtic fascination under Aurora's frigid border. All that is left, an easy birthing of street life's pornography. She, in trademark strapless, low cut red dress, matching heels and lips coated ever so rouge, her hair a loose mop of whitest locks, knots and scarlet ribbons, adrift yet still alive, immune to antics privacy gifts those sat smug behind doors, spitting two-faced grunts and groans to breakneck applause'.

I made mention of this dream of the previous night to Zada after we had both eaten and taken perhaps a glass or two too many. In my studio, blackboard and chalk inevitably the only mode of one-way communication. The girl held my hand as she read from the board.

Kissed my forehead when she had finished, then penned upon my mushroom and home-made bread satiated stomach, 'A GAME OF CHESS?' I had no idea we had a chessboard and pieces. Zada had, it turned out, discovered them lurking in the cupboard under the stairs in the hallway when she was tidying up there earlier in the day. In any case I readily accepted her challenge, regardless of my shortcomings when it came to playing The Royal Game. Time had not stolen from me the rules of chess, though I was never very good at it.

Back in the lounge, still cosy, although the fire now beginning to wane, we shared the last dregs of wine and set about the contest. For me the game was demanding. Notwithstanding the various sizes of the pieces, having to picture in my mind the 64 squares and memorizing the placements of both her pieces and mine was hard enough, discerning what exactly were my pieces from hers almost impossible at the outset. No doubt seeing my difficulties were making the playing of the game pointless she took it upon herself to grab a sharp kitchen knife and make cuts into each piece, one cut for a pawn, two for the bishops, three for the knights and so on in order that I could feel what I could not see. Frankly, it still was not ideal until she scored similar crosses in reverse on her own pieces meaning I could recognize her opposing army.

I lost both matches, after all she heralds from Romania where they are born with full knowledge of the game I understand. Even so, I think with a little practice I could master the pursuit and play, at least to an average level.

It was in the early hours; fast asleep I was awoken by the presence of another in the bed. Initially, I presumed my lover had come home sooner than expected. That however was not the case, for it was Zada who lay next to me. Carefully, under the covers she spelt out these words upon my chest, 'LAISSEZ-MOI ÊTRE VOTRE COURONNE D'ÉPINES JUSTE POUR CE SOIR' namely, 'Let me be your Crown of Thorns just for tonight'. Was it that she perceived my enduring suffering and wished to, in her eyes at least, banish it from my soul? That in the guiltlessness of her own ordeal she sought no reply, most likely thought that if I could speak my reaction would be a simple 'Amen' was like as not the truth of the matter. Come morning, neither she nor I made mention of the events of last night.

13.

AUTUMN 1952 – AMSTERDAM

Her: Under the unsympathetic blackest vault of a grieving heaven an agitated bulkhead creaks, butch stringers snap, robust rivets moan in metronomic rhythm and herculean girders groan as a remorseless nor'wester's kindred waves of replete urchins torment a rickety hull, of late in unbridled panic. Little wonder a weak-kneed full moon shies away. No place for clandestine romance by its silvery light on this old rust bucket ferry bound for The Port of Amsterdam. Certainly not on this night of 'fee-fi-fo-fum' overhanging salivating, ravenous crests impeding entry to the open wide gob of The North Sea Canal and the relief of safe moorings, a thing that would prove to be impossible until the contradictory calm of dawn's first light.

She sits, eyes shut tight, not in the debatable comfort of her box cabin but in the ships pedestrian bar along with the vexed hoi polloi, a fine cognac safe and sound in one hand, a Lucky Strike tentatively glowing in the other. Unruffled by the mumbled prayers, legitimate tears and ashen faces of those vomiting to the rise and fall of the bounding main, she merely contemplates The Devil incarnate in the form of the depraved doctor whose blood will soon be on her hands should all go to plan.

That this physician had escaped execution for reasons of lack of sufficient damning evidence at The Doctors' Trials in Nuremberg in 1946, a simple twist of fate. His guilt, his crimes against humanity were the stuff of uncontaminated legend among the few living specimens liberated from the death camps come war's end. Both the departed, also the somehow still alive, one and all were actual or potential guinea pigs to be experimented upon by the one who held no truck with any

Hippocratic Oath. His penchant toward the unspeakable mutilation of female inmates in the name of medical research, his speciality well known yet never adequately documented had tipped the scales of justice in his favour, afforded him an undeserved freedom in the safe haven of 'Mokum', the old Hebrew nickname for Amsterdam. 'Not for much longer,' her passing thought as she took yet another puff of yet another cigarette.

In truth, her employers wanted the doctor alive and had charged her to obtain by whatever clandestine means necessary a confession of past crimes. In that regard, and the very reason she had been chosen for the task was simply that she was the best there was when it came to information gathered through either the honey trap's sweet pillow talk or, as was more likely in this case, that she should inveigle herself into the doctor's company, maybe massage more than just his ego and set herself up to be his latest prey.
Autumn 1952 in the city had seen a number of worldly-wise prostitutes fall foul of elimination by way of multiple, despicable lacerations, their bodies and severed parts discarded within the canal system. New to the area, a course and distance man, the doctor was the prime candidate, the only plausible candidate. While his latter-day crimes were not the be all and end all to her client mattered not of jot. It was confirmation of war crimes they sought to discover. As to whether she was reporting directly to Mossad, a thing she would never disclose.

She had anticipated a 10pm arrival the night previous, yet it was 8am the next day when the jaded wayfarers were finally able to disembark. Solid ground had seldom felt better. Given the ferocity of the storm endured at sea she found it startling that this fresh Amsterdam morn was acceptably warm by any standards, a caught napping sun at a rush to cast longest shadows and barely a breeze in the air. In need of urgent sleep, especially so as she had to prepare for yet another long night ahead, she headed straight for Nieuwmarkt a charming, vibrant square situated aside the notorious since ancient times, Red-Light District where her client had booked suitable accommodation in a room with street facing floor to ceiling windows above a smoky café run by a discreet native go-between carefully selected and now also in the employ of her masters. It was at his café she enjoyed a light breakfast of just jam on toast, washed down with strong black coffee before taking of her rest. That Nieuwmarkt being in such close proximity to that Red-Light District known locally as 'De

Wallen' (a euphemism, intimating one should say "Wall" when alluding to the matter of 'paid for up front' sex) by any other name, a wise choice for it would be from that bedroom window at that very location she would be seen by whomsoever cared to look to appear to be hawking her exemplary wares as would any other indecent lady of the night. Not for her the hanging around outside the square's Old Church along with the cut-price, regular working girls. Better still, the depraved doctor himself had taken up residence nearby in one of the prepossessing much fabled leaning gabled houses. She would be more than just the bait to his hungry fish. She would be the fisher and intended to have him as her catch hook, line and sinker.

By late afternoon, a refreshed and wide-awake girl sat outside the café sharing coffee and Dutch apple cake with the owner by the name of Bastiaan, a strapping tiger of a man, albeit more than a little weather-beaten with a smile that could win a woman's heart from a hundred paces, let alone face to face. With a come-hither guttural delivery he advised that the sought-after doctor was a regular patron of his establishment and that he visited most evenings before presumably commencing his quest for new fresh flesh to slaughter.

"I'll give you the nod when he turns up. Just last night I let him, as per instructions from the top, know that a new girl, a rather special one at that, would be gracing the window of the flat above this evening. He seemed ecstatic at the prospect, especially so when I pointed out that the girl in question, namely you my sweet, are quite the most uniquely beautiful albino girl to ever have walked this planet Earth. Our doctor friend even pointed out that he had always desired the company of an albino, a thing good fortune had denied thus far in life adding that, and I quote, 'Even when I could choose any female I wanted never was there a specimen such as you describe In lIne from which to pick out as my own.' Also, I let it be known that you speak Dutch as well as English."

"As to the compliment you are too kind, Bastiaan. As to the doctor, I can't wait to avail myself of his company."

"You do understand he'll insist you go with him to his house? I understand that's what he does with all the girls, even the ones who come away unscathed, yet to date the police haven't been able to pin anything on him. Anyhow, should you find yourself inside you're on your own and, in my view, in great danger. I can understand why you have chosen to pose as a femme-fatale call girl; I understand why you are about to play the game as best you can to your own rules, yet what you're about to do is fraught with risk."

"Of course, I understand. Sorry if I come over brash, yet you can take it for granted I know exactly what I'm doing and the potential pitfalls. Anyway, I believe it's time I got dressed, or should I say, undressed, fit to kill!"

"By the way, I say again, do take care. I pray you really do know exactly what you're up to? Surely there's another way?"

"There is no other way and you'd be surprised to learn of some of the things I've done when facing down pure evil. Under the guise of a street girl I have by far and away the best chance of enticing him into my trap, a trap which by necessity will evolve, to some degree at least, on the hoof. Seriously, I must prepare myself now, there is no time to lose, dusk is nearly upon us."

Up above, curtains drawn and out of public view, she sought to change her persona to fit the task at hand. Recently she had read a full-length profile in Colliers regarding an up and coming starlet who exuded raw sex and passion by the name of Marilyn Monroe. Due note was made of Monroe's individuality, her own distinct panache. They shared, although she was a little slimmer than the starborn one, the same hourglass figure and although plagiarism of another's style was an alien thing to her she was taken with the photograph of Monroe in a strapless, lowest cut 'fit to fall out of' red dress with matching belt around her waist, red heels and, a must, several coats of gleaming crimson lipstick. That the actress had permed mousey brown hair dyed blonde and hers was snow white, straight and natural at least ensured she would not be thought of as a would be copycat or ever-hopeful doppelganger. Such a thing would simply be too much, hence her own locks would be held up with combs, pins and sticks, Japanese style. Regardless, when dressed and finally made-up, the words addressed to self, 'A red dress for red lights' brought forth a private grin. That, beside her outer layer she would wear nothing else at all save for her best new lucky threaded pearl ankle bracelet gave rise to brimming a wicked snort of approved disapproval.

It was as the last soupçon of sunlight was swallowed up by its neon nemesis she commenced her new and hopefully to be short-lived career as a polished prostitute seeking only the premium habitués. In reality, she had no intention to become enjoined with any such customers. She understood for all intents and purposes the various grade of gentlemen, and occasional arbitrary lady outside looking 'up and in' at her blatantly marketing her ample assets must believe she was the bona fide article. It was not a difficult thing. A pursed rouge lip kiss blown from the palm of her hand here, a raise of the dress hem revealing more than a just glimpse of thigh there, a flash or two of seductive feral cleavage ensured her authenticity as a seasoned professional. Bastiaan, acting as her as pimp, something he did for other girls at other times when acting as their authentic procurer had found himself as busy as a beaver, regularly making the excuse to the effect that the gorgeous girl in the window attracting all the attention already had a growing queue of men building up, all seeking to avail themselves of her own matchless services and as such turning disgruntled punters away. In different circumstances it would have broken both his heart and left his wallet empty to carry on thus. By the time he popped upstairs to advise that the doctor had finally arrived and was asking after her he felt compelled to add that, "If you were for real you do realize you'd have made a small fortune already tonight and it's only just gone 9pm." To that she merely smiled back adding, "I know, I've enjoyed myself but now the real fun starts."

"Fun?"

"Yes, fun."

"Our doctor friend wants to book you for the night...the whole night in the comfort of his home, but first he wants to wine and dine you at a little restaurant just around the corner in the Chinatown district. It's in easy walking distance. I hope you're hungry? He said, 'tell her to come exactly as she is' before handing over to yours truly, as per the usual practice here, your fee in hard cash...750 guilders, that's a lot of money by any standards."

"So, he values me at around 200 dollars. Is that good?"

"Most girls would bite his hand off for that sort of money. Yes, it's very good, very good indeed. He obviously expects a lot from you.

Just so you know I've locked away your money in the safe. As local gigolo I usually keep back 25%. Is that OK with you?"

"You can take your cut and share the rest with any of the other girls on your books, Bastiaan. His paid-up fee means absolutely nothing to me. This is it then? Best you introduce me to my first client!"

The doctor had waited patiently in the café doorway for her arrival. Introducing himself in perfect Queens English as Herr Maximillian an Austrian doctor on a long-term much needed sabbatical in Holland, he graciously lent forward kissing the back of the hand she instinctively raised to his lips. That he lied about both his name and country of origin par for the course in her experience. Chivalrously he, noting the chilling of the evening, draped his woollen overcoat upon her shoulders as the pair set off to make their way the short distance to what would prove to be an intimate Chinese restaurant, graced with only a few other lurking diners. As the pair wended their way he made a point of advising that, "The food there is par excellence, the place itself cosy enough for us to get to know each other a little better." Yet at just a stone's throw from the eating-house hideaway and without forewarning the heavens opened. With that, and without a care for his female companion, he snatched back his overcoat and let her get soaked to the skin, her dress now a near transparent figure hugging duplicate skin revealing all there was to reveal for all who cared to looksee. That she could not give a damn she hid well, tantalising him with a false modesty that appeared to inflame more than surprise.

Arriving at the restaurant, and with clinical Germanic efficiency, he grabbed tight her upper arm and frog marched her over to the proprietor, a wizened little Oriental man dressed in a blood and God knows what else stained long apron and without referring to him by name ordered, "Have someone sort the girl out. We got caught in the rain, she's sopping wet." Speaking with a cloying humility tinged with small insincerity, "For you, Herr Maximillian anything. As you may know my dear wife runs the laundry above this restaurant...come with me young lady, if you would."

The Chinaman's wife, an engaging woman was taller than her husband and by the look of her several decades his junior. Albeit that she tried not to show that she was plainly shocked that the German's date wore just the wet dress she was stood up in, it phased her not. Once out of the garment the combs, pins and sticks removed from her now brushed out wet hair, she was immediately temporarily concealed in a plain white traditional kimono. "By the time you've finished your meal I'll have you spic and span once more. Leave it all to me."

Now once more decent to the roving eye she re-joined her patron for the night at their table, discreetly hidden away in a candlelit corner of the restaurant. In his opaque defence the doctor pointed out with monotone distain, "I had no choice but to take back my overcoat. I'd not long since purchased this suit in Jermyn Street, London. It cost me a small fortune and I was reluctant to see it go to ruin," prompting her sardonic riposte, "It's worth more than me, then?"

"Much more, you were merely small-change and, I might add, I suggest you do not try to rise above your station. Certainly not at my expense."

"I'm sorry Herr Maximillian. I was only jesting. I know my place."

"Just make sure you do and we'll be fine."

In the awkward silence that followed she noted that her host was certainly much more handsome than he had looked in the photographs she had seen of him. Observing that the tall blue-eyed, golden haired Aryan she knew to be 47 years old with broad shoulders and carrying no excess weight, sporting the well-tailored charcoal check suit saved from the rain drops sat before her would, on the face of it, have made a fine catch for any woman seeking such a man of that sort. Although to her, notwithstanding his fine looks, he remained a cruel bastard worthy only of her contempt. Plainly, she was sure not to let her eyes or body language give her true feelings away. In the event, once the silence was broken, she made a point of openly hanging onto his every last word and by doing so intimated he would get value for money. Much of the ensuing conversation revolved around his morbid fascination with the congenital disorder named albinism and its genetic origins, on top of which his reinforced, boringly so, and time and time again throwaway remark as to how astonished he was that one of nature's imperfections such as she could be so remarkably physically attractive.

As to eating, in truth she was not hungry at all. At such times on any mission, dangerous or not, she lived on nerves alone. The prospect of food made her feel sick. Under the guise of 'looking after her figure' she got away with just ordering a Wonton noodle soup half a which she left in the bowl, while he filled his face with ostensibly all that Chinese cuisine could offer. Annoyingly, given her desire to remain as sober as possible the owner was forever topping up their glasses with overly sweet, yet thankfully, ice-cold lychee wine on the rocks. It was clear the doctor had a very sweet tooth.

The meal nearing its end had prompted the owner's wife to come over to their cloistered ill-lit corner table to meekly advise that the red dress had now been laundered and was ready to wear once again. At this so-called Herr Maximillian tilted his head saying with a lecherous look in his eye, "See to her here if you would. I shall enjoy my first comprehensive view of my first albino freak."

"Oh, I thought she'd be changing clothes upstairs with me, but yes Sir, your wish is my command. I'll go and fetch your lady friend's dress this instant."

The return of the dress to the restaurant area was taking a little longer than the now slightly stewed doctor had foreseen. It was during this lull in activity that he called out for the young male waiter, by the look of him the son of the owner, who rushed over on the double. "You boy, yes you, clear the table and move it aside." The boy dutifully obliged, leaving she and the doctor both sat opposite each other with no impediment between them. Having shifted the table as ordered the boy was about to flee in order to tend to other duties yet before he could depart, "Stay here boy if you would. I don't bite." Once more as loyal canine the half-pint waiter stayed put, a puzzled look upon his face. Herr Maximillian's next decree was aimed at his floozy playmate. "Stand up girl, take off the kimono, fold it neatly and hand it to the boy." Maintaining constant testy eye contact with he who would be her master she surrendered, did what she was told.

"There boy feast your eyes on an innately flawed Venus the like of which I doubt you'll ever see again. What do you make of her?"

Albeit visibly overwhelmed with a painful sheepishness he could but only reply, "She is very beautiful, Sir."

"I know. I imagine you're thinking it a shame she's mine to do with as I wish, and not yours?" A boast he wallowed in.

The boy, now head bowed, hugely embarrassed, "Yes, Sir."

At this, she felt bound to put in her two cents, hands on bare hips, adding with a disparaging yet gracious enough beam, "You really are a romantic devil, Sir. I'm yours for the taking."

She was almost disappointed that his response was a detached, "I know. I'm paying. It is good that you plainly know your place. I like subservience in my women."

"I can be whatever you want me to be."

"And, rest assured, before this night is out you shall indeed be whatever I want you to be. Now get dressed as before. Your clothing has at last arrived."

It took little time for the Chinaman's wife to make a show of not just dressing her client's client but also, and at her own behest, restore her hair Japanese wedding style, the latter perhaps better and considerably more authentic than previous. After settling the account the pair were off on their way to the leaning gable front property the doctor called 'home'. That he held her hand as lovers would all the way there a nauseous thing, although she saw no merit in doing anything other than surrender. Also, she wallowed In the satisfaction that if he thought for one moment that having her stand naked in a public place would humiliate or beset her in any way he was on the wrong track. In fact, she had delighted in the whole bizarre experience, more so that she arguably now had her own personal reason to destroy this slug of a man, let alone to do so on behalf of those souls who had suffered so very much at the hands of such a disgusting embodiment of the male species, a man who claimed, she had heard tell, to hold membership of the supposed 'Master Race'. Besides, she had done far more extravagant, some might say belittling things, in the basement clubs of Weimar Berlin in postpubescence's first flush, and later in

England when dancing as naked ballerina for, then bringing about, the execution of the estranged from St Petersburg Russian Grand Duke. By comparison, being nude in the darkest corner of a two-bob worth Chinese Restaurant in Holland barely counted as a significant event. At this she reminded herself that whatever she did was always of her own volition and that all she did or seemingly was made to do was simply a means to an end, namely the doctors demise.

The teetering, skinny leaning gabled houses of Amsterdam defy logic looking as they do as constructions likely to stumble and fall at the drop of a hat. Subsidence, Amsterdam's forever arch enemy, has had its own way thus far to no ill effect, yet perhaps one day may be victorious. Not this day though. Renowned as they are for having exceedingly narrow, steepest staircases ever reaching upward and beyond all she was introduced to when arriving at the doctor's home was the basement. This room served as his kitchen come diner. As she expected its layout was impersonal, antiseptic even and, unsurprisingly, everything was in its proper place.

Was it a smidgen of fear she felt entering this room? Were that the case she masked it well, commenting, "What a lovely home you have, Herr Maximillian or should I call you, My Lord and Master?"

"Yes, I'll settle for Lord and Master, I think. Would you care for something to drink before we start our little game?"

"I think not My Lord, you don't want me stewed under the influence of alcohol, when I'm sure you would prefer me under the influence of yourself," a reply that she hoped would not give away her concerns that he may well spike her glass.

"I don't mind either way. I shall take a schnapps regardless." With that he poured himself a large one, then invited her to the place he named as his surgery. "I think you'll be most impressed."

"You lead the way, My Lord." He did just that. Although most girls upon beholding what came next as overwhelmingly disturbing, she was exclusively intrigued. Access to the surgery, an unusual thing for a presently non-practicing medic to have within the confines of his residence, was via a plainly secret doorway that could only be accessed by sliding out of the way a wide kitchen dresser that was perched upon, almost hidden to the eye, tiny casters. Taking a key from his suit pocket he unlocked the door and with 'ladies first' politeness gestured that she should enter. She considered the point that the room she was about to infiltrate was most likely the place where the local girls had been murdered. Were she not on assignment there was no way on God's earth that she would have agreed to set foot in the place.

Once within, the dangling bare electric lightbulbs turned on, he made an extravagant, designed to cause alarm gesture of locking then bolting the door behind him. At this, she made a discreet and prudent point of observing the trouser pocket he placed the key in.

"There safe and sound, no one can disturb us now. I shall just hang up my jacket on the hat stand in the far corner and change into my white coat...I always prefer to wear it and look like the professional doctor I am when with you girls...why don't you look around while I do so? Feel free."

The room that constituted the surgery was large, much larger than she would have expected, although in truth she had not really known what to expect. Being below ground level there was no natural light, no windows. What immediately caught her eye was that on one side the whole wall had been shelved and served to be what she assumed was his personal library, yet on closer inspection all the works there had the look of manuals or perhaps diaries about them. Taking one slightly distressed, older manual from the middle shelf she opened it up at a random place and was taken aback by its content. Everything was penned in German in what she presumed to be his own neat handwriting. She was conversant with the language and spelling and thus had no problems speed reading. What she discovered felt like a severe punch in the gut. List upon list of numbers. Numbers she realized immediately were identification numbers of prisoners held in Nazi a concentration camp before and during the war. In the column next to the identification numbers there was a simple upper-case letter 'M' or 'W'. Männlich or Weiblich, male or female in other words. From the extract she was reading the vast majority of entries read 'W'. Additionally, there were dates, times of execution of the prisoner, times of arrival at the hospital where he presumably served and in some cases written in red ink a note to the effect that the prisoner arrived as living specimen of 'zero pedigree'. At a stroke she had found sufficient evidence to nail the doctor once and for all.

So engrossed was she in that thought, still rummaging through his back catalogues of tantamount admissions that she very nearly jumped out of her skin as, in a what was to sound as if in a curiously relaxed, overly familiar manner, the doctor stood only inches away from her and from behind remarked, "I thought you'd discover my little secret, most do, some sooner, others later. It depends upon how curious and intelligent they are.   If the Allies had known of this historical collection it would have been the death of me, firing squad most likely. I must confess I am not an Austrian doctor, I am a German one. I'll let that speak for itself," now placing his palms upon her shoulders as would father to beloved daughter, "The hospital I worked in was not far from a camp. You see I was not, am not just a physician, I am also both an anatomist, a histologist and I can add a cytologist to the list as well. The studying of microscopic anatomy, the cells, the tissues, particularly the organs such as the uteruses and ovaries, the female reproductive process my speciality. All these things must be understood far and wide and my findings acted upon if we are ever to succeed in producing only pure and perfect human beings. It is here, in Amsterdam, during this so-called sabbatical that my work is almost complete, my legacy soon to be assured. You see, as I was based in a hospital, not a camp for sub humans the prosecution at my trial could not, without plausible witnesses of which there were none, find me guilty. As such my ground-breaking work continues unabated. There, now you know a little more about me. The thing is I always find I need more and more fresh females or still warm to the touch corpses to put under the microscope. Back in the war I could pick out the specimens I wanted, set the time for their death in order that they arrived still nice and toasty; sometimes I would have them sent over alive and kicking should my line of clinical exploration demand it." Abruptly, turning her about face, adding, "You look a little flushed? I do hope you're not feeling unwell. We can't have that, can we. Certainly not now."

A burning question arose, one that deserved immediate consideration. 'Should she end the matter here and now?' After all, she had in front of her hard evidence of his guilt, and now he had put flesh on the bone through verbal disclosure. However, having come this far the matter of what else he had to say for himself was simply too tempting to just let go of. It was clear that he was comfortable locked safe and sound in his own private domain. The likelihood of learning more, his ideology, his methods, his innermost thoughts, these were things she could not bring herself to just cast aside.

Whilst her disgust at what she had read was manifest and sickeningly for real, she determined she should not let it show. Instinct told her that to cave in to his each and every demand would draw from an egotistic him all she felt she needed to know. Lost in deliberation, she was taken aback, when all at once he drew a primed revolver from his white coat and set it firmly under her chin. "I think a little walk about the surgery would be a good idea. Don't you? Yes, over here particularly. My operating table. You'll note it has wrist and ankle restraints, so handy for live carcasses. Not that I need to, yet I always gag the live ones. The place is sound proofed yet overt hollering can distract me when at work," then pausing for a moment, adding, "I can sense you're thinking that if I fire the gun the whole world will hear, rest assured they won't, my sound proofing is that good. I've even had the police visit the house attempting to find evidence linking me to the recent spate of dead prostitutes. I freely admit to you, some have indeed been locked down here and, despite their best endeavours, the officers of law never had an idea of what was going on down below. They want me so badly yet, as with the war crimes trial, without evidence there is nothing whatsoever they can do. My work continues. While we're on the subject of death, I was amiss in not advising you that no one leaves this room alive. Oh, I detect you wish to say something? Spit it out."

Hesitantly, and in difficulty as the revolver was impeding free movement of her jaw, "Bastiaan, knows my whereabouts. He knows because you told him that you'd invite me to your home. I take it as given that I'm next on your list, yet when I don't return tomorrow the authorities will be down on you like a ton of bricks."

"They may well pop by, yet I go back to my previous point. Without evidence, and there will be none, they cannot touch me. You, young lady are mine to experiment upon. The things I can learn from your specific albino physiology a vital ingredient in my overall research, especially so my current analysis of female fertility. Inevitably, we shall have to swap bodily fluids before I dissect you as one of my current research experiments, that experiment being that of the tracking the flow of sperm, it's twists and turns within the female body following male ejaculation. Most interesting don't you think? Mind you, back when the Führer was in control I'd have the guards rape the girls before delivering them to me there were that many. Still I have to say, no time like the present. Do not overly worry, I shall not be finally bumping you off for at least a couple of days. I believe, and given that you are my first albino misfit up for live research, it is essential you are more or less compos mentis to begin with. You my dear will be the vanilla icing on the cake that will celebrate my scientific achievements."

With that he removed the gun from her chin, yet now pointedly pointed it directly at her forehead as he carefully gesticulated she should be stood in front of his desk. Now sitting comfortably in his chair he poured himself yet another large one before saying, his affectation that of a kindly soul, "Now then, I am reluctant to shoot you dead, in many ways a damaged carrion would ruin my plans, but if I must I will pull this trigger so do make it easier on yourself and do whatever I tell, without question. As of now, it's time you got out of those clothes. You'll not be needing them ever again. First slip out of those hideous heels, they play havoc with a girl's general deportment in due course, you must know that, then allow the dress to fall to the floor rather than whip it off. I'd prefer it done that way," then, becoming visibly over-excited, "Tout de suite, tout de suite, girl, get started. I haven't got all night," adding with a laugh on the verge of derangement, "Well, perhaps I have."

Her compliance to his order, a given. She even made a show of it allowing, as stipulated, that her dress slip off her body seductively bit by bit revealing just one treasure at a time until it lay crumpled on the cold stone floor then, having spun around revealing all holding a 'please do not kill me' smile, saying, "There, I think you enjoyed that?" He looked delighted and nodded his approval. Then, as if confirming her deference, flamboyantly she kicked both gown and heels to the far side of the room permanently out of her reach prior to standing naked, proud and undefeated to attention as would any brave soldier facing a firing squad.

"My I'm impressed, most whinge, cry or scream at this point in the proceedings, while you just grin and bear it, or should I say, 'bare it'? Not that it will do you any good, yet such submission makes my life so much easier. I wonder if you'll be this good a girl when I tell you that I don't use anaesthetics when cutting open the abdomen. You see, I hate to use any substance that may pollute the internal parts of the body I'm working on. I'm sure you understand." If he thought that such a portent would have terrified this courageous captive, he was wrong. She detected a hint of bewilderment as to her matter of fact reactions in his quizzical facial expression. Undeterred, he filled his glass again took a gulp then topped it up, after which he spent the next half hour sat at his desk just sipping his schnapps, gun in hand, his feet resting atop the desktop, looking fixedly at the disrobed girl stood there still as a statue in a museum. Eventually, she could not help herself to do other than pass uninvited comment, "Are you a pathetic voyeur or red-blooded man, My Lord?" and then a hush until she added with a sour note, "and Master."

His voice now a little slurred, his demeanour more putrid than pure, "You must forgive me. I have simply been assessing your physique. You are in remarkably good shape. Tell me, although I guess your answer will be in the negative, have you given birth, had a back-street abortion or had a pregnancy that didn't make full term? Are you, although I know you are not, a virgin? I need to have this information you will understand." She failed to grace his question with any form of reply. "I'll take that as a 'no' then. I need to check your teeth and gums. They are a good barometer as to your general state of health."

The doctor's reluctant body stirred itself, his revolver still clutched tight now in his left-hand as he took the few steps around his desk to where she was masking what appeared to him at least to be obediently waiting. Breathing alcohol fetid breath over her, his nose almost playing footsie with hers, "Be a good girl and open your mouth wide. Put your head back some." She yielded to his instruction at which the fingers of his right-hand sought successfully to spread her lips far apart. For a moment he dallied freeing her lips, seemingly disgusted that his digits were covered in rouge lipstick. He wiped his fingers clean as he could on his white coat then proceeded from where he left off. "They're fine. I can report that both teeth and gums are in fine fettle." He returned to the comfort of his desk, drained from what was left of his bottle of schnapps into his glass and spoke the words, "Earlier, earlier when I said undress, you missed something."

"What pray did I miss? I'm stood her as naked as naked can be. I 'missed' as you put it, nothing."

"You'll find you were wrong on that assertion. And, I expect to be called 'Lord and Master' as we agreed. It has a nice cringing servility to it. Another thing I like in a woman." It became clear to her that the doctor was getting beyond tipsy, his speech now markedly garbled.

She, with a pinch of salt and picking up on exactly what he meant, and as ancient princess to betrothed King of all he surveyed, "Lord and Master, I believe you refer to my pearl anklet? I wear it always, never ever remove it. It's my lucky anklet, inherited from my great grandmother, it feels as if it's part of me," she lied, buying more time.

"I don't ever recall a pearl anklet being an integral part of the human anatomy. Remove it this instant."

Keeping up the pretence, "I shall do as you ask."

"Shall what? You're forgetting your manners again."

"My Lord and master."

"Well do it then."

Her senses painted a picture from both voice and body language that her doctor was not just three sheets to the wind but angry drunk also. She felt the tide of events turning in her favour. The desire to smile the full-blown smile she always felt when confident of a destined triumph, a thing she concealed well.

There is little dignity to be had when bending over naked to remove an anklet in front of a hawkeyed predator. It was a good thing she could not care less, especially so as he who would torment was watching, gawping from the comfort of his chair spurting out profound to him, idle to her, words that would never herald a truth, "I may have to remove your eyes at some point in the proceedings. They are a remarkable shade of violet worthy of scientific investigation. Far too good to dispense with. They might even brighten up the place pickled in formalin in a glass jar. A unique addition to the collection I have gathered over the years. You don't mind if I keep them, of course you don't when you've got no choice." She had become tired playing his silly games. The time had come to start playing by her rules. He had had his fun, certainly more than his monies worth.

"What on earth is taking you so long, girl? All you have to do is just take the bloody thing off. Get on with it." There was that anger again, manifesting itself as a cancerous temper growing inside of him.

"I'm having difficulty with the clasp, it's not been undone for ages and I don't want to break it," then hesitantly, although once more not telling the truth, "...My Lord and Master. Plus, these are white South Sea pearls and hideously expensive to replace," omitting to say that they were mere fakes, plausible from a good distance to be taken for the real thing and purchased cheaply in a branch of Woolworths just a few days ago.

"When will you get it into your head that you'll never put the damned thing back on. It'll be of no use to you again while you still live, and mean sweet nothing when you're dead." With that she, to his eyes at least, was seen to rip the fastener apart causing the pearls to bounce and scatter all over the surgery floor.

"For God's sake, what on earth have you just done. Look they've gone everywhere. I could slip and break my neck on one. Get on your hands and knees like the common whore you are and gather the hapless things up," an order he would so soon regret issuing.

On all fours, she searched for her fake pearls picking up those she could locate from every nook and cranny, holding those recovered tight in the palm of one hand along with the beading thread that was hitherto the thing the counterfeit pearls were held together with. However, the beading thread was unconventional in the extreme. The original had been ditched and it now consisted of a multiple twist of ultra-thin floral wire. A full yard of thinnest floral wire when unravelled and a thing of her own design just prior to setting off for Amsterdam. She had all along anticipated that given the role of prostitute she had chosen to play there was a better than even chance she would end up naked and seemingly defenceless. Ridiculous as it may have seemed the ultra-thin floral wire represented her preferred weapon, one that had stayed out of sight despite her nakedness.

The game of cat and mouse still in play, "I believe I've got them all now...no, wait a minute there are a few under your chair."

"And?"

She was getting sick and tired of this, "Your Lord and Master," game.

"And?"

"Pick the accursed things up, woman. You're boring me now and I'm not moving out of your way, I'm comfortable as I am. You can slither and stretch underneath the chair for all I care, and hurry I want to make a start with your initial examination...yet first I need to teach you a lesson." The doctor chose to give up the claimed comfort of his chair, red in the face as if to explode he stood up and demanded she also got to her feet. With that she deliberately spilled the pearls once more, faked a fear in mind and body that might appease his tyrannical trait, his violent temper. He sighed, beckoned her closer, dragged her by her hair to the mirror above the sink in one corner of the surgery. Held her fast, made her stare at herself, "Look, you're not human, the likes of you are a stain on humanity only fit for slavery and medical experimentation that might improve the lives of those like me, the thoroughbreds, the pure and the perfect. I will make you lie on your back on the floor, spread your legs and beg for mercy, make you plead with me not to fuck you senseless even though I've paid good money for that very right, make you grovel, scream for your life when I tie you down and open you up. Make you shed pointless tears, make you beseech me to be done with you." With that he slapped her face time and time again. Still she shed no tears, just looked at him blankly, emotionless until he let go, returned to his chair saying, "Now pick your fucking pearls up. And don't drop then again if you don't want to be cut from fanny to throat right now. And, I'm not a fool, I can see the so-called pearls are just costume beads. Don't think you can barter your way out with those. My how wrongly you have read me."

The one thing she noticed above all others when he blew his top was not the pain or any angst she might have felt, but the fact that he had left his revolver upon his desk throughout the whole incident. His obvious alcoholism his Achilles Tendon. Back sat in his chair, perspiring and clearly short of breath he now rested the gun upon his lap. Throughout the escapade she had kept the floral wire in the palm of her hand, had been quietly using tucked in fingertips unfurling it, unnoticed.

"I've got all the beads apart from the one's still under you chair," not bothering to add 'Your Lord and Master' as it was clear that that part of the game was now old hat. "I'll gather them now." He proffered no riposte, just stayed still in his chair, waiting.

Given that this time the doctor was not in the mood to move from his seat and make way for an easy task she had no choice but to crawl behind where he was sat for that was where the beads, not that she cared, were resident. Aborting the mission to recover them, her floral wire now completely untangled, she grabbed its ends with both hands and with haste passed it over his skull, then immediately around his neck, doubled it over and pulled with every ounce of strength she possessed, her own anger now taking hold, "Who's begging now, My Lord and Master?" He began to choke, his weapon falling to the floor as he floundered. "Answer me that you evil bastard, you cunt of the first order of cunts, answer me that." Searching for air as he was, he was unable to offer any reply, let alone beg audibly at this time.

It was after 4AM when she returned to her café lodgings, a sore face, as fully dressed as she was when she left the place last evening, her snow-white hair in a tangled mass, tired yet pleased with herself. Bastiaan had waited up concerned for her well-being, although he hid his anxiety well, pretending to be tidying up in the café as she walked through the open door.

"Is everything OK? Your face is bruised to fuck. Can I get you anything, you name it, I'll get it?"

"My cigarettes are upstairs. Coffee and a cigarette will be fine, Bastiaan, just fine."

"I'll get them, and an icepack for your face, it'll help that bruising? I'll run you a hot bath later if you wish?"

"Hold on the ice and the hot bath for a while, Bastiaan. Caffeine and nicotine are my priorities for now."

Having fulfilled her request, Bastiaan joined her at the window table where she sat looking out and up at a night sky in denial; a sky full of stars that soon would lose their game of bagatelle with a crafty sun.

"Well, I'm all ears. You look like you've been in the wars. Successful mission?"

"I've nothing wrong with me that won't heal quickly. As to the assignment, yes it was successful in every which way. I'm just a little tired, it's been a long night. Will you do me a favour and telephone our 'Lords and Masters' that I have achieved all they asked of me. It's a given that they'll know what you mean, and regardless I'll be meeting with them in Brussels later today for a debriefing, so nothing to add on that front. You have the codeword for verifying 'mission accomplished', don't you?"

"I certainly do."

"Then, thinking about it, just give them that, nothing more at this stage. It's all they want to hear and anyway that's what we all agreed at the outset. It's unwise to say too much about anything on the telephone."

Left alone while Bastiaan made the call, the first medicinal hit of caffeine cut through the barrier of a myriad of ruminations, reawakening one tired mind and body. She just wanted the new day now dawning over and done with, to be back home in England and in her own bed. That would represent a paradise whatever the weather the journey home may thrust her way, an immaterial minor nuisance.

When Bastiaan returned confirming the call had been made it was clear he wanted to hear the whole story, a thing she felt she could not deny him. They were, after all, colleagues on the same side. Making sure to give him the entrance key as well as the extra key, the one she had retrieved from the doctor's pocket before departing; the one that unlocked the door to his hidden surgery behind the dresser that she had put safely back in place in case the police, or anyone else for that matter, gained access to the premises.

"Bastiaan, I'll need you to visit the doctors home and recover his journals for they contain all the evidence necessary to prove, beyond any reasonable doubt the guilt, of this evil man, not just his current crop of murdered local girls but also his direct involvement mainly at his hands of the slaughter of hundreds of inmates at the camp. It would be best if you could personally deliver them to our paymasters...there are too many, and they're too heavy for me to take to Brussels with me. They are vital, important evidence so we can't take risks, and certainly if the Amsterdam police get their grubby mitts on them we'll not see their return for an age. Oh, he had a revolver. I placed it back in his desk drawer, also in the surgery. As I'm only wearing what I stand up in I thought it best to leave it there rather than walk across the city here holding a gun."

"Leave it to me, you needn't think about them or it again. I'll get over to his place before the city wakes up. How is the doctor? I imagine he's safely bound and gagged? What shall I do with him?"

"Well he is bound, in that he's tethered securely to his operating table. As to 'safely', it depends on how you mean the word."

"Explain? He's not dead, is he? You didn't?"

"Well, he certainly wasn't dead when I left, yet as of the here and now, I'm not so sure."

"You have me on tenterhooks, tell me more."

"When I left him, and as you will find him, you might want to prepare yourself for a shock."

"Very little shocks me, I've seen it all."

"This might! You see, after I'd manacled him to the table I gave him some of his own form of punishment, although he would no doubt call it a necessity of scientific, medical research performed upon the living. At any rate, you'll find his balls stuffed in his mouth, a mouth that I have double stitched up nice and tight. I was rather pleased with my skills, especially so as it was with his own needle and thread I used. I found that profound and satisfying. I even managed to get the surgical knots right by following the instructions from one of his old manuals.

Likewise, I used my discarded hair pins to fix his eyelids to his eyebrows ensuring his eyes were permanently wide open, forcing him to see all that I was doing. Another 'Oh' and yes, when I left he was bleeding profusely from the place where once lived his balls. As I said, he wasn't dead when I left him."

"Remind me never to upset you! I'm curious though. His penis? Is his penis keeping his balls company still or did you leave it in-situ?"

"Of course not. Not after all the things he has done to others. I took it with me when I left him behind. No doubt you heard the seagulls in the square riotously squawking just before I got back?"

"I did, and a bloody racket it was this early in the day."

"The gulls, I think you'll find, were fighting over which one should eat his cock for breakfast."

"Classic stuff, he deserved everything he got, although I thought the brief was to trap him alive?"

"It was, I'll just put his demise down to self-defence. I've used the same excuse before and got away with it. The others, when I meet up with them later today, will understand, and the evidence I have uncovered is more than they could ever have hoped for. You never know, from that evidence they might be able to discover the actual family names of some of the butchered ones. I hope they can at any rate."

"The bruising about your face? Did the bastard hurt you in any other ways? I can get you over to the hospital if he did."

"The bruising is nothing. Toward the end he was as drunk as a skunk. He's an angry drunk, the worst kind, although the fact that he was aided my cause as his faculties were faltering making his downfall inevitable. I'll be OK. I could do with that bath now if you don't mind. After that I'll grab a few hours' sleep. And lastly, in case I forget, when you are at his place I'd appreciate it if you could recover my comb, floral wire and cheap fake pearl beads, we don't want the local police to find those things when they eventually gain entry. Annoyingly the beads are scattered all over the place, a long story you don't need to know. Nothing must link me to him or his home. That reminds me, don't forget the pins through his eyelids and the hair stick, the latter you'll find within, how shall I put it? Let's just say, 'the place where the sun doesn't shine'! And again, as with the gun given I had chosen not to carry a bag last night, it seemed inappropriate to be seen carrying a mishmash of bits and pieces back here."

"Leave it all to me. I'll run that bath straight away. You don't want someone to wash your back, do you?"

"You know, another time, another place I might just say 'yes' to that, but not now, I'm wiped."

"One last question if I may? Do you ever feel fear, even just a morsel?"

"You may not believe me when I say this but in situations where I am facing malevolent scum fear becomes an alien thing. In those situations I'm the most dangerous woman alive simply because I don't care if I die."

14.

AUTUMN 1952 – SUSSEX, ENGLAND

Her: "Why the sad face, Zada? A dalliance with a worthy purpose, a therapy for a locked-out man with little to stimulate him when it comes to one-to-one contact. You should be proud of yourself. Imagine that you were as he hearing no sound, seeing no visions, speaking no words. When I suggested to you the idea it was simply based on the fact that making love, or whatever one cares to name it, is the only material gift of kinship you can offer him and in doing so you both have now a bond. I should add that he thoroughly enjoyed you and that he hopes you feel the same?"

"I do, very much so. I had to have more wine than I'd planned in order to build up a little Dutch courage, and even then I lay in bed in my own room until the early hours thinking 'should I, or shouldn't I'. I crept into bed with him in trepidation that he might reject me. Also, and even taking into account that since I've known you both; since I've lived on the Left Bank I've seen a whole new world, yet something of the peasant girl from a small Romanian village in the middle of nowhere, bought up on fresh air and religion – accepting that in these Communist days such religious beliefs have to be hidden from public eye – remains. Religion begets guilt when it comes to matters carnal."

"I can see that. Religion is the curse of the free spirited, yet the simple act of sex for the pure pleasure of it doesn't retract from love. The giant and I are in love. What I asked of you was not an act of love, it was, put simply and as I've already said, to create a connection twixt the pair of you. I know it was easier for him than you. You didn't have to. You shared the gift of each other simply because it suited you both and now you are friends for life."

"Thank you. What you have said reinforces the feeling in my stomach that says I shouldn't feel bad about it. By the way, he is something of a stallion isn't he. Certainly, more staying power than my former artist lover."

"He is that. More so I think since he became this inside out person I now have. Out of interest, why did you only sleep with him the one night? I was away for three nights, you both should have been having a whale of a time."

"The first night it was on my mind to make an approach, and I hadn't realized then that he knew a thing about it. He seemed from his body language a little on edge what with you being away so I thought it best to wait. It wasn't until the next night that I, as explained, plucked up the courage, and as of last night, well we were both...I certainly was...tired out from the previous night. I slept like a log last night."

"I'm glad to hear it although I have to say that tonight he's mine, unless of course you want to join us?"

"As intriguing as that idea might be I'm not sure that my mindset can cope with three in a bed just yet. God, I wonder what my grandmother would have said if she'd heard I'd shared a man with another woman all in the same bed. She would disown me."

"If you ever change your mind remember it's no big deal to me, or him. Certainly, back in the day before his injuries I suspect he'd view the things he and I... now sometimes he and you...get up to as unacceptable, yet when you consider the things he's been through, the state he was in when we recovered him; the way...even though he has got his functioning brain back...sex, adorned or unadorned is his one guaranteed physical pleasure. He has his art, he has his music, but they are activities that involve no others. He takes sex for the simple thing it is, you should do the same. Life is so much easier that way. I think he's already let you know but he did add, gorgeous as you are, that he thinks you much too skinny at the moment."

"I know. When he wrote that on my ribs I didn't know whether to laugh or cry."

"I bet he didn't get dressed even the once when I was away? He's most impressed the way you keep this house nice and warm. It puts my efforts to shame."

"Oh, we did go out for a longish walk the afternoon before I plucked up the courage to have my wicked way with him. We dressed for that because it was so cold outside. That's when I came across the mushrooms I went back for later to cook them up in the traditional Romanian way as a soup."

"Yes, he's told me about your cooking also. It seems you are the perfect housemaid, and I mean that you take that as a compliment not an insult. You really are a true treasure Zada even if you do need fattening up a little."

"I have prepared already, before you returned from Amsterdam, an old Romanian peasant dish called 'Ciolan afumat cu fasole'. I went into town first thing and used your ration book...hope you didn't mind...in order to buy a pork knuckle. I wanted it smoked but your local butcher didn't even sell it like that, or so he said. Well I think that's what he said, as my English is still very poor. But this meal you'll find is winter food, our soldiers love it and although its cooked at home with white beans I could not find any so you'll have it with red kidney beans, all in my special sauce."

"Well, no smoked pork knuckles indeed, I'll have to smack your bare bottom, Zada."

"I think I'm growing to like that idea."

"Well, I think your just teasIng me?"

"Sorry, I could not but help myself. Can I change the subject?"

"Of course, Zada, of course you can."

"I was just wondering how you coped without your lover during those war years. Were you ever unfaithful? I mean, I know already that you have a moral slant that differs from most others but was there a true love affair between you and anyone else? If you think I've got a cheek asking just tell me to shut up."

"Not at all, you've every right to ask. My mistakes could be your lessons in life. And yes, aside from a little amorous play, mostly of operational necessity, there was one I was nearly smitten with. Thankfully it came to nothing."

"Pray tell me more."

"I'll do better than that I have kept the only letter he sent me. I have it here in the dresser drawer. His tale is neither sad nor happy yet I can vouch its authenticity. I think in different circumstances... well anything is possible in different circumstances. I'll read it to you, he calls me Anna, which of course is not my real name. You would have guessed that any way.

Dear Anna,

Just an honest, old fashioned love note. I pray you do not mind. You see, I'll be away for a short while yet wanted you to know that so spellbound am I by you, you might be impressed if I wrote verbatim of the recent case we worked on together. You will understand that had I not been bowled over thus, such recollection would have been in the process of being lost to time. Please, please be impressed, dearest girl;

First a sip of champagne, then a rare girlish tilt of the head and in an instant, your naked iris, roseate eyes ambushed mine. Detained them for the duration. Not too long, yet likely just long enough. Was it contemplation as to my purpose of being? Mental telepathy? Thought transference? I never could translate the language of those conspicuous, yet most agreeable eyes.

A little earlier, not long after we had sat at our corner table and the waiter had taken our drinks order, you had insisted the candle be snuffed. "My photophobia demands it" your courteous reasoning. I obliged, killing the flame twixt wetted finger and thumb. You had me light your cigarette. I was keen to ask of you why you had chosen to wear a white silk cocktail gown upon your snowy frame, yet thought better of it. Felt it improper to delve. Notwithstanding, it was charmingly low cut, invitingly filled, both you and it, a heaven-sent, magnetic art form. In that regard, my own straying eyes would have, no doubt, published the daring workings of my desirous mind. Such poor form on my part seemed to bother you not. I guess it was a thing you were used to, the price to pay for blessed beauty bestowed. I would have liked to say it was me who first found you, although in truth the opposite was true. Such was the way of a fling in times of war. Times when only the losers surrender.

You picked at your food as if to not enjoy, made note of my quizzical glance, "A little over-generous with the calamari, the white bean puree was sufficient in itself. Worry not my appetite has never been that rife...unlike some!" Your soft gibe aimed at a palpably ashamed me. "Well, The Savoy is exempt from this wretched rationing, no reason not to have my fill. Thankfully, you'll not find dried egg and that dreadful chicory coffee here." You smiled. Just a fleeting smile. Sufficient to appease my self-evident guilt.

To the backdrop of the big band playing, appropriately at least insofar as I was concerned, 'In the Mood' we discussed the methodology of assassination. "So, you will help me then?" I nodded in agreement. You continued, "Good, that's settled. I am fully aware MI5 briefed you in this matter some time back and that you have the expertise to covertly gain access to his suite here. It is, as you will understand, in both our interests the pseudo human dies...by the way, it would be best you book a room here, you and I as wife and husband. That way you will be my perfect cover, no-one will suspect a thing, plus we can track his movements, find his weak spots before I make the kill...as such, we remove any chance of failure. In a place as grand as this, where the walls really do have ears, team work ensures a successful outcome. We can take up residence tomorrow." Your eye for detail was impressive.

Take up wedded residence we did. At your insistence we acted out our respective roles as if our marital status were honest. Your lovemaking was clinical, seemingly devoid of passion. I think you found sex a mere professional necessity, pointing out that the chambermaid, from the state of next day's sheets would be in little doubt as to our bona fide standing in the, albeit unlikely, event she was ever questioned thus. Additionally, you made sure your lipstick stained cigarette ends married those of my own in the ashtray upon the bedside cabinet. "One can never be too careful in such matters" your gambit and prerequisite to further entanglement. Whilst the creature in me did not mind your 'lay back and think of murder' approach, the lover, rake perhaps, that part of me was always left hoping for you to reveal an eagerness to explore in place of your 'if I really must' mechanics. Maybe just an old-fashioned fake embrace that had perhaps little meaning, though that was never to be. That you sought such union so often surprised, was contradictory. Your stock phrase, "It helps me think" did little to boost my waning spirit. Surely you must have known that I was besotted.

War torn London in June meant sunshine, showers and bomb shelters in equal measure, though whatever conditions prevailed you wore darkest sunglasses. Upon our picnic in Green Park, aside Piccadilly you had the added protection of a simple straw sunhat and the purest demeanour...the latter, no doubt, to signal that any hanky-panky on my part would be unwelcome. We discussed the task in hand in some depth. Your contempt for the one you had christened 'the pseudo human' was palpable. I prayed your sheer ferocity in that regard would not end up an Achilles Heel. Regardless, you advised that now we had established his movements about town, his habits and regular haunts, that tonight would be the night he would meet his end.

"You have the copy key to his suite...Good. Pass it me...also, I think it important we stay on a couple

more nights after the assassination rather than depart immediately the task is done and dusted...should we simply disappear the tedious uninformed constabulary might put two and two together...organise it if you would please. Other than that, I'll join you in our room after dusk"

I was lost in the previous day's copy of The Times when you, my gratified grinning liquidator returned. A grin of affirmation, duly noted. Just a well-placed single bullet apparently. I had the bellboy bring us up a bottle of bubbly...told him it was the occasion of our first anniversary, and... how shall I put it? Suffice to say, my indiscretion in spilling the beans was, I hope, forgivable, for you were not backward in coming forward that night. Good Lord no.

Circumstance has meant we never revived our carnal pursuits. Such is life for seasoned espionage agents such as you and me, Anna.

If you ever find you need me, you know where I am.

All the best my Love,
        Douglas

"Your paths never crossed again?"

"Never. I heard that he died just before the war ended. A nasty business I'd rather not talk about."

"I'm sorry."

"It matters not Zada, it matters not."

Him: An instance of the alchemy of revelation or one of failed obliteration? I have not the acumen to determine which, yet a phenomenon of ostensibly significant circumstance has come about. As yet I have felt compelled to keep the event under my hat; a secret from her just in case my judgement, a judgement born of the ruination of my senses is unsound.

My off and on befuddled mind thinks back to the first time my eyes gazed upon the one I still see in my mind's eye as an unadorned divine white messenger. I muse upon that debauched evening before the war whereupon, and in front of an audience of the slobbering stinking rich virile bozo's, she danced ballet enthrallingly naked to the accompaniment of a solitary enigmatic pianist. Then I leapfrog a decade or so onwards over the hurdles of life to my last immovable recall, my final reminder of being whole in body and in spirit when detained in Berlin, those last moments before the nothing arrived, when echoes of the immediate past were sent to time's own well fastened locker. For it was in a cell in Berlin the Jewish pianist came to me during the night and bestowed within me the unfathomable yet remarkable gifts of art and music. That he was an impossible ghost, a figment of my imagination or something tangible I do not know.

Nevertheless, following the restless night I had after the previous overly active hours of darkness courtesy of the grace of Zada, it dawned on me that my white angel's pianist from back when and my ghost of last recall are, or maybe perhaps better put, were one and the same person. Of that I am now certain. My new-found recall cannot separate them, they are identical, their images hanging next to each other in the gallery inside my head.

Long since I have accepted that ours is a love affair of necessary secrets. The very nature of our choice of similar covert careers has ensured that. That I worked for the secret services of my mother nation and she, or so it has always seemed, works freelance, a minor detail. Yet beyond the confidentiality of our respective assignments there has always been an unanswered question, a question I have always bowed to her insistence that such things she would not divulge and never sought an answer to. That question? In truth, it is twofold. Her name, her heritage. We are bonded, like mute swans, 'mute' perhaps being the operative word in my case, to mate for life, yet even after all this time I know not her name or whether she is of noble or yokel origins. It is a subject she had made clear from the very outset that would never be disclosed, was not up for debate. Nevertheless, the pianist whose path I have crossed on two occasions now must hold the key, knowing her before I ever did, and whether in dream or reality, visited me at a dark time and arguably let me inherit from him the means by way of which I could suffer my state of being more easily than any other alternative. Surely it would be only fare of her to acquaint me with sufficient truths to eliminate my puzzlement. I'm not angry with her at all, how could I be? She is my eyes, ears and voice; she has cared for me, made sure that the rotting vegetable I was is close to becoming a human once more and importantly she remains the love of my life yet I believe she should share her secrets, not just the tale of the pianist but also her own story, as she shares with me her entire essence.

Her: She thanked whatever God she should thank for the invention of the braille typewriter. He had asked certain questions of her regarding her real name as opposed to any nom de plume, additionally her ancestry, such as it was, given that behind her in the family tree there were but just two entries. As something of a throwaway line toward the end of his typed note he questioned, not in a fierce way at all, yet questioned nevertheless as to why she has never seemingly had qualms about being unclothed in public spaces. "I really don't mind at all. I've seen how lovely you are, hence even now I know how lovely you are, yet your raison d'etre as explained thus far is open to debate, methinks," his exact wording.

After some deep thinking she determined that yes, she was under a moral obligation to disclose a little more of herself. As she arrived at this decision she laughed. It was hardly the case that she had not disclosed all that she 'had' previously, yet this was different. This was important to her Titan giant. Would he believe a single word though? Most would think her a liar, others who ever got to read her words would likely take her away for scientific research including her dissection most likely.

Starting at the very beginning she wrote first of her mother, a woman who had been designated the identification 'Mayday', yet felt compelled to add that she accepted that he would think what she had to say a nonsense and would most probably never believe her. In that regard, she pre-empted any doubts he may have, begging his forgiveness in advance, adding that every word she was about to impart would be, as oath given as evidence demands, 'the truth the whole truth and nothing but the truth'. Fingers crossed.

15.

OF A GIRL NAMED 'MAYDAY' – MY MOTHER'S STORY

Prior to her exploitation Mayday had deduced she needed hard currency and friends. That to be immersed within this human race such things paid worthy dividends, yet time was not on her side, she would be carbon dust by dawn's first light, her incineration, the chosen method ridding the cosmos of the blight the wise men perceived as actual, for she defied all natures laws, overlooking entirely that she was testament to Aristotle's final cause. Given a choice in the matter she would never have opted to be one of a kind. Sadly, she was never afforded a say. In hindsight, and considering her current situation, her designer had come to a similar conclusion. That he should have kept her very existence a confidential thing until the time was right and if that time never arrived, then she should simply be his little secret kept safe from mankind.

It was at The Linnean Society of London, arguably once the epicentre of natural history and taxonomy he first let his, upon reflection, diseased self-esteem part company with sanity and had proudly presented her in all her glory to his peer group of esteemed biologists and interested academics. His presumption that his genius would bring forth accolades and plaudits across all corners of the globe, sadly ill-founded. Instead, he would be vilified by one and all as the creator of a monster that challenged the authenticity of the human species being at the very zenith of The Tree of Life.

Two poached eggs set upon a nest of saagwala her preferred last supper. That the duty officer acceded to her request, an act of startling kindness toward one who was merely a collection of handpicked organic cells encased forever the naked non-human as she had been since her creation, as of the moment, in a prison cell in a place far, far away from the public eye.

"I've heard tell you have the same emotions, same intelligence, same state of consciousness as a regular human being, yet you cannot catch a head cold?"

"You are correct, yet I am however, capable of crying, laughing and dancing a waltz when the mood takes"

"Why did he...that professor who made you name you 'Mayday'? Why no clothing?"

"In terms of my name, it is because that was the day he completed his work; the day I came into being. As of my lack of clothing, he deemed it inappropriate for a non-human to be afforded that luxury. I understand his major concern was that he felt his peer group, religious leaders, lawmakers, maybe even the general public would think it wrong that I should be passed off as a human being when strictly speaking I am not. It is of no concern to me. The embarrassment of a 'run to ground' Eve is alien to me."

"He's banged up doing forced labour in some archipelago now by the way. So, you never had a childhood; you just came into being"

"Yes, I was not born of a mother. I am 'unique' they say...well that plus the fact they see me as a threat to your species were I to breed with one of you. Many don't like the thought of a highbred I understand, as it conflicts with long held beliefs"

"You are the most beautiful creature you know; you deserve better than the fate that awaits"

"Thank you"

"Do you know why the professor just made the one version of you? I mean to say he could surely have come up with a male prototype to keep you company? Temptress or not, he could have called you Eve and him Adam!"

"If I recall he said, '"There is more scope for compassion within the female of any species, no place for a male in the new order I envisage' or words to that effect."

'Later, into the early hours, over more than a glass or
two of moonshine,
he shared memories with Mayday, told of his
childhood days, so sublime,
with that he unlocked her cell door, took her hand,
made good her getaway,
even now all that is really known of her is just her
name, the name 'Mayday''

She never laid eyes upon her 'creator' ever again nor ever discovered his fate. I often wonder if the fact she had a proven creator, a thing the human race has searched for and tried to prove the existence of since their claimed, 'beginning of time' was lost on her? I somehow doubt that the case.

At this point in the tale I must confess that the verse concluding this section of my mother's story is not entirely true, far from it. Her guard did indeed fashion her escape, even covered her up insofar as he was able in order that she would have a chance of getting away unnoticed by the public at large. The lie in the verse is its last line. Wishful thinking on my part. I shall now delve a little deeper!

The spring of 1914 in London, a time of tediously day upon day overcast skies, yet fortunately a relatively dry one. A polar opposite to the devil dark storm cloud 'July Crisis' soon to erupt in diplomatic circles across Europe that would spark 'The War to End Wars'.

Mayday, a girl who lived on her wits, now satisfactorily lost in the throng of humanity, was sat upon an Old Father Thames towpath's newly painted wrought iron bench lobbing pieces of crimping's from an obvious, to even his untrained eye, shortcrust Cornish Pasty to a mob of dabbling mallards to scoff upon on that day he first met with her.

A creature of habit, as ever upon his morning constitutional and as was his want, good manners ensured he delivered her a cheery, 'Good day' notwithstanding her self-evident lack of decorum. Bare feet indeed, plus a rather risqué double skirted mid-calf dress, bright orange in colour of all things, although it did match her locks and galaxy of adorable freckles. Plainly she was fashioned from an unusual mould.

Little did he know at the time her hair and freckles were merely a disguise. The chameleon within had been at play. Furthermore, he had no idea that she was not human, well at least not human as science would have it.

Whatever, for his part, he was walking on by, Kew Gardens bound, when he caught her almost impudent, "Excuse me Sir. I need advice and possibly you can assist in that regard."

Turning about face, his perfect English yet heavily accented riposte, "Should such advice be within my gift you are welcome young lady. Pray what do you need to know?"

"The sun is due to make an appearance later, I understand, and my desire is to get a suntan upon the soles of my feet. The thing is I find myself unable to decide whether or not to stand on my head or lie on my back with my feet in the air. I mean, either way the soles of my feet would face the sun, just not sure of the best option."

"I think the latter, as the former methodology would likely cause you a rush of blood to the head and that would never do, would it? Additionally, you may think in terms of common decency the undertaking of your intention would be better enacted within the privacy of your own plot."

At this she laughed aloud, afforded him the most captivating wide smile, "I'm an actress and when I said, 'Excuse me Sir. I need advice and possibly you can assist in that regard' I was merely reciting from memory my lines. That you responded allowed me to play a cheeky, idiotic game. You have my apology, kind Sir." She need not have expressed regret in this instance. Such is the once in a while alchemy of chance encounter, for he was by this time, smitten.

*The black satin blindfold was your choice
and at your insistence you led the way
along the corridors of vague revelation
to the concert hall where the freethinkers pray*

*Theatregoers witnessed with unusual blind faith
a farce marketed as sombre tragedy
she played the flawless protagonist*

he chose to overact nonsensically

Who was this man Mayday had become involved with? Indeed, why had she allowed herself to become embroiled thus?

By necessity, Mayday had evolved a mercenary trait. As such she kept out of harm's way yet would let little or nothing to stand in her way when needs arose. When her new gentleman friend had let it drop that he was of royal decent, a monarch in fact from a land across The English Channel, east of Gay Parie, north of Sevastopol, south of the Barents Sea, her whistle was well and truly whetted.

"You don't have the look of a King?"

"I'm hardly going to walk the towpath wearing a crown, am I?"

"I suppose not. Why are you telling me this?"

"Because you are the most adorable creature I've ever laid my eyes upon. I would love it for you to be my Queen."

"Haven't you got a Queen? You may not be in your dotage, yet you are not in the first flush of youth, Sir."

"Regrettably, I cannot tell a blatant lie. I do have a Queen, yet...," and grinning like the cat who got the cream, "...perhaps you'd consider being a royal mistress?"

"You mean a 'kept woman'? You have some cheek, Your Highness!"

"A lavishly 'kept woman' living in a palace all of her own. How does that appeal?"

Given the things she had been through, the thought of being safe and sound and lavished upon had a certain understandable appeal to Mayday. It was time she proffered her hand for he would no doubt kiss it and in doing so commence, albeit unknown to him, an extrasensory connection that would allow her to establish if he was for real, or was just a chancer seeking only to bed her and be off about more 'pressing' business. Being a creature born of invention, rather *than a fruit of fornication, had its advantages when it came to matters unaccountable to his kind. At the very moment he planted his kiss upon her mitt she discovered to her amazement that he was indeed telling the truth. Her swift foray into his mind...a beneficial perk endowed by accident to Mayday, a being of creation...also gave her insight to the fact that he hated his Queen with a vengeance and that she had yet to provide him with a boy child...any child...to further his dynasty. That by way of archetypical royal union born of pacts twixt nations he was stuck with she, 'The Barren Queen'.*

What then happened was that The King kept his promise. Although never feeling overly emotionally or physically attached to her new-found monarch lover she afforded him all the respect he deserved for he had been true to his word. For his part he adored her, squandering fortunes upon her by way of gifts of jewellery, acclaimed artworks, a wardrobe fit for any queen and a palace of sorts tucked away in as remote a part of a foreign land, namely this house we now live in here in Southern England. I bet that comes as a shock to you! For just a few months until war was declared it was here where he spent his every free moment. That he had an unsurpassed sexual appetite was not lost on Mayday. How could it be! She ensured he was allowed his illicit conjugal rights whenever it suited without ever once letting on that his chosen mate was of unique origin. Besides, to her the act of sex was little more than a mechanical process. By the end of July that year, and out of duty to his subject's, the King of a land across The English Channel, east of Gay Parie, north of Sevastopol and south of the Barents Sea reluctantly left for his homeland, not to return to these shores until early 1919 after the war to supposedly end all wars was done with.

The pair renewed their affair with even more vigour than before. A true love as far as he was concerned, mere tolerance and respect on hers. Much of the next few years were spent travelling hither and yon. The royal one, an accomplished artist and musician, would often play his violin to her flamenco dance, sometimes he would have her stand aside the grand piano while he played unaccompanied, but mostly he painted nudes of her, for he marvelled at the fact her perfect physique had not wearied in the slightest during the years conflict had kept them apart. His love for her was undoubted, his contempt for his queen back home similar for, aside her embittered demeanour, she had still failed to bare him an heir.

In the fullness of time Mayday fell pregnant. The fact that she could fall pregnant came, I understand, as something of a major shock. She had always presumed that while her mating rituals were more or less the same as his natural selection would, most likely, slam shut the door when it came to fertilization of her eggs from his sperm, at worst the possibility of non-viable or at best, a sterile progeny. Nonetheless, she was made of the same organic materials as humanities self-proclaimed Herrenvolk and thus perhaps should not have been nonplussed by the event. Sadly, story has it that Mayday died unexpectedly and unaccountably in childbirth, my birth, me the little albino girlchild. Once again, I suspect that as you read you will be more than a little shocked that I am but only one-half human! In truth, I have often wondered if that fact alone, especially so when considering Mayday's intrinsic predisposition to be undaunted when naked in public, is where I get the same trait from. Likely it is, certainly the thought makes me laugh. I wish so much that I had known my mother, she the only female of any species ever to have had the gift of a life empty of any form of childhood. I often think of the things she might have achieved if she had lived. Sadly, such a privilege was denied her because of giving birth to me. Her ashes were spread upon the lake here in this place where we now live. Its beauty aside that is why since moving in here I have spent so much time by the lake, best times I think, especially with you. I digress.

So, there we have it The King was robbed of the only woman he had ever genuinely, and for that matter, faithfully loved. It is said of him that he was understandably heartbroken yet never once did he cast blame upon his little albino daughter. Quite the opposite. She became the light of his life. Only the very best for his misbegotten love child, his Lilliputian princess, and in the absence of any offspring through his marriage to his queen, arguably the next in line to his throne.

Can you imagine that my giant. I might have been a Queen! By the way, the story is not over yet, I trust you are not dwelling on the fact I am not wholly mortal. More of that later. Once again, I digress.

From wet nursing, through to education, my training from early years in ballet and subsequently traveling the continents with my esteemed father, little old me had the best of the best. To an extent in my adolescence I let him down somewhat. All the physical and psychological trademark angst following puberty displayed themselves in riotous fashion. Even half-human me was not immune to the mood swings associated with the huge surge of hormonal activity bringing about sexual ripening. One night in a fit of teenage anxiety I packed a bag and made for Berlin determined to make my name as a ballerina any which way I could. If that meant starting out in low life clubs than so be it. Why Berlin? Berlin, to me was the place where art and the artists craft could manifest itself, gloriously in every way, yet in my rush to escape and find my way in life I had entirely over-looked, indeed had no real idea, of the rise of Hitler's new Germany and the sordid ascendency of the far-right. I simply, and selfishly, had come to worship the legend of Isadora Duncan, the wild dancer who had in small part made her name with the Berlin State Ballet before moving to the now communist nation of Russia. She was beautiful, flouted traditional morals, was bisexual and atheist. All things that were 'me'.

It was while I was working in some decadent, sleazy dive in Berlin, a den where I would dance without the merest hint of shame dressed only in my ballet shoes before my rapturous drunken audience of all-sorts, that a sleuthhound tasked with the job of locating my whereabouts, and long since in the employ of my father, finally located me. Taking me aside, insisting I get decent and put some clothes on and prepare myself for a shock, he advised me of the grave news that my father, while disguised and under an assumed name visiting Jewish musician friends in the German city of Weimar had been caught up in a wave of Jewish arrests. That he, his friends and many others had been taken to the camp at Buchenwald. It had always been the case that when my father visited his cronies he felt it appropriate that he not be recognized as a king, yet despite his protestations to the contrary his Nazi captors were having none of it. He looked like a Jew, had the papers of a Jew, was dressed as a Jew, played the fiddle like a Jew, sounded like a Jew therefore was a Jew.

This event took place in the July of 1937. The detective was later to advise The Queen of her husband's demise. I understand she made due note of his words, had her henchmen shoot the messenger on the spot, and was thus able to keep the true news of The Kings ruination out of the headlines, save for issuing a statement to the effect that he had met his end in a mountaineering accident in The Alps, claiming he had fallen from a ledge in bad conditions and that his body was yet to be found.

Whether in that year, the next or the one after I do not know, yet I take it as certain that my father died in that camp, starvation the most likely cause of death given that, in those early days and beyond, a lack of food was prevalent in the camp. I should add at this point that you will now understand my contempt for not just the Nazi's yet all doers of evil and how that hatred of such scum fashioned what perhaps is best referred to as my 'choice of career'.

Oh, I must not leave out The Queen. She was executed simply for having blue blood following an inevitable Soviet annexation not long after the war. In the circumstances, the monarchy was abolished. Any claim I might have had to the throne now an irrelevance. However, even though the homeland assets of the royals had been confiscated there remained this property we live together in right here. It remained empty all through the war and it was only as recently as last year, probate research I sanctioned on the advice of, how shall I put it, a well-placed American, ensured that as the only direct heir of The King ownership became mine. Additionally, whilst all monies and other assets from his royal portfolio of this and that in his homeland were frozen or lost to eternity, my father had had the foresight to keep considerable monies in the English banking system, had had shares in numerous businesses now becoming most profitable following the end of hostilities. I, the albino princess inherited the lot. That means you and I are rich, certainly beyond my wildest dreams but I imagine yours also?

As of now I need, for both our sakes, to discuss the pianist. The one you call, 'an impossible ghost, a figment of my imagination'. It may come as the biggest shock to you thus far, yet I agree wholeheartedly that the pianist was, well I shall add 'is' to that, my father. That night of debauched ballet dancing in Surrey before the war I had fully intended to dance naked to no accompaniment. There is art in silence and anyway my performance required no such accompaniment for the audience could not care less either way. They were not the slightest bit interested in my art, it was but my bare fresh flesh, my sex they came to feast upon, nothing more. Knowing well animals such as those in attendance, I anticipated one would be able to hear a pin drop. The execution of my act, in total silence, I still maintain would show more than a little artistic panache. Anyway, and as you would expect, I recognized my father in an instant yet we never spoke a single word to each other, just an exchange of knowing nods. For a moment when first hearing him start to play, then turning to see him there, a dead man manifested as if 'in the flesh' I presumed a certain embarrassment might strike me, it is not everyday a father catches up with a daughter in such circumstances. Fortunately, the professional within was in its ascendancy, and by happy chance had danced to the piece of music he played many times in the past, and besides my only purpose in being there was to assassinate The Grand Duke who I was well-aware was once an arch-enemy of my father. Albeit, on the wrong side during the Russian Revolution some years previous, The Duke saving his own skin had turned quisling and his new masters had benefited from the significant intelligence he had shared with them. The identities of many 'on the side of good' he had imparted to them, their deaths assured in the wake of such treachery. More importantly to my father, the duplicitous had taken it upon himself to guide many a Nazi on the run to South America, Brazil and freedom for the most part. I presume my father's ghost was there that night to both see The Grand Duke die and to keep a revenant ghost's eye out for the protection of his favourite girl. Exactly what he might have done if things had gone wrong that night I do not know save that maybe he could have spooked the audience in some way, maybe turning himself into a poltergeist. The thing is, while it is clear to me theism, deism whatever 'ism you want are ludicrous, meaningless mumbo-jumbo and that there can be no afterlife of bliss in heaven or torture in hell, there may well be realms, say parallel universes and/or a place for each and every one of us in another zone of existence, one that defies time meaning that those who are dead in our dimension may still be alive in another. That may sound like gobbledegook, yet there is some scientific basis. I shall shoot off at a tangent here for only this very year in Dublin in 1952, when the Nobel prize winning Austrian physicist Erwin Schrödinger gave a lecture in which he jocularly warned his audience that what he was about to say might "seem lunatic." He said that, when his Nobel equations seemed to describe several different histories which were "not alternatives but all really happen simultaneously." This is the earliest known reference to the multiverse. The multiverse is the hypothetical set of possible universes, including the universe in which we live. Together, these universes comprise everything that exists; the entirety of space, time, matter, energy and the physical laws and constants that describe them. The various universes within the multiverse are called "parallel universes". The structure of the multiverse, the nature of each universe within it and the relationships among these universes differ from one multiverse hypothesis to another. I know for certain that my mother's 'creator' held similar views. My father told me that, and that whilst he doubted their authenticity at first he had, over his time with Mayday, come to believe she was correct. Namely that we can be alive there when we are dead here!

So, there you have as much information as I dare provide. My name must remain top secret, the specifics of my heritage left concealed. There is too much at stake. My half-human status, were it to become general knowledge would, I truly believe, be my downfall. The powers that be would likely change my status and with it any human rights afforded me. There are no conventions protecting for the likes of me, just one of a kind. If news of my true self ever got into the public domain I would end up in the same boat as Mayday. As effectively 'an alien' I would be a mere cadaver, the subject of scientific research or worse. There would be no refuge for me, even The Vatican, and all other religions for that matter, would not be keen to support my cause and accept that I am capable of human emotions, have an intellect, nor would science accept that I am atop their tree of life in evolutionary terms. Philosophers would struggle with the concept of my very being, me part created; part evolved.

I know this note is in braille and not easily read by prying eyes, yet logically it would be best if you hand it back to me in order that I can destroy it as soon as you have fully digested its content. I also know you will fully realize the enormity of the matter and understand the importance of my secrets being kept safe.

I'll finish off by asking you, with tongue firmly in my cheek, do you still desire me? Love me still now you know I am, strictly speaking, not of your own kind?

After interpreting the tome his lover had transcribed, a thought, just a thought in defiance of keeping secrets safe between just the two of them struck her Titan giant, namely that it seemed grossly unfair that he be the only guardian of her extraordinary, yet taken as read, authentic tale. That there was Zada to consider. In layman's terms she was now 'one of the team'. As such, Zada should know chapter and verse and that not to include her would be to treat the girl as a second-class citizen. When put to his lover, she found she could not but agree, so before ridding herself of the manuscript of both her chronology and of how she came about, she took Zada to one side.

"I hope you are prepared for a shock, Zada, a mighty shock at that?"

"Should I sit down?"

"Let us both sit comfortably. You see these papers I have in my hand Zada. These recount the outwardly impossible story of how I came into being. All I shall tell is true. Not one word an exaggeration or a lie. You see, I am not entirely human."

"Sorry, I don't understand. How can an obvious human, such as you, not be entirely human?"

"I think it best I read aloud what I've have written here. Our giant has read it already. As part of the family now we feel you must be privy to its contents. Sadly, I do not have a Romanian or French draft so my voice in the tongue of your motherland will have to suffice...are you sitting comfortably?"

"I am."

The recital over, Zada was plainly taken aback, asking question over question as to exactly how it was her friend could be anything other than a conventual human being, muttering the word, "Impossible" time and again. Then pulling herself together she alighted her chair and purposely kissed her 'friend without a name' both on the forehead and lips multiple times, before concluding by saying, "Your story is safe with me; I'll not mention it to a living soul. Thank you so much for taking me into your trust. You don't know just how much that means to me."

"I think I do know, Zada. We love you, and love must never hide secrets. However, a favour please, Zada. For reasons I've already explained, you will understand that this manuscript is akin to a time bomb should it get into the wrong hands. It needs to be destroyed as soon as possible. You will, I feel sure, understand that. I know it's unlikely, yet it's best that it doesn't survive now that you know its contents. Can I leave that task to you? I suggest you burn it at your first opportunity."

"Of course you can. Leave it to me."

Although not by design, Zada remembering that the Irish stew she had on the hob was likely boiling over in her absence, and her mind racing like Billy-O thinking about what she had just been told put the task of destroying the document on hold; on hold long enough for to momentarily forget to fulfil her promise. It was only when she had the slow cook of the evening meal back on track she remembered the thing she had forgotten. By then, and despite a desperate search she could not immediately place where she had put it. Finally, it dawned upon her that the manuscript rested upon the peelings of the vegetables aside the kitchen sink. As her pulse rate subsided to one closer to normal, Zada took the view that the paper be used to wrap the peelings in and then be cast in the dustbin. She was soon to discover that that was not a sound modus operandi when destroying something so sensitive to her friend's wellbeing.

16.

WINTER 1952 - SWISS ALPS

Her: There are certain things, important things, things that would unsettle or scare shitless the asinine little brain boxes of the hoi polloi the world over, things they simply do not need to ever know. At least that was the prevalent view of the committee, a 'Baker's dozen' of top level diplomates, high ranking military, dogmatised archbishops and cardinals, curious physicians, chomping at the bit surgeons, retired right of centre judges and an esteemed research scientist, all under a metaphorical 'on pain of death' oath gathered together at the behest of a hurriedly formed McCarthyism secret fellowship aimed at protecting the peoples of the Western world from subversion of the social order. Needless to say transparency was not a thing high on their agenda and seemingly not a warm-hearted do-gooder amongst the lot of them. Not too much room for human compassion at this time, in this place, in this state of the art research clinic tucked away up high in The Swiss Alps, a location so restricted by it geography that access could only be made by narrow gauged railway, private cable car or gifted mountaineer. Certainly, to the one effectively 'on trial' there was more than a sniff of Mengele in his heyday in the clean, crisp wafts of ghoulish indifference toward the freak albino girl sired by one of perfect mortal pedigree, yet brought into this world of an unnatural birth mother, an anthropoid female of human creation but not strictly-speaking human biological make-up.

The proudly, and for the main part, bunch of zealots, not a doubting Thomas amongst their number, most conscious that they were at the very zenith of the survivals fittest, had decided prior to calling their meeting to order, and behind closed shut tight and guarded doors, that the questionable female human lookalike whose status and future they were to adjudicate upon could not, under any circumstances at this stage in the proceedings at least, be under any illusion, in any circumstance that she was their mortal equal either in body or soul.

Additionally, and reluctantly accepting that she was capable of speaking several languages fluently, it would be highly inappropriate to allow her to address the concourse personally, in part or at all on any relevant subject matter, or any other matter to be precise. In principle, no questions or request for clarifications of any sticking points were to be aimed in her direction. Such a thing would be not right; not proper and an impediment to free-thinkers train of thought. Sadly they were in short supply. Further, that there was absolutely no requirement for her to have advocate to represent her, as they deemed, after cursory private consideration that she be given the ranking of an animal; given the self-same rights, such as they are, of a scientific research animal and that until a judgment had been formulated, she be not just ranked, but also treated as if she were an animal, a great ape perhaps. Even that, to some of those collected together was a liberty too far. That human sperm had fertilized the nonhuman egg that prompted her gestation within a foreign womb they thought an irrelevance at this time in proceedings.

Spoilt for choice within the unlikely located and hellish difficult to construct, substantial and impressive marble stone complex styled in the flamboyant North Italian Baroque fashion, with its mass of oval columns and unconventional façades, those in attendance had chosen for their final deliberation not the main auditorium but a rarely used convention centre below ground level. Out of sight, out of mind in terms of meddlesome eavesdroppers. It was within that intimate room they took their respective seats, seats set out in a line, each with matching Scandinavian desks of minimal design and tapered legs for functional finesse. In short, 'less is more' work surfaces. Little need for the traditional when in the gloom of a corner sat a shorthand secretary to take down the minutes and make note of the final verdict.

Already they had formulated a short listing of questions that needed decisions apropos the female's fate. Earlier debate had allowed the scientists among them to choose a suitable Latin denomination for her genus, 'Genotype de femina ignota, sexualium phaenotypo distinction' or 'female of unknown genotype–phenotype distinction' by any other name. For ease of conversation and deliberation they had settled on naming her a rather lacking in imagination and distinctly unfeminine 'Albus' as an alternative to the originally proposed unsubtle, 'Snow White'. To her left ankle a permanent bracelet had been fitted bearing that name.

At the bidding of the centrally placed table The Chairman, a recently retired Supreme Court judge from Quebec, Canada one Pierre Chevrolet, smart even though casually suited for the occasion yet obscenely obese, called the meeting to order. Either side of him sat two others, both carefully selected former senior Judge's, one from Denmark, the other from the United States. As a trio, they would adjudicate and moreover be responsible for the irrevocable final verdict. The outcome they sought would be dependent upon the evidence, in reality mere suggestions, put forward by their ten partners in arguable crime, each a specialist in their own field; fields determined relevant to the serious yet informal tribunal that some discerning outsiders might be forgiven referring to as a Kangaroo court; a quasi-judicial assemblage.

Judge Chevrolet began his opening address, "My friends, as you will be well aware, we are gathered together here to adjudge the destiny of a unique specimen of a living thing. A lifeform alien to any that has gone before. A lifeform whose very existence has sparked a controversy amongst the high elite that must be settled here and now. Time is of the essence in that were we to dwell too long, procrastinate too much then the peoples of The Free World would arguably be discombobulated. First though, I need to confirm with you all that these proceedings will be conducted in the English language as it is the case that to some in attendance it is their mother tongue, and all others I understand are fluent in English as their second language?" As he glances to his left then to his right he notes nods of agreement all around. "Then I shall proceed." He pauses briefly to request of the bespectacled secretary in the corner that she pop outside to the corridor and issue the guard with the demand that 'Albus' be brought down from her present whereabouts for those assembled to view, as none had seen her in the flesh previous, sooner rather than later, then carries on expanding upon the point he was originally aspiring to, "Our purpose here is, put simply, to come to a decision as to what to do with 'Albus'. Each of you will have a fifteen-minute address, no longer, providing you with the opportunity to put forward your own case as to how you see the resolution of the matter at hand; to expound upon what you believe to be the appropriate course of action. In doing so you will need no reminders from me that we have been charged with this duty from the highest levels from almost all nations considered to be 'Western' in both outlook and, to an extent, geography," with that Judge Chevrolet casts a knowing smile toward Cardinal Bernard Smith, an Australian lately domiciled in The Vatican here on behalf of The Pope, "and additionally having digested your various standpoints my two fellow Judges and I will make our pronouncement. Such verdict will be final, most private to the extent news of the event must never be leaked and, importantly, with no scope for appeal. I should add that in the event the three of us cannot find unanimity then a majority of two in agreement will be sufficient, in the case of each of us favouring entirely different outcomes then I shall have the last say in the matter. I trust that that is clear...Oh, that was quick...I see that Albus has arrived...good...perfect timing...my thanks guard...please place the specimen we are to adjudicate upon before us...and Bernard, perhaps you would like to address us first." Cardinal Bernard agrees, yet stays seated for the moment while the guard positions his theatre trolley upon which an anaesthetized Albus rests, her body under the cover of a plain white sheet save for her face and feet. "Over to you, Bernard." At last, Bernard stands up but instead of staying upright and behind his desk he purposefully strolls over to a motionless Albus on her trolley, dismisses the guard with the wave of his sweaty hand then stops briefly as if to take a breather, makes to seem to loosen his bright red cassock yet instead grabs the sheet covering the otherwise naked girl robbing her of any modicum of tenable decency, then makes show of folding said sheet neatly before casting it aside as if swatting the Devil incarnate.

In an ever-increasing brooding temper that plainly shocks a few of the representatives the cardinal commences his sacrosanct homily, "Would an ape be covered thus? Would an ape be afforded a sheet, afforded human clothing? Would a cat, dog or caterpillar? If we are foolish enough to share the common-decency etiquette afforded to all the children of God since the eviction of Adam and Eve from Eden with a lesser being, a being not one of 'us', then we are already bowing to Satan himself who certainly would be laughing from his pride of place stoking the fires of Hell. The detrimental effect on our subconscious such emancipation of that damned sheet bestowed upon the creature before us sickens me. I would ask of the judges that they erase any notion beyond that on which we agreed earlier namely, that the creature here has equal status to the tailless primate that is the ape. Overlook her ability to stand upright; overlook her supposed intellect and consider this, after the flood God gave us the animals as food for humanity to eat...for the uninitiated you can confirm this in Genesis 9...and also, lest we forget, Albus's mother was created, yes created no less, by a flawed, hardly omnipotent scientist playing at being God. I believe that that abomination, the mother, was in hindsight appropriately named 'Mayday' and began her life as a fully-grown adult. I'm no scientist yet to me the fact that a non-human organism able to think and display emotions is something that counts for nothing. God never sanctioned her creator to imitate God's own design that is for certain and undoubted," the cardinal pauses once more, takes a deep breath all the time looking down upon the naked body of the sedated one, "Moving on, and if you need further convincing, I pose this single question. What if she were to breed with one of us and her offspring went on to breed, and their offspring bred and so on? What then? If we allow that to happen then we would be allowing the pollution of humanity. This creature, 'Albus' is a blight on humanity; an insult to God. I have no hesitation in recommending euthanasia forthwith. I rest my case." He makes to return to his seat, stops himself in his tracks, stands statuesque aside the trolley, his rigid digit forefinger pointing directly at her torso then adds as a parting observation, "At least God created the ape; a deluded mortal was responsible for creating this obscene monstrosity, this counterfeit human, this wolf in sheep's clothing."

The cardinal seemed to have created a trend for showmanship, for next up came Professor Marcus Vranitzky, a research scientist formerly of Harvard Faculty of Arts and Science, presently head of The Office of Science and Technology Policy (OSTP) adviser to the Executive Office of the President, also choosing to hold court beside the womanly 'Albus'. A man calm, exuding confidence, lean, impeccably suited and booted, at ease with his audience he takes little time to get to the thrust of the proceedings from his angle.

"Thank you for that passionate address Cardinal, although perhaps controversially I feel I must say I detected more than a little hark back to the Spanish Inquisition from days of yore. I trust you don't mind me saying that." By the testy look on Bernard's face he clearly does mind. "It will come as no surprise that my views on this matter cannot be compatible with the Cardinal's. Here, with Albus we have a phenomenon, one that needs to be researched rather than destroyed. Why? I'll tell you just why. Right in front of us now we have, on the face of it, a perfectly formed human adult female. Every last inch of her anatomy spells human being. Look see, if you did not know otherwise you would presume she is one of the collective 'us' the cardinal referred to. That her sire was a European monarch, her mother a marvel of science the construct of which has yet to be fathomed, a modern-day miracle, she perhaps his Aurora to her Tithonus...I trust you'll forgive me the 'miracle' analogy, Cardinal, yet it is the plain truth of the matter. It is our nature to be curious, for only the curious make discoveries and boy is there much to be discovered analysing Albus. My questions with regard to Albus are manifold. First and foremost just how was her mother formulated? Pure genius, yes, but that's not sufficient. We need to unravel the secrets of her mother's maker for one day, who knows when, for the sake of the preservation of our species there may be valuable lessons to be learned, let alone the reconstruction of lost limbs, a cure for paralysis perhaps and the like of those afflicted with such issues say from injuries in the theatres of war, or by tragic accident. Her immune system. Does it differ from ours? Her brain functions. Just how does that brain regulate and control of her bodily functions. How do her limbs receive and interpret sensory impulses and transmit information to the muscles and body organs? How did she come to be in a state of consciousness, able to think, retain memories and display emotions? How are her behavioural responses when compared to ours? How is she different to you and me yet functions as we do? Sure, with a human father much of what we need to know will have been diluted yet maybe researching her will provide clues, clues I and my team can work with. Also, I am curious with regards to her albinism. Albinism a congenital disorder characterized by the complete or partial absence of pigment in the skin, hair and eyes. Neither of her parents were albino. Why her? Was there a fault in her mother's formation that led to her albinism? I could wax lyrical for hours, yet this is neither the time nor the place. Another thing, as far as I am concerned, there are ethical issues to consider. Albus displays human emotions, is I am told, prodigiously intelligent. As such we owe her a degree of respect. The respect of asking of her if she is willing to offer herself up for research. If, as I suspect, she answers in the negative then we must ask of ourselves if it is right and proper to force her to comply for our sake, for the sake of all mankind. But it's not just ethics in terms of the moral values we apply to her, for on top of that we stray into the arena of bioethics. The ethics of, 'what if?'

The answering of questions that arise out of the relationships of all the facets of being. What if we discovered when researching her composition something that impacted on not just science for the future, but medicines, politics, the law even. Big issues with potentially big outcomes, yet if we don't try we'll never know, will we? In my considered view Albus should be handed over for research whether she agrees or not. I hope beyond hope that she agrees and our compassion trying to ensure she suffers minimal pain and distress wins out. Any questions? I think we have a minute or two for questions, Judge Chevrolet?"

"Professor, you do have just enough time left for me to ask of you one question. An important one, I believe. Are you able to conduct any useful research as to Albus' makeup from her corpse, or does she have to be alive?"

Albeit, and for the first time a tad hesitant, the Professor answers, "To an extent, yes. However, in terms of the full range of experiments I am minded to conduct certainly, in the short to midterm of such research it would be best that we ran tests and experiments on a living Albus, much like we do with animals in the lab. For example, for tests relating to breeding, and say, the immune system is only of value on living organisms. As to her component parts, yes there is some merit to be had in dissection and subsequent analysis, but only after a good degree of live research. Certainly, we will learn more about the structure of her brain if we had her brain in a jar to refer to. I jest, yet there is truth in my words. Also, I trust I do not sound too barbaric. I'm not recommending Albus be subject to terminal experiments. I feel I must make that point crystal clear."

"Thank you, Professor. You may take your seat once more. I believe you are next, Mademoiselle Fabienne Colomb."

Fabienne Colomb, a petit 60-year-old twice divorced former French Ambassador to the now dissolved League of Nations, famous in political circles for both her laid back though often cruel satire and retained good looks wastes no time making her presence felt. Arising from her seat, taking just a sip of water she, the only woman amid the assemblage, walks the catwalk walk of a seasoned model of Gaelic sophistication as she replicates her male predecessors, giving her address beside Albus.

"Where do I start? Um, yes," she smiles her sexiest smile at each stern face facing her in turn, looks to the sky, then takes a deep breath, "Even though I expect you boys won't admit it, I bet you are all wondering...well maybe not you, Cardinal...how I feel about having, for all functional purposes, a naked woman put on view in my immediate vicinity. I guess you seek to shock! Having said that, there is little doubt that she is quite the most beautiful living thing. My answer? I am not offended; indeed, it would take a great deal more than this to offend me," then theatrically, Fabienne lifts Albus's limp hand to her lips, kissing the back of it, then gently placing once more in situ, fakes embarrassment, then, "from what I understand by deduction and what I have been secretly told, in order that I am not blinkered in coming to my recommendation I have taken the immovable stance that she is the equivalent of a shop window mannequin, nothing more. Sad yet true. I anticipate that may disappoint one or two of you, I know how you boys love to corner the weaker sex; have us submit to your male superiority. Seriously though...take due note of that word, 'seriously'...personally I believe the brace of ethical, theoretical and theological arguments put forward thus far are pathetic in the extreme. Albus exists. Here, right now, she exists...full-stop. For God's sake we, well you gentleman in particular, are gawping at her. It is as simple as that and you are liars if you claim to be doing anything other than 'gawping'. Some of you having lustful thoughts? I bet you are! My view? She must be released from this pseudo zoo immediately and not treated like fishpond low life. You should, the bloody lot of you, feel ashamed of yourselves and, I might add, I am not saying this because she and I are of the same sex. These discussions are a farce! I would conclude by saying to you three judges set this woman free."

It is Robert J Wanamaker, an in-situ currently active, most senior officer reporting to The Directorate of Operations for the CIA who speaks next in the polished manner of one comfortable and at ease in front of an audience. Wholeheartedly and in a most professional slick, as only an American can be, style supporting the view of Mademoiselle Colomb, elaborating his position outlining the covert success Albus had achieved in the field, of how she has single-handedly rid the world of many evil characters intent to further their own devious causes or trying to escape, run and hide from justice; of how her intervention has saved countless lives of field operators engaging with our common enemies, when quite out of the blue, a startled Albus sits up straight on her trolley perch, looks all about the room, showing no obvious signs of the blind confusion accompanying that startled state one would expect of someone coming around from a drugging, aside from tilting her head and momentarily scrutinizing the bracelet affixed to her ankle. This prompts a collective gasp from the panel of onlookers, each with a potential role in settling her fate, that almost echoes about the room. Sedated as she was, no one had thought to restrain her in any way. Her awakening so soon, a most unexpected event.

Noting the close proximity of the impeccably dressed man stood over her, not realising he was there supporting her cause, in truth not knowing at all where she is, she lashes out in the calculated manner of a seasoned professional, displaying the information gathering darting eyes of one who would fight before fleeing any day of any week, revealing not the slightest concern for her naked predicament. Defending himself Wannamaker grabs hold of the forearm travelling at pace toward his jugular, then tries his level best to pin the girl flat on her back upon the trolley until assistance arrives. To all appearances, fortunately for him, a reinforcement does arrive in the shape of the gruesome looking guard, a man of some stature who originally delivered her up to the meeting and had remained on duty inside the room, stood to attention by the entrance door. Together the two men try their level best to hold Albus back in position however, such efforts prove to be of no avail. She is too nippy for the both of them. Her teeth penetrating Wannamaker's wrist, so close to the ulnar artery causing him to instantly release his hold, just before a well-placed forehand chop to the throat, worthy of an Ancient Greek wrestler, disables the guard who crumples to the floor and is left fighting for air intake. With that, and with a remarkable quickness, gut reaction motivates her to dismount the trolley and head straight for the exit door.

Wannamaker whines, the guard regains a modicum of decorum, the panel remain seated all in their own particular way, lost for an immediate reaction either in word or deed.

Alas, poor Albus is unable to make good her getaway for outside in the corridor a previously bored senseless small security team await her. Her escape to God knows where well and truly blocked she puts up a good fight, hits out, spits worse than feathers and writhes as angry as a snake as four of the team of five eventually grab a limb apiece and carry her back to the place from which she had run. Not without extreme difficulty for she twists, turns and contorts in their grasp refusing to yield, she is eventually presented spread-eagled before a trembling with rage Judge Chevrolet who has no hesitation on insisting Albus be carried away back to from whence she came, namely locked-up in the confined cage in the depository with the other bewildered animals hand-picked for scientific research, concluding his instruction insisting that they make sure they, "Put her in irons for both her safety and, importantly, for ours. Also, a medic is required for Mr Wannamaker urgently," despite said Mr Wannamaker maintaining he is 'Fine now', then said Judge adds, "And have the bloody anaesthetist report to me later, I want to find out both why and how such a thing as this could happen. Mark my words heads will roll."

Wannamaker insists upon remaining with the others so as to hear out the proceedings for there remain seven more yet to have their say. Judge Chevrolet regains his prior indifferent simulated sedateness. All around is a dispassionate taste in the air. The residual experts in their specific fields each, in turn, have their due say, one of Social Democratic Party persuasion and a onetime member of The Swiss Federal Council, an aging before his time Zoltan Dietiker, taking a considered humanitarian stance and completely unfazed by Albus' half-human state makes the profound conclusion to his address that, "From what I've learnt of this girl, I truly believe she could be considered one of a kind; one of a superior species, one that adds to, rather detracts from this race of human-beings we belong to and that she be allowed to live among us without restrictions. We may learn from her by simply tolerating her presence among us." From the indifferent body language and eye contact his words bring forth it is clear few, if any, entirely concur.

At this juncture, Chevrolet calls an adjournment suggesting that the others take light refreshments while he and his cohort judges deliberate before coming to, then announcing, their final pronouncement 'back here' in exactly one hour's time. True to his word the wily judge does indeed deliver his decision in the matter of Albus's fate on the hour.

"Firstly, may I thank all of you. To have such diversity of opinion so eloquently put forward has been most useful and just in case any of you are wondering why the Albus exhibit is no longer here before us, I can advise that following the earlier outburst and for the safety of one and all she presently remains under lock and key in her cage. Regardless, the matter at hand is to come to a decision about the destiny of the living thing labelled, 'Genotype de femina ignota, sexualium phaenotypo distinction' known to us colloquially as 'Albus'. I am able to say that both my colleagues and I have reached a unanimous ruling. In doing so we took account of the stark fact that Albus cannot be considered wholly human for the simple reason she is not. As such we are in new territory for, from a legal standpoint the tag we have titled her, namely 'animal' is strictly speaking incorrect. In essence she is an enigma, her birth mother having been born of assembled organic matter sourced...we do not know exactly how and likely never will...by a rogue scientist who is long since deceased taking his secrets with him to the grave although I am at pains to add her father was undoubtedly human in every which way. Importantly, the product of those parental loins is 'Albus', on the face of it a fully functional human blessed, as we understand it, with a cleverness that would put many of use to shame, and a loyalty to the cause of righteousness second to none. Her endeavours on behalf of her betters...in the genetic and anatomical sense...in terms of covert deed are laudable. Indeed, she has put her own life on the line on many occasions in supporting the cause of righteousness. We have seen with our own eyes a little earlier her fiery temper, her Machiavellian predilection toward protecting her life induces her toward violent response at any costs when the perception is that she is in grave danger. A commendable thing? Used in the right place at the right time, 'yes'. However, throughout her career, a successful career I might add, Albus has known all too well, yet kept confidential, her nonhuman status. Does such a thing constitute a crime? The answer is an across the board 'no'. The reason? An unambiguous uniqueness, never previously under examination in terms of her equality, or lack of same with those who she shares identical traits with. Mr Dietiker, Mr Wannamaker (albeit under physical attack from Albus) and Mademoiselle Fabienne Colomb have all concluded that, in principle, we accept Albus as one of our own and that hereinafter we simply get on with our lives regardless of a newcomer amongst our kind. Others, most notably Cardinal Bernard have...he from the theological standpoint...made the case that, in short, the very existence of Albus is a crime against God. From just a biblical perspective the Cardinal's reasoning is resistant to alternative argument. Yet should our finding be in tandem with the Cardinal the outcome would be the immediate euthanasia of Albus. We would be denied any other options; there would be no going back.

The unanimous decision of the three of us, and without sounding vainglorious in any way, vastly experienced and expert adjudicators in all manner of complex constitutional and ethical legalities leads us to conclude that there is only one course of action we can take, namely, that based around the proposals laid before us by Professor Marcus Vranitzky. Our verdict is that Albus be put under Professor Vranitzky's jurisdiction immediately in order that he and his team of scientists based here in Switzerland are able, under completely classified circumstances, to conduct the full range of scientific research proposed, up to any including euthanasia when the time is deemed right. In doing so, we determine that the benefits to humankind of such research far outweighs the moral and ethical issues relating to the subject of this case, namely Albus herself. In many ways, our view is that she is but collateral damage in our quest for knowledge.

I feel I must add that in coming to this verdict my colleagues and I deduced that there was no place for the unadorned compassion that human nature, by way of God's gift bestows us all with, such is the importance of the research to be undertaken upon her. I know that the professor will afford Albus the respect for her well-being the best he possibly can until such time as his analysis of her live body is accomplished.

In conclusion, I am of the view that there is another matter, one not subject to these proceedings yet nevertheless important, that you should be aware of and keep exclusively to yourselves. When taking Albus into custody, those agents acting on behalf of our free and democratic Western nations were compelled to detain two others, both in every respect entirely human, one was Albus' long term partner in life, the other her female friend. Her partner is well known in security circles having been an agent working on behalf of MI5 until that is the Soviets robbed him of his key faculties when under torture leaving him deaf, blind and mute. Her friend, who we know little of and is likely using a false name had, I have been informed, been assisting Albus with the day to day care of her partner. We surmise that both are fully aware of Albus' nonhuman state of being. Presently, the pair are in residence, albeit under lock and key, in one of the executive suites on the top floor of this very building. Plainly, and given what they know they cannot be allowed to mingle with the outside world. As to their eventual fate, I am pleased in many respects that that is something entirely out of my hands. Presently, as you and I would expect I am able to advise that the pair are being treated well, deprived only of freedom of movement.

These behind closed doors proceedings have been conducted less formally than in open court. However, that fact must not...not that I expect any of you would think otherwise...detract from the key issue, namely that the verdict as just announced is final, top secret and as far away from informal as any judgment on any subject matter ever before adjudicated on. I repeat, my word is final. I declare this hearing over. God bless you all."

No luxuries for the one pronounced fit for exploration's exploitations, the one they ironically call 'Albus', the one whose only crime is that of being sui generis; in a class of her own. She curls her shivery bare body into an awkward ball in a corner of her new home, an uncluttered locked laboratory box cage, with heavy iron side and ceiling bars, its carpet of straw upon a cold cement base and formerly housing its previous guest, a chimpanzee, without a given name. Measuring some twenty feet by eighteen the enclosure had been designed specifically and considered suitable for larger nonhuman primates.

A regiment of overhead fluorescent tube lights blaze twenty-four hours a day for seemingly no sound reason. In a marginally smaller cage of similar design neighbouring hers a frozen to the spot, fretful juvenile orangutan gawps askance in her direction no doubt disturbed that the simian next door is uncommonly, save for the whitest hair about her head, shorn of body hair and is perhaps curious as to whether similar mutilation will be his own eventual fate.

Sedation plays havoc when measuring time. She believes she has only been in residence some two, possibly three days or was it just now she came to be here? As yet she cannot be sure. In her mind only the misty recollection of turmoil in a room of crème de la crème unnamed persons. Her forearm is bruised, a scab is forming on the tip of her chin. Not ready to pick at any time soon.

A whistling close by. A male whistle, then a clamorous rattling of baton against iron bars. She looks up and ahead. Makes due note that a personable young man, conceivably Italian for he has a Roman nose, hazel eyes and olive skin, clad in a white coat is offering her a water bottle to drink from when, as should be obvious, her predicament demands the water bottle plus a warm blanket at the very least.

Speaking in Italian she requests of his kind face that a blanket, an old coat, anything warm would do, would stave off the chill. He, open-mouthed with surprise that she speaks his maternal language neglects to reply. Obviously under orders to take care, he prudently places the water bottle through the bars and on the cage floor before she decides to come anywhere near him. That is the way of things when dealing with perceived wild animals. One cannot be too careful and this one has already earned herself a reputation in that regard.

Unfurling herself she stands, walks as daintily as one can in a cage over to the bottled water all the time curious to know what kind of creature he thinks she is. It should be obvious from her naked form, yet thus far she knows not a thing of the proceedings that have determined her future as a lab rat. His eyes are firmly fixed upon her as if he cannot believe what he is seeing, yet he remains silent, failing to afford her common manners. He neither agrees nor rejects her simplest appeal for something warm to put around her. An agile girl, she climbs the vertical iron bars best she can, spreading herself feet and hands far apart as if an angry queen of the jungle and making known her perfect bilateral symmetry, then looks over to her new neighbour ape seeking his unfeasible approval.

Aimed at the Italian, "Like what you see? You seem to. Have you never seen a grown woman stripped before? Whatever, if you'd stop gawping like a pervert I'd feel more comfortable, or perhaps you are a pervert? Seen enough yet, have you?" Still he says nothing, just walks away as if vanquished, leaving her to the company of the anonymous orangutan.

While taking a sip of water, the feeling of cold worsening, she recalls the ankle bracelet. It has a tag affixed. On inspection the tag reads, 'Albus – nonhuman, property of SARC'. The motif, Swiss Animal

Research Centre is one she is familiar with. At this instance, she hazards a guess as to her fate. Knows for certain her predicament, simply not the manner in which it came to be.

A little later, for she still is not in tune with time, a spruce and attractive man of not quite middle years introducing himself as Professor Marcus Vranitzky stands outside her cage door, his opening gambit straight to the point, "Primatologists have long recognized that restraint methods may introduce an uncontrolled methodological variable by producing resistance and fear in an animal. Numerous reports have been published demonstrating that non-human primates can readily be trained to cooperate rather than resist during common handling procedures such as intravenous therapy or for blood sampling, injection and general veterinary examination. Cooperative animals fail to show behavioural and physiological signs of distress. I do trust you will be cooperative, and by the way I'm the head honcho here and you have been, if you haven't yet guessed, handed over to me for all-manner of scientific research."

"And what if I see fit not to comply?

"My dear, I am not as kindly as my comportment might suggest. I have a veritable myriad of common restraint methods that, whatever your behaviour, all serve to the self-same end, namely that of the success of my research. My, my, the list is endless from squeeze-back cages, manual restraint, restraint boards, restraint chairs, restraint chutes, tethering, and nets even. Not to mention the practice of chemical restraint. For example, a sedative may be given to an animal before a restraint procedure reducing stress-hormone production or we can be so kind sometimes if it means getting our own way, we can even offer psychological support in which an animal under restraint has visual and auditory contact with the animal's cage-mate. This usually ensures stability in blood pressure and heart rate responses. Whoops, I almost forgot, you don't have a cage mate. You're on your own in that regard. Shame, we shall just have to train you to cooperate with applicable restraint techniques when and if you behave unreasonably."

"You're a compassionate soul then?"

"When it suits, though to the outside world I am the very model of compassion. Here though, here in my domain I seek results at all costs and you're a once in a lifetime opportunity to me, 'Albus'...by the way that's your name now. My work with, or perhaps better said as 'on' you will be the stuff of legend. Indeed, I sense my Noble Prize will be in the offing in the fullness of time. As such your compliance, your complete surrender to both me and my staff is vital. So no more funny business, dear girl."

"Do I get the blanket I requested of your subordinate earlier?"

"No, we have no clothing for those deemed as equivalent to animals here. Yet to prove my compassionate trait I will however, ensure that the heat is turned up a few degrees. And as a 'creature' comfort we've provided you, in case you haven't already noticed, a slop bucket plus I'll have someone hose you down first thing each day. What more could a penned incumbent ask for? Aren't you going to say, 'thank you'? I've never had a specimen thank me before."

With inevitable reluctance, for she dearly needs that pledged extra warmth, 'Thank you."

"Not too warm though, I can't have the furry friends in my charge overheating!" With that he commences to leave for the time being, yet pauses for an instant, turns about face, looks Albus in the eye, saying, "Tell me something would you? I am puzzled, for it would be expected of any human female finding herself caged and naked would attempt to cover herself up best she could, you know a suitably placed hand here, a forearm there yet you stand before me brazen, arms behind your back. You, by rights, should be shamed, humiliated even. Why is that, it surprises me?"

"I am surprised you're surprised. After all, as you have already noted I am but an animal. I don't see my friend next door covering up." Chewing that fact he takes of his leave. Drained of immediate options, once more she curls in her preferred corner, into the foetal position upon the bed she has fashioned from pale yellow straw in view of all and any. Trembling when she should be shivering? A split-second contemplation, a thought swiftly dismissed strikes her that this time she is in deep, deep trouble. What to do?

In the isolation of cold solitude her state of full awareness reappears as if by magic. Where it has been resting she has no idea. One thing she realizes for certain is that her little secret, that of her genealogy is out! Just how did that happen? Also, the last thing she remembers before the rumpus and the cage is laughing out loud, faking fear, riding piggy-back on her blind giant's, giant shoulders en route to the lake back home. Her train of thought suddenly grinds to a halt in its tracks as she puzzles over what on earth has befallen her giant, and for that matter, dear Zada. Where are they?

Him: Initially, I had not the slightest idea as to what exactly was going on. In many respects I am still none the wiser. One minute she and I were quite literally enjoying a little horseplay, lake bound, the next thing I know is that my angel is on, what we call in the trade, 'the missing list' while Zada and I are shut away, confined in a secure yet, she advises me, plush suite of rooms with balcony views overlooking snow topped mountain peaks. We know not if my girl is dead or alive, yet from what poor Zada's ever so shaky finger upon my torso informs, the missive my lover had penned about her bloodline must presently be in the hands of whomsoever. She has no idea who that 'whomsoever' might be. She says the perceived enemy are keeping themselves to themselves as to their specific identity currently. Zada, of course, is besides herself with grief and remorse, admitting that in unthinkingly placing said forbearers braille missive in one of the estates dustbins, rather than torch it, she has brought about the current plight we find ourselves in. Enough said of Zada's foolish error of judgment

My best guess is that we are here, wherever precisely 'here' is, at the pleasure of a Western government agency, maybe MI5 though more likely the CIA, perhaps even a confederation of the lot. Certainly, were it the other side we would all be dead by now. I wonder just how long the undetermined 'they' have been searching through our rubbish. Certainly, all decent agents worth their salt have the patience of Job and now, for sure, they will be fully clued-up that we have a part-time human among us. Certainly, the Holy Joes won't like that and the United States has religious maniacs aplenty at the highest levels of government, let alone in general society. Couple that with the orgasms research scientists will have at the prospect of an all-new life form will, I anticipate, demand she be closeted within their confines for all manner of investigative procedures, the exact nature of which I am finding potentially too harrowing to even contemplate. I pray I am incorrect in my summation and that the situation we find ourselves in is both temporary and innocent of ill-intent, although I doubt that is the case.

I must admit, finding out about her extraordinary background came as something of a shock, yet it changed nothing. I love her and if necessary would die for her at the drop of a hat. Such insight changes bugger all. I always had an inkling she was not like the rest. It bothered me not then, certainly I care not a jot now. I feel certain my unique 'she' is alive and this deaf, dumb, blind waste of space that is yours truly is determined to find her and bring her to safety. As to how I need to formulate a masterpiece of a plan, perhaps using my weaknesses in the form of my afflictions to my advantage. A naïve plan? Most likely, it is. Zada will have to be my eyes and ears; will have to gather intelligence for me. Despite her calamity she is a capable girl I can call a friend, one I can trust in a crisis, plus she wants to make amends for that grave mistake.

Presently I can tell from the metronome vibrations of her breath that Zada is sleeping next to me on the immense bed we have been given to share. My natural investigators paranoia tells me that the fact that our captors have provided just the one luxury bed is indicative of them trying to 'divide and conquer' hoping she and I will become an item thus further isolating my unique whitest lover. Little do those in charge understand apropos the nature of the eccentric, Bohemian life we trio share. If this tactic be of 'their' design they are already wrong-footed. Regardless of anything else, Zada and I owe her one for there was a time not that long ago when she rescued us both.

A chink in the enemy's armour? Perhaps, or is it just that the ringleader has an unseemly weakness for the fairer sex? Whatever it is he, or for all I know perhaps she, has got wind of Zada's pleading to visit her friend were it the case that she is also confined within this seemingly palatial mountainous abode. Having begged of a chambermaid, likely one well briefed above and beyond the usual bed changing duties associated with the stereotypical skivvy, to speak with someone 'in charge', such a chap, she tells me, ostensibly fulfilling that tag turned up all smiles and bonhomie. A subordinate to the top man, no doubt, yet nevertheless Zada passionately and tearfully put forward her case and he agreed, while never admitting our girl was even in the building, to have a word with the powers that be.

The answer that came back was positive. Zada would be taken to see our girl as a guest of a Professor, the boss running this place, to who's office she would first be accompanied to by this Mr All-Smiles, before moving on to wherever it is our girl is presently in situ. In the light of my own predicament and with Zada playing up the case that with me unfamiliar to our suite of rooms I had not had the time to familiarize myself with the layout...a lie I might add...someone would be left to protect and keep a safe eye on me. In that small way, she was attempting to use my helplessness to authentic her case rather than raise eyebrows.

Time just creeps along when things are up in the air, when you know the intelligence you seek is out there; when you are in the hands of another's virgin instinctive skills to undertake the covert investigation you yourself would rather conduct. It is at these times I despair of my condition.

All the time in Zada's absence I tried to sleep and failed. The thought of someone new, unknown to me, looking over me fairly put pay to any prospect of hiding in the world of dreams.

Later though, after what had seemed like hours, Zada finally returned. I removed the dressing gown the staff here had gifted me for when I arrived in this unknown place I was my usual casual naked self, and laid surreally, although some might say doltishly nude atop the bed in order Zada could immediately have a sufficiency of my papyrus flesh to communicate upon in her just about adequate French and bring me up-to-date regarding all that had happened and exactly what undercover, snooping discoveries she had made in the time she was absent.

It seems that my first thoughts on the matter of our abduction and internment here in God knows where, most likely somewhere in The Swiss Alps I deduce, were unreservedly correct, namely that Zada's carelessness in not disposing of the note had brought about this event. Plainly, I cannot do other than to forgive and forget, for Zada could never have predicted the ghastly outcome when inadvertently not confirming beyond doubt that the manuscript was destroyed.

Over the next two days, taking only time out to sleep, a guilt ridden Zada scrupulously committed herself to the laborious process of laying down upon my bare flesh, having plainly absorbed virtually every last word this Professor chap had imparted, the things he had told her regarding his proposed research activities on his new nonhuman subject. Yet before getting to the meat of the matter, namely what I had predicted, that being so-called 'scientific research' she was at odds to paint me a picture of the man himself.

I understand that settled in his office and over tea from China and shortbread the Professor was the definition of a gentleman-at-arms. Fortunately, he spoke impeccable French, making allowances for her shortcomings in that regard. He softly quizzed her on the subject of her background, occasionally resting a parental hand upon her knee and perhaps thinking, hoping even, she was another wrong side of the blanket offspring of a monarch and a perceived monster. She parried his questions merely saying that she was of Romanian origins. At that she says his facial expression had an element of downcast doubt about it. After taking a sip of his tea he probed a little deeper asking if she could throw a little light as to why, from their discreet research, no person of her name came up in any records, reminding her that The Soviets were sticklers for accuracy with regard to keeping records of their plebeian populous. Not wishing to drop herself, or for that matter her family back in Romania, in any possible trouble Zada unaffectedly replied that she had no idea and was bemused why his people came up with no record of her, expressing concern that they had felt compelled to undertake any checking up on her validity in the first place. The Professor let the matter drop. Then, upon her changing the subject telling him, 'I am so angry. That when one of your soldiers turned up where we live in England...at least I think they were soldiers for they wore army combat uniforms...and fired that tranquilizer dart into my thigh...it still hurts by the way, look here at the bruising...as I was doing the washing up in the kitchen, they carried me off barefoot, with me just in this old smock, a smock that now needs a wash I might add. I don't think such behaviour is befitting of your reputation or of this establishment, do you?' At that the good Professor apologised profusely then advised that someone on his behalf would deliver Zada several changes of clothes and shoes before nightfall.

It was at this juncture he advised that Zada was owed an explanation as regards to the predicament, as he saw it, that had given rise to the three of us ending up guests at his establishment. He even donned a contrite expression when Zada pointed out that she felt more a prisoner here. However, he was at odds to firmly point out that, 'As you are already well-aware your little albino friend is not, how shall I put it...is not, as the righteous might say, of 'God's design'. As such we, you need not know who 'we' are, or why we feel compelled to learn of her essence, her substance and hopefully discover from scientific research all manner of things that might be of benefit to humanity. The fact that you and your male colleague were brought here with her is simply because you know her situation. The powers that be, at the highest level I might add, have determined no person outside of our very tight and privileged circle should ever become aware of the existent of the exotic creature among us, adding, 'If such news did get out just imagine the havoc that might follow as religions collapsed in the wake of any broadcast that God wasn't the only creator and nations tumbled into revolt, for the very existence of your friend, albeit most probably unknowingly, has the power to achieve that very thing. That, put simply, is why she is here. To maintain the equilibrium of mankind intact. In my own defence, there were some who would see her euthanatized tout de suite. It was only my personal intervention that has kept her alive.'

An aghast Zada then pointedly asked exactly what the Professor intended to do with his new plaything and established from his clinical reply that in terms of his proposed research it seems the initial approach will be to valuate her current state of health, and if nothing detrimental came to light then to undertake a more intense study of the basics such as body temperature, blood, heartrate, liver, kidneys, thyroid, lung capacity and such like. Following that, he would then make comparisons with human equivalents. If nothing untoward raised its ugly head and all was in order he would use her as, in his words, 'a guinea pig', firstly to seek to gain an understanding of her biological process with the aim to find new treatments for humans. Somewhere down the line, if such investigation threw up something of interest, something that might have possibilities, to devise drugs or treatment processes and where appropriate test them on her. Additionally, his unequivocal objectives included an improved cure for tuberculosis, better treatments for manic-depressives, even a cure for the common cold. With regard to the latter he grilled Zada as to whether the one he made mention of, who 'incidentally' was now known to both he and his staff as Albus, 'that's what we call her by the way,' had to the best of her knowledge ever suffered the sniffles, a question that provoked just a cryptic shrug, although the irony of the use of Zada's new surname 'Albus' being the same 'new' name for her friend was not lost on her.

That he got overly excited, like a Christmas morn child anticipating gifts when speaking of his possible plans for breeding experiments with her, likening them perversely to horses and donkeys came as a shock, as he went on the say, 'Also, the prospect of breeding experiments holds a particular interest', explaining further that, 'When say, a female horse mates with a male donkey the result of the copulation would be either an infertile mule stallion or occasionally, a few mare mules have been known to produce offspring when mated with a purebred horse or donkey, yet it is a rare thing. Just think Zada, what I could achieve with testing the possibilities on your friend. I don't deny that a Noble Prize has always been my dream.'

Zada freely admits she is at a loss to expressly understand why the Professor told her all these awful, frightening things. Bewildered, and not feeling able to contain herself she bravely asked of the Professor if he realized he was perhaps the sickest man to ever have lived. That was the point he revealed his true nature, no more Mr Nice Guy, and whether out of premeditated intent or just pure anger he gave Zada something of a real fright by menacingly pointing out he would ideally also require to test such drugs and processes that may evolve upon bona fide humans, not just 'his' Albus, continuing such dialogue noting, 'Say someone like you or that isolated freak who accompanies you, for example. You never know,' adding, 'The powers that be haven't a blind clue what to do with either of you. You know too much to be allowed to return to the public domain'.

Dropping the specifics of what could only be termed a threat, he changed tac and became once more his ever so polite original self as he asked, 'Would you care to visit Albus with me now you know a little of my ambitions?' Plainly, she answered in the affirmative.

It was at this point in the proceedings and much to my concealed chagrin that Zada beseeched of me to allow her to get a little sleep. The trauma of the events of the day, coupled with the sheer effort of scribing her words capital letter by capital letter had got the better of her and she was tired out. Whilst I could do with a rest myself, my mind was racing and not getting the whole picture was frustrating. Ever the gentleman, and upon the mammoth bed, I let her fall asleep, her head resting on my shoulder.

Come first light, both of us refreshed we set to work once more, pausing only to take a little of the breakfast the chambermaid had arrived unannounced to deliver us. I must say Zada noted that the girl looked somewhat bemused when unlocking the door, her armed attendant waiting outside in the corridor, at catching the pair of us with nought on, she bent over a prone me, mapping out words upon my upper body. Presumably, and to an extent worryingly, she would no doubt report back to the Professor what she had seen. Following our irksome interruption Zada continued her telling of the day previous tale.

She was taken from the office by way of staircase up several floors to a huge room, one that covered a whole vanilla, dull floor and accommodating what she could only explain as a whiffy indoor zoo containing a number of species, all caged, from small rodents, cats and barking dogs right up the size scale to a funny looking redhaired silent ape plus, our girl. 'She has the largest of all the cages and I had to fight back tears when I saw her curled up into what looked like a frightened, naked ball in the corner. The odd thing was that although she spends most of her time wearing nothing at all this was the first time I'd ever seen her stripped of dignity, naked to the world at large. Upon catching sight of her the Professor, noting my concerned expression, made a token attempt at allaying any fear I might have had by pointing out that she was kept clean and well-fed and although strictly speaking against the rules he had succumbed to her request for a blanket for night-time's when the temperature of the room was allowed to drop, adding pompously, 'We can't have her upsetting the apple cart and becoming unwell, can we. Such a thing really wouldn't do.'

With that he ran the back of his hand across the iron bars, called out the name he had given her thus alerting her to the fact she had company. 'Albus, you have a guest.' Albus didn't move. The Professor had to repeat himself a number of times before she stirred. Eventually she got onto her feet, brushed away remnants of the straw she had clearly piled up to make into a crude mattress of sorts and just gave him a hostile look of utter loathing. Then after rubbing the sleep from her eyes and spotting me at last she smiled an undefeated smile and blew me a best ever kiss as if to say, 'I love you and I'm OK'.

Zada could plainly not let the matter of her friend's confinement go without saying that the belittling treatment of her was disgusting and inhuman to which the Professor reminded her to look around at the cages all the other creatures lived in. 'Your friend, my dear, has been pronounced to be worthy of just animal status, not that of a human being. She must therefore get used to living with the animals. It is beyond my gift to afford her any other creature comforts, not that I'd feel inclined to anyway. Oh, by the way did the case of new clothing arrive last evening?'

'Yes, it did. I haven't had the opportunity to open the case yet. However, seeing what I see here you can shove them up your arse, you pig of a man.'

'Suit yourself, Zada. I heard tell you were busy playing little games with that wasted lump you share the rooms with. I'll have the case collected without delay and, as retribution for your insults directed at my person, you can hand over that disgusting garment you have on and join Albus in the cage for a while.'

Keen to get close enough to be able to speak with her friend, yet pretending otherwise, Zada's riposte was to tongue-in-cheek say, 'You must be joking.' With that the good Professor literally ripped the cheesecloth smock apart with his bare hands and watched it fall to the floor, leaving her bare. He had a guard in attendance unlock the cage and jostle her inside, adding, 'I'll be back for you later and by the way, even as we speak my secretary is drawing up documents that you and your male companion will, and rest assured you will, both sign and by doing so willingly hand yourselves over to be human guinea pigs available to me and my team of research scientists as we undertake worthy experimentation for the betterment of mankind. And don't for one moment think that you can decline, the hierarchy were looking for a solution as to what to do with you both and I've resolved the issue at a stroke. I merely await the legal bods give the contract the once over and then I'll even loan you my favourite pen to endorse your signatures thereupon. You can all live together here. I think I'll name you the

Notoriously Naked Flames.' As the Professor departed for the time being he could not help but to say what a pretty pair we made.

For my part, and given my shortcomings, I had had no idea that when returning to our rooms yesterday poor Zada had been left with nothing on. At this point I spent the absorbing of the remainder of the story fighting a red mist that was ever growing within. Yet from what Zada went on to explain, allowing both girls to spend some time in the cage together might just prove to be to our advantage.

Zada pointed out that upon overhearing all that had been exchanged twixt her and the Professor she thought it vital we sign whatever contract he wanted us to sign as it would mean we would be together in the same place and as such making it decidedly easier to implement whatever scheme my lover had already planned that would ensure our safe getaway from this God forsaken place. As to what that plan might be, she didn't get the chance to say, for the Professor had commissioned two sentries to escort her back here before the girls could conclude their conversation. Thankfully, she says they were well-behaved and showed her due respect save for staring at her as if they had never seen a naked woman before, although more likely, and hopefully, they were just enjoying the view. Had Zada reported that they tried any funny business then I think I might just have spontaneously combusted, such was that ever-blossoming rage inside. It seems to be the case from what Zada has told me that the guards working in this institution are few, yet all armed. She asked the chaps who accompanied her back here exactly why they carried guns in a place like this, to which one of them replied, "I'm not sure, we're new here, but think it is because of the girl in the cage and you two colleagues of hers. I heard a rumour that we have to keep an eye out for anything untoward in case the Russians get wind of your existence. It looks like you're all prized assets of The West."

In the light of all that I've been told I deem it necessary to accept the stark fact that patience is now the key. As we waited for the Professor to play his now predictable hand and reckless as it may seem, Zada and I made untamed spontaneous love releasing the tensions of the awful episode we were living through. I only wished my albino lover was with me now. For all the confidence I have in her abilities and for what has been to date an outright successful career in the field, getting us all safe exit from here was going to be fraught with difficulty.

For all my desire to formulate an escape plan it seems I am just a hopeless buffoon, impotent in a crisis. All I can do is pray the God's are smiling on us.

Her: The girl deprived of the luxuries of mortals awoke the next day having unexpectedly slept like a log on her thrown together mound of Nazareth straw and under annoyingly bright fluorescent light, pleased that Zada and her giant were alive and as far as she could tell were unharmed. That she had awoken to the prying eyes of the bland lab assistants clearly tasked to care as best they could for the caged animals did not phase her in any way. Most of them were weedy males, afraid of their own shadows. They never spoke a word and aside from delivering her food and drink largely ignored her. She found that being deprived of cutlery thus having to eat solid food with her fingers not to be as disagreeable as she had imagined. Runny food posed some difficulties though. Sat cross-legged on the floor cupping lukewarm porridge in her palms might be messy and not be quite the culinary equivalent of a delightful Eggs Benedict breakfast at Tiffany's yet all things considered food is sustenance, nothing more. The opposite applied to her post breakfast hosing down. Such hosing was undertaken by a brute of a man who from outside of her cage simply chased her around the pen with his water jets wearing a look of sadistic glee upon his face. He was unlike the rest of the underling wimps pottering about doing this and that. No, this poor example of chivalrous manhood offered her no soap, no towels and certainly no decorum. His kindest act was to deliver new straw after the wastewater had run away down a predictable centralized grate and the floor had eventually dried out of its own volition.

The water pressure emanating from the hose was powerful enough yet fortunately not too fierce, likely not fierce enough for the sadistic brute's taste. Although she had an issue with it being ice cold to the extent her teeth chattered and her goosebumps huddled together in a failed search of safe haven for a good half hour after the event. When asking of the brute if he could ensure that next time, 'Would you be so kind as to use warm water,' he merely blanked her, not giving her the courtesy of any form of reply or response. At least the vile Professor had been true to his word and upped the general heat. Naked and warm is one thing; naked and freezing cold quite another.

Getting used to her new surroundings, she made mental note of the fact that three uniformed armed guards had been working what she assumed, for there was no clock in view from her cage, were eight-hour shifts each. Much of their respective shifts involved, out of choice she presumed, walking around all four sides of her iron cube just watching her, never speaking. Occasionally, they would take a brief rest on a high stool by the entrance door from which they could conduct direct surveillance as to her continued residence within. The guards clearly had no interest whatsoever as to anything else going on, on this floor, just her. She wondered if they had been briefed and were aware that they were guarding a non-human in its forced, new environment. Probably they did know and their constant gawping was purely them marvelling at having been so lucky when drawing at straws and getting to oversee an immure stark naked girl, seducing their eyes by revealing all, yet perhaps perplexed that she cared not a jot about her own nudity, a thing that must be pure paradise to voyeurs and other perverts alike. If the deviant within them wanted her in coy or humbled state they would have a long wait. From what she had seen she took it that the guards had no direct access, likely no need, to hold any set of keys to her cage. For certain the Professor had his own keys and she had worked out that the namby-pamby assistants had access to keys from an area of the room, like the clock, out of her eyeline.

The orangutan had taken a liking to her and she, him. He would screech to high heaven in her defence was she was being hosed down, yet when she glanced his way, caught his eye and put her finger to her lips he would hush. He had noticed her ankle bracelet, touched his own equivalent then pointed his long twig-like finger at hers as if to say we share a common servitude. Her heart told her to free this wonderful beast upon her eventual escape; her head suggested such notions as out of the question.

It was as she hung from the cage bars imitating, to his clear delight, her new-found ally that the Professor arrived in the company of Zada, her giant and a man with a handgun at the ready. That the Professor was clothed, her consorts not, hardly came as a surprise.

"Well, my dear I see you have befriended one of your own. Good for you. Although, if I were you I'd take care not to get too attached. Young as he is, the fellow is due to be euthanised in a few days' time. He has served his purpose here, and besides your comrades here will need a place to call home now that they have agreed, even signed irrevocable contracts of their own free will, to obey my demands by way of which they will undertake to be human guinea pigs and assist me with my research. How decent of them don't you think? For just the price of board and lodging they've agreed we can test drugs, and do all manner of things about their person in the name of furthering our knowledge of life on earth. I thought that by giving them the opportunity of living with, and as the animals would, help us in that regard, hence and like you, they shall be penned up without a stitch on for the duration. It'll be a little cramped for a day or two until the orangutan is eliminated and his cage can be freed up, but I trust you don't mind lodgers for now? Of course, I'll ensure you have extra bedding straw and such like. I'm all heart when you get to know me."

With that he advised the armed guard to be at the ready in case of any shenanigans while he unlocked the cage and ushered the others inside. His impatience with the speechless one of deaf ears and blind eyes was palpable. Duly locked up together, the Professor sent for an assistant who brought with him a cine camera he was to attach to a tripod. "I don't believe you'll find this too obtrusive...well it doesn't matter even if you do...yet I am keen to see, and have permanent record of how humans react in the company of a new species. Just act naturally, the more 'natural' the better in my book; simply pretend the camera isn't there. You'll note I've placed it out of your reach, yet just close enough to capture a more or less panoramic view. My man here will be back to change the film every so often," adding, just before he left them alone, "I thought it might interest you that this little beauty also picks up sound, so take care what you say, girls. I realize this snippet of information is neither here nor there insofar as the monster among you is concerned."

Albeit under video and guard surveillance, the three of them were once more united together. Folly on the Professors part? Only time would tell.

Him: We sat as a circle holding hands in the cage, me frustrated that I could not take part in what was surely a coded conversation twixt the girls as to our escape. At one time, the very thought of being caged up with two beautiful women would have been an impossible erotic dream realized. Not now though. I felt I needed to know exactly what had gone on and what was currently going on. All I knew was that Zada and I had signed a ridiculous piece of paper that logically would have no meaning in law, signed as could be argued, 'under duress', agreeing to our respective subjugation.

While they planned, I was in the dark, lost to the world. I got to thinking that the dream I had had not long after the beginnings of my recovery, such as it is, whereby I was known by just the number 107345, was perhaps a premonition of my incarceration in this hellhole. Moreover, that when in the hands of The Major back in the Soviet Union, the tattoo on my wrist the girls advised me of and bearing that same bloody number, 107345, was no coincidence, for Zada tells me that the bracelet the Professor had his henchman affix to my own ankle bears the self-same number. Zada did attempt to reassure me that it was more credible that the Professor had named me thus after noting my wrist. Perhaps she is correct; perhaps my paranoia was hurtling out of control.

Later, to find myself being hand fed again, after having succeeded and got used to feeding myself by way of following a daily routine, knowing where things were, the most degrading thing. After all my recent triumphs it seemed I was back where I started. An incompetent, helpless plank.

As a triad, we eventually massed together to try and get some sleep. My gal planted a kiss upon my forehead, and by means of spelling out words with the tip of her tongue rejected the offer I had made during a little palm talk earlier, namely that the two girls should plan their escape and leave me behind as I was a liability. She had said, 'I would die before I'd leave you behind.' The girls, either side of me were quick to depart to the land of nod while I just lay there trying to work out just how three naked prisoners, one of them enfeebled and a hindrance to boot, locked in a permanently floodlit iron cage devoid of any privacy and always under the ever-watchful eye of armed guards, banged up as I understand in the cage in a secure environment atop the Alps with no easy way out, could ever prevail in taking flight. And, even if we were successful and made it back to Blighty, those powers that be with malice in their hearts would have no difficulties in establishing who and where we were. To me the situation we found ourselves in was beyond pointless, was nonsensical.

Her: Next morn, with bare backsides to the camera, weighing up the state of affairs and making credible plans to break free they spoke only in whispers. Occasionally, a quizzical guard would hover nearby trying to get wind of what they were talking about, but to no avail. No doubt the guard would report back to the Professor the subject of the indecipherable whisperings.   Essentially, such prying ears, as with prying eyes, was a thing both girls studiously ignored. One topic in particular was at the top of their agenda. Problematical as it might be, once an escape from the building itself had been accomplished, just how would they get back down the mountainside. Zada had seen for herself from the balcony in the rooms they had occupied only the day before that they were marooned at least a mile high and that the only way in and out was by way of pygmy train. She had already seen staff arrive and leave by such mode of transport, then added, "We were unconscious when we arrived here so I cannot be sure of anything or everything." This when put to her that surely there must be a cable car operating at this height, she was unable to say. Without question she had not spotted one nor overheard talk of one.

"Well then, Zada. The Professor throws the word euthanasia about with alarming regularity. My plan, ever since realizing the full extent of our dilemma has been to euthanize the lot of them, thus giving us full access to this entire building, its facilities, its lines of communication with the outside world and its contents, yet with you both hold up with me I might just have a better, easier for certain, plan."

"How on earth can we ever escape from here, locked up as we are?"

"Oblique as it may sound I'll just say 'soon' Zada, very soon. Be at the ready at all times. For your part, all you'll have to do is take charge of our giant, keep him safe, lead him wherever I point and leave the rest to me. By the way, it is clear he is down in the dumps presently, do you think it an act of worthy mercy to wake him up and spoil him a little even though I know for certain it took him hours to drop off?"

"Well, I don't mind, but what about us all being filmed on camera, the man who visits all the time to change the film and the snooping guard?"

"Zada, really. The wretched Professor dearly wants footage of how you humans react to the likes of me. Let's give our beloved big man a treat, and the evil one an eyeful recorded for all time on a reel of film. As to the guard and the cameraman, they can watch all they want. The irrelevant twerps will think they are in seventh heaven. You know what most men are like and remember also that our Professor has already named us 'The Notorious Naked Flames'. It's about time we lived up to our reputation! Plus, a big plus when we leave, that film reel in particular, along with the others to a lesser but still meaningful extent, will be dynamite in the right hands."

"How so?"

"Think about it. If we become escapees as we are we will be on the run forevermore. They will hunt us down like dogs and kill us, make no mistake. Whereas, when I hand over the footage to my Fleet Street contacts and make known of their existence to a former lover I remain good chums with who holds a very senior position at the United Nations no one will dare touch us for fear of their own fall from grace."

"I don't really get what you're saying?"

"Put simply, Zada, if ever those reels coupled with our story ever get made public the very things the Professor and the others fear would happen will happen. If our true story becomes common knowledge and their world; indeed 'the' world, would fall apart. If they try to murder us down the line, just think of the impact the front pages of national newspapers across several continents would have!"

"You really are a clever one. It's 'ShowTime' then. I'll follow your lead."

To the addicted one in a crisis a lack of nicotine, more than anything else, fudges sound judgment. Willpower can override its significance sometimes, yet when a cigarette is integral to the successful outcome of a well thought through scenario then a cigarette must be had. All three guards, she had noticed, imbibed in the habit of smoking while on their plainly tedious shifts overlooking the creatures in the cage. Of the trio there was one, the youngest in the group who, like the others, never spoke yet who's occasional eye contact and general manner conveyed a certain geniality. He likely was the one who just might succumb to the pleadings of a damsel in distress in need of her nicotine hit. At any rate, he was her best chance in that regard. Surely there is not a man alive who would not favour a reasonable request from a beseeching, beautiful naked girl. On top of that, her experience in the field of intense espionage told her that this callow youth was far from the finished article, indeed all three guards had the look about them that spelt 'novice' and were likely drafted in for what, on the face of it, was a task presenting little scope for trickery on the part of the imprisoned. It stuck out a mile that his newness had ensured he had been given the solitary role of the nightshift, meaning he and only he was on duty alone save for the various caged occupants of the 'zoo'.

"Guard, I see you're smoking. I'm absolutely gagging for a cigarette, I've not had one for days. I'll understand if you don't feel able to offer me a smoke, but do you think I can have at least a couple of puffs of yours?"

Not that it mattered in the circumstances yet the youthful guard felt compelled to look this way and that, ensuring there were no others in the room prior to making his approach. However, he was put off by the ever-rolling camera. His reticence born of not wishing to be caught out by his seniors was palpable, yet his body language suggested he was not entirely against fulfilling her request. Clearly, she was not going to get her smoke just yet, although she took on board a willingness on his part to comply.

Some little time later, the film reel predictably needed changing. Since being shown the rudimentary process of replacing used reels for new on day one the guards now had this duty to themselves. It suited the cameraman to have it this way. As is commonplace with artists, the cameraman had a passion for film and his mind was more on the video captured than the repetitious, in this instance at least, procedure of securing them. She sensed her opportunity. Like any red-blood the immature sentry had predictably fallen foul of the tendency toward unalloyed lust, a common enough frailty in the male species.

With the girls making due note that the change of reels, although a pressing issue, was not necessarily an immediate task, it was only a partial surprise when a tap on the cage brought to their attention they had a murmuring visitor in close proximity. To all but the desperate his request would have been unseemly, disgusting even, but yes, in exchange for a brace of cigarettes the soldier asked, "What's in it for me?"

"You get to take your pick. You can have your way with either Zada or me. If it helps you can, if you've sufficient time, have the both of us. Does that sound fair?"

"I'll have to be quick. The reels need changing."

"You can be as quick as you wish."

"I'm not allowed to open the cage, you'll have to suck me off through the bars. You, the whitehaired haired one tonight, the other one tomorrow night. Suck me off first, then get your fags after."

"No chance. How do I know you aren't lying? A lit cigarette each for Zada and me and you've got a deal. Just think, for the price of those cigarettes you can play your little game with us night after night for as long as you wish."

It was likely that that last tantalising sentence was perhaps the trigger that made him acquiesce to her more than reasonable terms of engagement. What a foolish young man she thought, more so that so engrossed was he in prospect at hand that in his excitement, apropos his quest for fellation, he had completely missed out on the fact that there had been a brief exchange of quiet words twixt the girls.

Moments prior to the carnal experience he hastily passed Zada a lit cigarette, saying, "I've lit it for you, can't trust you with matches, can I? Anyway, here's the one for your friend, I'll light it for her as soon as we're done."

Yet the young man's sport was not to be. What he was unaware of was that Zada was already primed to reach through and lift the guards gun from its open holster about his waist as he was otherwise engaged in undoing his fly buttons.   He had no idea that this was so. Such an easy task when the owner of the weapon had his mind fully focused on the commencement of employing that other 'weapon' of his elsewhere.

On her knees, mouth open wide she could not resist coaxing him along with a little unmerited homage, observing, "My you are a big boy," before taking delivery of the penis her teeth were about to clamp down upon with all her might. The guard, now screaming in pain and wild with fear at the thought of being separated from his manhood made to unlock her jaw with his bare hands, until he noticed Zada had his gun primed and aimed directly at his forehead.

Just prior to taking Zada's lit fag from her lips and tossing it to the dry straw laden floor she could not help herself to pass comment, saying, "What an inefficient soldier boy you are. Your trousers around your ankles, a half bitten off penis pumping out blood and a gun, your own gun, aimed straight at what little brain you possess. Look see young man I shall fan the thing you call a fag and set the cage alight if you don't this very instant go use that telephone on the wall to call the Professor, and tell him there is an emergency and that he should get here right away and to bring with him the keys to this monstrous coop. Be quick boy, you've turned whiter than me and I suspect you will pass out any minute. We can't have that can we?"

"You fucking bitch, look what you've done to me. You can all burn as far as I'm concerned, cow."

"You'll more than burn if the Professor finds out you've let his prized asset, namely me, burn to death. Do what I say. You're in serious trouble now, it'll be worse for you, believe me, if you dally he'll have your guts for garters. Do what I say right now or you'll end up another lab rat just like my friends here."

It was not long before a bleary eyed agitated Professor arrived in his swish silk pyjamas, undoubtedly furious, yet armed with a gun of his own in one hand, a mass of keys on a large ring in the other. A disdainful look at the humbled guard sobbing and incapable, curled up against the wall under the telephone in a pool of vital fluid told him all he needed to know. Moreover, with Zada having handed her gun to her non-human ally the Professor found that it was she who was aiming it directly at him'. The situation was one of standoff.

"Drop the gun Albus. You girls may have smothered the fire but the conniving pair of you will be severely punished for what you've done, make no mistake."

"I think you've not got your sleepy head around the situation Professor, you drop yours then shove it over to the cage with your foot where a grateful Zada will take possession of it, then go unlock the cage door if you've got any sense; if you don't want me to kill you, that is. Of course, you can take the risk but you must understand I am a crack markswoman. I feel sure you've read and heard all about my talents in that regard. And you would be well advised that I care not a jot as to the threat you name as 'consequences' for by just being here I face them whether you are alive or dead. In short I don't care what I do."

"You wouldn't dare shoot me. Do as I say."

"I'll count to three...one...two..."

The Professor had spoken a better game than he played. Steadfastness alluded him. He blinked first, dropped his shooter and moved it across the floor in the manner decreed, whereupon Zada reached through the bars and took possession of it.

"Now unlock the door, but before doing so take off your pyjamas and hand them to Zada."

"My pyjamas! You've got to be kidding me."

"No kidding Professor. They might be a little short in the leg yet will just about fit my giant colleague here. I believe they will rather suit him nicely. Hurry along."

The Professor, albeit grudgingly, succumbed, undressing and as with the gun, using his foot to kick his nightwear close enough to the cage for Zada to gather up. In advising the giant to put them on, she took the opportunity to make palm contact and in doing so made the unsuspecting giant aware that the escape was on.

"There, that wasn't so difficult Professor. Now the keys please. The same delivery process will apply."

With the cage door now unlocked Zada took it upon herself to invite the Professor to join them within. He had little choice but to once more acquiesce. Although not instructed to do so, the girls were rather proud of their giant who took matters in hand, automatically reaching out for the Professor and making a good fist of gagging him with the pyjama top and tying his hands behind his back with the bottoms prior to punching him in the solar plexus causing him to drop to the floor. It was then that the girls transferred the ever-amiable orangutan from his cage into theirs to watch over the Professor how so ever he wished. Once accomplished the prisoners took flight, locking the Professor in their former home, then ensuring the keys were hidden away in one of the empty film reel cases. As to the balance of the reels, Zada charged the giant with the task of carrying them away, letting him know that they were integral to a successful escape.

With the giant carrying a significant quantity of reels Zada simply stood behind him, her hands resting on his hips and, following the non-human's lead, guided him toward the exit door.

"Zada, it was jolly good our man used the PJs to bind rather than wear. I'm most impressed he was that alert. Whatever, I think we can take it as read that there will be an armed guard if not in the corridor, certainly in close proximity. I'll likely have to disable, perhaps even kill him. You two hold back by the doorway until I give you the nod."

There was indeed an armed guard outside. She spotted him stood looking out of the window at the end of the corridor into the moonlit night sky. Given that she had been at odds to open the zoo door silently, and given that her feet were as bare as she herself, it was with little difficulty she crept up behind him. The guard felt the rigid barrel of the gun in his back the same instant as he heard the words, "I bet you haven't been taken from behind by a naked female assailant before, matey boy? Lead me and my colleagues out of here and I might just let you live. I'm thinking the fire escape might do us nicely. Comprehend?"

Before obeying instructions the guard asked, "The Professor?" and was advised that said Professor was likely being dismantled by an angry orangutan presently.

17.

EARLY 1953 – SUSSEX, ENGLAND

Her: Back home in England's scorched pastures once green, now turning brown, a still mute and deaf giant, yet now with restored eyesight, cracks open the first of more than just one celebratory magnums of Moët et Chandon champagne. The fizz of the freed cork as it flits as if an escapee wasp past Zada's left ear at a rate of knots has the girls giggling like happy girls should giggle. The inevitable small spillage from the bottle top irks the giant to some degree, yet save for a giveaway drop of his bottom lip he tries not to let it show how he hates any wastage of such a fine nectar. Flutes at the ready he pours and shares the glasses around.

Earlier, on this undoubtedly fine spring day and certainly not a day for clothing when privacy is guaranteed, he has spent the last hour or so on the tennis court giving a few much-needed tips to his female companions as to exactly how the game should be played as opposed to how they had been playing it. Whether the pair fully took in his sound advice, a matter for conjecture. Now they toast the return of his seeing faculty and of their ensured freedom.

It was early morn when the overly animated giant had announced to the two drowsy girls curled up either side of him in the ginormous bed that his eyesight had been restored and that he could see both them and the world at large. At first, they did not believe his words; thought he might have gone insane. Then, coming to their senses the pair in unison first hugged each other then him, all the time crying their eyes out in perfect joy. Again, in unison and in delicious French they bawled, "Comment?" ... 'How so?' by any other name...not realizing at first that sight was the only sense to have been reinstated. It mattered not, he had lip read their question. By way of swift hand gestures he made it obvious enough for the two of them to understand that sight was the only one of his lost senses returned to him. That he had sight, in essence a miracle in itself.

Climbing over his lover, stumbling and almost falling on the floor in his enthusiasm he rushed to his studio returning with pen, clipboard and paper. Rolling Zada over onto her tummy, he placed the clipboard on her bare backside and began to write as she squealed in amicable, feigned protest. His initial words, 'I COULDN'T TELL YOU I COULD SEE DURING THE NIGHT FOR FEAR OF RUINING YOUR SLEEP, BUT THIS I AM ABOUT TO WRITE IS IMPORTANT! IT CLARIFIES WHY I CAN SEE AGAIN'. Then in the form of a letter he wrote these words;

My lover and dear Zada who we have come to love,

In the supernatural dark of deepest night, as you both slept like the dead and in spite of my deafness, my 6th sense...if such a thing exists...caused me to stir. I was awoken by the waves of resonance of exquisite euphony emanating from the piano. Not painful to behold, just pianissimo vibration perfection. Initially confused, I crept out of bed careful not to disturb either of my two delicious mermaids. In my world of darkness I rarely feel or fear the dark, it holds no potential horrors to me these days, yet this was something quite out of the ordinary. Familiar as to the layout of the house I made my way to its logical source, the drawing room. Without rushing and in case we had an interloper in our midst I crept ever closer, sure my bare feet upon carpet would go unheard. As my post-sleep befuddled brain began to accept my state of consciousness, my wide-awake self detected that whomsoever was at the piano was performing, more than merely fooling around, the exquisite Liebesträume No. 3 known generally as 'Dreams of Love' in A-flat Major. Don't ask me how I knew that. It is a thing I just do. I have no explanation as to how or why. Anyway, it is one of Franz Liszt's works I have come to enjoy playing myself in recent times. Getting closer to the source of the sound waves I became aware that whoever it was playing had abruptly come to a halt. As if in the realm of fairy tales a kindly, familiar voice spoke inside my head. "We meet again, my friend." It was the same voice I had heard with my own ears when in the hands of the Stasi in East Berlin prior to my internment in the Ukraine; the voice of a man whom I recognised in that Berlin cell that night prior to my defeat; the one who was identical to he who had played piano accompaniment for your beguiling naked ballet in the days before the war, namely your beloved father.

Logically, the house was in the self-same total darkness I had come to know so well. Had I eyes with purpose I would have been in the same 'exempt from reality' state of being as I have been inflicted with. Words almost fail me at this point for what I was altogether unprepared for was the unexpected sight of a match being struck, and before my previously dead eyes I found myself observing the lighting of the candles in the three-arm candelabra sitting upon the piano top. For a moment I was frozen to the spot, then as a moth to flame I moved closer, then closer still as the magic of opaque illumination took hold. To my great shock, the pianist alighted the stool, and with an air of almost female grace and serenity strode toward me stopping just an arm's length away. A ghost or of substance I could not tell then, nor even now. He reached out and handed me a parchment upon which in perfect calligraphy were written the words that opened with a quote from Liszt himself, 'It is impossible to imagine a more complete fusion with nature than that of the Gypsy' continuing thus, 'May I first thank you, Zada. Your loyalty to my daughter in times of need and when in danger have fairly touched this old wraith's fraudulent heart'. Dumbfounded yet riveted I was compelled to read on. 'And you, yes you, the one she calls her 'giant'. There is no motive hidden within your love for that girl of mine. Despite your colourful relationship your love for each other has you both joined at the hip. Watching from afar, I have seen how she has come to care for your well-being as only a true flame is capable. Yet, I fear in time such caring will wear the poor girl out, will one day crush her spirit. I cannot allow that to happen nor, I know can you. Additionally, you Sir, deserve a better fate than the one handed you. I have it within my gift to repair your eyesight, a gift as you will have noted I am sure, has already been bestowed. Were it the case that I could mend your remaining frailties then believe me when I tell that that would have been done. Sadly, I cannot. Long since out of pity for a good soul in a tight spot I entrusted you with the gifts of painting and music. I see you have treated both with due respect. Now you have back your sight. The divine trinity is now yours. Last time we met I suggested that our paths would never cross again. At that time, I spoke a truth. Events have reawakened this weary shadow one last time. She, my daughter, was once in my eternal care. As of this moment I step down for now she is forever yours to watch over. Whatever labels surly mankind might tag her with I know that under your guardianship I will be able at last to rest in peace.' With that his physical substance faded away, he became immaterial.

Your thoughts, my darlings,
   Titan

Close to tears born of something indefinable and seeking to be left alone a white Princess stood by the bedroom window, curtains drawn open allowing the first 'red sky in the morning's' daystar beams to guide her in absorbing the content of the epistle while down in the kitchen the Titan giant waited for the kettle to boil, as Zada danced alone to the crooning of Bing Crosby on the gramophone, a facile euphony that might just as well have been the music of the spheres such was her rapture.

Up above and having devoured, then savoured her dead father's words, she neatly tucked his parchment within the pages of her diary for safe keeping, then joined the others on downstairs. With the gramophone now respectfully silent, the tea brewed an air of bewilderment ensnared one and all. It was Zada who spoke first, "Do you not think that we should show a little consideration for your father and at least don dressing gowns?"

"Worry not, he's God knows where by now. Besides he wouldn't care a damn. Anyway, I think it only fair my man can at last see us both in all our glory. Look Zada, he is enthralled. At last he now sees what before he could only touch." Pointing at her empty cup indicating that a top up would be well received served to brake his gaping trance. With a corrupt smile embracing a hint of innocence he duly obliged, yet not before mouthing to his girl in English (she swiftly translated to Zada in French) the words, "Tell me this isn't a dream. You are both the most beautiful girls the universe has ever spawned." At last, all was well in their unconventional world. This day would be a good one.

Him: The first medic to visit me following my mishap in the Ukraine I am advised diagnosed my loss of speech and hearing as most likely permanent. The signs of deliberate damage at the cruel hands of my warped captors were all to obvious. However, the chap was unable to determine the cause of my blindness. On the face of it there was no obscurity of vision, no obvious deliberate damage to my eyes. He was perplexed. All he could suggest was that I may have been suffering from a thing named 'Hysterical Blindness' whereby the trauma of my torture had likely caused my brain to block off all visual impulses. My delirium at being unfairly impaired had given rise, perhaps, to an affliction of the sensory organs that are my eyes. He had added that during the two wars a number of soldiers suffering appalling injuries or being traumatized by one too many close by explosions had either permanently or temporarily suffered complete sight loss. Beyond that he could say no more. It is thus, more so with the passage of time, that I had come to presume my condition would be with me till Doomsday.

In the solace of her private folly, the girls having dressed up and gone into town seeking provisions without having to worry about my safety for the first time since whenever, I got to question whether my cure was born of their efforts in ensuring I could live as natural a life as possible, thus easing my distress, instead of the implausible meetings with the mentor of what were more probably just dreams. However, if so then what of the material evidence to the contrary documented in the form of the missive, proving to our satisfaction otherwise? I had never held sway with religious beliefs. While I have taken the name 'God' in vain in colloquial terms as one does, generally to combine truth with disbelief at the passing of an event, I've never believed in the fellow. An afterlife, ghosts and things that go bump in the night I had always previously associated with the doctrines of foolish, blinkered clergy and their all too easily swayed followers.

The sanctuary of that lost folly within the estate that she had allowed me to visit just once previous, prompted thoughts beyond the mundane obvious. Even back then in my imposed 'darkness' its air of the necromancy kept the workings of my mind on its tiptoes. It's feel of bleakness; its lurking, latent inducement toward all things intimidating guaranteed to keep an active brain darting this way and that. This time, taking what she had said previous literally, I chose to leave my gandoora outside and ensure my experience within would be one of solitary optimum intensity that only being naked and vulnerable in the face of dark danger can render. It was thus, in this instant decision-making environment I came to accept that it is possible my all-knowing view of the ways of the universe may be more than a little pompous. The God concept, I determined, remained as ever just a mere legend, manmade to suit the ways of men, yet above that I now accepted there are matters my hopeless self-proclaimed omnipotence and that of many of my kind should keep an open mind about. The contents of the parchment represented a 'living' proof that all was not known to mankind.

Having rehashed my world view on things I started thinking of my albino girl and all that she, with the help of Zada, had done for me in my time of greatest need. Without due warning I found I had buried my head in my hands and was weeping as would a lost child. Experience from having been in the field of action told me that I was in a state of shock yet, knowing that was of no consequence, the tidal wave tears would not abate. Eventually I calmed and once across the horizon of tears I reflected upon the fact that I would never hear or speak words again, yet in the vernacular of a common navvy I, 'couldn't give a flying fuck' because, I now had my eyesight back.

It was on my way back to the house that it occurred to me that as yet I had not chosen to examine the artwork I'd painted while sightless. The fear inside of me that all the praises the girls had bestowed upon my work might just have been given out of pity. I determined that this was a fear I must put to bed and get on with my life. I confess I allowed myself a mute chuckle at the fact I had two perfect muses to model for my seeing eyes to paint in the future.

Perhaps, after all my previous reticence that proposed exhibition of my work in London might become a reality now that I had lost the feeling of being a freak of nature. For the first time in an age I felt an air of excitement. A good feeling, for sure. It was then I recalled that I had entirely forgotten to collect my gandoora upon leaving the folly. Another of my mute chuckles for I had wondered as to why I was so damned cold!

Her: Since their return from The Alpine clinic the subject of their escape had been off the agenda. Had not been a topic of analysis or even wry humour. The giant had followed the girls lead, yet remained keen to be brought up to date with regards to what exactly had happened. His key area of interest was to be able to make some sense of the events post their exit from the clinic, as to him at the time it had felt as if they were lost in a maze. Feeling a little cheated, and more than a little curious, he suggested by way of a note joyfully written in pen and handed to Zada over dinner that the girls should tell all and that, for one last time, they impart the story using their previous tried and tested method of finger upon bare flesh. He had made clear that he was not looking for chapter and verse regarding the escape, as that would take an age. The salient points alone would be enough for now. By way of a codicil to the proposal he further insisted he be allowed to keep his eyes wide open and that they, the girls, scribe upon him naked in order that he could savour the dazzling view. In the event, and despite their compliance to his reasonable request the task proved to be a complete disaster as he was unable to focus his mind on the invisible words being dished out upon his torso and, for their part, they discovered that a mutual fit of the giggles was not conducive to imparting an accurate account of the escapade. Finally, they all agreed that the mission should be aborted and that it would be a wiser thing to simply write him an account that he could read in his own time and at his leisure.

Next day, while Zada gave the house a spring-cleaning and his lover sat at his side on the veranda, he finally got to read the tale of their escape after having left the clinic.

My Darling Giant,

Firstly, both Zada and I wish to say a simple sorry for not enlightening you earlier. We agreed that so amiss were we you may smack our bare bottoms if you feel compelled to punish us thus! More seriously though, you must take account of the fact that the exhilaration and excitement brought about by the sudden return of your eyesight made it nigh impossible to concentrate and convey to you the inside story of our homeward bound adventure.

While locked away in my cage after Zada's first visit and prior to you and she becoming incarcerated housemates I puzzled over the intelligence she had gathered from observation and her speaking with that wretched Professor. It was clear that once we had bid farewell to what was for all intents and purposes our prison cell, and if we could survive the cold of night, then I could foresee no major impediments to prevent an uncomplicated getaway and ensure our secure future together. You see Zada had noted that many of those working at the institution arrived on the little train each morning. That crucial piece of information indicated that at the bottom of the mountainside there must surely be a township and such a town would be the place where those incidental workers who formed the vast majority of the staff complement...who most probably did not even know our true reason for being there...lived. At this point you must remember that our presence within the institution was so secret, even at the highest political levels across the globe, that certainly locals would know nothing of my status as a half-human or the actual reason of us being in-situ or indeed the planned research the Professor intended to inflict upon us. In short, getting to any such town would be the first significant step toward freedom.

Armed with that gen, I worked around a hypothesis that the three of us would leave the premises naked...I assumed that that would most likely be the case unless out-and-out good luck was on our side as there would be insufficient time for us to locate and steal suitable clothing... and as such we would have the look of disorientated strangers who had been stranded on the mountainside when we turned up in town. Based on that assumption it was clear that on balance, we would be cared for and helped on our way by the townsfolk rather than be arrested for public nudity.

Assumption can be a dangerous thing if one makes the error and overlooks costing in the possibilities of pitfalls and, to the uninitiated, is often par for the course. Risks however, we all live with. I was implementing a plan not just to escape but to do so with minimum risk based on what I had learned from Zada. Having the corridor guard held hostage, the Professor dead or disabled and the youthful cage guard damaged to the extent he became a quivering irrelevance, coupled with the fact that in the middle of the night the staff levels in the building were minimal gave us the edge providing we were long gone come morning. Also, the benefit of holding the two handguns we had purloined afforded us a little extra security should things turn sour along the way.

Once outside that awful place I was well-aware a key to a favourable outcome had to be the cutting off of all communications twixt the clinic and the outside world. Certainly, that decision was fraught with risk, yet being aware of the Professors massive ego I thought it odds-on that he had kept news of the problems we had caused quiet as, undoubtedly, he would not want his bosses thinking he had a weakness or was inefficient in any way. I guessed right as it turned out. Regardless, the moment we were out via the fire escape I had the hostage lead us first to the telephone's junction box, then severe the wires with his own knife, a knife he had wrongly thought I overlooked when abducting him. Indeed, the only reason I hadn't taken the knife from him in the first instant was 'where on earth does a naked girl keep a knife?' I jest!

With communications down I read our captive his fortune, pointing out that if he couldn't or wouldn't guide us to a cable car then I would cut his throat. I *just knew there must be one as I couldn't believe that the top brass would share the narrow-gauge railway with the local plebs. Sure enough, such a thing existed. A mono car system, a thing I have previously operated in the line of duty. Better still, within the cabin and in the storage space under the seating were blankets, plus miniature bottles of brandy, although sadly no St Bernard dogs... that reminds me, I want a dog soon, the estate here deserves at least one dog. There were flares and a first aid kit to boot. It took little time to deal with the guard, and the bandages from the first aid supply were sufficient to gag and bind the poor chap, having previously undressed him in order that you could have his uniform, a little too small for you I know, yet in a panic in the dead of night no one would notice that minor shortcoming. That he had a few Swiss francs and perversely $500 dollars in his back pocket, an extra bonus of sorts, plus it confirmed we were in Switzerland and that the guard was most likely on the fiddle somehow, not our problem. Having had the good fortune to find the cabin atop of the town and previously had the guard under my instruction power up the system from the powerhouse, we were on our way. The methodology of the breaking system, fortunately another thing I was familiar with. Sure enough, with both Zada and I warmed up and our debatable modesty protected under woollen blankets, you with your all-important film reels looking handsome in the guards discarded uniform, we looked to all and sundry as two rescued damsels in distress. I felt a little sorry for the guard, leaving him naked on the cabin floor, yet what the hell, he was one of the enemy. I presume come morning someone found him and cared for him unless, of course, that someone thought he knew too much!*

All that aside, when knocking loudly and crying out for help upon the door of the first 'bar come hotel' we chanced upon I was at odds to explain to the landlord...after we'd finally roused him from his slumber...in suitably broken Norwegian, with just a sufficient soupcon of French thrown in to help him *understand our plight, that Zada and I had been very silly girls trying to ascend to the top of the mountain in pitch black conditions and having lost our inadequately packed back packs and bivouac sacks to a gust of fierce wind whilst stupidly changing clothing...hence we were naked under the blankets we wore. Furthermore, that you, our hero had at least saved us and the film reels of scenes we had filmed on our mountaineering travels, could not add anything useful to the conversation as you were, although in the employ of the institution up top, a Russian with just your Mother tongue to your name. As was to be expected the landlord shook his head with dismay and a hint of scorn, yet warm-heartedly offered us a bed for the night. Politely I refused his kind offer saying that ideally, first I would like to make an international reverse charge telephone call and secondly the use of a motor vehicle and a map book to guide us to the nearest city...not knowing exactly where we were on the map...was a necessity. At first, he looked most doubtful...I find that often the case when imparting an outrageous story such as the one I spun him...but at the appearance of $400 of the 'luck that favours the brave' $500 clasped tightly in my paw he almost bit my hand off, allowing me to make two calls and offering there and then to drive us to the town of Vernier on the border between Switzerland and France. From the moment I had made those calls I knew we were forevermore safe. With the few Swiss francs left over, after having paid our Vernier hotel bill in advance the night before, I was able to telephone my bank manager in England, who fortunately knows me and the tight spots I regularly find myself in, who then forwarded via a bank transfer sufficient funds for us all to buy clothing and more importantly perhaps, an old Citroen to drive back to Boulogne from where the Folkestone crane loading ferry boat would deliver us back to England. The rest is now history.*

I must add that the Swiss Hotel manager, although surely perplexed at the state and late time his customers arrived, save for suspicious eyes, never once revealed he felt thus, or questioned the authenticity of our dubious plight. I think we should visit his place again one day, I suspect it more than a little risqué! In conclusion I must say that the Professor may well have been the consummate scientist, albeit sick in the head, yet in terms of his team I feel they left something to be desired. They were plainly amateurs in the ways of espionage. I found it all rather disappointing. Although you, my gorgeous Titan giant must be made aware that the reels you safely looked after all the way home, were our hero, for our continued safety depended upon them. I bet until you got into the guards uniform the tins were freezing against your skin. And, by the way in The Times just this morning the Professor's obituary stated that he died at work of natural causes and in all probability, although without a nomination, it is anticipated he will be awarded a posthumous Nobel Prize.

PS. I feel, for the sake of eliminating any doubt, I ought to add that had our hostage not held a mass of doubtlessly illicit cash, my original plan would have been put in place, namely, following any reverse charge telephone call, to steal any vehicle I could lay my hands on, and...an important 'and'...had there not been a cable car available, the trainline would somehow have had to do. As I've already said, luck favours the brave.

Your Half Human Fancy Bit

18.

AND IN THE END

As the days turned into weeks, the weeks into months the unique threesome rediscovered impetuous passion within the curtained off paradise they called home. Not for them the mind-numbing day to day routine of the suburban commute or the pain of internal office politics. Each was now filthy rich in his or her own right. Most days, of choice, Titan would paint. For their part, the girls would be painted any which way that suited the demands of the fussiest of artists. Exhibitions of his work both those compiled in blindness and latterly with sighted eyes became exalted, the critics adored his exclusive expertise, the challenges he had faced that generated his peculiar take on the representation of exclusively nude art. Fortunately, unlike many artists, his income from his endeavours materialized while on the living side of the grave.

No longer compelled to hide-away in his divine abode in perpetuity he initially, and at the behest of the girls, later out of personal choice travelled in their company promoting exhibitions in London, New York, Berlin and especially so, Paris. Paris became their home from home. They even purchased a property there. Nothing too grand, an apartment with a balcony in Montparnasse sufficed.

Now fond of her first ever, only spoken in jest nickname 'Albino freak,' she and her Titan now shared a combined wealth beyond the wildest dreams of normal folk. As for Zada, she too amassed significant riches in her own right having been awarded a weighty royalty in respect of each painting for which she posed that had been sold, plus the bonus of being most likely the best paid house 'skivvy, come chef' of all time.

Life had been kind to one and all. The former secret agent lovers, at the back of their minds, were always concerned that one-day Zada may see fit to move on, make a new start or perhaps seek out or stumble upon a true love. For a galaxy of reasons the pair simply did not know what they would do without her.

They need not have worried, for they had overlooked the stark fact that Zada was content where she was in life. More so when she found herself pregnant by Titan, a pregnancy born of his lover's suggestion and impassioned approval. A planned pregnancy, no less. As to his sweet albino, she had long since taken the decision that she would not upset the apple cart and breed a brood of her own. Besides, the trauma of having lost a child, albeit one conceived of rape to fetal death in the tragic days of war, had killed any desires she might had had in that regard. Certainly, she had no desire to see the fruit of her loins potentially go through the things she had had to suffer; that it was best this way, best that they shared a willing giant who had made it clear from the start, loved only his angel, yet was happy enough to deliver to Zada a maverick kind of love and caring most women would never know of in a thousand lifetimes. That the trio saw fit to share each other as the mood took was inevitably the thing, given their hankering for all things artistic and Bohemian, that made them the talk of the town, and perhaps, also served as the best form of unpremeditated marketing of his wares. The label, 'Notoriously Naked Flames' was theirs to keep; was as good an unofficial brand name as any.

Over time, with sign language perfected in English, French and even Romanian meant instant communication had become the easiest of things. No more braille typewriters, no more the finger to palm or torso that had inspired in part, maybe consolidated in reality, their respective zest for nakedness.

When away from paradise wherever they were in the world, be it a hotel, a restaurant or any place else in the evenings over dinner Zada was, as if a child seeking a bedtime story, a glutton for her friend's compelling espionage tales of days of yore. They fascinated her beyond measure, had a magnetic effect. It was ensconced within a Parisian restaurant that Zada asked, "Tell me again that one about The Old Lag. I know you've told me so many times before but the baby is nearly due so I'm allowed to be samey in my cravings," then signing toward the giant she asked him whether he minded if his lover friend spoke the tale out loud. He minded not, just smiled and nodded approvingly, content to take in the view of being sat twixt female beauty personified both in sexuality and evolving motherhood a veritable feast for gentle, creative eyes.

Having had the waiter top up glasses of champagne for two, mineral water only for the expectant one, she began, yet not until she had pointed out that it would not be that far into the future before Zada herself would be telling stories of her own adventures to her small child. Zada's riposte? "Our small child; always it must be 'our' small child, not just 'mine'."

Whatever, the tale of The Old Lag was told once more, *"More out of sheer boredom than real interest I told him that the boys back at RAF Tempsford had christened him an 'Old Lag'. That he was an experienced airman I had little doubt, after all he walked with the requisite bail out limp, sported a handlebar moustache and, by the smell of his breath, had a taste for the hard stuff. 'An Old Lag you say, do they by Jove? Bloody penguins the lot of them,' he bellowed over the thrash of the propeller and the angry bumble bee constant hum of the engine. Although sounding the worse for drink, to his credit and my relief he seemed to have total control of the willowy, matte black Westland Lysander flying by the light of a silvery moon low over The English Channel toward a field 'somewhere' in Northern France. Being a little naïve when it came to slang I felt compelled to pose a question, "Penguins?" "Yes, my dear, 'penguins'. I presume you are talking of those bloody ground officers with no operational experience, birds with wings that can't fly, in my book." Then I got his drift.*

'May I ask what you were doing before you joined Special Opps?' I contemplated taking the easy route; telling him a lie yet to kill time settled for the truth, 'I worked in Paris in 'a place more marvellous than any other,' at 31 Boulevard Edgar Quinet in Montparnasse to be precise.'

'Well, well, well...you surprise me. 'Le Sphinx' no less, to my dishonour I know it ever so well from back in the day. Is the lovely Madame Martoune still in charge? I heard tell that Wehrmacht have commandeered the place for exclusive use of the military? Don't recall

seeing you there though, mind I was somewhat tanked up most visitations.   Wonder if they still keep that dwarf chappie who gift wrapped the gals in Cleopatra garb, such as it was, in a rolled-up carpet? The little chap had the finest job imaginable I'd say.'

I explained I had no idea as to the current welfare of Martoune, her bordello or the dwarf adding that I had no recollection of her pilot either, 'I left Paris in June 1940, the very day the Hun marched in... I was one of the lucky ones I suppose...and by the way, I merely served drinks, just a waitress, never a working girl...they said I was too pale and skinny,' my roughly true explanation.

'You're not French, your use of English tells me that; your diction perfect.'

'True, yet I am not English either, although if you heard me speaking French you would think me French...that is why they recruited me.'

He chose not to delve into my origins any further. 'So, it's a bit of clandestine skulduggery with the Resistance in occupied territory, no doubt a bridge to blow up or such like. You must be a very brave gal going back there when you could be safe and sound, well as safe and sound as one can be in these wretched times, staying on home territory?'

'I do not think of myself as brave, I simply take satisfaction from naked revenge and pay no heed to the consequences should my mission fail.'

'You owe the Gerry one then...payback time?'

'Very much so.'

Now over the solid terrain of La Belle France it was not long before the pilot announced that he had spotted the burning torches lighting the covert strip of field where we were due to land. 'François and his cronies will no doubt be ready to whisk you off to the safe house. Take care my lovely.'

'I'll do my level best.'

Come next full moon above a cloudless crystal clear navigable night sky the Lysander returned to take me back to England.

'You did your duty I take it?'

'More…much more than that I can assure you.'

At that time of my life I felt no affinity with kith and kin anymore, I had lost all to the firing squads or the ovens. The tribalism born of lines on maps left me bemused. The perceived requirement for flags and anthems an alien thing to a girl of Royal descent; now a traveller who knew no boundaries; who took no prisoners."

Zada beamed the beam of one enjoying a stability in her life, "I love that story, just love it. You never did say what happened to The Old Lag?"

"I like to think he hasn't aged a bit. That he's somewhere up in the sky flying his Lysander and as pissed as a rat."

It was only a matter of a few weeks later still off home territory in the Montparnasse garret that Zada, with a little support from her whiter than white midwife, gave birth to a girl child. A 7lb 6 ounces small, yet healthy girl child, who would find herself blessed with triple nationalities, given that, as was somehow appropriate she had been born in Paris, her father English and her mother Romanian. Moreover, she was born with the proverbial silver spoon in her mouth, as throughout Zada's pregnancy Titan had been at pains to create a series of remarkable paintings of her mother that covered each wonderous and in equal measure beautiful stage of her ripening. He was well aware that such was the demand for his work and the popularity of his muse the series would fetch, when sold at auction, a pretty penny. They did!

By strangest fortuity at Sotheby's, only the day prior to the girl child entering the world, a cloaked in mystery buyer, his bidding handled by an unnamed black-veiled female of Hellenic stature and indeterminate age, referring to herself his 'associate' out bid all others. Rumour had it that the one she acted on behalf of, by all accounts, was once long ago a much-celebrated pianist with royal connections. Certainly, he had parted with a King's Ransom for the entire portfolio. As was Titan's want all proceeds from the sale were gifted to his baby daughter, although such monies would be held in trust until she came of age. She certainly was a lucky little girl, blessed also with, for all practical purposes, two untamed mothers, a rock-solid father and a weeping willow beside the lake she would grow to love and one day to learn swim in.

Asked exactly, by Titan, where the purchaser resided the buyers reticent concealed associate would only say, "He watches from afar that's all you need to know, save that he asked me if the opportunity arose to remind you that today is 30th. April 1954. The year is irrelevant however, the day and the month you may think noteworthy, depending on the events of tomorrow."

Titan himself was flummoxed as to what significance the next day, the 1st May might have vis-a-vie anything at all other than it being a still-celebrated lecherous, pagan spring festival until upon his arrival back in Paris the next evening, just moments before Zada went into what would be perhaps the most expeditious labour in modern history. Chatting over the events and what he had been told the day previous at the auction his albino lover merely smiled, saying, "Wait and see". The wait was not long. The child arrived well before midnight.

The little one would have the wildest formative years, both loved and allowed to be the imaginative, feral princess all girls should be. Her name? 'Mayday Albus', perplexingly, an albino girl some say more beautiful than the half human she calls 'mother'; a girl who never once caught a common cold.

It was some years later Mayday Albus commenced the monumental undertaking of penning the life and times of her parental troika. Her book would be entitled, 'Notoriously Naked Flames'; a phrase plagiarized from the words once spat in the direction of her immediate forbearers in cruel satire. Her book would end as it had begun...

Sometimes, just sometimes, the intoxicated Time devil, drunk on his own success, slumps into a benighted stupor and time itself is fleetingly fractured. It is upon the occasion of such seismic cracks; a tsunami of memories comes to flush out what has passed; a double-take much better than before.

By plea of frozen tears, the mind's eye gallery opens its cryptic doors and as mayflies to an ominous dusk, excited habitués race here, there, everywhere to assimilate that which has long since been archived, now dusted off, displayed.

A rendezvous perhaps? Two soon to be lovers, a chance encounter born of fate oblivious as yet of the unsullied bond twixt vivacious flesh and abiding soul, no care in the world over anything or everything, unaware of walking canes and deathbed musings that one-day will unmask a fault in fortune's haughty wheel affording them a brief escape when Time takes of its wasted rest.

Twixt thus far stainless sheets those green lovers and the one circumstance had invited in; the one they had come to love, scramble to discover and invent, knowing then, forgetting now, that sometimes, just sometimes, nothing is impossible.

ACKNOWLEDGEMENTS

My thanks to Ted Giffin, Bachelor of Fine Arts from Indiana University, the Herron School of Art for his sublime original cover and reverse side art.
Ted can be found at www.tedgiffin.com

Also, to the lovely Rachel Carrera for all she has done including the cover and reverse side of book art adaptions and without whom I would get nothing done.

To George for the promotional video he kindly took time out to produce.

Finally to dearest Shirley, forever my muse.

ABOUT THE AUTHOR

Mike Steeden, a fast aging juvenile born of a London suburb in the times when smog was expected rather than rejected has previously written two poetry books, *Gentlemen Prefer a Pulse – Poetry with a Hint of Lunacy* (2015) and *The Shop That Sells Kisses – Poetry with a Hint of Magic* (2016). *Notoriously Naked Flames* is his first novel.

25006268R00153

Printed in Great Britain
by Amazon